*Here For The Cake*

# JENNIFER MILLIKIN

Copyright © 2024 by Jennifer Millikin
All rights reserved.

This book or any portion thereof
may not be reproduced or used in any manner whatsoever
without the express written permission of the publisher except for the
use of brief quotations in a book review. This book is a work of fiction.
Names, characters, and incidents are products of the author's
imagination or are used fictitiously. Any resemblance to actual events, or
locales, or persons, living or dead, is entirely coincidental.
JNM, LLC

ISBN: 979-8-9868099-9-1
www.jennifermillikinwrites.com
Cover by Okay Creations
Cover art by Rosie Fables
Editing by Emerald Edits
Proofreading by Sisters Get Lit.erary

*To those of you who like a warm breeze, sandy toes, and the sparkle of the sun on the water.*

# Prologue
PAISLEY

*Eight years ago*

Who knew writing a story could feel *this* good? Like releasing a caged exotic bird, and watching it fly to freedom. All these words, inside me for days and months and years, and now here they are, on paper and tucked in my backpack.

Nobody of importance will read them, but that was never the point.

Their release was the point.

The snipping of their hold on me.

Goodbye, good riddance.

Hoisting my backpack higher, I tug down the hem of my jean shorts from where they've ridden up my legs and bounce up the steps to the English building. I'm not an English major, but this creative writing class is making me wonder if that's where I'm headed.

Electricity zips through me at the mere possibility of figuring out what I want to do with my life. My dad was wrong. I won't be crawling back to North Carolina with my tail between my legs. I'd passed on Notre Dame, his alma mater, in favor of Arizona State University. In doing so, it seems I've passed on being his daughter, too. He wants little to do with me, at least for the time being. The feeling is mutual.

Being out from under his thumb gave me the freedom to try something new. The creative writing class in the course catalog caught my eye, and the description tugged at the strings of my curiosity. Did I dare try? The cardinal question released an exhilaration that served as my answer.

Cut to now. One month into the semester, and the verdict is in: I love it. Especially this most recent assignment.

The parameters were simple: a short fiction story, anonymously authored and anonymously critiqued by a classmate. Constructive criticism? Sign me up.

I'm proud of my work in a way I haven't been in a long time. Years of advanced math classes and studying the metrics at my father's hedge fund didn't feel a fraction as good as what I extracted from my heart and crafted into a story.

I want words. Moldable, buildable, powerful. Emotion evoking.

Numbers are *boring*. Too precise. My father once informed me numbers tell a story, but I'm an avid reader, so I understood his idea of what constitutes a story differed from mine.

Declaring a major that has nothing to do with finance or business will make my dad's skin melt off his face, but that's an outcome I'm willing to shoulder. I'm already persona non grata. All those years of occupying the role of protégé, gone because I'd defied him.

Ironically, I'd never have gone against his wishes if he hadn't done what he did. He'd made a terrible choice and asked me to lie for him. After that, well... It's hard to look up to someone when they display low behavior.

Not all my bravado rang true. An enduring ache took up residence in my chest, soothed at last by my words, poured out on the page.

A twinge of nerves pokes at me now, this fear of letting someone else read my work. Anonymity is my saving grace. I'm safe. My story won't leave this classroom. The author won't be known by the reader.

Pushing my way into class, my gaze zeroes in on a lone figure. *Klein.* Adrenaline sparks in my limbs, rolling through me the closer I get to his seat near the front of the classroom. He's a serious student, his ever-present notebook open like always, scribbling away like a mad scientist of words. Hair the color of wildflower honey, full eyebrows atop stunning green eyes, lower lip captured between his teeth as he concentrates. A pencil sits trapped behind his ear, and as much as I try not to, I find it endearing. Cute, even.

The guy is too good looking for words, even in a room full of creative writing students. Could any of us properly describe him? I cannot. There's something about him, an essence, that holds him apart from the rest of us. Not only his talent with the written word, which he has in spades, but something else.

It's not a social glow, because he's not particularly

friendly. Strangers don't gravitate toward him, attracted by an unnamable quality.

Except for me. I'm the stranger, attracted.

Same as I was that night seven months ago, in my apartment, when he showed up with a friend of my roommate's.

We'd talked for hours, and I'd thought *here's someone who understands me.*

We'd kissed, too.

And then, nothing. Not a word from him, though I'd given him my number. The disappointment was crushing. What's the word for a one-sided connection?

Leech?

Barnacle?

Well, I wasn't going to be one of those.

Every time I saw him after that, I ignored him. I made ignoring him my second job. My preferred pastime.

Thanks to being placed in the same class, I'm given the chance to exercise my ignoring muscles every Tuesday and Thursday, and by now, I'm swoll.

Per usual, I keep my gaze laser-focused on the lectern as I drop off my short story. The professor accepts my paper with a curt dip of his chin.

My answering smile is perfunctory, my head lowering just in time for my hair to cover my face so a certain someone isn't on the receiving end of my adulation.

I haven't felt this buoyant and happy in a long time. The last thing I need is to catch Klein's eye and risk him thinking my smile is for him.

No.

This smile is for *me*.

For the words I have written, and all the words I have yet to write.

# CHAPTER 1
*Paisley*

My college sweetheart's wedding invitation arrives in my mailbox on a Thursday afternoon.

I'd been expecting it, but still. It smarts, snapping at me like a rubber band that has reached into the past before zinging back into the present.

I'd prepared for the invitation's arrival by telling myself my feelings don't matter to anybody but me. They simply *don't*. But preparing for an eventuality, and living through it, are two different things. You can tell a person they will one day feel angry, but when that one day arrives, anger doesn't come solo. Erratic heartbeats, sweaty palms, a decrease in common sense, *those* are the feelings that accompany the emotion.

That's how I feel now, and it's not only anger. Add humiliation to the mix. Also, a splash of anger's close cousin, indignation.

Abandoning the small stack of mail in the mailbox, I take only the large envelope with me as I hurry up my driveway. I live on a block full of cute, tidy homes and even cuter, tidier neighbors, most of whom love to chat.

Today is not the day for chatting. Or answering curious but well-meaning questions about why I'm using a two-fingered hold on the corner of an elegant-looking envelope. *You'd think she's holding a used gym sock*, Bill would joke. *Or my sports bra after hot yoga*, his exercise-addicted wife Jessica would add.

Head down, I make it to my front door without incident. Tossing my purse on a side table, I drag a deep breath through my lungs, releasing it noisily. With zero poise I flop onto my couch, one leg tucked beneath me. My finger slides under the flap of the fancy envelope with the gold filigree in the corner. A paper cut seems apropos, but no such injury occurs. I am undamaged by the invitation. Physically, anyhow.

I remove the invitation, turning it over in my hands. Ivory cardstock, heavy and textured. The text in black ink, the font a readable serif with a touch of whimsy. Classic, simple, tasteful.

Like my sister, the blushing bride-to-be.

*Wine.* I need wine.

I'm up from the couch, gliding into the kitchen and uncorking a crisp white kept in the fridge. After a long, decadent swallow, I deposit the bottle on the counter alongside the offensive invitation.

A deep breath crashes through my lungs as the sweet sting settles into my belly. I am fortified. If a girl can't use booze to numb the indecency of her little sister marrying her ex-boyfriend, when can she use it?

Bent over the white quartz counter, I remove an insert

from the envelope. It's a personalized note from the happy couple, the text printed in shimmery copper.

> *You are cordially invited*
> *to make the event of the summer*
> *even more memorable.*
> *Please be on the island*
> *one week prior to our nuptials*
> *to accommodate a forthcoming itinerary.*
> *Xoxo,*
> *Sienna and Shane*

Gag me. Now. With a spoon. A *serrated* spoon. No! A spork.

Did my sister just refer to her *nuptials* as the 'event of the summer'?

I eye the trash can in the corner. What would happen if I threw the invitation away? Claimed it was lost in the mail? It would be a lie, but a lie told solely for the purpose of self-preservation surely isn't as bad as one told with cruel intentions.

Yep. That's what I'll do. I didn't get the invite, therefore I couldn't book a flight, and now *oh shoot, I'm so sorry* I can't make it. I have a non-refundable trip to Anywhere, U.S.A. planned for that same week.

Except, I can't.

I knew this invitation was coming. I was one of Sienna's first five phone calls after she touched ground following the ultra romantic hot-air balloon proposal.

Also, I'm a bridesmaid.

An anvil named reality crashes down upon me, and I resign myself to my fate. I live across the country from my family, but there's nowhere on earth I could go to get away from this wedding. Soon I will be on an island off the coast of North Carolina, watching my little sister pledge everlasting love to my ex.

My phone rings and I retrieve it from my purse.

Sienna's name displays across the screen. My stomach drops to my knees. Is that sweat beading at my hairline? Can't be. It's January, for crying out loud. It's sweater weather even here in sunny Scottsdale, Arizona.

Sienna's name continues to flash angrily. I know where this is going, and there's only one way to face it. Head on.

Another swig of wine and I'm doubly fortified. I got this. I'm good. I'm *fine*.

I tap the screen, and without me greeting her, Sienna's exuberant voice fills my kitchen. "Hellooooo did you get the invite?"

"No." I didn't intend to lie, but it's a damn smooth delivery, if I do say so myself.

"Oh," Sienna says, disappointed. "Check your mail. Mom received hers two days ago, so yours should be there. It doesn't take *that* long to go from North Carolina to Arizona. It's not like it's being ridden on horseback."

*I wish it were. Maybe it would've taken an unfortunate dive out of the postman's saddle bag.*

"It doesn't matter if you get it, because obviously you're coming." Sienna pauses, giving me the opportunity to chime in with an appropriate response, something like *Well, yes, I'm a bridesmaid!*

Here's the thing about my sister's relationship with my ex: it's my fault. I could've put a stop to it from the beginning. But on that day when she'd called to tell me she ran into Shane, I was too shocked to use my words. My ears were in working order, so I listened and nodded my way through her almost unbelievable story.

There Sienna was, sauntering over the tree-lined streets in downtown Raleigh, the fall leaves scattered over the sidewalk, when she bumped into Shane. *Can you believe it?* she'd said with an incredulous gasp. I thought she was going to tell me he looked awful, that I'd dodged a bullet when he broke my heart two years prior, *blessing in disguise* and all that jazz. I didn't need my ego stroked, only pacified.

"He moved here from Phoenix about a year ago. He looks great," she'd said, and it was the way she infused the word 'great' with a smile that told me all I needed to know. Across the miles, I heard the want in her voice. "He asked me out. I said no, of course." She took a deep breath. "But Pais, I kind of want to."

I felt as if a cartoon rubber mallet swung from offscreen and walloped me over the head.

We should've been laughing about the fact he asked her out, mutually agreeing about his cretin status. Sienna should *not* have been holding her breath, waiting for me to give her my blessing.

And that's when it hit me. She'd do what she wanted, no matter what. My choice was to make a fuss, or acquiesce.

"You can go out with him if you want to." *So mature! So agreeable! Paisley never causes problems or makes waves!*

Deep down, there was a part of me hoping she'd change her mind. That she'd choose me and our sisterhood over whatever attraction she felt toward Shane.

But, no.

And here we are. I'm cordially invited to the event of the summer being held at my favorite place, my sanctuary, my childhood hamlet. *Bald Head Island*.

So I say what Sienna is waiting for me to say, because what else is there to do? "Of course I'll be there, Sienna. Obviously."

She makes a squeaky, joyful noise. "An entire week on the island, Paisley. All our loved ones, days and days of wedding shenanigans." A dreamy quality envelops her voice. "It's going to be ah-mazing."

If I thought I was dreading this wedding, it's only a fraction of the feelings I have about returning to Bald Head Island. As wonderful as it was to grow up vacationing there, it wasn't always perfect. Correction: the island remains pristine. The actions of certain individuals tainted a handful of my memories there.

"One more thing, and it's kind of late notice." Sienna takes a deep breath, her gusty exhale crackling the connection. Excitement oozes from the phone. "Paisley, will you be my maid of honor?"

## CHAPTER 2
*Paisley*

"You know what your problem is?" Paloma, my best friend and second-in-command at my digital marketing firm, stares at me from four feet away. She raises her eyebrows, one hand on her hip while her other arm extends to hold up her side of the mylar photo backdrop we're affixing to the hotel room wall.

"No," I grunt from my side, using a disproportionate amount of strength to push a thumbtack into the wall and wincing at the dull pain it sets off. "But I bet you're going to tell me."

She blows a strand of black hair from her face. "You're the floor."

I frown as I suck the pad of my thumb between my teeth. "I'm the floor?"

"People walk all over you."

I hold back my smile. Paloma moved here from Brazil when she was eighteen. She has nearly perfect English, but the idioms and phrases give her trouble.

"I'm a doormat," I correct. It's true. When it comes to

my family, I have the damndest time asserting myself. It's far easier to let them walk all over me than it is to address our issues. I view it as risk versus reward. Do I want to tell my family I have thoughts and feelings and opinions and fight that fight, or do I want to keep living across the country and fake it when I visit? I'm all for doing hard things, but maybe not right now. My focus now is on getting through the wedding.

Paloma waves a hand, her painted-red fingernails twirling. "What-*ever*. Don't be a doormat, Paisley. Tell your sister you don't want to be her maid of honor. Tell her you don't want to be in her wedding at all."

That would be ideal. At that rate, I might as well not attend. It would save me from another forced outcome I don't want: seeing our father. There'll be no avoiding him at the wedding, unless I decide to make a break for Western Europe by freestyling the Atlantic. Our relationship never fully recovered after I declared marketing as my major following my short-lived stint in creative writing. Now I see him when I go back to visit on major holidays, where we share a late dinner at a snooty restaurant after he's left the office. During appetizers he levels remarks that veer more aggressive than passive, and by the time entrées arrive, I count the minutes until dinner is over.

I promised myself I won't agree to a dinner like that again, but I know I will. I'm not a weak person, or a masochist, but I fear what will happen if I sever the tenuous string holding us together.

Nodding to appease Paloma, I push the final tack into place. We step back to survey our handiwork. Glimmering strands tumble down the wall to a basket holding photo props and inflatables. In a few hours, my sister and her 'I do' crew will be here, posing in front of the mylar while effervescent champagne sparkles in their glassware.

Paloma shoulders me. "You're not going to tell her, are you?"

"Not at her bachelorette party."

Paloma's eyes narrow. "That you're throwing her."

"They wanted to come here," I argue meekly.

"There aren't any bars in Raleigh? Or Charlotte? Savannah? *Florida?*"

A sharp ache begins at my temples. "I'd like you to remember," I say, dramatically swiping the packaging trash off the coffee table, "that I've been rebellious in my own way."

Paloma grabs the inflatable penis from the photo prop basket, smirking. "Kind of, yes. You could have been far more devilish than this."

I smile unabashedly, pleased at my act of defiance. A cursory glance around the space confirms the hatching of my devious plan.

Penises *everywhere*.

Sienna is going to lose her mind. She had only one instruction for her bachelorette weekend, and it comprised three words.

*Keep it classy.*

Here's what I heard: keep it classy *with penises*.

Paloma flicks the tip of the phallic inflatable and tosses it into the bin. "What I wouldn't give to stick around and see your sister's face when she walks in."

Paloma doesn't know my sister well, but she's heard

enough of my stories to know Sienna prides herself on being elegant. What she doesn't know is that while my sister has a tendency to be vain and egotistical, she can also be sweet and kind.

"You can be my plus one," I remind Paloma, but we've been through this already. Twice I've begged Paloma to be my guest at this sham of a bachelorette party, but it's her dad's sixty-fifth birthday today. She has strict instructions to be on a video call with her family at eight p.m. Also, she doesn't want to go, and unlike me, Paloma is excellent at boundary setting and enforcing.

She plucks her purse from the side table near the hotel suite door, ignoring my offer and hitting me with a one-two punch instead. "Speaking of plus ones, you need a date to the wedding."

I'm shaking my head before she finishes her sentence. "Who's going to be my date to a wedding on the other side of the country? On an island. For a week?"

Paloma frowns, acknowledging the uphill battle I'm facing. "You're screwed."

"Exactly. So I'll go alone"—cue internal cringe—"and I'll play up the independent woman schtick. I own a booming marketing company that was recently featured in the 'companies to watch' section of Young Entrepreneur magazine. I bought a house last year. I wear high heels every day, dammit."

Paloma snort-laughs. "High heels?"

"When I was younger, I thought if you wore high heels to work it meant you were someone important."

"Strippers wear high heels to work."

"Shut up," I groan, but I'm laughing.

"Ok, Miss Independent." Paloma opens the door and sashays out, blowing me a kiss as she goes. "Send pictures of you and the inflatable dong."

The door swings shut, and my best friend disappears, taking all the good energy with her.

Heavy dread settles into me. Paloma is right. I'm the worst kind of doormat, the kind who knows what they are but doesn't fix it. It's my job to keep everyone in my family happy, because I'm a part of why my parents are no longer together. I didn't keep my father's lie, and it cost our family.

As much as I feel responsible for the general climate of my family, this bachelorette weekend was not my idea.

It was my mom who arranged that I would be the hostess, and good luck to anybody who goes up against Robyn Royce. She can talk anyone into anything. She'll take your argument, which you'd previously believed was solid, and tear it to shreds until you're unsure of what you were refusing to begin with. All it took was a five-minute phone call where my mom lamented I missed the bridal shower due to distance, then claimed Scottsdale was recently named the most popular destination for bachelorette parties and Sienna would *just love* to have it here. Wham, bam, thank you ma'am.

Sienna called later that night, gushing about how sweet it is that I offered to plan her epic weekend of bride-to-be bliss. Then she sent me a picture of our mom's credit card. Her instruction to *keep it classy* went through my resentment-soaked listening filtration system, and... *here we are.*

Dick city, baby.

The theme is 'Last Rodeo, but make it phallic'. Lined up on the table in the common area are pink fluffy cowgirl hats, the one in the center bedazzled with rhinestones spelling out 'Bride'. A large sparkly banner announces 'Let's Go Girls' on a cow print background. Six cowgirl boot shaped cups hold six penis shaped straws. The banner over the mylar background reads 'Same Penis Forever'.

Honestly, it's amazing what you can find on the internet.

After the bar is set up (rosé, champagne, vodka, and sugar-free mixers), I take a shower and get myself ready. I'm shaking, either from lack of food or the stress of the day, so I mow down a protein bar I threw in my purse before I left my house this morning.

I have done a good (scratch that, *great*) job of pretending the whole situation is fine with me. My acting skills were good enough that I led my family to this point. If I'd been honest even once about how I felt about my sister dating my ex, I wouldn't be in this Spanish-tiled bathroom with the lighted mirror, holding back tears while I apply more eyeliner than I usually wear. My olive skin wouldn't be this pale. Thank goodness for bronzer and blush.

Gripping the edge of the marble countertop, I stare at my reflection and see Sienna by my side. We share the same shade of blonde hair, though hers is highlighted brighter than mine. Our eye color is different; mine a blue-green, hers a toffee brown. She got my father's round face and prominent eyebrows. My face is heart-shaped, my nose straight and pert, gifted to me by my maternal grandmother.

Sienna and I look alike, but there are differences. It makes me feel a smidge better. Shane is not dating my carbon copy.

I do not still love Shane, but once upon a time I believed I did. He broke up with me because he said I wasn't the right woman for him (his words). Not that *we* weren't right for each other. *I* wasn't right for *him*.

For me, it was out of the blue. He claimed he'd been wanting to do it for five months. I was flabbergasted. He stayed in a relationship with me for five months without actually wanting to be in a relationship with me? That was worse than him realizing I wasn't the one for him and ripping off the bandage. I felt pathetic.

Shortly after, he was offered a job in my hometown of Raleigh, of all places. He moved. I buried my nose in my work, and I've hardly looked up since. I have a lot to show for it, too. Professionally, at least. My personal life resembles the desert in which I reside.

And now, because my sister is not in possession of a fully functioning frontal lobe, and I'm lacking a backbone, soon Shane will be my brother-in-law.

···🐚🐚🐚···

My mother, Sienna, and her flock of three bridesmaids arrive at five p.m. precisely. I hear them in the hall, inserting a key card and shuffling their luggage. Two of the bridesmaids are friends from childhood, one is a college roommate, and all I've met at least once but don't remember with much detail. I'm four years older than Sienna, but it felt like light years when we were growing up. She entered high school, and I was leaving it. She started college, and I had recently graduated. The gap is even bigger for my brother, born three years after Sienna. Spencer feels like a distant relative sometimes. I've lived across the country from him for almost half his life. That's a lot, considering he doesn't remember his first five years.

I'm waiting a few feet inside the hotel room when the door swings open. Sienna is first, striding in looking fresh from a runway, not a four-hour flight. Her recently highlighted blonde hair is wound in the most depressingly perfect messy bun. Her black silk romper is probably soft but also makes it impossible to use the plane's lavatory. A white sash wound around her body reads 'Bride' in gold lettering.

*Classy.*

My mom and the rest of the 'I do' crew file in behind her. We hug, kiss cheeks, re-introduce (Wren, Maren, and Farhana), and then I watch with bated breath as Sienna steps into the living room. The suite has a view of Camelback Mountain and the waning sun, but she's staring at the décor. The moment, horror mixed with disgust, is camera-worthy, but I've left my phone in the bedroom. Paloma will be pissed I didn't capture the reaction for her to cackle over.

Sienna recovers, swallowing hard and forcing her petal pink lips into a smile. "Paisley," she says, "I should have known you'd outsource the preparations, as busy as you are with work."

She wraps an arm around me, and it feels like the hug is meant to console, like she's saying *It's not your fault the place looks like a nude sausage fest. It was those pesky perverts you hired.*

I'm not sure what it is about this hug, or maybe it's not the hug at all. Maybe it's the fact that I'm the floor and she's standing on me with those Gucci sandals, but I open my mouth and admit, "This is my handiwork."

She steps back, surveying me with wide brown eyes, and I almost feel bad about the *classy with penises* thing. Her left hand lifts to brush hair from her eyes and a pear-shaped diamond the size of a mythical giant's teardrop blinds me with its brilliance.

Never mind. Not sorry.

I gesture out at the room, looking at the bridesmaids and my mother, who are standing at the edge of the living room, waiting to follow my sister's cue. "Work came second today. These decorations are courtesy of yours truly. And mom's credit card, of course." That rectangular piece of plastic and fifteen digit code also paid for this hotel room, and is already on file with Obstinate Daughter, the restaurant where we have reservations tonight.

It's a trendy restaurant, with beautiful emerald green tiled floors, textured ivory walls, and copper accents. A hot spot with live music, it also serves a full dinner of upscale comfort food. The people-watching is superb, and that's my favorite part. If I don't see a sixty-year-old millionaire parsing through a group of twenty-somethings for his next ex-wife, I want my money back. Later, after our bellies are full, we'll move on to a second place for more drinks, and dancing if that's what Sienna wants.

My mother picks up a penis straw and glares at me. I bite back a grin. I don't know why this offends her so deeply. There are phallic shapes in all corners of everyday life.

Like, *ahem*, the plane she flew on to come to Scottsdale for the weekend.

Her eyes widen, accusing me, like she's saying *You knew what you were doing.*

My mouth opens, a habitual apology at the top of my throat, but I swallow it down. My jaw clenches as Paloma's words float through my head, and I find I don't want to apologize. I don't want to be a doormat. I want to get through this weekend, and then one week on Bald Head Island, and skedaddle my way back across the country where I will only have to see my sister and Shane on major holidays. *Maybe.* I hear St. John is lovely at Christmastime.

Sienna recovers, smiling brightly.

A whoosh of relief dips through me as she takes it in stride. I wasn't aiming to ruin her bachelorette party, only push her buttons a little.

She snatches the inflatable penis from the prop basket and pretends to kiss it. "The number one rule for this weekend, no posting pictures of me with this thing!"

The tension breaks. The bridesmaids leave us to deposit their luggage in their rooms on the same floor, and my mom and Sienna settle into the other room in the suite.

I sit on the bed and watch them unpack.

"How's Ben?" I ask my mom. Sienna rolls her eyes behind our mom's back.

Ben is my mother's boyfriend, fifteen years her junior. She tends to make inappropriate comments about their sex life, and Sienna probably hears more about it because they live five minutes apart and spends the most time with her.

A smile lights up my mom's face. "He's the best. Sweet, kind, generous"—her perfectly shaped eyebrows lift—"*if you know what I mean.*"

My cheek muscles work overtime to keep from making a face.

Sienna rolls her eyes a second time, giving me the *You knew it was coming* look.

I grin. So does she. Something in my chest fractures. I needed this interaction, this dose of sisterly bonding. I've built her up in my head to be the marrier-of-ex's, but she's still my little sister.

Sienna pulls two dresses from where she has recently hung them in the small closet and holds them out to me. "Which one?"

This is the time-honored female tradition of asking for fashion advice as a way of determining the climate of a relationship. It says *I'm not a threat, are you?*

I point left. "The white, obviously."

She nods happily. The sisterly warmth returns, and a well of hope springs up inside me. Maybe the weekend won't be so bad after all.

Maren, Wren, and Farhana return from their rooms, freshened up and dressed in their dinner clothes.

They're nice, but it's clear I'm on the fringe here. They know Sienna in a way I don't, and I can't help the stab of envy in my heart. If I'd never left North Carolina, stubbornly refusing to go the path my dad laid out, would Sienna and I be closer?

My mom plays bartender. She hands me a glass of champagne, and I force myself to sip when I want to gulp. By the time we're ready to leave for our dinner reservations, everyone is tipsy and drinking champagne from penis straws.

## CHAPTER 3

*Klein*

I keep a paperback book tucked under the bar. Not because I have time to read during my shift (that never happens), but I like to have it when I grab a five-minute break in the back of the restaurant. Usually I'm shoveling bites of whatever food the chef has placed on the metal break table while I read a few pages.

There's been no opportunity for a break yet tonight. Obstinate Daughter is slammed. Every seat at the horseshoe-shaped bar is taken, with even more people crowding around the backless teak stools. Every table in the dining room is booked throughout the evening. The DJ, here on weekend nights, sets up his station in a corner of the bar. He doesn't play pulsing club music, but more of a low-key background sound to match the hip, upscale vibe.

I'm on my first hour of nonstop drink making, and between the bodies jammed around the bar and the number of drink orders spitting out from the machine, it won't be slowing anytime soon. When I was sixteen and working my first job as a host in a little Mediterranean place, I found the bartenders aloof and cool. Then I became one and realized they were aloof because they had to save their socializing for all the patrons at the bar.

"Excuse me," someone screeches, a female, probably Lexi.

Five-foot-one Lexi emerges from a group of tall men standing near the bar, all holding icy beers. She wears a murderous glare as she barrels toward the drink pick-up station.

I close the lid on the cooler holding bottles of beer. "You look ready to commit heinous acts."

"Ugh," she groans, throwing down her drink tray on the rubber mat. "Why must they stand there?"

I line up all the glasses I'll need to make Lexi's long ass drink order. Grabbing a shaker and loading it with ice, I set about making lychee martinis for the thirty-seventh time tonight.

"If you haven't noticed," I glance up at Lexi briefly before continuing my work. "There's nowhere else to stand. I don't think I've ever seen it so busy."

The live DJ starts his music at that exact moment, taking the scene and ratcheting it up to nuclear. "It's that bachelorette party," Lexi yells.

I shake the steel mixer, give it a good thwack on the edge of the bar to loosen the top, and pour the mixture into the waiting chilled martini glasses.

Lexi leans over the drink station so I can hear her while simultaneously threading her long midnight black hair into a ponytail. "The bride is a piece of work. She won't shut up about the groom. Anybody who talks that much about their fiancé doesn't mean a damn word of it."

I nod and say nothing. I know better than to speak against Lexi. She divorced her philandering husband six months ago, and vociferously informs people he'd screw a cardboard box if it had a nice rack. That's verbatim.

Lexi loads up her drink tray with my freshly made martinis. "They're drinking like fish. At this rate, they're going to float out of here."

"Make sure you don't over-serve them," I caution, and for my care I am repaid with Lexi's middle finger made longer by her lime green fake nail.

My feelings are far from hurt. Coming from Lexi, the middle finger is a sign of love.

I palm my chest and pretend to gaze at the heavens. The moment is over and I grab Raul, my barback, and ask him to aid Lexi in her treacherous sojourn across the bar to where the drunken women await.

More tickets spill out from the printer. I'm reaching for the new orders when I catch sight of Lexi's finished ticket on the counter and realize she's missing a mixed drink. Lexi will undoubtedly give me grief for making her walk back through the crowd to deliver the missing drink. In the name of protecting myself from her verbal assault, I whip up a quick vodka with soda and round the bar.

I stand at precisely six feet tall, and unlike Lexi, my wide shoulders make it easy to navigate the sea of bodies. In no time I've made it through the bar patrons and into the only slightly more tame restaurant area.

The bachelorette party is easy to spot for many reasons, not the least of which is the woman at the center of the table wearing a hot pink cowboy hat that reads *Bride*. Shockingly, there isn't anything that resembles a dick anywhere in sight. At this point, I've seen it all. Obstinate Daughter is usually the first stop of the night for bachelorette parties. Carb-loading to start the festivities, I guess.

I get Lexi's attention by lifting the missing drink in the air. She hurries around the table and takes it from me, whispering, "Thank you, but now you need to get out of here. One of the bridesmaids said she's DTF, and her standards are low." Lexi delivers a small shove to go along with her warning. "You'd be right up her alley."

"I don't know what that stands for." I'm aware Lexi issued a jab, even if I don't know what DTF means. Current pop culture, and its common vernacular, is something I stay away from. Give me books, my laptop, my family, and my weekly soccer scrimmage. In none of what I listed is the acronym DTF.

Lexi makes a little ferocious sound that's not at all scary. "It means *down to fuck* you bookworm, and the longer you stay here, the more likely she's going to harpoon you."

So we're continuing with the under-the-sea metaphor? I like it. "Well—"

Lexi shoves me again, harder this time, and for her diminutive stature she has some power.

My weight shifts, and I spin with the intention of returning to the bar. But then I see... *her*.

Paisley Royce.

A woman who has haunted me for years. A dream, but in the flesh. A story I relive too often. Beautiful Paisley, with her unique blue-green eyes and her rosebud mouth.

Once upon a time, she and I shared a very messy, very drunken make-out session our freshman year of college. It was a terrible kiss, the kind you look back on and outwardly cringe. I grope-smashed her breast, our teeth clacked, and who knows what else happened. She was a friend of a friend, and I wound up at her off-campus apartment, a little high and a lot overwhelmed by how pretty she was. She smelled like orange blossoms, an all-time favorite scent of mine thanks to the three orange trees still growing in my mom's backyard.

Paisley was special, different, an electric connection. I'd never, and haven't since, felt pulled to someone with immediacy and urgency in equal measure. We talked for two hours, ranging from her obsession with Laffy Taffy (disgusting, in my opinion), to our shared love of Lord of the Rings and early aughts rom-com films.

She said I had lips like Peter Facinelli (I'd watched Can't Hardly Wait recently, and felt proud I knew the actor she was talking about), and I replied with a suave *But do my lips taste like his?* She said she didn't know what his lips tasted like, and I suggested she give mine a try so if the day ever came that she kissed Mr. Facinelli, she'd be able to compare.

The grope-smashing commenced.

The next day, fully sober and one hundred percent mortified, I sent her a text. Shooting for levity, I said *Hey, it's Klein, the guy you probably hoped to never hear from again.*

I must have hit the bullseye with that joke, because she did not respond. I waited a week, feeling more and more like an idiot with every day that passed, then deleted her number. What was I even thinking, a guy like me and a girl like Paisley? She had class and sophistication oozing from her pores. She sat with good posture, well-spoken and well-mannered, and I thought maybe I'd hit the lottery, or that God had decided to make my dreams of finding the perfect woman come true.

Yeah. *No.*

Reality was more than an ice bath, it was a caveman's spiked club across the head.

The experience taught me a valuable lesson: never get so drunk you cannot properly kiss a woman.

But that's not where the story of Klein and Paisley ends. It gets worse. Way, way worse.

The following semester, we found ourselves in the same creative writing class. She pretended I didn't exist. But me? I loved her from afar with a burning desire that consumed me. I lived for that twice a week seventy-five minute class. I went rain or shine, sickness or health. A gnarly cold didn't keep me away, but it did keep me at the back of the class, a polite distance from people. I could never get up the courage to talk to Paisley, not after that kiss she clearly regretted.

The regret gnawed at me. A connection like that doesn't come around often, and never so effortlessly. It wasn't the mind-altering substance either. Paisley herself was the mind-altering substance, a woman sent to complete me.

Did I know all this from one evening with Paisley? Yes, I did.

Except I'd squandered it.

And my misstep? Another dude capitalized on it.

Shane Michael (really? Never trust a guy whose last name is a first name) was meticulous about his clothing. And his shoes, which were too clean in my opinion. He made his move. Paisley began walking with him to class, then one day he was sitting beside her.

And me? I felt like I'd been gut-punched, only the fist never left my gut. It was lodged in there, a thorn, the pain a fresh wave every Tuesday and Thursday.

Until the day we handed back our assignment to anonymously critique a classmate's story. To be fair, I didn't know it was Paisley's story I tore apart. I was convinced the class was full of people who weren't serious about writing, like I was, people who took the course because it sounded easy.

The professor taught many of the classes in the creative writing program, and considering my life goal was (and still is) to be a writer, I saw an opportunity to impress him, and I took it.

I eviscerated Paisley's story. She cried. That's how I knew it was hers. She knew it was me because I'm the only asshole who took the assignment seriously enough to use a red felt pen, and guess who had that pen out on the table when her eyes performed a search for evidence? Between that and the sheepish look giving me away, I was toast.

And the look in her eyes?

I'd expected the hurt, but the disappointment had confused me. She looked like she didn't want to believe it was me who'd said what I'd said about her work. I didn't apologize, because I didn't know how to. Mortification from what I'd done to her writing, paired with her not responding to my text, swirled into a mass that left me unable to speak to her.

Which was tragic, because my infatuation did not wane in the months that followed. The semester ended, and it was like Paisley dropped off the face of the earth. Two serious girlfriends later, she became a figment of my memory, a stalwart in my daydreams.

Unbelievably, here she is now, situated to the left of the bride. She wears her hair loose, meandering curls falling over shoulders left bare by her dress. I bet the royal blue fabric makes her eyes more blue than green, and suddenly I'm insatiably curious to know if this is true.

She's still the most beautiful woman I've ever seen, and the memory of sitting beside her, of being the recipient of her thoughts on life and basking in her ebullience when she liked something I said, hits me hard in the center of my chest.

She's drinking one of those damn lychee martinis, and looks bored. Or sad. It's hard to tell. Her shoulders are stiff, and the corners of her mouth turn down, and that could mean a lot of things.

Lexi's push at my lower back knocks me from my reverie. It's good to be literally shoved back into reality; I could stand there and stare at Paisley all night.

I allow Lexi to urge me through the crowd for two reasons. One, there are probably an astronomical amount of drink tickets to work on. Two, I don't know what point there is in saying hello to Paisley after all this time. Probably best to let sleeping dogs lie.

Two cocktail servers send me death glares when I

duck behind the bar. I don't explain my absence, because it's too loud for them to hear me anyway.

After a solid twenty minutes focused on slinging drinks, I've reached a point where I'm caught up.

My pocket vibrates at the same time Raul says he's going to run to the back and tap a new keg.

"I'll do it," I offer quickly, stopping him. Usually I let all calls go to voicemail, but I'm waiting on one in particular.

Using the key on the ring in my pocket, I let myself into the keg room and pull out my phone.

"Dom," I say my cousin's name in lieu of a greeting.

"Where are you at?"

"Don't end your sentence in a preposition."

I can almost hear him rolling his eyes at me through the phone. "Where are you at, asshole?"

I don't have time for chit chat. "Work. I only have a minute."

I've been anxious all week. Dom's not only my closest cousin, he's also my literary agent. Recently he sent my book proposal to editors at all the major publishing houses.

"Good," he replies, "because it's not going to take more than ten seconds."

I deflate. Good news isn't delivered that swiftly. But bad news is.

"Nobody wants the manuscript?" I knew better than to hope, but I've been doing it quietly anyway. I press my phone to my ear with my shoulder and check to make sure the keg is empty.

"It's not your manuscript that's the problem. You're a debut author and you don't have any social media.

Publishers need you to at least have an online presence. They don't want to be solely responsible for your marketing." Dom clears his throat. "Also, everybody is online, so the fact you're not looks weird."

I hold my tongue as I turn off the $CO_2$ supply line. I'm weird for not sharing pictures of my dinner with strangers?

"I told you this might happen," Dom reminds me.

Right now, I want to take him by the neck and wrestle him to the ground like I used to when we were kids, before he moved to New York City for college and never left.

"Yeah, I know." I lift the coupler handle at the base of the tap where it joins the keg and rotate it counterclockwise.

I can't believe it. I've worked on that manuscript for four years. My soul is on those pages. And now it won't get the opportunity to be considered, because the price of admission is an online presence.

FML.

Take that, Lexi. I know an acronym.

"I gotta go," I say, reconnecting the coupler on the new keg.

"Consider social media," Dom says, not-at-all gently. "You can't win if you don't play."

"That's what people who buy lottery tickets say."

"And twenty-six year old writers who are one disappointment away from watching their dreams go up in flames."

"Dickhead," I mutter, stepping from the keg room and locking the door behind me.

"Go mix some drinks, cry baby. Call me when you're ready to put yourself out there."

He hangs up, and I slip my phone in my pocket. Dom gives me a fair amount of shit, but nobody has ever believed in me the way he has. He spent years letting me read my stories out loud to him. I am part of the reason he became a literary agent. He is part of the reason I continued writing.

*Go mix some drinks, cry baby.*

His harsh words accompany me back out to the music, the hordes of people swaying in place and laughing. It'll calm down soon, once everybody moves on to the row of bars and clubs a few streets over.

Crestfallen, I resume my job on autopilot.

Tending bar in a trendy restaurant isn't the worst, but I don't want to do this forever.

## CHAPTER 4
## *Paisley*

Everyone is hammered drunk, including my mom. They're talking about the next place they want to go, but I'm dreaming of returning to the hotel. Comfortable sweats, a glass of rosé, and a remote control sound like my idea of a perfect Friday night. I also would not like to waste the luxurious suite my mother shelled out for. The robe hanging in the hotel closet is softer than newborn kitten fur, and coincidentally has my name on it.

I've stuck around the restaurant to pay the bill using the credit card I placed on file to hold the table. I'm supposed to meet the rest of the party out front, but what are the chances they'll be too drunk to remember my instructions and wander off to the next destination without me? Pretty high, considering I feel extraneous to the group as it is.

Just like in the hotel room earlier, they're not intentionally placing me on the outskirts, but it's where I am. I don't have funny or cute stories to share about Sienna and Shane, like the other four women in our party. I fake smile and laugh my way through their tellings, but otherwise I'm quiet.

The server, Lexi, brings me the receipt to sign. Gratuity is included, but I add one hundred dollars and total out the bill. Somebody might as well have something good happen to them tonight.

I knew this weekend would be the ultimate test in my patience, but it's already more difficult than I thought it would be. If it's not the bridesmaids and how they're hanging on every word my sister speaks that's obnoxious, it's my sister and the way she won't stop gushing over Shane. I tuned her out halfway through dinner, then finished her chile-dusted fries out of spite while she recounted the time she was sick and he brought her soup and crackers and sparkling water.

Making my way across the restaurant, I march into the women's room and slip into the only available stall in the middle.

Two doors on either side of me open, heels smack the tile, and sink water runs.

A voice rings out. "It's pathetic, right?"

A second voice sounds in response. "Oh, totally."

I freeze. I know those voices. It's two of my sister's bridesmaids, but I'm uncertain which two.

"I mean, how is she even surviving tonight? I thought she was going to *die* when Sienna said Shane's nickname for her is 'Blondie'."

My elbows hit my knees, and my head drops into my hands. They're talking about me. How embarrassing.

For what it's worth, they're wrong. I did not feel like dying when Sienna said Shane's nickname for her is the very same nickname he gave me. What I really wanted to do was land a punch on that smooth jaw of his. Not because it hurts my feelings, but because my little sister deserves better than my nickname leftovers.

The shrill sound of a zipper fills the air, followed by the noise of rifling through something. A purse, probably. I stare at the honeycomb-shaped tile, waiting for them to finish and leave.

"I wouldn't be caught dead throwing my sister a bachelorette party when she's marrying my ex."

"I know, right? Sienna said she's not bringing a date to the wedding, either."

A pause follows, and I'm imagining an expression of shock and horror.

"Ouch."

"I think she works all the time and doesn't have a life."

"Did Sienna say that to you?"

"It was more that I was hearing what she wasn't saying."

My head snaps up. My hands shake and my face heats, Paloma's words from earlier mixing with this current gossip. I might let my family walk all over me, but that's where I draw the line. I'm going to step out of the stall and watch those girls' mouths drop open when they realize I've heard every word.

Except I had three glasses of water with dinner, and this is taking too long. As soon as I'm done I hustle through adjusting my dress, taking one precious second to twist my gaze around and make sure my dress isn't tucked into my underwear. A wardrobe malfunction would be icing on the shit cake that is this night.

Taking a quick, deep breath, I throw open the door, poised to deliver the biggest shock of their week.

They're gone.

I meet my gaze in the mirror above one of the sinks. My dress is as short and tight as the event and local trends necessitate. My hair is blown out and curled, my makeup is on point. From the outside I appear young and carefree. On the inside, I feel emotionally haggard, a person who's had too much asked of them.

I finish washing my hands as a buzzing comes from inside my purse.

My sister texts.

> We left a few minutes ago, meet us at the next spot. Love you!

Exiting the bathroom, I make my way toward the front of the restaurant. I glance left, and in a split-second decision, decide to steal an open seat at the bar. I just *cannot* anymore. I've reached my limit of being the sad sack on the periphery of the night.

I adjust my dress as I settle on the stool, tossing my purse on the bar top. The crowd is thinning, which is perfect because it's way easier to people-watch when I can see out.

My eyes rove around the horseshoe-shaped bar, landing on a man coming around the bottom curve. He's dressed in black jeans and a gray T-shirt with sleeves that stretch, straining against his biceps. He is tall, trim, his jeans doing something to his thigh muscles that should be illegal in at least forty-eight states.

My gaze finds his, and I gasp.

I know that guy.

I *despise* that guy.

Klein Madigan.

Indignation heats my fingertips, spreading up my arms and over my chest. My pulse skitters, galloping away like a horse in a tornado. My teeth sink into my bottom lip, a welcome pain spreading. I never got the chance to tell him off. To look him in his (annoyingly beautiful) green eyes and tell him how bad he made me feel. This guy is the reason I ever fell for Shane in the first place.

Which led to me introducing him to my sister.

Which led me to here, this night, *this moment*.

Everything wrong with my life is Klein Madigan's fault.

*Yes! That's right!*

A tiny voice inside me rejoices at having discovered the source of all my current problems. A gift, if you think about it.

Recognition flares on Klein's face, and he stops in his tracks.

My fight or flight alarm bells ring in my head.

*Run.* Now.

I'm reaching for my purse, calf muscles tense as I prepare to flee, when someone pops into my field of vision.

"What can I get you to drink?" she asks. Her magenta hair is parted down the middle and slicked back into a severe bun. On her it works, especially with those woven gold hoops in her ears.

This is it. Stay or go? My gaze flickers to Klein, but he's gone. I didn't imagine him, did I? It's not without possibility. There are times when I'm alone, when my thoughts turn to daydreams, that I see his face. But that's my little secret.

"A glass of rosé, please?" The part of me that says to run has been superseded by my curiosity.

"Be right back," she announces, turning on her heel and extracting a wineglass from a shelf above her head.

I watch her pour the wine, appreciating the shapely gold-rimmed glass, the laser-cut on the body. I have a thing for pretty stemware.

My phone rings at the same time the bartender sets my wine in front of me. I nod my thanks and pull my phone from my purse, assuming it's Sienna or my mother.

*Shit. No no no no.*

It's Shane.

My heart pounds in my chest as I stare at the screen, my brain scrambling for what to do.

Ignore. He's the last person I want to speak with.

Wait! Does ignoring him communicate something silently? Would he perceive it as something it's not? That I'm nervous? Overwhelmed?

That's the last thing I want him to think.

I take a healthy gulp of wine and answer before I can talk myself out of it. Here goes nothing.

"Hey," I answer, but it's almost a bark and comes off as defensive. Really not the impression I'd want to give if I'd had any warning about his call and could've had the chance to prepare.

"Pais," he says, his voice smooth, shortening my name like we saw each other last week.

"What's going on?" It's suddenly occurring to me there

might be a problem with Sienna. But if there were, wouldn't my mom have called me?

"Don't worry, everything is fine." He chuckles warmly, like worrying is just so *me*, like he remembers this detail about my personality and finds it endearing.

I want to smack him.

"I talked to Sienna a few minutes ago. She's having a great time. I thought I'd call and say thank you for throwing her this bachelorette party." He sounds so high and mighty, like he's reaching down from his bejeweled throne and patting the top of my peasant head. *Tap, tap.* "It was big of you."

"Big of me?" I parrot. The audacity has me flummoxed and unable to form my own coherent thoughts.

A second chuckle rumbles over the line, and I have a second urge to inflict bodily harm on him. "Yeah, you know, because we used to be a thing."

I'm two seconds from hanging up when Klein strides back around the bar. His green eyes zero in on me, affixing me to this moment, tethering me to the center of the emotional hurricane swirling around me. He hesitates, and then, despite me being on the phone, comes closer.

My heart batters my breast bone. Why do I have to like the way he walks? Who does that?

Attempting to get my bearings (and failing), I make the asinine choice to once again repeat Shane's last words. "We used to be a thing," I say slowly. Great. Shane probably thinks I'm so overcome by his phone call I cannot form original thought.

What's keeping me from using my brainpower is, unironically, the same person who caused me angst a long time ago. Klein stops directly in front of me, and he's all bronze with forearms that have the right amount of hair and corded muscle. His T-shirt dips and swells with his muscled chest. He is not supposed to have aged this well. Does he not know the rule of hated persons? Why is he not less attractive than he was the night I pulled him into my bathroom and attacked his face?

The corner of his mouth quirks, and *oh great* he thinks he's caught me ogling. It matters not that I was, in fact, ogling him. I cannot have him convinced of it. To rectify this, I shoot him a dirty look.

He snaps his fingers and points. "Now I remember you."

Channeling my inner six-year-old, I stick out my tongue. His eyes squint, like *really?*

Shane's voice breaks through. Whoops. He'd been speaking and I hadn't noticed. "...I think it's great you're coming to the wedding. I know things could be weird, but we don't have to let them be that way. It's all up to us, you know? We are the masters of our destiny."

Something tells me his shelves are still crammed with books about mindset mastery.

"Right," I agree, my gaze locked on Klein, but I'm not sure I fully understand what I'm agreeing to. My past has come hurtling at me from different directions and I'm busy drowning in the convergence.

Music from the DJ in the corner wraps around me, the sound breaking the spell. I blink twice, grasping at my loosely tethered bearings. Klein turns to go but I hold out one finger, imploring him to wait. I don't know why. It shouldn't matter to me if he stays or goes.

Shane drones on. "It would be great if you could bring someone with you, but Sienna said you aren't seeing anybody?" The inference hangs, heavy and irritating. *Poor, sad Paisley.* "Don't worry, Pais, you'll find someone."

The unwelcome platitude, offered with a tone of patronizing comfort, is the last straw for me. My molars grind. Angling the phone away from my mouth, I lean over the bar and curl my finger at Klein. He sends me a quizzical look but comes closer.

His nearness almost derails my thoughts, stopping my idea in its tracks, but I hold tight to my resolve and say, "On three, will you please say something a boyfriend would say to me?"

He makes a face. "What?"

"Please, just do it. You owe me." I give him an imploring look, but truth be told this is the boldest request I've ever made in my life.

He stares long enough I'm certain he's going to deny me, but then a little twinkle flits across his eyes. I'll take that as acquiescence.

Placing the phone back at my mouth, I say in a louder voice, "I must've forgotten to tell Sienna I'm seeing someone. He's here with me now."

I count off on my fingers and hold out the phone. Klein's lips hover an inch from my screen. His green-eyed gaze grips me as he says, "Paisley, baby, get off the phone. I'm done sharing you."

I swallow. Hard.

Did *Paisley baby get off the phone I'm done sharing you* just become my favorite ten words in the English language? Yes, but I'll never admit it out loud.

"Oh," Shane replies, and I detest how surprised he sounds. "I didn't realize—"

"Ok, bye now." I hang up, covering my mouth as I cackle from sheer relief at the severing of the connection with Shane. Klein looms in front of me. Another ghost from college past. Shoving the phone in my purse, I begrudgingly mutter, "Thank you."

A small machine on my right prints a drink order, and he jumps into action. He reads the paper for three seconds before laying it on the bar and preparing the drinks.

"You're welcome," he returns with his own mutter.

I'm quiet, sipping my wine as I watch the way he moves, confident in his maneuvering in the small space. He tilts a glass at an angle and pulls the lever on the tap. Amber beer spills into the cup.

A memory hits me. *The edge of the counter digs into my lower back as our mouths collide. The kisses are sloppy, hasty, the alcohol elongating our limbs and rubberizing our lips. Someone bangs on the door, breaking the spell.*

It was objectively the worst kiss of my life. But we were young, and sweet, and handsy, and for these reasons I look back on it fondly. When I pressed my nose to his neck, he smelled like spiced apples and something I couldn't name but immediately made me a different kind of drunk.

Impossible though it seemed, I felt a deep and immediate connection to Klein. It sounded crazy, and felt even crazier, but when I looked in his eyes there was a future. It didn't have form or shape, but it was there. It was Klein by my side. My friend, my partner, my lover. By then I'd spent the better part of two years hurting following the break up of my family, and Klein's smile was like spreading magic salve on a wound.

The connection was one-sided. He didn't use the number I put in his phone. Then he took my short story, which wasn't fictional like the assignment was supposed to be, and ripped it to shreds.

I finish my wine, because I don't know what else to do. I've never randomly made out with someone, hated them, and run into them eight years later. Is there a protocol for this sort of thing? A standard operating procedure?

Klein uncorks the rosé bottle and gestures to my glass.

I nod, not because I want another glass of wine, but because I want to keep him here. I haven't decided if I'm going to let him have it. If he disappears on me now, I won't get the chance.

"Where's the rest of your crew?" he asks tightly, stowing the bottle in the fridge below.

"You saw us?"

He nods. "You're hard to miss."

Flipping the tiny plastic switch on my light-up ring, I lift my right hand in the air. "Was it the flashing penis?"

He grabs my raised hand, holding it still between us. His other hand moves for my elbow, fingertips slowly trailing up the inside of my arm. Goose bumps rise on the sensitive flesh, a ball of heat forming in my stomach. The intensity in his gaze highlights the gold threads in his green irises. The heat in my core blooms, spanning up and out, through my chest and into my arms. I force in a shallow breath, pushing it out with effort. What is Klein doing to me? And why is my body, the treacherous traitor, responding in such a way?

Klein's touch skims my wrist, bumps over the heel of my palm and, using two fingers, he removes the strobing ring and tosses it in the trash.

Devious! The man used the power of distraction to disarm me.

My annoyance soars as I realize the sizzle of heat between our hands wasn't attraction. I don't know what it was, but I know what it wasn't. I snatch my hand from his grasp. He smirks. It makes him even more attractive, and incenses me.

"I despise those things," he says matter-of-factly.

"What a grump," I shoot back. I'm actually glad to be rid of the accessory, which only annoys me further. I bought the rings, but I expected Sienna to refuse them. A couple drinks and she was insisting we all wear them to dinner. We'd ended up turning them off because they cast colors over our faces when we took pictures.

I hold back a sigh and assess Klein. Maybe we should clear the air. Just get it out in the open. Or maybe it doesn't matter. I can go on my merry way and haul my rear end across the country to an island and fake smile my way through a wedding and never see Klein again.

Also, maybe I'm tipsy. More than tipsy. Topsy-turvy.

"Topsy what?" Klein folds his arms in front of his chest, biceps popping, and looks at me like I've lost my mind.

I clamp my mouth shut. The fewer words I say right now, the better. I cannot trust that my inner thoughts will not become audible.

Klein opens his mouth to speak, but a woman comes

from out of nowhere and throws her upper half on the bar.

"I'd like to order a desert beetle," she says breathlessly.

I lean back, but only so I can better take her in. She's pretty, with brick red nails that match her lip stain. Her dress leaves little to the imagination, but that's par for the course where we are. Her eyes are imploring, like she's attempting to communicate something to Klein.

He offers a terse nod. "Coming right up."

Instead of making a desert beetle (gross), he rounds the end of the bar, stepping out from behind it. He strides our way, and it really is unfair how good he looks. His shoulders stretch on forever. His chest is muscled just right, giving way to a tapered waist. He was handsome back then, but this is... well, this is something else entirely.

"Come on," he says, stopping beside me and the woman.

"Me?" I ask, pointing back at myself. I am beyond confused. Didn't this lady just order a drink from him?

Klein makes a face at me, and I shrink back. "No," he grunts, clearly irritated at my question.

"Oh gee, sorry, I guess you were talking to someone else you drunkenly sucked face with eight years ago."

He gives me a sharp look. I ignore it. The wine is hitting me now. So is the embarrassment at thinking it was me Klein was inviting to join him to some unknown place.

The woman steps away, and Klein takes her by the elbow. I know this is the least sexual part of the body and so it shouldn't matter that he's touching her. It also shouldn't matter because *I don't even like him*, but I can't help feeling slighted. I was in the middle of verbally sparring and she ruined it.

*Wait a damn minute.* Is 'desert beetle' a bizarre code for a hookup? Is Klein a part of a tawdry club of individuals who order sex acts using code words?

I'm going to be sick.

The pink-haired bartender who I feel too intimidated by to ask her name comes my way. She doesn't know Klein poured me a second glass, and when she gestures with the bottle I nod my head.

I cannot begin to understand the last thirty minutes of my life. I give up.

## CHAPTER 5
*Klein*

"Get home safe." I tap the hood of the white Honda Civic.

The driver, Saul, gives me a two-fingered salute and pulls away from the curb. The woman, safely tucked inside, waves from the back seat.

*I'd like to order a desert beetle* is code for *I'm on a date and I don't feel safe, please escort me out.*

It's posted on the inside of every stall door in the ladies' restroom. We are under strict instruction from management to drop everything we're doing, no matter what it is or how busy we are, and help the person out to their car.

Tonight was the third time this has happened to me. The woman, Annie, didn't have a vehicle to drive home, so I waited with her until the Uber came. Luckily there was one nearby, and the wait was only seven minutes.

I'm stepping back into the restaurant, preparing myself to address Paisley's *sucking face* comment, just in time to catch Paisley's beautiful face with her eyebrows drawn, stiff pointer finger extended, say to a group of young guys, "Nice matching hairstyles. You know who else gets perms? Your great-grandmas."

I pause long enough to rake a hand down my face and push away the reluctant smile tugging at my lips. She's not wrong. All five guys probably turned twenty-one in the last year, and all five sport matching unnaturally curly hair.

Hustling to the bar, I place myself between Paisley's indignant eyebrows and the death stare she's sending their way.

"Pais," I start but she transfers her ire to me.

"Do not call me that," she thunders, a storm brewing in her blue-green eyes. There's a softness there too, a fragility that tugs at my chest, stirring me.

I hold up my hands. I'm not interested in pissing her off. Not any more than I do simply by existing. "No problem."

I hurry around the bar and return to where I'd been standing before the blonde showed up. Peeking at the tab in front of Paisley, I see Halston has added a third glass of wine.

Wow. Ok. Paisley is probably pretty drunk, and I know she had at least one lychee martini with dinner.

Her arms cross, her eyebrows tugging together. "Those guys—"

I wave off her explanation. "They've been mouthy since they arrived. I'm sure they deserved it."

Leaning her elbows on the bar, she rubs at her eyes and admits, "I'm drunk."

Pushing down my laugh, I say, "I know." To busy myself, I grab a towel and wipe down the bar beside her.

A loud breath vibrates her lips, and she says, "My sister is marrying my ex-boyfriend and I'm her maid of honor."

My cleaning halts. "Why did you agree to such a thing?" Why would someone put themselves through that? Doesn't Paisley have the word 'no' in her vocabulary?

"Because I'm the floor," she wails, dramatically tossing a hand in the air.

Wow. She's really drunk.

Paisley's elbow connects with the bar top once again and she catches her forehead in her hand. I use the opportunity to snatch her wineglass and pour a majority of what's left in it down the sink.

"Can I get you a ride home?" I ask.

She straightens up, squinting at me suspiciously. "Where did you go with that woman?"

I pull a face. "What woman?"

"Busty McBusterton."

Alright. Something besides wine and lychee martinis is in this woman. She's hallucinating.

"I have no idea what you're talking about."

She sends me an exasperated look. "The woman who ordered a *bug*."

Ohhhh. Paisley's lower lip puffs out the tiniest bit. Is she jealous?

*Busty McBusterton.* I smash my lips together to keep from laughing in Paisley's face. Ok, yes, the woman had what my mother would call an 'ample bosom', and anybody with two working eyes would see it because there wasn't a lot to that dress.

"I was helping her get a ride home."

"Sure." Paisley crosses her arms, making a face that demonstrates how little she believes me. "You probably took her out to your car for...for...lascivious acts." Her nose scrunches on the word 'lascivious.'

I scoff, only to cover up my intense desire to roll on the ground and laugh until my sides ache. "Are you a fiction writer? Because you should be. That's a great story you just dreamed up."

Paisley looks like she wants to come over the bar and knee me in the balls. "I quit my writing career before it ever started because *someone* took a torch to my very first story." She sniffs. "You ruined my career."

"What? That's ridiculous. I did not ruin your career. *You* ruined your career when you let one person hurt your precious feelings. If anything, I did you a favor. If a critique of your first story hurt your feelings this badly, you'd never hack it in the writing industry. You don't only need thick skin, Paisley, you need calluses. So"—I step back and bend at the waist, sweeping one arm sideways and bowing—"You're welcome."

When I straighten, Paisley is dragging her purse off the bar and sliding from her stool. She steps away and wobbles.

Shit. Shit shit shit. That was too harsh. My bad news from Dom has me acting out.

I whip around, keying my employee number into the computer. When I'm finished clocking out, I yell to Halston on the other side of the bar. "I need to walk someone—" Does Paisley have a car here? If so, she can't drive. "—somewhere," I finish.

Halston rounds the curved part of the bar, eyebrows tightly drawn, hands glued to her hips. "I hate closing alone. You owe me." Funny, it's the second time tonight a woman has said that to me.

"Eternally," I confirm, already chasing down Paisley.

She's striding through the front door of the restaurant by the time I catch up to her. From behind, she looks like my type. Long blonde hair, athletic legs, and an ass that makes me want to bite my fist. Paisley sounded envious of that other woman's chest size, but I'd take Paisley's backside over—

Nope. Not even going there. Those thoughts have bad idea written all over them.

She doesn't know I'm behind her, and that makes me feel like a creep until she stumbles walking down the three concrete steps leading to the sidewalk on the main road.

One quick jump to the pavement and I'm there, catching her before she can fall. Paisley doesn't know it's me, so she screeches, a banshee in close proximity to my face, and attempts to hit me with her tiny excuse for a purse.

I bat away the less-than-accurate attack. "Calm it down, She-Rambo. Your face almost kissed the pavement." I step back, but keep a grip on her upper arms. "Where are you headed?"

"Agave." She squints one eye and points in the wrong direction. "It's that way."

Of course she's staying at Agave. It's the newest, swankiest luxury resort in downtown Scottsdale. Phoenix hosted the Super Bowl last year and guess where one of the teams stayed? Agave.

I rotate her shoulders the right direction and release her. "Lead the way."

She makes a face. "Why the hell are you following me there?"

"Accompanying," I correct.

One hand on her popped hip, head swaying as if on a pendulum, she sasses, "Again I ask, why the hell are you following me there?"

So damn stubborn, this woman.

"You're drunk, and I don't want you walking alone."

"I'm not alone. I'm going to find my sister." She takes her phone from her purse and brings the screen too close to her face. After reading something, she frowns and puts the phone in her bag. "They're back at the hotel."

*How nice of them to leave you behind.*

I gesture out with an open palm. "Start walking."

Paisley says something I can't hear, stares at me for three full seconds, and then, at long last, marches away.

Agave is close by, and it takes all of three minutes to reach it. Paisley's navigation of the sidewalk is impressive, considering she is both drunk and wearing at least three inch heels. Maybe four. Who the hell knows.

She reaches the sliding glass door entrance, flanked by potted desert flora, and whips around to face me. "You owe me a flashing penis ring."

My gaze goes to the teenage valet to see if he's overheard. He's looking away pointedly, so I'm going to assume he did. I blow out a gusty sigh and answer. "Never going to happen."

"You"—Paisley steps closer and pokes my chest—"are just jealous because yours doesn't light up."

With one eyebrow cocked, I look down at her. "How do you know it doesn't?"

She gasps and takes a step back, her palm pressed dramatically to her chest. "Was that a joke, Mr. Serious?"

"I would never joke about phallic light shows."

She releases an annoyed breath. "Literally cannot tell if you're joking, because your face looks ten kinds of stern."

"Paisley, there is only one kind of stern. Stern. That's it." I hold up a finger. "Just the one."

She rolls her eyes. "You're as repugnant as you were back then."

That actually hurts, but I'll be damned if I show it. Mental note: use the word repugnant in my next novel.

Her chin juts out, head sideways. "I made it in one piece, so yay. Bye."

Her dismissal sits between us. She doesn't move, other than to cross her arms in front of herself.

There's no reason to prolong this, to offer a perfunctory but well-meaning *call me sometime.* She knows where I work. If she wants me, she can find me. Not that she's going to want me at all, for any reason, ever. She is under the impression I ruined her future, and why work to disabuse her of the belief? I probably won't see her again after tonight.

With my hands crammed into my jeans pockets, my shoulders reach for my earlobes in a silent *There's nothing left to do here but go* motion.

Paisley says not a word as I turn to leave. I've taken

two more steps away when there's a commotion at the hotel entrance.

A group of women pour out the sliding glass doors. They're dressed in expensive clothing, talking over one another. One holds her phone in the air and makes face after face as she snaps selfies. Another woman catches sight of Paisley and halts, obviously relieved. "Where have you been?"

Paisley's gaze falls on me, as do five other pairs of eyes. Everyone looks curious except for the woman wearing the 'Bride' hat. She looks delighted.

She approaches, peering at me and clapping her hands twice. "Pais, you didn't have to get me a stripper." The fact that she belts out the word 'stripper' as if she's in a Broadway musical takes the horror of this moment and makes me want to find a hole to crawl into.

I wait for Paisley to correct this woman I'm assuming is her sister, but the correction must be stuck inside her throat, because she isn't saying a word. Paisley's sister circles me, a lioness preparing to leap at a gazelle's jugular.

"Paisley, do you think I could hang from his arm if he flexed? This guy is jacked." She paws at my arm, peering at her sister. "Good choice."

"Hello?" I urge Paisley. I could make the correction myself, but I don't want to embarrass her sister. Did she just squeeze my bicep?

Paisley grins, enjoying this show far more than she should. "Hi."

I release a hard breath of annoyance and shake my head. If Paisley's not going to make the correction, I will.

Holding up my hands, I step away from Paisley's prowling cat of a sister. "I'm not a stripper, I'm—"

"He's a police officer," one of the girls in the group yells, jumping up and down and pointing at me. "He's here to arrest you, Sienna, because you've been bad."

Someone else hollers, "Watch out for the long arm of the law."

The group of women cackle. I snap my head at Paisley. Her hand presses against her mouth, eyes sparkling like this is a comedy skit.

Fine. She wants to leave me out here to fend for myself? No problem. Two can play this game.

Gently, I remove Paisley's sister's hands from my forearm. "Actually," I say, my voice raised enough that it gets their attention. Closing the space between me and Paisley, I place my hands on her hips and roughly haul her into me. Her hands land on my chest, and before she can protest, I say loudly and with confidence, "I'm Paisley's boyfriend, and my strip shows are meant for an audience of one." Then, to really add to the moment, I boop the end of Paisley's nose.

Murder flares in her eyes, and that should be a warning sign, but I'm distracted by the ocean color of her irises. They are probably even prettier when they're not shooting death rays my direction.

"Paisley?" An older woman steps around the shocked group.

I release Paisley, but only enough so that she can turn and address the person I'm assuming is her mother.

"Yes, Mom?"

The woman's gaze darts from Paisley to me and back again. "Is this true?"

Any moment now Paisley is going to spin this into a joke, so I'll just wait.

Paisley's gaze lingers on my face, and I can tell somewhere in those eyes she's making a decision. She looks back at her mother. "It's true."

What? Panic shoots through me. Now what do I do?

I'm still looking down at the top of Paisley's head, but I feel her mother's eyes burning holes into my temple. An automatic smile appears on my face, but it is tight-lipped and tense.

Why is Paisley lying? I honestly didn't know what I was thinking when I decided to slot myself into the boyfriend role, but I guess somewhere in the back of my mind I'd assumed there was no way Paisley would go along with it. It's not like I gave it that much thought or consideration before I opened my big mouth, but the real question is why Paisley is letting the lie exist?

I could be a real dick and announce the lie myself, but contrary to popular belief, I'm not an asshole.

So, I smile at Paisley's mother and offer my hand. "I'm Klein. It's nice to meet you."

Her mother eyes me suspiciously as she takes my offered hand. "Robyn. Why am I just now hearing about you?"

"It's new, Mom," Paisley answers from beside me.

Paisley's sister pushes in. "I'm Sienna. Sorry about the bicep fondling." She looks different from Paisley, despite sharing a vague similarity. It's the eyes, I think, and not only that they're different colors. In Paisley's eyes is a depth that does not exist in Sienna's.

I'd like to ask her how she justifies marrying her older sister's ex-boyfriend, but it's not appropriate. I won't lie though, I'd like to know. My sister has thoroughly educated me on girl code, and I'm positive this goes against it.

"No worries," I answer. "Just to be certain, are you expecting a stripper?" If so, I'd really like to be absent for the entertainment portion of the evening.

Paisley shakes her head. Sienna looks relieved. "Phew. I told Shane there wouldn't be any of that happening this weekend. He's so possessive." She grins slyly, telling everybody she likes this facet of his personality.

Lexi's complaint from earlier comes back to me. She'd said the bride wouldn't stop gushing about the groom. But now I know the groom is Paisley's ex, which probably makes comments like the one Sienna just spoke pretty hard on Paisley.

Without giving it too much thought and talking myself out of it, I thread my fingers through hers, squeezing her hand lightly. She flinches like I've caught her off guard, then relaxes and I feel the tiniest amount of pressure against my hand.

It's...nice.

So is that scent of hers, the orange peel and vanilla that makes Paisley smell too damn good.

"We're headed to a diner a couple blocks over," Robyn says to me. "If you'd like to join us?"

"He can't," Paisley rushes to say. "He needs to get back to work."

I don't tell her I clocked out. What's the point?

"Oh?" Robyn raises her eyebrows as much as she can. Her forehead is stiff. "What do you do for work?"

It's clearly a test to see if I'm good enough to be dating her daughter. That's laughable, considering the last ten minutes have been nothing but lies. Briefly, I consider telling her I am a circus clown, but decide not to, because that would probably only serve to embarrass Paisley. And even though I started all this with the goal of embarrassing Paisley, at this point, I'm beginning to feel sorry for her.

"I'm a bartender."

Robyn nods curtly.

If I were actually dating her daughter, and cared what she thought, that would sting.

It's annoying, though, so I add, "I'm doing that while I wait for my agent to sell the publishing rights to my novel."

Paisley's gaze bores into the side of my head. Considering she believes I am at fault for ruining her illustrious future writing career, she's probably not super happy to hear I've written a novel.

Robyn does not appear to be impressed. "Hmm. A starving artist. How... artsy."

What the hell? I'm not over here painting a rock the color red and then calling it a masterpiece. I poured over that manuscript for years. I skipped social engagements, typed bleary-eyed scenes at two a.m. only to delete them eight hours later when I woke up.

The group is silent, and it seems to clue Robyn in to

the fact that she has been rude. She scrambles, saying, "Are you working with Paisley's marketing firm?"

Marketing firm? Now that's interesting. Marketing happens to be the thing I'm worst at. It pains me that I can write all those words, but I don't know how to talk about them.

"We're working out the details," Paisley answers, sounding like she can't wait for the end of this conversation. "Anyway, Klein needs to go back to work. And there's a plate of onion rings with your names on it."

The group waves goodbye, but Sienna turns back, forming a megaphone around her mouth and yelling, "I'll see you on Bald Head Island, Klein."

I scratch the back of my head with two fingers and try to figure out what Sienna is talking about. I come up empty. Paisley's eyes are wide, saucers, telling me she's horrified by what her sister said.

Paisley watches the group disappear down the street. "Obviously she's not going to see you on Bald Head Island."

I shrug. "I don't even know what a Bald Head Island is."

Paisley shoots me a withering look. "It's a *place*."

"A noun, in either case."

The corner of her mouth quirks, but she bats away the tiny semblance of a grin. "I'm dead on my feet. I need to rip off these high heels immediately and fall into bed." She points down to her feet. "Unless you want to come upstairs and keep playing the role of boyfriend and rub my feet."

Does that sound appealing to me? Yes it does.

I'm not a foot guy, but I'm also not *not* a foot guy. I admit, the idea of caring for Paisley intrigues me. She was joking though. Of course she was.

Taking the hint, I say, "See you around, Paisley."

She steps away, a mischievous glint in her eyes. "See you around, Klein the stripper."

Laughter steals up my throat. I like her dry, teasing sense of humor.

She disappears into the fancy hotel, and I'm left out here on the sidewalk shaking my head.

Tonight has to be the most confusing night I've had in a very long time. Possibly ever.

Even more confusing is the overwhelm in my chest, the odd feeling of loss.

Paisley has never been mine.

There was nothing to lose.

## CHAPTER 6
### *Paisley*

I will never ever drink again.

If I open my mouth wide enough, balls of cotton may tumble out. My brain screams at me, the sound reverberating through my head and making everything worse.

My mother is currently passed out on the other half of my hotel bed. I found Sienna asleep in the bathtub, mascara streaking her cheeks. To be fair, the bathtub is large enough to fit Hagrid from Harry Potter, and his giantess girlfriend.

As for the rest of the 'I do' crew, I'm assuming they made it back to their respective hotel rooms.

And here I am, braving the outside world. I would still be snuggled in bed if I hadn't realized I left my credit card at the restaurant last night. I'd been so busy mouthing off to those curly haired assholes who teased me about Klein choosing the big boob woman over me that I'd forgotten to put my credit card in my wallet after I paid my tab.

Obstinate Daughter opens at nine for brunch on

Saturdays, according to the website I looked at before abandoning the ridiculously high thread count bedsheets.

Pushing my sunglasses on top of my head, I step inside the restaurant. Half the tables are seated, the scent of rosemary potatoes and spicy chorizo wafting through the bright space. It's easy reconciling last night's trendy spot with this morning's more low-key but still hip brunch vibe. My gaze swings to the bar. The pink-haired woman pours tomato juice into a pitcher, then adds some spices.

I send up a quick *thank you* to God for answering my prayer. On the walk over I asked this to be a non-Klein event, and so far that head of wildflower honey hair and expansive chest are not present. I cannot handle seeing him this morning. Not after last night, when he, for whatever reason, decided to tell my family he's my boyfriend. And then I, for whatever additionally stupid reason, decided to go along with it. It would've been so much easier if I said he was joking, but I was tender after that conversation with Shane and overhearing the bridesmaids in the bathroom. My ego was bruised, and my mind was inebriated. Calling Klein my boyfriend was just the stroke it needed. Unfortunately, my sober self will pay the price later today when I have to tell the truth and spin it as a joke that went on too long, instead of a lie. If they know I lied, the most natural follow up question would be, *Why?*. After that, it would be a fountain of words I don't want to say. Some worms are better left in the can.

My little sister marrying my ex-boyfriend qualifies as a worm in a can. And there it will stay.

"Hi." I wave, approaching the bar. "I'm sure you don't remember me from last night, but—"

Her gaze flicks over to me, her hands never stopping their task. "I remember you."

Eesh. I get the feeling it's not good she remembers me.

"I think I left my credit card here?"

She stops stirring the tomato mixture. "You think? Or you know?"

Intimidated but in desperate need of my credit card, I open my mouth to answer. A deep voice from behind me answers instead.

"You left it. And I found it."

I whirl around. Klein, dressed in dark gray joggers and a light blue V-neck, stands three feet away. He holds my credit card out between us.

"Thank you," I breathe, taking it and dropping it into my purse.

Why does he have to look good enough to eat, while the only thing I look good enough to be eaten by is a dog? I'm not even the good, fresh food. I'm kibble. My hair is piled on top of my head, and not in a cute way. I'm positive my makeup is smeared under my eyes just like Sienna's, courtesy of falling asleep before washing my face last night. And honestly, my head hurts too much for me to care.

But I still do. A little.

"I saw you left it behind last night when I came back in to grab my car keys," Klein explains. "I was going to swing by your hotel later and drop it off with the front desk. I didn't think you'd be up this early or I would've done it right away."

"I didn't think I'd be up this early either," I grumble, "but my mom was snoring."

Klein breathes a laugh. "I have a hard time picturing your mom snoring."

"It only happens when she's had too much to drink. Also, Sienna fell asleep in the bathtub."

"Picture?"

"Already added it to my hidden 'blackmail Sienna' folder in my photos app."

Klein nods. "Always a solid idea to conceal the evidence."

I purse my lips. Are we...getting along? Flirting, even? Unacceptable.

"Well, Klein the stripper. Thanks for saving me from certain credit card fraud." I move to side step him.

"You're a good liar," he says, making me pause.

"My fibbing abilities appear to be on par with yours." I give him a meaningful look. He holds up his hands in acquiescence. "I guess I'll be drawing on those lying skills again today."

He adjusts his stance, his shirt sliding to accommodate the movement. I'm just going to pretend his chest isn't straining against the fabric more than it was before. "Why is that?"

"Because I have to come up with a break-up story. Either that, or explain why we were joking, to which they will want to know what about all that I found funny."

Klein shrugs. "So don't tell them we broke up."

I snort. "What exactly am I supposed to tell them when I attend my sister's wedding without my boyfriend on my arm? That he is afraid of water, and therefore cannot be on an island?"

"Since when do you have a girlfriend?"

Ok, whoa. I forgot there's a third person standing nearby.

Klein looks over my shoulder. "Halston, how wonderful of you to enter the chat."

She flips him off. "I'm standing right here. How rude of you to ignore me." She bends to put something in a fridge, then straightens. "Two questions. One"—she looks at me, eyebrows raised—"This is not your girlfriend, so who is she? And two, why did she refer to you as *Klein the stripper*, and can I pretty please make that your nickname?"

"That was three questions." Klein passes me. He pulls out two barstools, gesturing for me to sit.

I'm settling on the stool when Halston says, "Answer all three and I'll view it as an apology for not introducing me to your new girlfriend who is *not Megan*."

Blood rushes from my head, pooling in my stomach. Of course he has a girlfriend. Why wouldn't he?

Klein drops onto the stool beside me. With one shoe propped on the bottom rung, he presses his forearms to the bar top. "Megan and I broke up, Halston. Six months ago. You know this."

Is that relief I feel? No. That wouldn't make sense.

She crosses her arms and raises her eyebrows. "Is that why she was in here last week, giving you puppy dog eyes?" She peers at him, waiting. I have to admit, I'm peering at him also, and not just because his five o'clock shadow is the perfect blend of rugged masculinity. I am inappropriately invested in learning whether or not this Megan person is really his ex.

"Where is duct tape when you need it?" Klein mutters.

Halston smirks. Pushing Klein's buttons appears to be a favorite pastime of hers.

My attention ping-pongs between them.

Klein, looking supremely irritated, says, "She found a writing book of mine that had a bunch of notes and highlights, so she thought I'd like it back."

Not missing a beat, Halston volleys. "Did she think you might like her back, also?"

An involuntary laugh escapes me. Klein side-eyes me, but says to Halston, "Not that it's any of your business, but no."

Halston's eyes settle on me, but she looks less combative than she was when I walked in. Maybe it was me laughing at her joke. She seems defensive of Klein. Not in a way that makes me think she likes him, but that she cares for him as a friend. "New girlfriend?" she asks, eyebrows raised at me.

My nose wrinkles. "No way."

Halston nods, glancing back to Klein. "I like this one. Anybody who thinks you're gross is a friend of mine." She turns to me. "Do you want breakfast? I bet you're hungry after last night."

An embarrassed warmth fills my cheeks. "Starving."

"Perfect, I'll order two of Klein's breakfast."

"You have your own breakfast?" I ask Klein. His elbows rest on the bar, his chin nesting on the heel of his right palm.

"She calls it that because I come in here every Saturday morning and eat before I go to soccer."

"You play soccer?" I ask, pouncing on this morsel of information. I don't know why I find it so interesting.

"I play matches for fun once a week, but on Saturdays, I coach my nephew's recreational team. Or I used to, anyway, before my nephew joined a club." Klein glances at his watch. "Today is his first game with his new team."

I stare at him without meaning to, trying to decide if he's lying about coaching his nephew's soccer team, or if he really is quite possibly a nice guy. The thought makes me shift in my seat. In my memory, he has been a villain. But coaching his nephew's recreational soccer team? That's hero uncle status, and it does not fit inside the box I've put him in.

"Hmm," I say, because there's no way I'll say what I'm really thinking.

Halston watches me from her computer with shrewd eyes. I am almost positive she sees right through me. "It's really too bad you guys are already breaking up," she says, fingers tapping at the screen as she places our breakfast order. "You have chemistry."

Klein pretends to elbow me. "No, we don't," he argues.

*Yes, we do.* Hence why I pulled you into my bathroom once upon a time and suctioned my lips to yours.

Halston ignores him. She makes a water for each of us, placing them on the bar. "Explain to me why you are both good liars, and why you have to tell people you're breaking up when you weren't together in the first place?"

I drink all my water in one go, then deliver the story. Klein interjects to insist he didn't mean for everyone to believe us last night. He didn't fully think of what he was saying until he spoke.

"I hate to break it to you," Halston says when I finish telling the story, "but you can't show up to your sister's wedding to your college sweetheart without a date. Even worse, fresh from a 'break up'. Double loser status."

I suck in a horrified breath. "Why didn't I think of that?" I turn on Klein.

He's ready with a palm extended to block me, eyes wide in defense. "You asked me to say something a boyfriend would say, remember? To whomever you were on the phone with last night?"

He has a point, but I'm unwilling to budge. Besides, I could've turned that into a story, told my sister I'd roped some random guy into saying that. "You made this worse. They put eyes on you." I groan into my hands. "Seriously? I run into you after all this time, and you immediately managed to make something in my life worse."

He stares at me like he's trying to decide how to respond, and then he shocks me by admitting, "You're right, I did."

"Way to go, Klein," Halston adds. "Now you have to clean up the mess you made."

He raises his eyebrows at her. "And how do you suggest I go about doing that?"

She smiles slowly, savoring whatever idea has just popped into her brain. "You're going to be her fake date to her sister's wedding. On an island. Across the country." Halston grins broadly.

Klein shakes his head. *No*. Halston is already nodding. "Yes."

I'm on Klein's side, shaking my head right alongside him. But then… The wisdom of Halston's suggestion sinks into me. On its face, sure, it's a terrible idea. But when you disassemble the idea and look at it for its parts, well… It may actually be ingenious.

"Listen to me," I say, grabbing Klein's shoulder and shaking it. "Do you need help marketing your book?"

He nods reluctantly.

"I'll help. I own a digital marketing firm."

His eyebrows cinch in the center. "You own it? Your mom made it sound like you worked at a marketing firm."

At least my mom will talk about my career. My dad prefers to act like it doesn't exist.

"It's mine," I confirm. The plan forms in my mind as I speak. Excitement snakes through my limbs, soothing my hangover in a way nothing else could. "I will market your book in exchange for you pretending to be my boyfriend for one week."

"Social media," Halston adds. "The guy isn't online at all."

"I know," I say, before I can stop myself. Dammit.

Klein's eyes are wide as he drinks his water. It's quiet as I wait for him to finish because I know, *I just know*, he's not going to let that admission pass without comment.

He makes a show of finishing every drop in his cup before he says, "I am most grateful for the ammunition you've handed me."

On a rumbled groan, I say, "Don't pretend you haven't searched my name online."

"Looking you up was the last thing I wanted to do."

Ouch.

But it's good that he's hurting my feelings. We don't need any of this getting messy. If we're too nice to each other, we might end up exchanging more bad kisses in a bathroom. If we're really going to do this, it's best to keep things clean.

Halston leaves the bar to go to the kitchen and check on our food.

"What do you think?" I ask.

Klein pushes his hair off his forehead, and it falls back into the same place he pushed it from. "I think," he starts slowly, the tip of his tongue coming out to brush over his bottom lip, "it's an idea fraught with peril."

I gesture with my hand between us, like *keep going*. "And?"

He frowns. "I'm never going to get a publishing deal if I don't have an online presence."

"Who told you that?"

"My cousin, who is, sometimes regrettably, also my agent."

"Your cousin/agent is correct."

"When is the wedding?" he asks, rubbing his thumb over his lower lip. It's distracting, setting an ache to the tops of my thighs.

I uncross, then recross my legs. "Six weeks from today, but we would fly out in five weeks."

Halston appears, sliding two plates of steaming eggs, corned beef, and hash browns toward us across the bar, along with a side of green chili sauce and flour tortillas.

The delicious smell curls around my face, and I know I said I was starving, but this is on a whole new level of ravenous. I dig in, paying no mind to the people around me. It's just me and this plate of food now smothered in green chili, and I will be the victor.

"Let's do it," Klein says after a minute.

A thrill races through my body. Is this for real?

I've just taken a huge bite of food, so there's nothing for me to do but shake my head in agreement while my mind races at the prospect of taking a fake boyfriend to a weeklong island wedding and parading him around my loved ones.

Halston, who I'm learning in addition to being protective of Klein, is also an instigator, grabs a napkin from somewhere beneath the bar. Pulling a pen from a cup next to the register, she writes out a short and not at all legally binding contract.

She shoves the pen at Klein. "Sign," she instructs.

Klein reads it out loud. "I, Klein Madigan, agree to accompany Paisley—" He purses his lips and glances up to Halston. She urges him on with a nod of her head. "Paisley *WhatsHerFace* to an island for one week where I will pretend to be her boyfriend."

He takes the pen and crosses out WhatsHerFace, writing my last name above. "Royce," he informs Halston.

"Proceed," she instructs.

He slides the napkin to me. I swallow my bite and read. "I, Paisley WhatsHerFace, agree to create and run a social media profile for Klein Madigan for the duration of six months." I frown. "Six months?" That is far longer than I want Klein in my life. I pictured being done with this by June, shaking his hand at the airport, and going our separate ways upon our return.

She raises an eyebrow at me. "Do you want to show up lonely to that island paradise, participating in whatever it is people do during an entire week of wedding festivities?" A grimace develops on her face as she speaks, making it clear a week of wedding festivities is a fate worse than death to her.

"No."

"Then you have to make the deal so sweet Klein won't be able to say no."

I eye Klein. He tips his chin to the ceiling, but his gaze stays locked on me. "Can you do sweet, Royce?"

My gaze narrows, and I lean in, until my breasts meet his upper arm. I brush them back and forth in the tiniest movement. "I don't know." My voice softens, my eyes widen. "Can I?"

"That"—a muscle in his jaw tics, and he looks like he would very much like to push me away—"was not at all sweet. That was devious."

Grinning broadly, I pick up the pen and sign the napkin.

Klein does the same, and Halston whisks away the napkin. She drops it into a black leather purse and grins with far too much enthusiasm.

I push my plate away after finishing every last morsel. "Give me your phone."

Klein removes it from his pocket, enters his passcode, and slides it over.

I hold it in the air between us. "Your background screen is a treehouse?"

"A *library* treehouse."

"Isn't that kind of like feeding a pig bacon?"

Klein's nose wrinkles. "I'm not making a treehouse out of paper."

"Just out of wood, I presume?"

Klein rests his chin on his hand and peers at me. "What it must be like in that brain of yours."

I ignore him and dial my number. Handing him back his phone, I quiet the vibrating inside my purse. "Now we have one another's phone number." I wag a finger at him. "No dick pics. I do not want to know if your thingy lights up."

Halston sputters on the water she'd been drinking. Wiping the back of her hand across her chin, she says, "What the fuck?"

Klein's gaze remains fastened to me. "Don't write my number on a gas station bathroom wall, Royce."

"I'd planned a spree. You've ruined my plans for the evening, Madigan."

His focus drops to my lips, and I watch him force back a smile. "Don't your plans include more bachelorette shenanigans?"

I groan. "Speaking of," I pause and pull my wallet from my purse. "I better get back."

Halston waves away my credit card. "This one's on the house. Consider it my thank you for making Klein's life more interesting for a while. All the guy does is write, read, work, and play soccer."

"Noble pursuits," Klein adds in his own defense.

"Thank you for breakfast." Tucking away my credit card, I say, "I love your name, by the way. It's unique."

"My mom named me after a fashion designer. She was obsessed with owning a Halston dress, but she never got a chance to before she died last year."

"I'm so sorry," I say, pressing a hand to my heart. My

mom might drive me nuts, but losing her so young? I can't imagine how much that must hurt.

Very clearly, an image crosses my mind. My mother's closet, three vintage Halston wrap dresses hanging on velvet hangers. When was the last time I saw her wear one?

"Way to bring down the mood," Klein says, and I gasp. Halston reaches over the bar and lands a medium-effort punch on the top of his arm. She's looking at him in this annoyed but affectionate way, and I gather it means their relationship typically consists of all this teasing.

I climb off my stool and thumb behind myself. "I better get going. All those sleeping beauties might be awake by now."

"Spa day?" Halston guesses.

"In matching silk robes embroidered with our names."

Halston cringes.

To Klein, I ask, "Can you come to my office on Monday at ten? We'll nail down the specifics of your half of the deal."

He nods.

"I'll text you the address."

Halston forms a megaphone around her mouth with cupped hands, and bellows, "Let the games begin."

## CHAPTER 7
*Klein*

What the hell did I agree to?

From every angle, no matter how I examine it, the idea screams *likely to fail.* Just how exactly are Paisley and I supposed to pull off a charade of this magnitude?

I've been unable to think about much else since leaving Obstinate Daughter and driving to my nephew's soccer game. So much so that I'm distracted from the game playing out in front of me. Shoving aside the vague feeling that I was conned into agreement (thank you, Halston), I force myself to focus on the game.

Oliver charges down the soccer field, toe-poking the soccer ball away the first time his teammate passes it to him.

"Take a touch, Ollie," the coach yells from the sideline.

"Why is the coach yelling at my nephew?" I grumble, even though he's correct in his instruction.

A grin stretches across my sister, Eden's, face. "That coach is Oliver's future stepdad."

I shake my head at her. "Be real."

After Eden's douche canoe of an ex-husband, she deserves the best. Oliver's soccer coach is probably not that. Don't ask me how I know. It's a feeling.

"Check this out," Eden says in a low voice. She pulls out her phone, taps and swipes, then holds it out to me.

On the screen, a young guy performs bicep curls in a tight shirt while his muscles pop and flex. I frown at the atrocity. "Why the hell are you showing me that?"

She points across the field. "That's Oliver's coach."

I look at the dude standing next to the team bench, clapping his hands and yelling instructions at the kids, then back to the guy on the screen. "Seriously? Why is he doing that?"

"He's working on becoming a fitness influencer."

Loud laughter bursts from me. Eden smacks my arm. "Shut up," she hisses.

"You knew what my response would be before you showed it to me."

She makes a show of rolling her eyes before tucking her phone into her back pocket. "Dom called me this morning. He said you're dead in the water without social media," she pauses to drill a pointed finger into my chest, "so I'm trying to show you there are other people, other *guys like you* putting themselves out there."

"Let me guess. Dom asked you to talk some sense into me." It would be just like our cousin to do that. Always telling my big sister when I dug my heels in about something. It's been that way my whole life.

She nods once. "Precisely."

"Eden, I have a negative percent chance of posting a video of me lifting weights."

"Well, duh. You'd do something related to your field. Like, reading a passage of your book, or—"

"Never gonna happen," I interrupt.

She does the sad eyes thing, where she feels sorry for me.

"Quit doing that." I wave a hand in front of her face. "I'm a perfectly capable reader now." As a child I'd had dyslexia so severe I eventually found myself in a school specifically designed to meet the needs of children with the diagnosis, and teach ways to overcome the learning disability. But not before being teased relentlessly in my first school, where I'd clam up and stutter when it was my turn to read out loud. "It should please you to know I'm going to start an account."

Eden's eyes widen, excitement dancing in the light brown.

"But I won't be running it," I add.

Her eyebrows pinch in confusion.

"A marketing firm will do it all for me." I think. Right? A tingle of trepidation trips down my spine. I don't fully know what I've gotten myself into. I'll learn more on Monday at the meeting Paisley invited me to attend with her team.

"With what money?" Eden asks. Paisley's mother hit the nail on the head when she called me a starving artist.

"Well, here's the thing—" I cut off, every muscle in my body stiffening as Oliver gets the ball.

He takes one touch. Then two. Fakes out a defender with a step-over I taught him last season.

He winds up, kicks the ball, and it sails into the net, just out of reach of the goalie.

Eden and I jump up and down, arms pumping the air as we shout. Oliver looks at us and beams. He points at me and recreates the step-over.

Cupping my hands around my mouth, I shout, "Way to go, bud!"

The game resets in the center of the field, and Eden says, "You were saying?"

"No money is exchanged," I answer, my heart still battering my chest bones as the excitement fades. "The owner of the marketing firm is someone I know from college. We bartered."

Eden's eyebrows shoot up her forehead. "Bartered? What did you have to offer? I highly doubt anybody wants your collection of pewter Lord of the Rings figurines."

"Ha ha," I deadpan.

Eden stares at me. "Spit it out. What did you offer this person?"

"My..." My brain scrambles for a word. "...services." I wince. That was a poor word choice.

Eden's face twists in horror. "Like a stud?"

Rolling my eyes at my sister, I shake my head. "No. I—"

She holds up a hand. "Never mind, I do not want to know."

"Paisley's ex-boyfriend is marrying her little sister, and a joke went sideways, and now her family thinks I'm her boyfriend, so I'm going to be her pretend boyfriend for a week while she handles my book marketing." I explain to her the logistics and location.

Eden stares at me. "That's either really smart, or really stupid. I'm not sure which."

"I'm aware."

Eden punches me lightly in my arm. "What's Paisley like? Maybe you should try real dating her, instead of *fake* dating."

Crossing my arms, I say, "She kind of dislikes me."

Eden shakes her head as if she's heard me incorrectly. "You're going to spend one week on an island pretending to be attracted to somebody who kind of dislikes you?" She throws her arms in the air. "What could possibly go wrong?" Sarcasm oozes from every word. "It sounds more like a bad idea than a good one, Klein."

I shrug, feigning indifference. Bad idea or not, I made a deal. Also, there's no way I'm touching social media. "It's low risk, high reward. I want to make my dreams of becoming an author a reality. All I have to do is fly across the country and spend a week on an island watching the wedding shenanigans of the wealthy. There will likely be loads of top-shelf alcohol and good food."

Eden taps her chin, considering my words. "And cake," she adds, getting on board. "You do love a good cake."

I nod. "Precisely." It's a running joke in our family that as a kid, I was the first in line for every birthday cake, even if it wasn't mine.

"And the girl you're doing this for? Paisley?"

Something in my chest flexes at the mention of her name. "I'm doing this for me," I remind Eden. "For my future. For my dreams of becoming a published author." Am I though? The thought of Paisley suffering through the wedding all alone ate at me after I left her last night. If Halston hadn't been the brilliant brain behind this scheme, I might have volunteered to go with Paisley without recompense.

Eden waves away my reminder. "Right, right. But Paisley benefits, too."

Not as much as me, in my opinion, but what do I know? Maybe showing up with a boyfriend weighs as much to Paisley as my career weighs to me.

"Sure, yes. Paisley benefits."

"Are you positive there isn't something there? Between you two? You say she dislikes you, but she wouldn't be hauling you across the country and introducing you to her family if you were truly the bane of her existence."

I'm already shaking my head before she finishes her sentence. "No way."

"So, there's no chance you're going to get swept up in the sultry island vibes and happily ever afters and fall in love?"

"Zero percent likelihood."

"Why do you say that with such certainty?"

"She was in my first creative writing class in college. We were assigned to anonymously critique a classmate's story, and I got Paisley's. I didn't know it was hers, and I tore it to shreds."

My sister gives me a look that has *you are such a dumbass* written all over it.

"It was awful. She figured out it was me. I figured out it was hers. She cried. And she still hates me for it."

Eden crosses her arms. "There's more to the story."

I frown. "How so?"

"Unless she's the world's best grudge holder, there's something more. A reason it hurt her that deeply."

"Or maybe it's exactly what it sounds like."

Eden rolls her eyes. "Don't be such a dude, Klein." She taps my head. "Use your noggin."

Huh. Could it be? Does it go deeper than embarrassment? The thought toys with my imagination, pushing me to consider. When I develop characters I layer their emotions, starting with the surface and working deeper. Anger is never simply anger, but a reaction to the emotion underneath.

Maybe Paisley wasn't only embarrassed.

*Oh man.*

Across the field, Oliver's coach calls the water break. With the boys gathered around him, he talks and stretches his hamstrings at the same time.

"Coach Kissy Face is getting limber for his next photo shoot."

Eden grins. "You mean Oliver's future stepdad."

I shake my head at her.

Eden drops the subject of Paisley, and we focus on the remainder of the game. Despite Oliver's goal, his team loses by two.

He trudges off the field, dejected. When he gets to me, I muss the mop of brown hair on his head. "Next time," I say, trying to make him feel better when I know very little will in this moment.

"Sure, Uncle Klein. Thanks for coming out to watch me. Sorry it was for nothing."

He shifts his black and white soccer club backpack, and I take it off him, slinging it over my shoulder. "I didn't come to watch you win, Oliver. I came to watch you play."

Oliver looks up at me, gratitude shining in his eyes.

"Also," I add, not bothering to look at my sister because she'll try and tell me no, "I need somebody to share one of those ridiculous milkshakes with me."

Oliver smiles. "The kind they top with whole candy bars?"

"And chocolate straws."

Eden blows out an annoyed breath, but I pretend I can't hear her. She complains I load Oliver with sugar, and then leave just in time for the sugar high to really get going. But hey, what are uncles for?

Oliver rides with me to Sugar Shoppe, and Eden meets us there. She eats one single scoop of strawberry, while Oliver and I polish off a large Mud & Worms milkshake topped with marshmallow fluff, cookie crust, and gummy worms.

History repeats itself when I take off soon after. Oliver is kicking his chair as I back out of the store, and Eden mouths *Screw you*.

Ten minutes later my phone dings with a text from Eden.

> I told Mom about you fake dating. Expect her call.

I'm at a red light, so I let my head hit the steering wheel. *Shit*. My mom.

This plan Paisley and I have hatched is going to delight her. She loves romance. She loves love. She inhales romance novels, and owns a T-shirt that says 'Book boyfriends do it better'.

She has even—

*Ring!*

*And there goes my phone.* One guess as to who it is.

I press the button and answer the call on speaker. "Hi, Mom."

"Eden told me."

What is the word for what she's doing with her voice? Oh, right. *Trilling.* The sound fills my car.

"That was kind of my big sister to tell you all about my fake date before I got a chance to."

"Pfft. You weren't going to tell me."

"Sure I would have."

She ignores my lie. "Don't be so reductionist, Klein. It's not a fake date. It's a weeklong fake-out on an island."

Oh, man. The way her voice grew in excitement the longer she spoke her last sentence tells me I'm in for it.

"I want to meet her," she announces.

"No, Mom."

"Yes, Klein."

"There's no point."

"You're going to fly across the country to a little island off the coast of North Carolina and stay with people I've never met. What if they're serial killers and this was all an elaborate trap?"

"Do you really believe that?"

"Not for a second. Did you know they don't allow cars on the island? Just maintenance vehicles and things like that. Everybody drives golf carts."

"Mom, how—"

"And there are alligators!"

How fast are my mother's search fingers? I'm picturing her hunched over her keyboard, smoke rising from her rapid internet queries.

"Klein, I want you to have dinner here Wednesday evening. Check with your lady friend and make sure that works with her schedule. Eden told me she's a big shot marketer, so you need to make sure she's not busy marketing something."

I stare at the phone, offended. "You forgot to ask if I'm free."

"Are you free?"

I blow out an irritated breath. "Yes."

"Lovely. Ask your lady friend and—"

"Paisley."

"Paisley," my mother repeats. "Like the pattern. I like it."

"I'll make sure to tell her you like her name."

"Don't be caustic, Klein. It's unbecoming."

I laugh. My love of words came from my mother. She's the reason for my large vocabulary as a child, even when I couldn't read.

"Wednesday," my mom echoes. "Ask Paisley and let me know."

"I will."

"Love you, Klein."

"Love you, Mom."

The connection ends.

I spend the rest of the afternoon reading about Bald Head Island and online shopping. I have nothing to wear to a wedding, and next to nothing for a week on a beach.

I quickly tire of online shopping, because, well, I hate it. I make a brief run to the grocery store, then get ready for the craziness that is a Saturday night behind the bar.

## CHAPTER 8
*Paisley*

I wait to text Klein until the bachelorette weekend is over and I've dropped everyone off at the airport. As promised, I send him a simple text with the name of my company and the address. I follow it up with a second message detailing when we're heading to the island and what the weather will be like.

Two hours later he responds.

> I filed that napkin with the Arizona Bureau of Contracts.

If I were in his presence, I'd shake my head in exasperation. But since he can't see me, I laugh. I type out a message and hit send.

> That's not a thing.

> There's one point we left out of the contract.

> What's that?

Three little dots appear. Disappear. Reappear. The message pops up.

> You can't fall in love with me, Royce.

> Wouldn't dream of it, Madigan.

# CHAPTER 9
*Klein*

Paisley's office is smack dab in the center of downtown Scottsdale. She's a stone's throw from the waterfront area, bracketed by an architectural firm and a luxury art gallery.

Pausing, I double-check the name on the glass door. *P Squared Marketing.*

I catch my reflection in the door as I reach for the handle. I'm embarrassed to say I spent too much time considering what to wear to this meeting. After all the deliberating, I ended up wearing my typical uniform of jeans and a T-shirt.

A middle-age woman smiles brightly from behind her desk when I walk in. "Hello. You must be Klein."

"Uh, yeah. Hi. Hello." Why do I sound nervous? I'm not nervous. Am I?

The woman gestures at the waiting area. "If you'd like to take a seat, I will tell Ms. Royce you're here." She takes a step away, then turns back as if she's remembered something. "Can I get you anything to drink? Coffee? Water? Kombucha?"

I refrain from rolling my eyes at the third option, then politely pass.

She leaves to tell *Ms. Royce* I'm here. The waiting area is trendy, modern, with low-slung cream leather chairs, and a glass coffee table with rounded edges and matte gold legs. Abstract art in earthy emeralds and deep blues decorate the walls. On the coffee table is a stack of pamphlets, the outward facing flap reads *What can P Squared Marketing do for you?*

Thumbing through one, I find the page listing photos and bios of the employees. Paisley is last, below a photo of a woman named Paloma. Paisley wears a red blazer and matching red lipstick, and I would never say this out loud because it's definitely not the look she's going for, but she looks like a supermodel.

The woman is drop dead gorgeous on her worst day. Time has done nothing but turn her into a woman with lush curves and a sharp wit.

I happen to be a sucker for both.

To make our deal successful, I'll have to show up with invisible weapons. The first of which is a promise to myself not to allow any shenanigans to develop with Paisley Royce. The others I'll figure out as I go.

"Klein," Paisley calls out.

I whip around and find her smirking, arms crossed. She knows exactly which page of the pamphlet my gaze had been trained on. Today she wears a tight, white skirt, spiked heels, and lavender short-sleeved top that looks soft to the touch. The woman is a masterpiece, a smoke show sent to test my resolve.

An uncomfortable feeling slips over me when I realize it has taken me too long to respond to her. To cover up my unease, I mockingly say, "Hello, *Ms*. Royce."

Her tongue runs the length of her upper teeth as she gazes at me just long enough for it to be awkward. For me anyway. I'm pretty sure she's doing it on purpose. Arching one eyebrow, she asks, "Are you ready to make your entrance online?"

I walk closer, closing the distance, trying not to drown in her ocean eyes. "It's social media, not a presidential inauguration."

Paisley laughs derisively. Gone is the red lipstick from her head shot, replaced by a petal pink that might look even prettier on her. She crooks a finger my direction. "Follow me."

She pivots, walking back the way she came.

I nod politely at the receptionist on my way by, hurrying after Paisley's confident strides.

Even with all that time we spent not seeing one another, I like to think I know Paisley somewhat. I've seen her drunk, I've seen her sad, I've seen her sassy, and I've seen her uncertain. The Paisley walking in front of me now is new to me. She's a boss, a trailblazer, an expert.

I am an aspiring author with low numbers in my bank account. I ate ramen for dinner last night, and it wasn't even the good kind.

"Here we are," Paisley announces, sailing through an open door.

I follow her in. One long table that seats eight takes up

the center of the room, a TV hangs on the wall, and a beverage cart lurks in the corner.

Two women are already seated on the same side of the table, and Paisley introduces them as Paloma and Cecily. "This is Klein," she says, gesturing to me. "My... friend from college."

Paloma rolls her eyes. "Just call him what he is. Your fake date to your sister's wedding."

Cecily laughs behind a cupped hand while Paisley sends a death glare at Paloma. My neck heats as I take a seat opposite the women.

Paloma gazes at me intensely, undeterred. "You'd better do a good job. Make it clear to that stupid ex of hers that not only is she better off without him, but she's better off with *you*."

Oh shit. Paloma is... *scary*. "I'll do my best." I offer her my winningest smile.

She arches an eyebrow. "You'll do better than that."

Paisley pulls out a chair beside Cecily and sits. "Paloma, stop scaring him."

"It's not my problem if he feels frightened by being called to greatness." She sends me a long look tinged with dislike.

*Ohh*. She knows why Paisley dislikes me. And she, in solidarity, dislikes me, too.

Paisley moves the meeting forward. "Klein is a debut author who does not currently have a social media presence."

"Professionally, you mean?" Cecily asks.

"And personally," Paisley answers, gaze shooting at me before bouncing back to Cecily.

Satisfaction warms my chest at the brief memory of Paisley admitting she searched for me online.

Cecily's gaze narrows, eyebrows tugging in the center. "Is there a reason you're a social ghost?"

Social ghost? What the hell kind of term is that?

I shrug. "I don't feel like telling people what I do every day. And I really don't care what other people do every day."

Cecily starts to roll her eyes, but stops herself.

"Revolucionario," Paloma mutters.

Paisley presses her lips together to keep from laughing. "Ok, ok." She presses her palms on the surface of the table. "Klein is a client. No eye-rolling, and no name calling."

Her gaze locks on me. *Damn, but she's pretty. Wide-eyes, dark lashes, slender neck. How else would I describe her if I wrote a character profile?*

"Why don't you tell me what your goals are for your brand?"

Paisley's question yanks me from my errant thought. "My brand?" What kind of question is that? I'm a person, not a *thing*. I'm not Nike.

She leans back in her chair, considering me. "Tell me about your book."

Here's the thing about being a writer. You can write an entire book, in my case 110,000 words, and be unable to summarize it in five sentences. It's like an overflowing sink and you're using a paper towel to clean up the water. There are too many plot lines and ideas and character struggles and conflicts to capture it all in a paragraph that also sells the concept.

"Well," I begin, my palms growing clammier by the second. It's only an audience of three and I'm losing it. I lean forward. The chair creaks. "It's a romantic suspense/mystery set in the 1920s."

Paisley motions for me to continue.

"An influential family arranges a marriage for their daughter to a local mafia family, but when she turns up dead they have her twin sister secretly take her place while they scramble to solve the murder."

Paisley's eyebrows lift. "That actually sounds good."

"You sound surprised."

She shrugs, writing something on her notepad. "Is there on-page intimacy?"

"Why?"

"So we know the tone of the novel. We don't want to present your book in the wrong light."

That makes sense. "Yes."

Paisley makes a checkmark on her page. "Does the murder take place on-page, as well? Is it descriptive?"

"Yes. But, Paisley," I glance at the other two women as I rest my forearms on the desk. "Is your plan to talk about my book on social media? Because I really don't see how this is all going to get off the ground and—"

"Actually," Cecily speaks up. "I have a different idea for how we should approach all this." She raises her eyebrows at Paisley, as if she is asking for permission to share.

Paisley nods, urging her to continue.

"I think we should use your situation to gain interest in your book."

I'm confused. What situation?

"Like, the fake dating situation you are both in," Cecily

says, catching on to the fact that nobody is following her line of thinking.

Paisley raises her eyebrows. "You want *me*"—she points at her chest—"on Klein's social?"

"Sort of," Cecily explains. "It doesn't have to be your face. It could be your legs stretched out in the sand. It could be a far away shot of you swimming in the ocean. It could be your backs while you ride bikes."

"This is why I hate social media," I mutter, rubbing my eyes. "So damn contrived."

Cecily shakes her head. "I'm not done explaining. You would be honest about what you're doing. Be upfront about how you're fake dating."

I'm already shaking my head. I should have known better than to get my hopes up. This idea is as crazy as it sounded from the beginning. It's better to put an end to it now. Paisley can tell her family she caught her new boyfriend cheating on her or something similar that I would never do. I'll be the bad guy so she can save face, and we can both move on. I'll figure out how to publish my book on my own. Authors do it all the time.

"Paisley—" I cut myself off when I see her smiling. No, *beaming*.

"I love it," she says to Cecily. To me, she asks, "Klein, what do you hate about social media?"

"It's fake."

"Then don't be fake. Be authentic. Honest. Be yourself."

"Be honest about fake dating? That's called an oxymoron."

Paisley's lip twitches, and I imagine she's fighting the urge to use the word 'moron' in a different way.

Excitement glitters in Cecily's eyes. "The investment in a story like that would be money. Think about it. Don't you automatically want to know what's going to happen?"

I already know what's going to happen. I'm going to take my ass on a trip across the country to an island where there's going to be a bunch of stuff to do, and out of it I'm going to get professional marketing help that will, in turn, make me more attractive to an interested publisher.

There's still something tripping me up, though. "How does all this tie into my book, exactly?"

"You're going to show that you can tell a story." She waves her hand. "Spin a yarn."

"Lie?"

"Isn't that what writing a book is? The world's longest, most intricate lie?"

I bristle. "No. It's creativity at its peak."

"Anyway," Cecily says forcefully, "the point of all this wouldn't be to talk about your book yet. We'll state in your bio that you've written a novel, but we'll save the book push for later, after you get a publishing deal. And how do you get a publishing deal?" Her eyebrows reach for her hairline as she waits for me to answer.

"I show up on social media." Do I sound as reluctant as I feel? Yep.

"And how do you show up on social media?" She's using a tone suited for a four-year-old who refuses to relinquish a stolen cookie.

"I exploit my personal life."

Cecily blows out a hard breath, thumbing at me. "I can't with this guy."

"Klein," Paisley says my name patiently. Too patiently. Once again, I feel like a four-year-old. "This is not exploitation. This is working with what you've got. And I have to agree with Cecily, what we're planning to do is harebrained enough that it'll pique curiosity."

"All publicity is good publicity?" My sarcastic tone gives away my opinion.

Cecily looks at me like I'm hopeless. "No, Klein. All publicity is not *good* publicity. You can't go running around with your schlong flapping in the wind and call it good publicity. This is *strategic* publicity. You're inviting the masses along on your escapade." She sits back, looking pretty damn pleased with herself.

I drag a hand down my face. "And this is going to help me get a book contract?"

Paisley responds. "It's going to help you get noticed, Klein the—"

I cut her off with a warning look before she can say 'stripper'. She grins, finishing her sentence with 'writer.'

Cecily claps her hands once, the sound reverberating through the room. "I think we just found your handle."

"Is that a euphemism for *schlong*?"

Cecily glances at Paisley. "Did you travel back in time to find this guy?"

Paisley chuckles. "A 'handle' is your name on social media. And KleinTheWriter is pretty much perfect."

Cecily grabs her phone from its face down position on the table, flipping it over and swiping rapidly over the screen. "It's available," she announces.

"Perfect," Paisley responds. Her eyebrows lift as she looks my direction, waiting for me to say something.

"Fine," I grumble.

"Fine?" she prods. "Or, amazing? Stupendous. How about"—she taps her chin—"thank you?"

"It's not like you're doing this out of the kindness of your heart," I remind her.

In my peripheral vision, I see Cecily and Paloma creep out of the conference room. The door shuts softly behind them.

Paisley pushes forward on the conference room table, using her palms for leverage. "You have four weeks to get to know me, and one week in which I expect you to hold up your end of the bargain. I have signed up for the next six months, and my firm will be doing this without compensation. So not only will I not be receiving payment, but I will still be paying my employees. Do you know what that means, Klein?" She leans closer, and it takes just about everything I have not to let my eyes wander down into her blouse that has fallen open. Even now, as I will my gaze to meet hers, at the bottom of my vision I note her nude bra that is anything but boring. It is scalloped lace on the top, delicate and feminine.

Mimicking Paisley, I press my palms to the table and lift myself up, until our noses are less than a foot apart. "What? That dear old mom and dad aren't going to get paid the same amount this month?"

Fire lights in Paisley's eyes. "Do you think"—she swirls a lone finger in the air—"my parents pay for all this?"

"Are you trying to tell me they didn't at least give you the money to start a business?" I cannot imagine in what world Paisley would be so young and have a business like this already. She comes from a wealthy family, isn't it a safe assumption that they would've at least given her the seed money to start this marketing firm?

"My dad blocked my inheritance, and me, because I refused to go to the college he had chosen, and then I doubled down on my refusal and told him what I wanted to major in."

Oh shit. I do not like where this is headed. Resigned, I ask the question I'm positive I already know the answer to. "And that major was?"

"Creative writing."

I look down at the table, trying to gather all the thoughts in my head, so I can form a sentence that is worthy of Paisley's revelation. "Paisley, I—"

"Don't," she says in a low voice. "Don't be sorry. And don't feel bad for me. I switched to marketing, and—"she motions out around her—"it seems to have been the right choice for me."

Though her tone of voice is strong, it wavered once while she spoke. What would she do if I reached out, if I ran my knuckles across her cheek?

The longer I look at her, the more the fire in her demeanor diminishes. Vulnerability softens her eyes, her whole damn face. And what a face it is. Pert nose. Heart-shaped. A triangle of freckles at her temple.

I could be in a crowd of people and still know Paisley's profile. In our creative writing class, I spent more time memorizing every dip and curve of her profile than I did paying attention to the curriculum. If only I could go back in time and stop myself from going overboard on that critique, or choosing a different one when they were laid out on the teachers desk. Would my life be different today if I had?

We stare at each other, the twelve inches separating us electrified. I want more than anything to erase her memories of my red pen and that one sophomoric kiss in her bathroom.

"My mom would like to know if you're available for dinner on Wednesday night."

The spell breaks. Paisley blinks twice. She stands upright, her thighs pressing against the edge of the table. I do the same.

She crosses her arms and bites the corner of her lip. "I guess it's probably a good idea. I need to get to know you, so I don't look like an utter fool in front of my family if they ask a question about your upbringing or your parents."

"Parent," I correct. "Just my mom."

She nods, but refrains from asking about my dad. "I'll be there. Text me the time and address." She takes her phone from the table and slips it into her pocket. "Would you like a drink for the road? Water, coffee—"

I raise my eyebrows teasingly. "Kombucha?"

A smile plays on her lips. "Have you ever been to a barbershop that offers beer to its clients?"

"Yes."

She strides to the conference room door and opens it. "That's because they know their audience."

"And you know yours?"

"Precisely."

I go to pass through the door, but something happens.

She doesn't move aside in time, and I end up brushing against her. She quietly gasps, and I pause to look at her. My nearness awards me an upfront view of her chest, rising and falling in an unnaturally fast rhythm.

As is mine, but add in clammy palms and a lump in my throat. "Paisley—"

Her head shakes quickly. "I'll see you on Wednesday. Cecily will be in touch to get the ball rolling on your account."

I take one last look at her, then leave.

The sun is bright, harsh, ripping me from the haze I felt in Paisley's presence. It's probably a good thing. She disarms me.

## CHAPTER 10
*Klein*

Dom's reaction when I tell him about the harebrained plan disappoints me. I'd needed someone to back me up, to tell me I'm doing the right thing and this will one hundred percent get me that publishing deal. I wanted a hype-man. Instead, he says:

> Isn't this the girl you had a massive crush on in college?

> > Yes, but that's been over for a long time.

> If you say so. Just seems like playing with fire.

> > Do you have a better way for me to fix my social media problem?

> Problem, or phobia?

> > <middle finger emoji>

> I'll bet you a hundred bucks I make it through the week with nothing but an expanded waistline from all the food and drink.

And the cake.

> You sound like my sister. What's with this family and cake?

It's CAKE.

> Forget the cake. What do you think about the plan?

There's nowhere to go but up. Unless you crash and burn. But let's not think about that.

I tuck my phone in my pocket. It's a good thing Dom doesn't live down the street from me like he used to. I'd show up at his door and pop him on the jaw.

It doesn't matter that I ever liked Paisley, because she has made it clear she is far from my biggest fan.

And now there's a hundred dollars on the table, plus being able to brag that I knew what I was doing all along.

This is all going to be a piece of cake.

Wedding cake, to be exact.

# CHAPTER 11
## *Paisley*

I'M TRYING MY BEST TO PAY ATTENTION DURING THIS VIDEO call with a coffee chain out of Seattle, but how can I when I feel so… so… unsettled?

My palm glides over the gleaming table, the very same table Klein and I faced off across earlier this week. Over and over in my mind, I see the way his shoulders slumped, the fight draining out of him when I told him I gave up my inheritance.

A text message from Paloma flashes on my screen. I glance at her across the table, my eyes squinting with question.

She looks pointedly at my phone, indicating her message.

Without being obvious, I swipe open her text.

> Thinking about Klein?

I give a tiny nod.

> I can see why. He's gorgeous.

>> I know.

He's more than his good looks, though. A lot more.

Paloma holds her phone below the table, out of eyesight of the woman on the screen. Her message pops up.

> Like Brad Pitt in Troy but his hair is shorter and not as blond. And he writes books. And he's bigger.

I fight to keep a straight face as I respond.

>> So, not at all like Brad Pitt in Troy?

Paloma rolls her eyes only a quarter turn.

> Ok, fine. He looks like he should play football.

>> Quarterback! Because he throws his words out there. Get it?

Paloma shakes her head solemnly.

>> I'll see myself out.

We stop texting after that, focusing on Stephanie, the store owner, as she takes us through the results she sees day-to-day following our marketing initiative.

Stephanie's biggest problem when she came to us was

branding. She hadn't yet figured out the soul of her company, and we helped her distill it down to a few words, then rebuild from that idea.

Paloma and I finish up our call. Paloma turns off the video while I snap my laptop closed and surreptitiously glance at my phone. I'm looking for a text from Klein, the one that is supposed to tell me what time dinner is tonight and his mother's address. I don't like that this is the fourth time today I've looked at my phone hoping for a message from him. Or that I did the same thing seven times yesterday.

I'm sipping my late afternoon mocha cold brew with two pumps of raspberry when the long-awaited text comes through.

> Hey, Royce.

> You're not going to be able to call me Royce in front of my family, so you might want to start kicking the habit now.

> I decide when I kick a habit. Royce stays.

I flick the phone screen with my middle finger.

> Stubborn ass.

> Can I pick you up at six?

> I'm capable of driving myself.

> You're capable of plenty. That doesn't mean other people can't do something for you.

> My mom lives across town. So, again I ask, can I pick you up at six?

Briefly I consider putting my foot down and insisting I drive. It would keep some degree of separation between us. But then I fire off a text that says *yes,* because I wouldn't mind being chauffeured. We live in a driving city, no mass transportation except for a light rail that moves through downtown Phoenix, and I happen to hate driving.

> Address, please?

I send him my address and tell him I'll be ready at six.

Paloma walks into my office, throwing herself in the chair opposite my desk. "I hate that man," she wails, a touch of venom in her tone.

"What man?"

She points a stiff finger to her right. "The guy who owns the architecture firm next door."

I suppress my smile. It's never a good idea to show mirth of any form while Paloma is mad. "What did Daniel do now?"

"What didn't he do?" she seethes. "That man is on my last nerve. All day long he stands in front of his store, *right next to my office*, and yammers away on the phone. It's like he's scared of his own desk." Her hands fly into the air, exasperated. "I want to pour boiling water in his ear."

"That would kill him."

"Exactly."

"Murder is an offense punishable by law."

"Ahh, but that's the beauty of this method." She mimes pouring water, then brushes one palm against the other. "It leaves no trace."

I study her. "You're terrifying."

She half-grins and shimmies her shoulders. "Thank you." She stands abruptly. "That's it. I'm finished complaining. What about you? Do you have anything to complain about?"

"Other than the fact I'm going to meet Klein's mother tonight?"

"You're meeting your *friend's* mom, not that you can call him that. Big deal."

I don't like how much emphasis she puts on the word 'friend'.

"Right," I nod, shrugging one shoulder. "Big deal."

Paloma gives me a knowing look, and I'm not loving how much she appears to be enjoying my discomfort.

"Tell your word slinger quarterback I said hello."

"He's scared of you, I think. At least a little."

She pauses in my office door. "Good." She repeats the pouring water motion. "He should be."

···🐚🐚🐚···

Is there a dress code for meeting your fake boyfriend's mother?

Moreover, is there a handbook for how a fake girlfriend should behave?

Klein will be at my apartment in fifteen minutes. I am on my seventh outfit change. The wide leg trousers and tank top was too 'cocktails after dinner'. The flouncy floral patterned sundress was too 'walk on the beach at dusk'. Don't even get me started on the plum colored joggers. They lasted all of three seconds before I ripped them from my legs.

"Argh," I groan, shaking a fist at the small pile of clothes on my bed. I'm not usually indecisive when it comes to dressing, but tonight I seem to be having issues.

I'm standing in my underwear and bra when there's a knock at my door. "Dammit," I mutter. Klein is four minutes early.

Marching into my closet, I grab the closest thing on a hanger and pull it over my head.

I pause at my front door, dragging a deep breath into my lungs. "Everything is good," I coach. "You're fine."

And I am fine. I am slap-my-ass fantastic. Whatever that means.

I wrestle open the door, and there is Klein. All six foot *something* of him, leaning against the wall next to my potted hot pink Hibiscus flowers. With nothing more than the strength of his upper body he propels himself forward.

He's so handsome it causes actual physical pain. A squeeze in the center of my chest.

He steps into the space made by the open door, gripping the top of the doorframe and leaning forward. "Were you talking to yourself?"

My words tangle in my throat. It should be illegal for a man to grip the doorframe and lean forward like that. He must know what he's doing, the way his biceps pop and flex, the way it takes an expansive chest and expands it even more.

He knows, right?

He knows. He has to. And if he doesn't, I will not be the one enlightening him.

Crossing my arms, I ignore his question and say, "You're four minutes early. I really could've used those extra four minutes to decide on what to wear." His gaze drops, starting with my bare feet and lifting *up up up* the rest of my body until he meets my eyes.

"You look fine," he grunts.

"Don't sound so enthusiastic."

"Do you want me to sound enthusiastic?"

I give him a dirty look. He smirks. "Thought so. Are you ready?"

"Let me grab my shoes and I'll be on my way. Unless you want me to show up shoeless."

"You can show up however you want. My mom won't care."

"Well then, I'll change into one of those giant trash bags used for landscaping trimmings. Much more comfortable."

"Lovely," Klein counters.

I growl, throwing up my hands and spinning around. Should I be concerned about how crazy this man makes me? Probably. But considering I'm low on men raising their hands and offering to join me in a weeklong sham, I'll have to put up with Klein.

Leaving him in the open doorway, I head for my room. I grab a pair of heeled sandals and slide my feet in them, then wind my purse over one shoulder. When I come back out, Klein is standing in my living room, looking at a family photo I keep on my shelf. He points at my little brother.

"Is his name Scooter?"

My lips tug into a frown. "No. Why?"

Klein shrugs. "He looks like a Scooter."

"How does a person look like a Scooter?" I gripe, joining Klein to examine the photo. I've seen the picture a hundred times, but maybe I missed something. The photo is of me, and my brother and sister, attempting to bake an apple pie in my mom's kitchen at Thanksgiving three years ago. It was my first holiday after Shane broke up with me. My brother wears a Burberry polo with pressed shorts. Ok, yeah, he could be a Scooter.

"His name is Spencer," I tell Klein.

"I was close," Klein says.

"When he was little we called him Spencer the Terrible because he was a rotten toddler." I poke at the smirk on my brother's face, the mischievous glint in his eyes. "He's seventeen. Has no idea where he wants to go to college. Claims to be uninterested in higher education. Doesn't do well making any meaningful conversation with adults." A heavy breath slips from me. "He has a little bit of a Peter Pan thing going, and my mother doesn't appear to care." She's too busy living her best life post-divorce.

Klein nods. "A refusal to grow up."

"He claims to be waiting for the right time."

Klein laughs and I elbow him. "See? You already like him. It's kind of hard not to, even if a majority of interactions with him consist of him grunting most of his responses or teasing people."

"And your sister?"

"You've already met her."

Klein looks down at me. He's awfully close. "Yeah, but what about her? I'm going into this thinking she's not a very good sister. Is that the case?"

I sigh heavily. "She's... selfish. But I guess we all are, to a degree."

"Some more than others," he says amicably.

"She's not a bad sister, though," I hurry to defend. "I told her it was ok to date my ex."

Klein doesn't have a response. His gaze wanders away from my eyes, slipping down over my cheeks, lingering on my lips. Eventually he makes his way back to my eyes. His thorough inspection elicits a feeling deep in my belly, a coiled snake unraveling.

"Do I have something on my face?" I run my finger pads under my eyes, in case there is mascara built up underneath them.

"You're perfect," Klein says. Panic flips through his eyes when he realizes what he said. He steps back. "Your outfit, I mean. For what it's worth, it looks nice on you."

Try as I might, I can't help feeling a bit of a glow at his compliment. Looking down, I smooth my hands over the mint green short-sleeved knit sweater dress I ended up pulling on. "Thanks," I murmur. "It's nothing."

Klein has already turned away, but I swear the deep timbre of his thick voice mutters, "It's something."

## CHAPTER 12
*Paisley*

Klein drives a late model 4Runner. I spend the majority of the drive to his mom's house learning about his mom and his childhood. We cover the basics, like where he went to high school (Chaparral), and his childhood pet (many, he says, but his favorite was a Corgi named Peanut).

"My mom is going to love you," he cautions, slowing as he pulls up to the house and shifts into Park. "She is already way too invested in us fake dating."

I turn sharply. "She knows?"

"Uh, yeah," Klein rubs at his chin. "I guess I forgot to tell you I told her. Actually, my sister told her."

"Here I was all afternoon getting myself worked up thinking about how I was going to meet my boyfriend's mom and what level of physical touch that requires." I blow out an annoyed breath. "I guess all that angst was for nothing."

"There was angst?"

I give him a flat look. There's no way I'll be describing the tornado that is my room after all those outfit changes. "Please do not become stuck on my usage of the word."

One side of Klein's cheek tugs fractionally, and I take this to mean he would very much like for me to describe my mental distress. My arms cross. Too bad.

"I figured it was safe for my mom and sister to know the truth, considering the fake dating thing is for your benefit, not mine."

"You have a point."

He nudges me with his elbow across the center console. "You can still show me affection. I can tell you're dying to, and I would never deny a woman what she so desperately wants."

"Hah!" I send him my best withering look. He doesn't wither; his eyes dance with laughter. "Touching only when it's required, Madigan."

He opens his car door. "Duly noted."

I step from the car and study the house in the light of a rapidly setting sun. It's cozy, made of stucco, with a wall of Bougainvillea growing on trellises. In the center of the yard stands a lemon tree, its trunk painted white.

I gesture at the tree as Klein rounds the front of his car and steps up beside me on the sidewalk. "Did you use the lemons from that tree to make lemonade when you were a kid?"

"I cut them in half and sprinkled sugar on the inside, then squeezed it right into my mouth." He smiles at the memory.

"Savage."

"Pretty much. There are three orange trees growing in the backyard." He glances at my neck when he says this, and I raise a hand, palming it self-consciously. There goes that odd feeling of uncoiling in my stomach, and this time, in my chest.

"Ready?" he asks.

"Let's do this."

Klein uses a key to open the front door, shouting, "Mom, we're here," as we enter the foyer.

"Kitchen," she hollers.

Klein leads me through the small house, past a living room with a typical couch and coffee table set up, and a fireplace with an outdated façade. The smell of garlic and onion grows stronger as we go, and then we reach the kitchen. The cabinets are painted the prettiest shade of cerulean blue, with ivory handles. Klein's mother, standing at the stove, gives something in a large pot a final stir, then turns around.

Her smile is ready, and the first word I think of when I see her is 'warm.' It's followed closely by the word 'happy,' as she looks at her son, then at me.

"Paisley, like the pattern," she says brightly, coming forward. Her hair is darker than Klein's, closer to auburn.

I laugh. "Exactly."

I extend a hand, startling when she wraps me in a hug. My limbs melt and I relax into it. I love my mother deeply, but her affection has never been this demonstrative.

Klein's mom pulls back, her eyes twinkling. "I'm Rosemary."

"Klein has your eyes," I say, staring into the deep green, shot through with amber.

She winks at her son. "He sure does. But I refuse to take any responsibility for his grumpiness."

"Hah," I laugh.

Rosemary gestures to a four-person table on the opposite side of the room. "Sit," she says. "Klein, pour your fake girlfriend a glass of wine."

Her frankness takes me off guard, but the teasing grin on her face tells me she's being sassy. With a grateful nod I accept the glass of red wine Klein sets in front of me. "Rosemary, I take it you're ok with the plan we've hatched?"

"I was taken aback when I first heard about it, but then Klein's sister told me about your sister's choice of groom, and after that"—Rosemary shrugs—"I'd say it's a fair deal." She stirs whatever is in the pot on the stovetop one more time, then pours herself a glass of wine and joins me at the table. "Plus, Klein's never been to the East Coast, or an island for that matter. Should make for an interesting story."

"I think he'll love it there." I glance at Klein, gauging his reaction to our conversation. He has taken a beer from the fridge, and he settles himself in the third chair at the table, twisting off the top and taking a long pull.

"What's not to love about alligators and golf carts?" he asks, swallowing.

I smirk. "You've done your research."

"Plenty more research to do." He points his bottle at me. "Pertaining to you."

I sip my wine. "Tonight's research is about you," I remind him.

Rosemary claps her hands excitedly. "How in-depth is

this research supposed to go? Do I get to break out the embarrassing baby photos?"

"No," Klein says.

"Yes," I counter.

"Photos it is," Rosemary declares.

"Mom, no," Klein says firmly.

"Klein, don't be such a stiff. What's a little baby butt between friends?" Her gaze shifts from Klein to me and back to Klein again. "That's what you are, right? Friends?"

Beer bottle poised at his lips, Klein says, "In a manner of speaking."

"Paisley, have you forgiven him for his cruel critique of your story?"

My mouth drops open.

Klein's eyes bulge. "Remind me to tell Oliver's soccer coach about the time Eden dropped her shorts in a public place and tried to pee on a palm tree."

"You weren't born yet when that happened. You can only repeat embarrassing stories if you were alive and aware enough to remember them yourself." Rosemary pats the top of my hand. "Klein's sister is very thorough when she gossips about him."

I don't have to meet Klein's sister to know that every ounce of gossip about her brother sits on top of a gallon of love. This home has love and acceptance seeping from its walls, as if anybody who grew up here automatically absorbed those qualities.

Klein included. It must be why, after almost eight years, he still feels bad about my story.

"To answer your question, Rosemary, I have not

forgiven Klein yet. But I might consider it after I see those baby pictures."

Rosemary belts out a laugh. She pats her son's shoulder and says, "It's too bad she's not your real girlfriend. I like this one."

Klein's lips form a grim line and he says nothing.

Rosemary puts the finishing touches on the beef stew she has made, and tells me about her job as a florist assistant at a store called Nice Stems.

"Last week we had an order for a dozen black roses. The card read, *Fuck you both, you deserve each other*. The delivery address was to a fancy hotel."

"Cheating, I assume?" Klein asks, placing spoons beside the bowls he has set out.

"Safe assumption," Rosemary responds.

"I can't understand why someone would do that." Klein shakes his head.

"My dad cheated on my mom," I blurt out, immediately regretting the admission. It's this home, I think, and its coziness. The general feeling of acceptance leeches the secrets out of a person.

Klein, bent over the table as he lays napkins out, freezes. His eyes are on me, watching. The color drains from his face. Is he waiting for me to cry? To become visibly upset?

Rosemary breaks in with a wine refill. "I'm sure that was difficult for everyone involved," she says diplomatically.

I nod. "Yes." I grab my glass of wine and take a long drink to nurse my vulnerability hangover.

Klein ladles stew into bowls, and Rosemary hands out chunks of crusty bread lathered in butter.

The meal is delicious. Rosemary is witty, sharing stories about Klein as a teenager. More than once I find myself thinking about how odd this all is, like taking a class about a person who just a few weeks ago I would've thought of only in my memory.

Rosemary does most of the talking. I pepper her with questions, and Klein steps in here or there to offer a word of defense or addition to what Rosemary has to say.

"He was a difficult teen," Rosemary says, looking at Klein with nothing but the purest of a mother's affection, "but that was only because he spent so much time when he was younger being—"

"That's enough," Klein says, eyeing her meaningfully. Rosemary nods in immediate understanding.

My curiosity is piqued, but I know better than to pry.

As promised, Rosemary shows me a few baby pictures after dinner. "He was chubby. His dad called him Brutus."

The mention of his father rolls easily off Rosemary's tongue, but Klein, seated beside me on the sofa, flinches.

I pretend not to notice.

Rosemary passes me an open album. Baby Klein, sitting inside a gigantic cardboard box, stares back at me.

She taps the photo. "He liked to crawl inside there and hide from us."

"I'd crawl inside one now if it were available," Klein mutters.

Rosemary ignores him. "Turn the page," she instructs. "The next one is him in the bath."

Klein tries to close the album, but I'm too fast. I angle

my body away, and the only way for him to overcome me is to reach around me.

Which he does. His hand snakes between my arm and my midsection, fingers making a desperate grab for the book.

Too bad I've already turned the page.

Klein's hand falls slack. He starts to pull it away, but he pauses at my waist. Hidden by my bent arm and angled body, he squeezes my hip lightly and tugs.

He releases me just as quickly, as if it never happened, and I swallow my gasp.

Getting ahold of myself, I peer at the album. "Look at that dimpled baby booty," I coo, and Klein sighs.

We go through a few more, until I'm positive he's ready to come unglued.

Returning the photo album to Rosemary, I say, "That's enough for one night. Klein's head might explode if we keep going."

"Fine, fine," Rosemary says, replacing the album on a shelf. "I guess it's almost my bedtime anyway. I'm opening the store in the morning."

We say our thank yous and goodbyes to Rosemary. She hugs me, and this time I'm ready for it.

Klein pulls his mom in for a hug, and I step back to allow them room. There is nothing perfunctory about his embrace. He wants to hold his mom and show her his love and gratitude.

I've never seen my brother do that to our mom. The thought both saddens and depresses me. Hopefully he does it, I'm just not around to see it.

Klein opens the passenger door of his car, standing

back so I can climb in. I settle in the seat, adjusting my dress that has ridden well past mid-thigh. I glance at Klein as I make the adjustment, and watch his eyes as they watch my thigh.

"Eyes up here," I remind him, but my voice is far too throaty for the words to be much of a warning.

He closes the door with excessive force.

The drive back to our side of town is quiet. My mind is filled with thoughts, images, the feeling of witnessing firsthand a warm and loving family. My own family means well, mostly. They don't mean harm, I know that for certain. But they're fractured. And every one of them except my mom believes I'm to blame.

Klein's silence is driving me crazy, making me wish I could reach into his mind, parse the contents. What is it he's thinking?

I've seen his cute baby rear, yet I don't know him well enough to know what to say right now. So I stay quiet, my thoughts locked in my head, until we pull up to my house.

He shifts into Park and I reach for the door handle.

"Wait for me, please." He opens his door, and I watch him get out and round the front of his car. He opens my door and stands back. The filtered light of the crescent moon descends over his face.

I can't decide if he's more handsome with or without that sliver of moon illuminating him.

I swing my legs over the side and pause, feet dangling. It's the beginning of May, and the night air is starting to tighten its hold on the warmth of the day. The cicadas will arrive later in the summer, so for now it is only the crickets serenading us with their intermittent chirps. A low hum from a busy street nearby simmers in the background.

Klein's hands go inside his pockets. "Are we good?"

My head tilts. "I could ask you the same question."

His lips purse, and he nods slowly. "I want us to be... *good*, Paisley. Everything we're doing here, trying to get to know each other and act like we're together, it'll all be easier for me if you don't hate me anymore."

"We've been through this. I said if I got to see your baby pictures I'd forgive you for what happened." I'm trying to make light of it because Klein looks torn up. I guess what I should really be doing is trying to understand why I care that Klein looks torn up.

He ignores my attempt at levity.

"Listen." He takes a step into the space left open by the passenger door. I lift my feet, propping them on the bottom of the doorframe. I don't want to break eye contact to look down and make sure my dress is covering all my parts, so I settle for assuming if I don't feel a breeze everything is copacetic.

"I apologize for what happened in college. I never should have torn apart anybody's story, but especially yours. I was being an asshole. If I could go back in time and change what I did, I would."

"I appreciate that." And I believe him, because I know at his core Klein is a good person.

"Can I ask you a question?"

I nod.

"Your story... Was it about your dad? You wrote about a teenage girl catching her father cheating on her mom."

He remembers my story?

My stomach lurches. I'm torn between remembering what it felt like to see my father passionately kiss another woman, and astonishment that Klein remembers the details of my story after all this time.

"Yeah, it was."

"The assignment was supposed to be fiction."

"I didn't listen."

Klein huffs a breath of disbelief. "Not at all."

"I guess I didn't make it easy on whomever ended up with my story to critique. That's not how I saw it at the time, though. It felt good to get it out of me and onto the page."

Klein closes his eyes slowly, shaking his head. "I said your story was overly-dramatic."

"You called it a bad soap opera."

Klein pinches the bridge of his nose. "Fuck me, that was cruel."

"You weren't wrong, though." I hate admitting that. "It hurt, but the truth often does. I'm a far better marketer than a writer." My foot taps the doorframe. "Besides, I still get to be creative, so it all worked out in the end."

He nods slowly, a look on his face like he's trying to decide if he accepts my words. "Last Friday night you said it's my fault you're in this position. What did you mean?"

I'd forgotten I said that. "I started dating Shane after the story debacle. I was really upset, and he smelled my vulnerability like a shark smells blood in the water."

"The guy with the annoyingly clean shoes?"

"Umm…" I prefer not to spend too much time sifting through memories to think about Shane's footwear and its level of cleanliness. "I guess so?"

"Weren't you already dating him? He was always walking you to class like an overeager puppy."

"You sure noticed a lot for someone who ignored me." My eyebrows lift, challenging him to refute my claim.

"What else was I supposed to do? You didn't respond to the text I sent after we kissed."

My mouth falls open. "I did not receive a text."

He gives me a *come on* look.

My spine stiffens. "I'm not lying!"

"Neither am I!"

We exchange defiant stares.

He breaks first. "One was sent. I promise."

"Do you have evidence?"

"I deleted your number."

"Harsh."

"I didn't want to be tempted to make an even bigger fool of myself if I had too much to drink and called you or texted you."

I shake my head, flummoxed. "If I'd received a text, I would've answered it."

His hands go into his pockets as he absorbs my claim. He nods once, accepting it, and says, "Tell me how clean shoe guy was my fault."

The news that Klein tried to reach out to me after our kiss is still sinking in, but I manage to arrange my thoughts enough to say, "Objectively, I understand nobody forced me to date Shane. Or take him to Raleigh and let him meet my family. Which eventually led him to liking it enough to move there for a job after we broke up, and then run into my sister and fall in love with her." I picture Sienna's stunning cheekbones, her rosy lips and typical pleasant demeanor. "I even understand why he fell in love with her. Who wouldn't? She's beautiful and sweet—"

"And a few lychee martinis turn her into a fan of male strippers."

"She let loose last weekend. You'll see once we get to the island, she's really different than how she was when you met her."

"She's marrying your ex-boyfriend, and here you are defending her."

I bristle. "So?"

He rubs his hand over the back of his neck. "Forget I said anything. Family is complicated, right?"

I finger the hem of my dress. "Sure is."

There's a different sound right then, like a thump of air, and an owl settles in a nearby tree. Yellow eyes stare at us. "Creepy."

"It's a sign I should quit while I'm ahead." Klein steps aside, allowing me space to exit the vehicle.

I gather my purse and step out. "I had my Klein lesson tonight. When are you going to start your Paisley lessons?"

Klein leans back, letting the car catch him. "Do you still separate your M&Ms by color before you eat them?" A cocksure smile appears on his face.

I blink hard, grappling with how him remembering details about me makes me feel. "Yes…"

He dips his chin at me, like he's saying *there you go*. "I guess I already know one of your quirks." Pushing off the car, he motions at my house. "I'll walk you to your door."

I point at my door, only thirty feet away. "That door right there?"

He sighs at my passive argument.

"Fine," I murmur, throwing up my hands as I deny the flutter of pleasure rippling through me. Might I have a thing for chivalry?

I pivot, and Klein matches me step for step. Halfway to my door, I feel a press against my lower back. A guiding palm I don't need, but... *Oh*. I want it. I like it.

Miracle of miracles, I make it to my front door without melting. Unlocking the door, I push it open an inch and turn back to Klein.

He drops his hand from my back, putting a bit of space between us. His tall frame blocks the porch light, casting an ethereal glow around him. Does he know how handsome he is? He must. How could he not?

Clearing my throat, I force thoughts of his heavily-fringed green eyes from my mind. "Thank you for walking me up," I say, prim and proper. "It was very gentlemanly of you."

One corner of Klein's mouth quirks, like my forehead is transparent and he can read my thoughts like a book. "Get used to me being a gentleman, Paisley."

"Let me guess. That's how your mother raised you to behave?"

"Yes, but also because you deserve to be treated that way."

Instead of saying thank you like I should, my gaze meets the floor. I'm not sure how to stand before a compliment delivered so brazenly.

Maybe Klein senses my unease, because he keeps talking. "I have a lot more to learn about you, Paisley. How about Saturday afternoon, before my shift? I'll come over."

A thrill races through me. "Saturday works."

Quiet falls over us, until he points at my door. "I'm not going anywhere until you're inside and I hear your lock turn."

I fight a smile. "So if I walked inside but forgot to lock it, you'd—"

"Sleep on your porch."

I chuckle. He can't be serious. This is his poetic, writer's soul talking.

"Don't worry, Wordsmith. I'll make sure you get your quality beauty sleep." Pushing open the door, I step inside and turn around.

"Good night," I say, allowing an extra lilt in my voice.

From Klein comes a single, heavy exhale between closed lips. "Good night."

The door closes. Out of sight, I press a hand to my chest and release a held breath in one long, slow stream. My head droops, my muscles thawing. The tension from the mental and emotional tightrope I walk with Klein is on par with—

"Paisley."

His voice reaches through the door, surprising me enough to elicit a surprised yelp. "Yeah?"

"Lock the door." He sounds bemused.

Grinning to myself, I reach out and flip the lock loudly.

The night falls quiet, and then his car engine roars to life.

Dazed, I make my way to my room and lie back on my bed, staring at the ceiling.

Klein, who I believed never looked my way in that class we were in together, remembers the way I'd empty my bag of M&Ms onto my paper and group them by color.

Why, after all this time, did he retain that unimportant detail?

And why, oh why, do I like that he did?

## CHAPTER 13
### *Paisley*

Klein arrives on Saturday afternoon at 3:55.

He wears jeans, like always, but this time his T-shirt is forest green. It deepens his eye color, and requires real effort for me not to stare too deeply into them.

"You're early again," I chide, holding open the door.

One hand is hidden behind his back, and when I swerve left to look at what it is he's concealing, he veers right. "Five minutes early is on time."

"Says who?" I coax back the grin bending my lips.

"The time police." He rocks back on his heels, eyebrows lifting. "And guess what?"

I bite down on a square of flesh inside my lower lip. "You're the sheriff?"

Klein makes an aggrieved face. "You stole my punchline." He moves the arm he has bent behind himself. With exaggerated fanfare, he holds out a bag of Laffy Taffy. "Maybe this will make up for my under-appreciated punctuality."

I take it from him and step back into my house,

fending off feelings as ooey and gooey as the bag's contents.

"They're a passable jumping off point. Come sit," I say, leading him to the living room and settling on one end of the couch. I gesture at the opposite end for Klein.

"Do you still like that candy?" he asks, passing me to get to where I've indicated.

"Mm-hmm." I try to keep my response blasé. There aren't any heart tingles happening from that little act of kindness. Nothing to see here, folks.

Klein attempts to fit his tall frame on my couch. He turns around, giving my throw pillows an accusatory stink-eye when they stop him from sitting comfortably. He elbows one, asking, "Why do you have so many of these?"

"Because I like them."

"Hmph," he grunts.

"So," I bring my legs up and tuck them underneath me. "Where should we begin?" I break into the bag of candy daintily, like I'm only eating it to be polite. But in my body, there's a different story. I haven't had Laffy Taffy in forever, and I can already taste its saccharine and artificial flavor on my tongue.

Klein extracts a piece of folded paper from his back pocket. "Well," he unfolds it, hesitating as he sends me a worried glance. "I made a list of things I would probably know about a girlfriend."

I nod calmly, but on the inside, I am trying not to freak out. Why do I find it so endearing that he made a list? I pop in a strawberry flavored piece of candy. The sugar hits my taste buds in a delightful assault.

I hold out a hand for the list. "May I see?"

He places it in my outstretched palm.

1. ***Musical preference***
2. ***Karaoke song***
3. ***Relaxation method***
4. ***Favorite food***

Clearing my throat, I push out the breathless feeling and tell myself this is only Klein being organized. Not kind, sweet, or thoughtful. *Organized*.

He plucks the list from my hand and removes a small silver pen from his pocket. Uncapping it, he lays the paper on his thigh, pen in the ready position.

I beat back a grin. Again. I'm having to do that a lot with him. "Are you afraid you won't remember my answers?"

He shakes his head. "I like to study."

"Right." I remember that about him, the way he would drape over his desk in class, his dark blond hair sweeping over his forehead. Sometimes the tip of his tongue poked out from the corner of his mouth when he was concentrating hard.

I sit up straight, swinging my legs out from underneath me because my knees are beginning to ache. "The answer to number one is whatever is on top hits."

Klein stares at me.

"What?" I challenge.

"Terrible answer," he grimaces. "We are going to need to do some work on your taste in music."

I palm my chest, pretending to be offended. "I like what I like."

"I'm adding 'expand Paisley's musical horizon' to our contract."

My eyebrow quirks. "The one you filed with the department of contracts?"

"*Bureau* of contracts," he corrects.

I start to laugh, then stifle it with a cough.

"You can laugh at my joke, Paisley." His voice grows huskier, chin dipping my direction. "It's allowed."

Oh-kay. We need to get back on track here. "I'll remember that for next time." Glancing down at the paper, I ask, "What was the next one?"

He doesn't have to look at his paper. He already knows. "Karaoke song."

"Easy." I relax back into the couch cushion. "She's In Love With The Boy by Trisha Yearwood."

"Never heard of it."

My mouth opens in what is likely extremely unattractive bewilderment. "Dealbreaker. The agreement is off."

Klein reaches behind himself, removing two throw pillows and, making use of the name, tosses them on a nearby chair. He leans back on the couch and looks up at the ceiling. "Sing it for me."

Umm...excuse me? I sing, but terribly, and only when nobody can hear me. "That's a hard no."

"Come on, Paisley. There is no worse singer than I, so you're already better than me."

"Look up the song. It'll take ten seconds."

"Probably less, but I would rather hear you sing it."

"Why, so you can take the knowledge and add it to your little stockpile of ammunition?"

His head turns and he looks at me. "What?"

"I let it slip that I looked you up on the internet, and then I saw you mentally tucking it away for later use. Gunny sacking, I believe that's called. And," I widen my eyes at him, "you made sure to tell me looking me up was the last thing you wanted to do."

The comment still smarts.

He sits up, bending a knee and bringing it between us. He's so big that he takes up almost the entire cushion. With an expression of utter seriousness, he says, "I said it was the last thing I wanted to do. Not that I didn't do it."

The clarification hits its mark. "You looked me up?" What a relief to know it wasn't only me haunted by him. By what we could have been if we'd talked after that kiss, or at all during that semester.

His arm has been resting on the back of my couch, and he bends it now, pinching his bottom lip between two fingers as he considers how to say something. "I looked you up twenty-two times. And every time I did it, it was the last thing I wanted to do because I knew it would lead to nothing but regret."

I mirror his posture. Mere inches separate our knees. "Regret? About the story critique, you mean?"

His lashes are long and full and his eyes are laser focused on me. "Sure," he answers slowly, and I'm almost positive it's a partial truth.

"I'll have to remember you're a wordsmith. I'm not used to paying special attention to what people are saying.

Usually words are words, but with you—" my head tilts, "I get the feeling they're more."

"Words are everything." He speaks clearly, strength pulsing in his tone. "I'm willing to put myself on social media for the chance to have my work out in the world. My words."

"But isn't that exactly what you're already doing with your book? Allowing people into your mind? Your heart? That sounds a hell of a lot more intrusive than posting on social media."

"They're characters." He taps his head. "I made them up. A work of fiction. All resemblances to persons, places, or things, both living and dead, are entirely coincidental."

"Thank you for reciting your copyright. No, but seriously, think about it. Maybe this will help you wrap your mind around the idea of being on social." I sit up straighter, excited. I'd rather Klein be receptive to our marketing initiative, or at the very least not despise it. "Authors put a piece of themselves into their work, even when they write fiction. It's like...the book is a woven piece of art. What are those things called? With a loom?"

"Tapestry."

"Right, that. It's like you're sitting at a loom, and you're *looming*." I mime weaving.

He laughs.

"And you're inserting microscopic pieces of your soul into the words. Onto the pages. Then you're giving it away, to whomever picks up the book. You have no control over that. You do not know who's picking up your soul vis à vis your book." My shoulders lift, hovering near my ears for a second before dropping. "It's not all that different from social media."

"Social media is performative. I hate that."

"Don't be performative. We talked about this. Be unapologetically honest."

"While posting about fake dating you?"

"Yes. Tell the world this is fake." I tap his knee. "Just don't tell my sister. Or her friends. Or my brother. Or my parents. Or my ex."

"Wouldn't dream of it," he responds. "But have you considered the possibility they might somehow come across my account?"

"I have. And I don't think it's likely to happen. The platform has two billion users. And while we'll strive to give your account traction and make it one to follow, it will be within the right space and for the correct audience. My family does not fall into that category." About this, I'm certain. I climb off the couch. "I feel like having a glass of wine. You?"

Klein shakes his head. "I'm good. I'm headed to work pretty soon."

"Do you want something to drink? Water?" I bat my eyelashes. "Kombucha?"

He smiles. "No, thank you."

I indicate for him to follow me, so he gets up and trails behind me into the kitchen. "What's it like working in a bar like that?"

"Loud," he answers, wandering over to my collection of cookbooks. "Do you cook?"

I answer with a nod as I'm on tiptoe, pulling my favorite wineglass from a top shelf. A small part of me wouldn't mind Klein coming up behind me and reaching for the glass. Would he brush against me, his front to my back? Would I feel his chest pressing into my shoulders? I remember all too clearly what it felt like to have his heated chest under my seeking hands. Sloppy or not, I liked having Klein under my palms.

He stays put, and that's a good thing. This situation has the potential to be messy enough. Why throw gasoline on an inferno?

Taking the bottle of wine from the fridge, I pour half a glass and turn around, leaning back against the lip of the counter.

I'm stunned, but only briefly. Is this really *Klein* in my kitchen? Asking get-to-know-me questions so we can pull off a week of fake-dating hijinks?

I swallow a mouthful of wine. "What was the next question on your list?"

"How do you relax?"

"I guess that depends on what kind of stress I'm experiencing. If it's just the everyday stuff, I watch videos of people making fancy ice."

Klein's eyebrows cinch dubiously. "Fancy ice? You mean like nugget ice or the square cubes?"

Pulling my phone from my back pocket as I walk closer, I tell him, "Prepare to be amazed."

But then it's me who's amazed, or maybe *dumbfounded* is the better word, because I'm so close to Klein now that his scent overwhelms me. The warmth coming off his body is distracting. Disarming.

Shaking my head and forcing myself to behave, I bring up the video, then press play. "This is my favorite one. She has seventeen molds, and she keeps them organized in her freezer."

Thirty seconds later, the video is over. "But why?" Klein asks. "What does she do with them now? Does the flower shaped ice go in pink lemonade? Does the diamond shaped ice go in a top-shelf vodka tonic?"

I squint at him. "You're weird."

"I need to know what she does with it."

I smirk. "You mean you need a resolution to the story she has presented in a thirty second short form video?"

"That"—he points at my phone—"is not relaxing. Too many unanswered questions."

"Why don't you tell me what you do to relax? I'm sure it's not always easy to deal with drunk people at night, and sling words during the day."

"Easy," Klein shrugs. "I watch videos of dogs throwing temper tantrums."

Now it's my turn to have pinched and dubious eyebrows. "Dogs throwing temper tantrums?"

Klein extracts his phone from his pocket, excitement twinkling in his eyes. He copies me by saying, "Prepare to be amazed."

He pulls up a video and offers me his phone. "Dom sent me this yesterday."

I'm already smiling and we're only three seconds into the video of a golden retriever lying on what appears to be an asphalt street, refusing to get up. The owner stands a few feet away, holding onto the leash and attempting to coax him from the ground. A young girl walks by, sparking the dog's interest enough to make him stand up and lick her hand. Relief takes over the owner's face as he believes they will now be able to continue their walk, but the dog lies right back down. The exasperated owner finally bends down on one knee, scooping up the dog who at this point could pass for a sack of potatoes. The owner staggers away as upbeat music plays in the background.

Klein slides his phone back into his pocket. I take a step away, inserting some space between us now that we've exchanged silly videos (and he's one-upped me).

Appraising eyes on me, he says, "You should see your smile right now. You look way happier than you did watching ice being made."

I wipe the smile off my face. "You're seeing things. I'm not smiling." Except I'm literally fighting a smile while saying it, and Klein's knowing look makes it even harder to keep a straight face. I take another sip of wine. "What was your final question on your list?"

"Favorite food."

"Tacos."

"That feels like a gimme."

"A gimme?"

"Everyone's favorite food is tacos."

"What's your favorite food?"

"Tacos."

I roll my eyes. "I guess it'll be easy for us to choose a restaurant sometime."

Klein glances at his watch. "Speaking of restaurants..." He pushes off the counter. "I better get going."

I nod, but find I don't want him to go. Do I *enjoy* his company? Our conversation?

Geez. I'm going to have to watch out for that. No need to muddy the waters.

I walk him to the front door, holding it open for him while he steps through.

He stands on the threshold, hands tucked in his pockets. "It was nice getting to know you. A little, anyway."

"It was only a little nice getting to know me?" I tease.

He offers a lopsided smile. "I mean, we've hardly broken the surface."

Disregarding his words with a wave of my hand, I say, "Nah. I'm boring. There's not much to know about me."

He arches an eyebrow. My breath sticks in my throat as he captures a lock of my hair, pinching it between two fingers. "I think you're very wrong about that." My hair glides through his grasp, his finger turning in a circle so my hair spirals around it.

Then he drops it. And lopes off. Just like that.

No goodbye. No backwards glance.

Inside my house with the door closed, I spy his short list lying on the couch where he'd been sitting. I swipe the paper, tracing my finger over his neat handwriting.

When I agreed to the idea of Klein being my fake date for the week, I'd only thought about it on a surface level. The logistics, and what each one of us will get out of it.

I didn't consider what it would mean for me to get to know him, or how it would feel to let him know me.

I like it.

And I don't care for that.

> Are you awake?

>> Yes. How was your shift? Any more lascivious acts in the parking lot?

> I told you nothing happened with her.

>> Sure, sure.

> You're stubborn.

>> As are you.

> I stopped for tacos on the way home. It made me think of you.

>> How thoughtful.

> And then I realized you never told me much about Clean Shoe Guy.

>> Uhh ok??? He has a name.

> Satan, correct?

>> Close. Shane.

>> What do you want to know?

> Do you still carry a torch for him? Just trying to ascertain what exactly I'm getting myself into when I arrive on the island.

> I'd rather chew off my own big toe than have a remotely romantic experience with Shane/Satan ever again.

I bet you said the same thing about me after our bad kiss.

> We were barely adults when that happened. I forgive us.

So no lingering feelings for the ex, then?

> What do you get when you multiply zero by a zillion?

Zero.

> Bingo!

## CHAPTER 14
*Klein*

What do you think about going to Oliver's soccer game next weekend? You could meet him and my sister.

> You want me to meet more of your family? Don't you think we're moving too fast? We've only been fake dating a few weeks.

You afraid?

> Nooo.

Don't go soft on me now, Royce. This is for believability. Oliver's an important person in my life. It'll look weird if you've never met him. What do you say?

> One question...should I bring my trusty foam finger??

Paisley arrives at the game ten minutes before it begins. She wears ripped jeans, a V-neck lavender tee, and sneakers. As much as I appreciate her work attire and those heels she favors, I like the casual look on her, too. She spots me standing in the grass near my parking spot and waves.

I stride her way, and she comes mine. As she walks she reaches into her purse, producing a white baseball cap that she fits onto her head.

My stride nearly breaks. I've always thought baseball hats on girls are cute, but on Paisley? It's on a whole new level, and on that elevated level the descriptor is no longer *cute.* It's sexy.

Sexy as hell.

Sexy as fuck.

Sexy as if she were standing in front of me in something lacy and barely there.

She stops in front of me. There's a smile on her face, no makeup that I can tell, and two gold hoops dangling from her earlobes. The delicate purple shade of her shirt makes the green in her eyes stand out more than the blue.

Curling a finger, I tap it against the bill of her hat. "Nice hat. Wrong sport." Maybe lighthearted teasing will keep me from telling her how attractive I find her.

"No such thing as a soccer hat," she trills.

Is she… *nervous*? No way. Not Paisley.

My hand cups her elbow. Immediately I regret it, wishing I'd gone for a place less asexual. I could've at least touched her shoulder. Too late, but I'm mentally kicking myself anyhow. "I'm glad you made it," I say, hoping my internal agony isn't showing on my face.

She blinks up at me. "I told you I'd be here."

I release her elbow and take a step back. "I know. But it's a kids soccer game." Now I'm the one feeling nervous. Did I really invite her to my nephew's soccer game? What a chump. Paisley's probably used to far better, well-planned dates. "I'm sure you have a lot of other things you could be doing with your morning."

"I do," she says, tilting her head. "But this is important, too. Believability, and all."

"Right," I nod along. "Believability."

"Uncle Klein!"

We turn in tandem toward Oliver. Decked out in a navy blue uniform with red lining around the collar and red knee-length socks, he runs at me full speed.

I catch him easily, swinging him around. Eden's a few steps behind.

She walks up to Paisley and extends a hand. "You must be Paisley. I'm Eden, Klein's older sister."

I set Oliver on his feet. Eden reaches over and musses his hair. "This wild man is my son, Oliver."

"It's nice to meet you both."

Oliver unwinds a backpack from Eden's shoulder. "Gotta go. I don't wanna be late for warm-ups. Coach is strict. He says I'm on a club team now and I have to act like it."

I frown. These kids are ten. What does it mean to 'act like it'? As soon as Oliver is out of ear shot, I tell Eden, "I think I'm going to have to spend some time making that social media model less attractive in the facial area."

Eden bursts out laughing. "I fear a crooked nose would

only give him a dangerous edge, and you know ladies love a dangerous man."

My frown deepens to a scowl.

"Backstory, please," Paisley sings out.

I run a hand through my hair, wishing I'd kept my mouth shut. "Oliver's new coach is an aspiring fitness influencer." Even I hear the disdain in my tone.

"Klein is jealous," Eden teases, pinching my cheek.

"False," I declare, deepening the timbre of my voice to make my sister laugh.

Paisley looks out to the field, her eyes zeroing in on the coach leading fifteen ten-year-old boys through warm up exercises. His thigh muscles strain against his shorts, and the sleeves of his T-shirt appear to be suffocated by his biceps. Does he not own clothing that fits?

"All right, all right," Paisley says. "I'm gonna need some proof."

Eden whips out her phone. She has the soccer coach's social media profile pulled up in fewer than seven seconds.

"Wow, Eden," I gripe. "You didn't even have to search for it. You keep it queued?"

She thrusts the phone in front of Paisley's face, but her eyes shoot death rays at me. "Have a modicum of respect. This is Oliver's future daddy you're talking about."

Paisley's gaze rakes over the screen, pointing at a video that appears to be him demonstrating hip stretches. "I think maybe you should make him your daddy."

"That's it," I mutter, annoyed at Paisley's open appreciation. "You're kicked out of the game, Paisley."

"No way," Eden interjects. She loops an arm around

Paisley, tugging her into her side. "Paisley is my new best friend."

I rub my temples. "I should have known introducing you two was a bad idea."

The referee's whistle blows, indicating the start of the game.

I swat at Eden's phone. "If you two are done slobbering over him, there's a game starting."

Eden takes Paisley to the sidelines while I retrieve chairs from the back of Eden's car. I return with two, setting them up and gesturing for Paisley to sit.

"Where's yours?" she asks.

"Klein doesn't sit during games," Eden answers. "He's too high strung."

"Coaches don't sit," I inform my sister.

"Former coaches," Eden corrects.

Paisley grins widely, far too amused by my sister's responses.

I spend the next forty-five minutes showing Paisley exactly what Eden meant about me being high strung.

"Can you calm down?" she asks, craning her neck to watch me as I pace behind her.

I throw out an angry arm, gesturing across the field. "The coach is an idiot. Why doesn't he tell them to stop passing toward the middle?"

Eden looks at me reproachfully. "Maybe he said something to them while they were on the sidelines but you couldn't hear it because you're not there? Because you are no longer Oliver's coach?"

"Maybe I should be," I retort, growling.

Eden's eyebrows lift. "What, now you're going to get a third job?"

"Hold up." Paisley's head swivels to my sister. "A third job? You mean because he's a bartender and also a writer?"

"Maybe I should've said fourth job," Eden says. "Add home remodel to that list."

Confusion lands on Paisley's face. "Home remodel?"

Annoyance fills me. I wish my sister would stop talking. "The owner of Obstinate Daughter is in the middle of remodeling his house. I've been helping him out here and there."

Paisley tips up the brim of her hat so she can see me better. "Now you're an architect?"

My arms cross. "No, I'm good at swinging a sledgehammer around and knocking shit down."

She stares up at me, lips pursed.

"What?" I look down at her. She's probably scrambling to figure out how she's going to explain to her mother that her boyfriend is also a swinger of sledgehammers. Is she wishing she'd stumbled onto some other guy with a better pedigree to be her fake date? The thought puts a sadness deep in my chest, and a layer of scorn on top. "You don't like the fact your fake boyfriend has callused hands? Are you having second thoughts about parading me around in front of your family?"

She lets out a little breath, offended. "That is *not* what I said."

"Geez, Klein," Eden interjects. "It won't be your calluses that get you kicked off the love train, it's going to be your bad attitude."

Paisley crosses her arms and glares at me. "She's right."

In the center of the field, the referee glances at his watch and slows his pace. He brings his whistle to his lips and blows a cadence signaling the end of the game.

The adults clap, shouting, *Good work, boys*, and *It's OK, you'll win the next one*.

Bummer. The disappointment I feel is similar to that of Oliver and his teammates trudging off the field.

"One scoop, Klein," Eden instructs, warning in her tone.

I refuse her with a head shake. "It is a two-scoop day, Eden, and don't try to tell me otherwise."

"Fine," she grumbles. To Paisley, she explains, "Klein takes Oliver out for a treat after soccer. Win or lose."

Oliver comes off the field, backpack weighing down his already hunched shoulders. His gaze meets mine, and his lower lip quivers.

I wrap him in a hug, ignoring the sweaty smell coming off him. "You played well. Be proud of that."

"We lost," Oliver says irritably.

"There are lessons to be found in losing."

"Uncle Klein, right now I just can't see what they are."

I nod, eyes squinting like I'm thinking deeply. "Do you believe a double scoop of ice cream will help your vision?"

One side of Oliver's mouth curls up in a smile. "Only if there's marshmallow fluff and crumbled Oreos on top."

Eden huffs. "If you insist on giving him all that sugar, you're taking him for the afternoon."

I offer a high five to Oliver. "Told you I could get her to let you come over for the afternoon, and have a treat the size of your head."

Oliver beams, his lost soccer game behind him now that ice cream is in his future. He slaps my palm with as much force as he can muster. "Uncle Klein, you're the best."

Over Oliver's head I point back at myself and mouth to Eden, "I'm the best."

Eden less-than-gently taps the center of my chest. "Best uncles facilitate the building of dioramas. That we don't have the materials for." She pretends to shake pom-poms. "Yay."

Oliver groans and swings his body around like this is the worst news he could receive.

I wink at him. "It's a good thing I double-majored in creative writing and diorama construction."

Hoisting a folded chair on each shoulder, I lead the way across the grassy field toward the parking lot.

"My little brother played soccer," Paisley tells Oliver. "I remember going to his games. You're way better than he was."

"Thanks." He squints one eye and looks up at her. "Are you Uncle Klein's girlfriend?"

"Paisley is my friend," I answer.

Oliver has his next question ready. "Have you ever watched him play soccer?"

"Nope." She pops the 'p' sound.

"You should. He's *really* good."

I grin at Oliver. You'd think we had an agreement the way he's talking me up.

We reach Eden's car and I fit the chairs into the trunk. To Paisley, I ask, "Are you up for ice cream?"

She shakes her head. "I'll let you guys have some family time. Besides, I have work to do."

Oliver makes a face. "On a Saturday?"

She grins down at him. "I'm afraid so."

"You should at least eat some ice cream before you work," I cajole, drawing out the last word.

Her gaze lifts to me. "Shouldn't the treat come after the hard work is finished?"

"No," my sister, Oliver, and I say in unison.

Paisley laughs, and Eden waves goodbye. "It was nice meeting you." She fixes me with a pointed look. "Hope to see you again soon."

Eden walks around the side of the SUV, Oliver in tow. "See you there, Uncle Klein," he yells, adding a wave.

I walk Paisley to her car parked nearby. "You should come with us."

A *hmm* sounds from her throat. "For believability? So I can report to my family your nephew's favorite ice cream flavor?"

We're stopped at the back of her car. My hand comes out between us, reaching for her, and I realize what I'm doing and drop it. I'm going to have to be careful. With Paisley it's almost too easy to forget this is all fake. We're too good at bantering, at teasing, at getting along.

Forcing a smile, I shrug and say, "Because I want you to."

She worries her bottom lip with her teeth.

I wish I could retract my invite. Why did I say anything at all? Going to Oliver's soccer game so she can meet him and be able to speak about him is one thing, but getting ice cream with my family, just for the sake of spending time with them, is another. We're not together, and let's be honest, I'm not the guy she'd choose.

Apology spreads through her gaze. "Klein, I—"

My lips draw into a hard line. "I get it. Don't worry about it." I put a step between us, because I need space. I can't be that close to her right now. It hurts.

She reaches out, but I'm not there to touch, and her arms fall limply to her side. "I don't think you understand."

"I understand perfectly." I keep my voice even. "This"—I gesture between our bodies—"is strictly business. No fraternizing beyond what's necessary."

She frowns. "It's not that."

Hope, persistent and irritating, sparks in my chest. "What is it then?"

She opens her mouth, but nothing comes out, and her facial expression shifts into quiet panic.

The hope is extinguished.

Paisley makes a sound of frustration, a strangled cry, and without thought I reach for her, grasping her forearm. She looks down at where I'm touching her, a quick breath slamming to the back of her throat.

My calluses.

I helped knock down walls three times this week. My calluses are prominent, more than when I've touched Paisley before.

She's disgusted. By my touch.

It *wrecks* me.

As if her skin is a hot stove, I jerk back my hand. Here it is again, embarrassment covered up by anger. "How dare I touch you with my calloused hands." It doesn't sound angry, just insecure.

Paisley's nose wrinkles, lips pressing together like an accordion while a determined 'v' appears between her eyebrows.

"Those hands." She points a stiff finger at me. "Stop talking about those hands as if they're a turn-off. They are a badge of honor, a trophy, an emblem of an honest man doing a hard day's work. The fact you assume I think otherwise is insulting."

She grabs my hands, whisking them under her T-shirt. I jolt at the feel of her warm, smooth skin, the dip of her belly button under the pad of my middle finger. She guides my hands over her stomach, fire burning in her blue-green irises. "Do I look like I care about your calluses?"

Shock holds me, but soon I'm moving on my own, running my hands over her sides, curving around to her lower back. Feeling Paisley's body. She shivers. She has… *goose bumps.*

Could it be? She likes my rough touch?

My hands remain in place on her back, frozen but for my thumbs gently stroking her soft skin.

"Paisley." My voice tumbles out, a deep and rumbly whisper.

"Yeah?" Her voice is shallow.

"I'm sorry. I'm…"

"Sensitive?" She arches an eyebrow.

"Yeah. I have a bit of a chip on my shoulder. We didn't grow up with much, and…" my voice trails off. There are things I haven't told her. Memories I prefer not to relive.

"Don't worry about it," she assures, stepping away and causing my hands to fall from her shirt. "Are we good?"

It's the second time we've had to determine that we are, in fact, still good. I'm beginning to wonder if 'good' is a stand-in for the word 'friends.'

I hold back my sigh. "We're good, Royce."

She walks to her car door, throwing me a tentative smile as she opens it. "See you soon, Madigan."

She climbs in, and I go to my vehicle. I'm sure Eden and Oliver are almost to the ice cream place.

As for me, the feel of Paisley's skin remains on my hands.

## CHAPTER 15
*Paisley*

I fibbed. I don't have to work. I have my final bridesmaid dress fitting, but that's not for a few more hours.

I needed space from Klein.
Klein the guy I drunkenly made out with in college.
Klein the guy who tore apart my story.
Klein the writer.
Klein the uncle.
Klein the man with work-roughened hands.
Klein my client.
Klein my fake boyfriend.
Klein
K l e i n
K L E I N

> This is what I'm wearing for the wedding ceremony.

Your picture-taking is worse than Oliver's.

> Rude.

You cut off your head.

> That was on purpose.

You didn't want me to see your face? You are aware I already know what you look like, right?

> Maybe I've been wearing a mask this whole time, like in the movies. The kind that go around my whole head and neck and part of my chest.

Weird way for you to ask me to put my hand down your shirt, but ok.

> If you put your hand on my chest and yank on my skin, I will poke you in the eyes at the same time I karate chop your windpipe.

> Don't test me. I took a self-defense class, so I am, in fact, certified in eye poking and windpipe chopping.

I'm terrified.

> Lovely. That's right where I want you.

I'm playing in a soccer match next Thursday. It's supposed to be friendly, but it's more of a grudge match. Young Bucks versus Dad Bods. Do you want to come watch?

> After Oliver bragged about your skills? I'd be a fool to decline.

Bring the foam finger.

> Will do. Do you like the dress?

Does it matter if I like the dress?

> No, but I need to be told it looks good on me. My sister isn't answering her phone right now.

The dress doesn't look good on you…

YOU make the dress look good.

> KLEIN THE STRIPPER you are THISCLOSE to a windpipe chop.

## CHAPTER 16
*Klein*

"Are there naked girls over there?"

My head whips to the asker of the nonsense question. It's my boss, Jeremiah, who is also my soccer teammate. "What?" I ask, a hard enunciation on the *t*.

Jeremiah's chin is lifted, his eyebrows raised. He has hair the color of a flaming hot Cheeto, and freckles from head to toe. He shoulders into me. "You missed a pass because you were looking at the sidelines. *Again*."

I shake my head in remorse. "Sorry."

"Are you expecting someone?"

Another head shake. "No."

The game is half over, and Paisley still isn't here. No reason to tell Jeremiah about her now. He'd give me all kinds of shit for being stood up.

Jeremiah lopes off to retrieve the soccer ball from where it rolled after I missed it.

I shouldn't have expected Paisley would come tonight, even though she said she would. It was dumb of me to invite her in the first place. I'd been high on happiness, on catching a glimpse of her cheering on Oliver, and I'd overstepped. The invitation I'd extended her had nothing to do with getting to know each other better, and she sensed it.

"Get your head in the game," Jeremiah instructs, placing it on the sidelines for Dad Bod's throw in. "We can't let these middle-aged men win. We're young, we're strong." He flexes his biceps and grunts.

"In case you've missed it, they want it more than we do. The will to win makes them more formidable than your arm muscles."

Jeremiah jogs backward, pointing at my chest. "An attitude like that ensures you will be a loser."

Taking my place on the field, I do everything I can to push Paisley from my mind. We're exchanging favors, nothing more and nothing less. It shouldn't matter that she no-showed.

I play the next thirty minutes with supreme focus. Flow state, it's called. A space where everything flows, where distractions are nonexistent.

Young Bucks win handily, 4-1.

Dad Bods use the bottoms of their T-shirts to wipe the sweat from their faces. In all fairness, only a few of them have midsections that live up to their team name.

"Who's buying the first round?" Jeremiah asks, looking around to the men from both teams. "I could use a beer, and whoever wants to go is welcome."

The guys discuss where to go for a drink, and half of the Dad Bods beg off, citing the wife and kids as their reason.

I might as well get in on the action. Better than going

home to an empty apartment and feeling like even more of a loner. "There's this cool place on—"

"Klein!"

I know that voice. A smile drags up the corners of my lips. The men crowded around me look over my shoulder, getting a glimpse of the woman calling my name.

I turn around and there she is, walking double time. She waves, looking only at me. "I guess I missed the game," she says, breathless, stopping in front of me. "There was a fire drill at work. One of our client's websites crashed. I may or may not have gone ten over the speed limit to get here."

"No worries," I assure her. I'd rather not cop to the amount of relief cascading through me. She didn't stand me up after all.

She's still in her work clothes, slacks the color of blood red, and a white blouse. A cursive 'P' on a delicate gold chain rests around her neck. Her hair falls around her shoulders in graceful waves.

"Hi," Jeremiah says, stepping around me with an extended hand. The rest of the guys have gone back to their previous conversation.

Jeremiah doesn't wait for me to introduce him. "I'm a friend of Klein's, and I own Obstinate Daughter."

He's expecting this to impress Paisley, but her face is a mask of polite interest. "How nice," she says, shaking his hand. "I'm Paisley." She offers nothing else, though she could tell him about her marketing company, and how she owns it.

Jeremiah glances at me, then back to Paisley. "Klein

was having a hard time concentrating during the game. I guess now I know why."

I level him with a hard stare. "That's enough out of you."

To Paisley, I explain, "You were late, so I worried. That's what I do."

She nods in understanding, but her eyes soften at the corners, and if I had to guess I'd say she likes the idea of being worried over.

"Paisley, are you joining us?" Jeremiah asks. "We usually go for a beer after a match."

Paisley looks at me hesitatingly.

"No," I answer. "Paisley and I have other plans."

"Cool." Jeremiah backs off. "Enjoy your night. Paisley, it was nice to meet you."

"Likewise," she says politely.

I retrieve my water bottle, keys, phone, and wallet from where they lie in the grass, and walk with Paisley to the parking lot.

She nudges me with her shoulder. "I really am sorry I missed your game. I wanted to watch you. Especially after Oliver talked you up."

"Maybe I should be glad you missed it. He probably oversold me."

Paisley looks up at me with that blue-green stare. "Probably not."

A car approaches as we walk through the parking lot. It slows to allow us to walk across, but Paisley hustles and waves apologetically at the driver of the vehicle.

"Uh, Paisley," I say when I catch up with her. The car passes behind me. "Are there ants in your pants?"

"No."

"Why did you hurry for that car?"

"To be polite."

"And the apologetic wave?"

"An apology."

"For what?"

"Walking in front of them."

"But you didn't do anything you needed to apologize for."

"Klein," Paisley says my name with exasperation. "I am a courteous pedestrian. I need that stranger to see me and be like, *that courteous pedestrian is a ten out of ten.*"

I shrug. "It's a little much, but ok."

We reach my car first. "I need to go home and shower. Do you want to follow me home? We can decide where we want to go from there once I'm no longer sweaty."

"You're not going to turn into a psychopath as soon as your front door is closed, are you? Lock me up and throw away the key?"

"I was planning to, but now that you're on to me, I'll save my villainous plans for another unsuspecting victim."

She runs the back of her palm across her forehead and pretends to flick away sweat. "Dodged that bullet."

We climb into our respective vehicles, and as I'm pulling out onto the neighborhood street that will lead to the bigger road to my place, I try not to think too hard about the bloom of happiness in my chest.

Yes, this is Paisley Royce in the car behind me following me to my apartment.

Sure, there was a time when I would've laid on a mud puddle to keep her from having to walk through it.

So what if I remember how she used to take notes with a multicolored pen, then became distracted, and drew flowers in the margins?

We are adults now. Adults whose only reason for being in one another's lives is to help each other out.

Friends for the time, not for the road.

## CHAPTER 17
*Klein*

"Your place is nice," Paisley murmurs as she noses through my book collection. Her neck bends awkwardly to read a book title.

Bookshelves line one wall of my living room. Paisley walks its length, her fingertips running over spines, pulling one out here and there to inspect the cover.

I wasn't expecting company, but I'm a tidy guy. A surprise visit to my home doesn't induce panic. I vacuum my floors, clean the dishes before they smell bad, and dust semi-regularly. I even own a throw blanket, of sorts. It's a quilt sewn by my grandmother and great aunt, and I never throw it because it's precious.

Despite knowing I'm a clean and otherwise socially acceptable man, Paisley perusing my shelves incites a nervous excitement. For every book spine she runs a finger down, a corresponding thrill shoots down my own.

I like her in my space. My home. Watching her learn me, my book preferences, puts a squeeze to my heart. Those red pants she wears only magnify her presence.

They do things to her backside that make it hard to look away from. She walked ahead of me up the stairs to my apartment, and I missed a step and narrowly avoided a fall that would've made it onto my list of top five most embarrassing moments.

Paisley looks over at me, a Stephen King book in her grasp. "Did you always know you wanted to be a writer?"

Her question is perfectly innocent, even expected given where she's standing and what's in her hand. She could never know how painful the answer is.

In a book, backstory is meted out, dropped like morsels along a path. A little something to introduce what made the character who they are in the present. It's never dumped on a reader like a deluge of cold water.

Hidden backstory is what the writer knows about the character, but never shares. As of this moment, I have no plans to share with Paisley the emotional pain I endured on my way to becoming a writer. Like every other time I've been asked this question, I deliver the sanitized version.

"My mom read to me when I was a kid. Big books, with even bigger words. I kept a dictionary next to my bed so I could look up the meanings. She instilled in me a love for story, and"—cue the shrug—"the rest is history."

Paisley likes my response, if her smile and hand over her heart are any indication. "That's sweet."

If I filled out the story, gave it sinew and marrow and muscle, she wouldn't find it sweet. And though I have no intention of doing so, in my chest is an odd ache to tell her.

No way.

I thumb at my bedroom, saying, "I'm going to take a quick shower," and hightail it from the room.

When I finish cleaning myself up and return, I find Paisley draped across my favorite chair.

It's deep, the cushions thick, and the right height to accommodate me. Paisley appears to have been swallowed by it, compensating for the size difference by sitting in it sideways. Her legs dangle off the arm of the chair, feet bare and shoes lying haphazardly on the floor below her. Her head leans back on the opposite arm, a book poised in the air.

She looks like a poem, a painting, maybe even the subject of an aspiring author's fantasy.

"Hey," I say gruffly, walking away so she doesn't catch me adjusting the front of my jeans. "What do you think about staying here and ordering dinner in?"

Behind me I hear the sounds of Paisley closing the book, climbing up off the chair. "Hmm," she says, "what do you have in your fridge?"

I'm turned away from her in the small kitchen, squeezing my eyes shut and willing my erection to play nice. At least I chose jeans instead of the more comfortable option. *Sweats.* Those don't hide a damn thing.

Paisley's voice grows louder and louder behind me, until I know she's only a few feet away. Not turning around now would seem rude. I take a deep breath, focusing on keeping my shoulders from moving so she doesn't know what I'm doing, and turn around slowly.

Paisley is staring at me with curiosity, her gaze strong and clear, and I can tell by the look in her eyes she's trying to work through the odd behavior I'm presenting.

"You good?" she asks.

I nod quickly, trying and failing at the attempt not to enjoy what has already become a little inside joke.

"Oh-kay," she draws out the word. She comes closer, bypassing me and going to my fridge. "Cute magnets," she comments, tapping a few with the tip of her pointer finger. "Who gave these to you?"

"My mom. Or my sister. It's kind of become a thing."

Paisley pulls one from the fridge and examines it closer. "They were pets?"

"Every dog we had growing up is now represented in magnet form."

She replaces the magnet. "That's really sweet." She removes the Corgi and holds it up. "Peanut?"

She remembers the name of my favorite pet, a name I mentioned once, briefly?

"The one and only."

"You had a lot of dogs."

"My mom had a thing for going to the pound and choosing the dog nobody else wanted."

"That's sweet, but it also sounds like you had to experience a dog passing away more than most people."

"Once I understood how much we were doing by giving them love and care in the final months or years of their lives, the grief I felt when we lost them became more manageable."

Moisture forms in the corners of Paisley's eyes. "I don't know if I could do something like that."

Her emotion has me longing to reach out to her. I cross my arms to stop myself. Would that be well-received? "You could if you understood what you were giving. You'd be surprised how much pain the heart can hold."

"I'm no stranger to pain."

Her voice is low, deep, almost gravely. Like me, she changes the subject before I can ask any follow-up questions. Stepping up to my fridge, she says, "I like to play this game with myself where I see what I have in my fridge and come up with something to make from the ingredients." She looks up at me. "I hate wasting food."

"What if all I have is," I grab the door handle, and Paisley shuffles aside as I swing it open. "Ground beef and tricolor cauliflower florets?"

"Hmm," Paisley taps her chin. "Do you have an onion?"

Pointing to a basket on the counter behind us, I nod in the affirmative.

She bends down to get a better look at my fridge. Do I take the opportunity to appreciate the curve of her backside, the dip of her lower back? Damn straight. "You have wine," she smiles up at me, and her eyes narrow knowingly. "Everything's better with wine."

"Even tacos?"

"Tacos are magnificent on their own, but they are enhanced by a spicy red." She pulls the ingredients from the fridge. "And yes, I caught you checking out my ass."

"Would have been a crime not to."

She laughs and shakes her backside at me. "I don't blame you. It's a nice ass."

I chuckle and take the ingredients from her, moving around the kitchen to assemble cooking tools.

Paisley and I work side-by-side, cutting the cauliflower

into small pieces and browning the ground beef. Paisley declares dicing the onion my job because it makes her cry. She looks through my pantry while I cut, coming away with a can of enchilada sauce. "Let's throw this in there."

By the time we've added chili pepper, cumin, salt, and pepper, my kitchen smells pretty damn good. I give it a taste, and lift my eyebrows in surprise.

Paisley grins. "I guess if it were terrible, you'd be frowning."

"Taste," I offer the wooden spoon, one hand cupped beneath to catch anything that falls.

Paisley leans in, lips parted and pressing against the tip of the spoon.

*Lucky spoon.*

"Oh my gosh," she breathes, "that is delicious." She holds out her hand for a high five. "We should be on one of those amateur cooking competition shows."

"I'll stick to spinning yarns."

Paisley laughs, rummaging through my cabinets until she locates bowls. She does the same thing with my drawers until she finds silverware. I could've told her where to find those things, but I was busy enjoying watching her get acquainted with my kitchen.

"All right," I say to Paisley as we settle at my small table. "Tell me about your mom and dad."

"That's a loaded question." She takes a bite, pausing to chew, then corrects herself by saying, "It's more like the answer to that question is loaded."

Lucky for me I don't have to go into detail about my parents. It's not me who's taking Paisley to a landmass accessible only by boat and having her spend the week with my mom and dad.

I stay quiet, taking another bite and waiting.

"My mom and dad are divorced. He cheated, as you know." Her gaze flicks to mine, then back down. She takes another bite, chews and swallows, then wipes her mouth with a napkin. "You also know I caught him cheating." She sighs, like whatever it is she's about to say still weighs heavy on her. "We were on Bald Head Island when it happened. It was with the woman who was staying at the house next to ours. When his infidelity finally came to light, everyone sort of blamed me for what happened as a result. The divorce, and all the ugliness that went with it."

I nod calmly, or at least that's how I hope it comes across. My thoughts are a little more *what the fuck* mixed with *who's delusional enough to blame Paisley for her dad's behavior?*

"That's awful," I say, which isn't enough, but I can't think of what to say that isn't derogatory about her father. At the end of the day, the man is still her dad, no matter what he did.

That thought has my fork stilling midair, the realization of my words slingshotting against my brain, reverberating down into my heart.

Do I really believe no matter how badly a mom or dad behaves, they're still your parent?

A minute ago I would've said absolutely not, but that errant thought snuck up on me, and now I'm not so sure.

I rest my fork on my plate, indignation spurring in my chest. My polite initial reaction is fading fast. "Actually,

Paisley, that's more than awful. That's cruel and selfish. Please help me understand how your family blames you."

"Not my mom. Just my dad and my siblings." She sits back, crossing her arms. "They said it was only a kiss, and I blew it out of proportion. I can see where my brother and sister were coming from, because it was a total disruption to everyone's lives. I get that it would've been easier for them if it had stayed buried."

"Paisley, it's not your fault no matter what anybody says. Your siblings were young and probably responded with a commensurate level of maturity, but your dad blaming you is unbelievable." The longer I spoke, the more ardent my tone grew, and now I sound like I'm delivering an impassioned speech. But I'm not done. "He's also wrong, and I bet he really blamed himself but his ego couldn't take it. Has he grown up since? Apologized?" I fear I already know the answer.

"No, but maybe this trip he will. He's kept me at arm's length for so long, you'd think…" She shrugs, but there's hurt behind her eyes. "So, anyway, you'll get to see the whole fam in all their glory. My mom hates my dad, but she's moved on. She has a boyfriend now, and he's young. Like, *young*." Paisley says this with wide eyes.

"How young?"

"He could be *my* boyfriend."

"Whoa."

"Yeah. And she isn't shy about their, uh"—Paisley searches for the word—"*enjoyment* of one another."

Once again I'm nodding calmly, but on the inside I'm throwing up in my mouth.

Paisley continues. "It gets more interesting. My dad

didn't want the divorce. He claims my mom's having a mid-life crisis and he's waiting for her to"—Paisley makes air quotes—"come back home."

"Then why did he cheat?"

"A momentary indiscretion. A lapse in judgment." Paisley rolls her eyes. "Those are his words, not mine."

"I'm sorry you were the one to find him. That's really shitty."

"That part gets worse, too. He knew I saw him, and he asked me not to tell. Stupidly, I listened to him, but it ate me up inside. The anxiety and guilt made my stomach hurt, and then I actually became sick. I had a physiological response to the stress of keeping his secret. I wrote it down on a piece of paper just to get it out of me, and my mom walked into my room. I tried to hide it from her, but she saw that I was nudging the notebook under a stack of schoolwork, and she snatched it up." Paisley laughs once, an empty sound. "I think I would've eaten that piece of paper before I let her read it. How fucked up is that?"

"Pretty damn bad."

"So," Paisley takes her last bite. "My mother will be busy parading her young, hot boyfriend around in front of my father. My father will be busy making disparaging remarks. It'll be grand."

"That would be great in a future story."

Paisley grins wryly. "Just change their names and locations and it's all yours, Wordsmith."

I finished my dinner while Paisley was speaking, so I push the empty bowl away from me and say, "The story you wrote in college didn't go exactly that way. You changed some details."

I don't like bringing up The Unfortunate Thing in my and Paisley's past, but we can't ignore it either. It's there. It's a part of us, of how we came to be the way we are with each other.

"I didn't want to use the real details. I wanted to give it different circumstances. At the time, I thought it would help me process everything that happened. It was all still fresh. By the time I got to college, my parents divorce had only been final a few months. But writing that story did not help me like I thought it would."

"Especially not when somebody came along and ripped it apart." What an asshole I was.

Clearing our empty bowls, I take them to the sink and wash them while Paisley tidies up the kitchen. I'm not necessarily surprised to find myself liking her in this space typically only occupied by me, but I am surprised to find just how much I like it.

Placing the clean dishes on the drying rack, I turn around and find Paisley perched on the counter. She grips the lip of the counter with two hands, legs dangling. She smiles at me, her face open and bright, and asks, "What's next?"

Am I crazy to be contemplating what it would be like to step between her legs? To weave my hands through her hair and ease her body into mine, pausing for a breath with our lips nearly touching?

I would make up for that failed drunken kiss so long ago. I'd make up for it tenfold.

Her eyes are on me. Watching, waiting. For what? For me to make the move? Does she want it? Does she want me? Does Paisley Royce want a struggling writer, a guy who tends bar and slings words and feels too much?

Her chest rises and falls with her breath, her breasts straining against that silk button-up shirt.

I take a step in her direction. Then I take two more. I stop a foot away from her, taking in the moment, waiting for her to say or do something that will alter my trajectory. The air between us is charged, electric, a current running over my body.

Paisley speaks. "At some point we should probably get used to kissing each other. It might be awkward if our first kiss happens in front of my family." She blushes. "Aside from that other time when we were young and very drunk. That one didn't count."

"So you're telling me you want to practice kissing?" I attempt to keep my voice neutral, like this isn't the best news since I typed THE END on my manuscript.

"We don't have to." The words hastily trip out of her mouth. "If you'd rather not show any affection in front of my family, I understand. We can tell them we're not a PDA kind of couple. It's totally fine."

"No."

"No?"

I might be getting six months of pro bono digital marketing, but the real win is getting to be affectionate with Paisley.

"Practice," I draw out the word, stepping up between her legs, my hands on the cool countertop flanking her thighs, "makes perfect. Preparation is essential to the success of any good charade." My eyebrows rise, waiting for her response. Internally, my whole body holds a breath.

She leans closer, teasing the tip of my nose with her own. Her eyes are wide, vulnerable, waiting for me to make a move, telling me she wants me to.

With a low rumble in my throat, I say, "I think practice is—"

A knock on my door steals my attention. I'm not expecting a visitor, and anybody who knows me knows better than to randomly drop in.

I back off, pinching the bridge of my nose in frustration. Disappointment colors Paisley's expression.

I try not to stomp to the door, but I fail. Behind me comes the soft thud of Paisley hopping down off the counter.

"This had better be really fucking important," I grumble, opening the door.

I flinch, surprised to see a familiar face. "Megan?"

"Klein, hi." She smiles. It wasn't too long ago that smile made me happy, and frustrated when it went away. The longer we dated, the more elusive that smile became, and the harder I worked to bring it back. Funny how something I put effort into is now something I don't care to see.

All I care about right now is my near-kiss with Paisley. *That was interrupted by my ex.*

I lean against the door, hoping my irritation isn't obvious on my face. "What's up? Did you come across more of my books?"

"Uh, no," she shakes her head. "I was actually hoping we could talk."

"About?"

She swallows nervously. Nervous is not a place Megan finds herself in often. This alone has me on high alert.

Megan points into my apartment. "Can I come in? I'd rather not talk in the hallway."

"Uh, no." I glance behind me. "I'm busy." I don't know where Paisley is, but she's staying out of sight.

A frown works its way between Megan's eyebrows. She peers around me, searching, and her gaze stills.

I turn, thinking I'm going to see Paisley, but nothing is there.

*The shoes.*

Paisley's red-bottomed spike heels lie on the ground beside my chair.

Megan clears her throat. "Your new girlfriend knows her way around shoes."

"Yeah." I don't know what else to say, and I am not about to correct Megan. If we're letting Paisley's family think I'm her boyfriend, I sure as hell don't mind letting Megan think the same.

Megan stands there, uncertain, then laughs softly and says, "Wow, this is awkward."

My hand rubs over the back of my neck. "It's not great."

"I guess I shouldn't have come here."

I'm scrambling for something to say that won't hurt her feelings, and all I can come up with is, "Probably not." *Wow, Wordsmith. Impressive.*

She thumbs toward the stairs. "I'll guess I'll just go."

I nod and give a halfhearted wave. "Take care, Megan." Then I step back into the apartment and close the door.

"Umm," Paisley says, suddenly appearing. "That was weird to witness."

I run my hands through my hair. "Where were you hiding?"

"In the kitchen. I walked out when I heard you closing the door. Halston was right. Your ex wants you back."

"Megan's probably bored," I argue, going to sit on the couch.

"Or she realized she made a mistake," Paisley counters.

"Too bad." I settle in and weave my fingers together behind my head. "I'm someone else's boyfriend now."

Paisley rests that fine ass of hers on the arm of the couch. "The deal was that you'd be my fake boyfriend on Bald Head Island. Not here." A playful look wrestles over her features. "Is this violating some kind of location clause in the contract?"

I shrug. "The provision wasn't made. Moot point."

"Moot point?"

I nod.

Her nose scrunches. "I think I dislike the word 'moot.'"

"Moot," I try it out, then say it twice more. "Agreed. I hate it."

"Strike it from the English language."

"I don't have the authority."

"You're a wordsmith. Of course you do."

Our banter makes me a happy man, makes me laugh and feel a lightness in my limbs that I like having there. "So stricken," I say, deepening my voice.

I work to keep the wistful smile from sliding its way onto my lips. My mind cannot believe this is the moment in which I've currently found myself. I'm in my living room, watching Paisley perch on the arm of my worn couch, one arm behind her propping her up. Her hair falls down her back, her silk shirt shines in the indirect lamp light, and those red pants cling to each curve and dip of her lower half.

She is stunning, and you know what happens when you're stunned? You cannot speak.

That is precisely where I've found myself.

Paisley twirls a lock of that pretty blonde hair around her finger. "What happened between you two? If you don't mind me asking. You don't have to answer, but I'm curious."

"Why? Are you sussing out the possibility of an untenable fatal flaw?"

Paisley wiggles her eyebrows. "Maybe."

Unhooking my hands from the back of my head, I adjust myself so I can face her more full-on. "Megan and I dated for a little over a year. Things were going well, and then she got a job in finance. She changed after that, which I didn't mind so much because she's about four years younger than me and just starting out in her first job. The changes were subtle at first." I rub my chin, parsing through my memory to find an example. "She stopped saying fi-nance and started pronouncing it fin-ance."

Paisley crooks an eyebrow.

"I know it sounds like a non-issue, and it was. But it built on itself from there. She'd mention people she was meeting, but their names had iterations. Alexander became Alex. Robert became Rob. She started going out for regular happy hours." I hang my palms in the air between us. "I know it doesn't sound like much, because it was subtle. I started picking up on hints, like how *Alex* was going skiing for the weekend and had invited a group of them along. Things like that. We began spending less time together because she was building a robust social life outside of me. She never invited me. I felt like an afterthought."

"Geez, Klein. That's awful."

"I spent a good portion of our relationship feeling bad. One day I decided I'd had enough. I broke things off, and she looked relieved. She didn't want to be the one to do it, I guess."

Funny how hurt I was at the time, and how over it I am now.

"I can't imagine choosing *Alex* and *Rob* over you," Paisley says their names with disdain.

I smile gratefully. "I appreciate that."

"Sounds like she regrets it, too. What do you think changed?"

"Moot point."

Paisley's nose wrinkles. I laugh.

"I'm going to take off," she announces, pushing off the couch. "I have an early meeting tomorrow morning." She strides to her shoes, sliding her feet into the high heels with practiced ease.

Like the baseball hat she wore the day of Oliver's soccer game, I've most definitely found a new move I find dangerously sexy.

I wish I could rewind time, take us back to the moment we were in my kitchen before the spell was broken, when I was only seconds away from kissing her senseless. Holding her in my arms would be a full body exhale, something I've waited a very long time for. An opportunity I never believed I would be presented with again.

I get up to open the door for her. "Thank you for coming to my soccer match. Or, trying to make it there, I mean."

"Thank you for dinner." She pats my chest on her way out the door. It is a careful, perfunctory touch. I'd like to trade it in for something far better. "See you around."

Instead of continuing down the hall, she turns and looks back at me. "When this is over, and we're back from Bald Head Island, you can call her. Your ex. If you want to." She shrugs in this adorable way, like she knows she's talking too fast. "Find out what changed. By that point, you'll only be my client."

She turns and walks down the hallway before I can say a word to the contrary.

I want to tell her I don't like that idea. I am officially rejecting her suggestion.

HARD NO.

# CHAPTER 18
## *Paisley & Klein*

> How did Oliver's diorama presentation go? A++, I'm assuming, considering he was aided by someone holding a degree in the subject matter.

He earned a 95.

> Respectable.

He was robbed.

> Ahhh so you were a stellar student growing up?

Not quite. But I aspired to be stellar.

> Wanting to be something is half the battle.

Then I guess it's a good thing I desperately want to be a writer.

> You already are a writer. Now we're going about making you a published author.

> Cecily driving you crazy yet? She can be strict.

I like her style. She means what she says. Yesterday we were brainstorming my bio and she called me a reticent fool.

> ???

She was right. I was being a reticent fool.

> Good to know her tough love style works well with you. I have to go. Paloma and the architect next door are arguing.

---

What happened with Paloma and the architect yesterday?

> Words were flung like knives. Fire shot from her eyes. I'm positive she's in love but won't admit it. The architect though? He knows he's in love. He asked her to have dinner with him this weekend.
>
> I hope he has final instructions set up. Paloma has the most creative and untraceable way to off someone.

??

> That's an ace I'll keep tucked in my back pocket, thank you very much.

Finally found your nickname.

> And that would be?

Ace.

---

Hey, Ace. How was Paloma's date?

> She's been out with him two more times! She swears she's only letting him buy her dinner because I don't pay her enough.

Are you a bad boss?

> Hardly. I can tell she likes him because she starts talking fast when the subject of him comes up.

She already talks faster than I can keep up with.

> You'll get used to it the more time you spend around her.

---

> I'm assuming you saw your plane ticket I emailed to you?

Yep. Send me your info and I'll reimburse you.

> Let me buy your ticket. I roped you into this.

Six months of digital marketing is more than enough compensation.

> You haven't met my entire family yet. Just wait until my mom and dad are in the same room together. You'll be charging me for pain and suffering after the week is over.

Somehow I doubt that.

> You're going to eat your words, Madigan.

...🐚🐚🐚...

Royce, you available? I need some guidance on clothing. Shopping currently.

> Just got out of a meeting. Send some pics.

Too late. I hope you're ok with me wearing a speedo on the beach. Just figured since Bald Head Island is closer to Europe...

> I just pictured you in a speedo.

I know, I know. It was too much for you and now you're hot and bothered.

> More like tepid and unruffled.

Going to have to change your tune now. Picture incoming.

> Please be joking!!

<picture>

> Oh, thank God. I really like those shorts.

## CHAPTER 19
### *Paisley*

"Why are you smiling like that?"

It takes me a moment to realize Paloma's addressing me. Is it the sound of restaurant cutlery and exuberant lunchtime chatter from the tables around us that have made it hard for me to hear? Perhaps it's the video of ice Klein sent that I was watching for the seventh time.

We're at our favorite lunch place after a morning of meetings, but I couldn't resist peeking at the message Klein sent an hour ago.

> A video to cool you down in case you're hot. Have a good day, Ace.

A link to an ice-making video followed.

*Ace.*

I love the nickname. Adore it.

Stowing my phone in my purse, I drop kick the upturned position of my lips and lift my gaze with its freshly applied poker face. Paloma and Cecily's curious expressions stare back at me.

"I'm not smiling."

"You *were*," Paloma insists. "Like a stranger who sees a bulldog puppy in a Trader Joe's and wants to pet it but doesn't want to seem weird so they leer at it with heart eyes instead."

I lean away, giving her an exaggerated head to toe look of concern. "That was oddly specific."

She waves halfheartedly. "It's me, hi. I'm the heart-eye woman at Trader Joe's."

Just when I think I've cleared the hurdle of admitting what had me gooey smiling at my screen, Paloma firmly bats at my open menu. "So, why were you smiling?"

I jab in her direction with the thick plastic. There's no point lying. Paloma's bullshit detector is top-notch. "Klein sent me an interesting video."

"Word Daddy?" Cecily peeks out from behind her menu, eyebrows raised.

I frown. "What kind of nickname is that?"

"The accurate kind," Paloma not-at-all helpfully adds. "What kind of interesting video did Klein send you?"

I sip my sparkling water and look away. "Ice."

"Ice?"

I nod.

"Wow," Cecily deadpans. "Don't get too wild. Ice is dangerous. Frostbite. Hypothermia. Whatever the fuck else."

Paloma frowns. "I expect more creativity from a writer. Maybe he's washed up before he got out of the gate."

"He has plenty of creativity," I defend. "He only sent

me that video because I told him I like to watch different types of ice being made."

"Hold up," Cecily raises a hand. "We'll come back to your weird ice fetish later. For now, let's discuss him sending you something he thought you'd enjoy."

I shrug. "He came across it and sent it to me. What's the big deal? It's not like he offered a kidney."

"He didn't *come across it*," Paloma says, running her finger underneath every item on the menu as she reads. She'll have the salmon, as she does every time, and still, she'll read the whole menu. "He went looking for it."

"Oh wow." Placing the back of my hand on my forehead, I pretend to swoon. "He typed three words in a search bar?" My hands dramatically drop to my chest. "Be still my heart."

"Downplay it all you want," Cecily says as she locks eyes with the server, nodding when he gives her the universal *'are you ready to order?'* facial expression. "In today's dating landscape that's like trudging uphill both ways in the snow to deliver a single rose to your beloved."

Paloma gives her a withering look. "It's not that bad out there."

"Correct," Cecily nods. "It's worse."

The server arrives to take our order. Cecily and I order the bacon and tomato grilled cheese with a side of tomato basil soup.

"I'll have the salmon," Paloma announces with gusto, like she's going out on a limb and trying something new.

"Surprise, surprise," Cecily mutters, gathering our menus and handing them over. "Let's talk more about Klein."

"I really don't want to."

"Why not?"

"There's nothing to say. We've been doing what we need to do to get to know each other as much as we need to."

"Klein the writer would vomit all over that jumbled sentence."

"Not my best," I admit. "Our relationship is professional. We're not even friends."

"Dumb," Paloma says bluntly. "You might want to be friends with the guy you're flying across the country and staying on a secluded island with."

"There will be lots of people on this island. Family, friends, and strangers."

"And Word Daddy." Cecily pops her eyebrows, just once, while the rest of her face remains impassive. This is all I need to see to know that Cecily thinks well of Klein. "You know," she says slowly, like the idea is occurring to her in real time. "You're kind of checking the same boxes of people who are really dating."

"How's that?"

"Getting to know each other, meeting his family." She counts off on two fingers, unfurling a third finger and adding, "texting videos you think the other might enjoy."

"Well, yeah," I defend. "This farce needs to be believable."

"Cecily's right," Paloma cuts in. "Why don't you two date for real?"

"His ex wants him back." Removing a cut lime from the little dish in the center of the table, I squeeze it into my drink. I'm wearing a solid mask of nonchalance on the outside, but my insides are a swirling mass. Standing in his kitchen, still reeling from our near-kiss, I'd had to listen to his ex shoot her shot. I detested each second of it, too. At first I felt bad for her, the way her voice wavered. But that stopped when Klein told me what happened between them. My sympathy ground to a halt.

"Does he want her back?" Paloma asks patronizingly.

"It doesn't appear so."

Paloma gives me an exasperated look, so I add pointedly, "It's none of my business."

"You know," Paloma says, pulling a lip gloss from her purse. "For someone so intelligent, you can be a real *idiota*."

"No translation needed for that one," Cecily says with far too much enthusiasm.

Ok. Time to steer away from the topic of me with Klein.

"You've been working with him, right?" I ask Cecily. "Getting his social media set up and all that?"

Cecily sips her hot tea. "I've already put time on your calendar to go over the set up and our approach."

I nod, slipping out my phone and pulling up my work calendar. Angling my screen away, I try to sneak a peek and see if Klein was invited to the meeting Cecily set up.

I haven't seen him since the night of our near-kiss. He's been working more shifts at the restaurant to make up for the week he'll be on the island, but we've managed to talk enough through text messages that if I scrolled through our history, I would have to keep going and going.

It's not that I miss him, because I totally don't, but I'm

wondering if his hair is still the same. Did he get a haircut? Does he have a five o'clock shadow? How about his thighs? Are they still obnoxiously well-defined?

"I sent Klein a meeting invite," Cecily says.

"Oh, that's nice," I respond airily. Nothing to see here. The information means nothing to me.

Cecily narrows her gaze. "You have the worst poker face."

The server approaches with our food.

"Saved by the soup," I say, digging in with an inappropriate amount of fervor.

---

Two days later, Klein appears in the conference room at P Squared Marketing.

He wears a tan shirt, black shorts, and to my great relief, his thighs are as defined as ever.

"Royce," he says, a head nod accompanying his greeting. He says my last name formally, as if we haven't maintained a steady stream of text messages the past three weeks. As if I haven't met the three most important people in his life. As if he hasn't sent me half a dozen ice-making videos, to which I responded with my own dog temper tantrum videos.

As if he didn't give me a nickname. *Hello?! The name's Ace!*

As if he didn't almost kiss me the last time we saw each other after I spilled my guts about my parent's marriage and divorce.

"Madigan," I say cooly, my gaze locked onto him as he

settles in a chair opposite me at the table. He looks at the ceiling, the tabletop, the artwork, his gaze finally resting on something out the window.

Cecily breezes in, her dark hair flowing behind her. "Hello."

"Hi," Klein replies, his voice all puppies and kittens.

I frown. I got mangy alley cat. What the hell?

Twisting my hair up on my head, I secure it with a pen and wait for Cecily to cast her screen onto the monitor on the wall.

Hurt darts through me, but I'll never show it. Hell, I'll barely let myself feel it.

Maybe it's good he's acting this way. We are two people whose paths are crossing a second time. We're not friends, we're not lovers. We're little more than business partners with a not-legal contract signed on a paper napkin. There's no need for me to feel hurt by his cool response to me.

For the next twenty minutes I sit and listen as Klein and Cecily volley conversation and ideas. Klein appears to be far less uncomfortable than he was when we first started this process.

"Posts began two days ago," Cecily says, biting on the end of her pen. "As Klein requested, we started with utmost honesty. I drafted the captions with Klein's help, keeping in mind that he is a storyteller at heart, and we want each caption to feel like a story." Cecily scrolls on her trackpad, bringing up the social media account. The first photo is of Klein sitting on a couch, leaning forward with a laptop open on a rustic wood table.

"Nice picture," I comment, careful to keep any

emotion from my voice. "Earthy, moody, it's giving me academia vibes."

"I got coffee with Eden last weekend," Klein explains. "She took it."

He says it carefully, like he wants me to know who took the photo. Who he was with. It doesn't fit with how aloof he was when he walked in here.

Cecily continues. "Here is this morning's post. Klein's home bookshelves."

I recognize them immediately, though I've seen them only once. Organized by author, the books are mostly hardbacks, except for a section of leather-bound journals. The caption reads *Trading in books for the beach. See you in paradise.*

"He already has a hundred followers," I comment. Grabbing my phone, I press and swipe the screen until I am one of KleinTheWriter's followers. The number on the screen on the wall increases to a hundred and one.

Cecily nods. "The response has been more than I'd hoped for. To be fair, I've been pulling some strings. Sending his account to my friends and asking them to follow and interact. They've sent it on to their friends, even though I didn't ask it of them. It's because, like I told both of you"—her gaze flits between us parentally—"people are interested in what you're doing. Your *authenticity* and *honesty* caught their attention."

"Is this where I say you were right all along and I shouldn't have argued?" Klein asks.

"Sure," Cecily responds, looking at her screen and logging in to her content planner. She opens a folder to show fifty stock photos, mostly books and bookish flat lays. "Here's what I have for filler until you leave. What I need from both of you are photos while you're on the island. I set up a shared album and added you both to it. You don't have to do faces, but I want beachy goodness. Think sand on Paisley's shoulder while she gazes out at the ocean." Cecily eyes Klein meaningfully. "We're telling a story." She snaps her laptop closed. "I have a call in five minutes, so if you don't need anything else from me...?"

I shake my head.

"Take photos," she repeats firmly. "Copious amounts. When you think you've taken too many, take more." Addressing Klein only, she says, "Have a safe flight. Enjoy your trip."

And then she's gone, the conference door closing softly behind her.

Silence descends. It's so unlike our recent interactions that I'm starting to panic. My mind hurtles twenty different directions, but mainly it's screaming out *how are you going to fly across the country with this guy when he's pulled a one-eighty?*

A deal is a deal, and my alternatives are none. In a brittle voice, I say, "I guess I'll see you at the airport on Saturday morning."

Reaching up, I yank the pen from my makeshift updo. My hair tumbles down around my shoulders.

Klein stares.

"Do you have something to say, Madigan?"

"You used to wear your hair like that in class."

I clear my throat. "I never remember a hair tie."

"Are we good, Ace?"

I bristle at the name I love. "Why do we keep having to ask that question?"

"Because we keep doing awkward shit."

"You were so weird when you walked in here."

"I was nervous."

His honesty knocks me sideways. Relief floods me. *He was nervous.* It takes a few seconds for me to regain my train of thought. "What were you nervous about?"

"Seeing you."

"But we've been talking nonstop for three weeks."

"I know. That's why I was nervous. I'm far better in written word than I am in person."

"That's a matter of opinion."

"And? What's your opinion?"

I stare at him, my stubbornness a stronghold, before shrugging one-shouldered. "The jury is still out."

A glint shimmers in his green eyes. "Pretty soon we have a whole week to tip the scales."

I stride to the door and open it, gripping it with one hand and placing my other hand on my jutted out hip. I am all sass, and judging by Klein's appreciative expression, it's hitting just right. "Ahh, but which way will they tip?"

An amused smirk broadens his cheeks. "I'm competitive, Ace. Be careful."

"Good to know. I like my opponents qualified, Wordsmith."

I strut away, leaving him to see himself out.

## CHAPTER 20
*Klein*

PHOENIX SKY HARBOR INTERNATIONAL AIRPORT IS NESTLED in the center of the city. Halston has offered to drive me, and for that I'm grateful because it will save me a lot of money in parking fees. It will cost me in terms of owing Halston, and when she reminds me of this, I tell her to add it to my tally.

She drops me at the departures curb with a wave, yawning as she pulls out into airport traffic.

I've been sitting next to the gate for twenty-five minutes when Paisley walks up. Her hair is tied in a messy knot on top of her head and she's wearing sweats and a tank top. No makeup.

"Klein the writer," she grumbles when she sees me. "I need coffee."

"Vast improvement from Klein the stripper."

A flick of a gaze is the only way I know she has heard me.

Wrestling the camel-colored leather backpack off her, I say, "You are awfully zombie-like this morning."

"I'm a delight." She squints one eye and looks at me suspiciously. "Are you a morning person?"

Pushing down my zest and zeal, I say blandly, "Yes."

"Ugh," she sighs. "Of all the bars in all the towns, I walked into yours."

"It was your lucky night."

"Was it?" Her head moves back-and-forth as she speaks, her messy bun careening precariously.

My head tips as I study her. "You're kind of mean early in the morning. Add that to the list of things I just learned about you."

"Caffeine," she says, by way of explanation. "I haven't had any yet, and it's the only thing that makes me human at this hour."

Placing my hands on her shoulders, I steer her in the direction of a coffee shop. "Let's get you caffeinated so you can start being nice to me."

Paisley orders the tallest coffee they have, plus a bagel with cream cheese. "Make that two, please," I say to the cashier, handing over cash.

Paisley's arm shoots out. "I can pay for mine."

"You bought my plane ticket. The least I can do is buy you a coffee and a bagel."

She nods. "I'll allow it."

By the time we have boarded our flight, Paisley has finished her coffee and is almost one hundred percent human again. From her bag comes a tattered paperback, corners bent and spine cracked. She stows the leather backpack under the seat in front of us with her foot.

I peer over. "What book is that?"

Paisley presses it to her chest, blocking me out with a curved shoulder. "Don't worry about it."

"You do realize all you've done is pique my interest in what you're reading."

Paisley digs her heels in, stubborn as always. "I told you you can't see, and now all you want is to see it."

I fight a smile. "Yes, Royce, withholding makes me want it more."

Her eyes flare.

"Double entendre."

"What's that?"

"A double entendre is a word or phrase that's— " I swallow the remaining portion of my explanation. Paisley's nodding way too enthusiastically to be authentic. "You're trying to distract me so I'll forget about the book."

She doesn't argue the accusation.

I narrow my eyes at her chest, where the book is tightly held. "Show me the book."

She doesn't move. "I always read it before I go to Bald Head."

"Always?"

She nods. She looks so cute right now. Messy and a little mischievous.

"Starting when?"

"Since I was fourteen."

I nudge her with my elbow. "Why can't you show it to me?"

"I can," she says, "I just feel a little bit shy about it."

Huffing a breath, she opens her shoulder so it's not blocking me and moves the book away from her chest.

"Summer Sisters?" I check out the author name. "Why are you shy about it? Judy Blume writes novels for middle grade and maybe young adults who are more younger than adult."

Paisley points at me. "That is precisely what I thought when I first picked it up. But this book right here?" She lifts it, shaking it just enough so the well-worn pages flap. "Taught me about"—she lowers her voice—"hand jobs."

I eye the cover. "Seriously?"

"Yep. My fourteen-year-old brain exploded."

"Not so much that it kept you from re-reads," I tease, flicking a dog-eared corner.

She scoffs. "It's a beautiful story about friendship."

"Sure, sure."

Paisley rolls her eyes. The flight attendant assumes her position in the aisle. She begins the safety instructions, and Paisley puts down her book, hands folded in her lap as she watches everything the flight attendant does.

When she finishes, Paisley picks up her book. I lean over. "You were without a doubt the only person making eye contact with her."

"It's rude to ignore someone who's speaking to you. Besides, she's teaching people how to save their lives, and the lives of others. You should be thanking me, because I know what to do if the air masks drop, and you don't and I'll end up having to help you." Paisley fixes me with a sharp glare. "You, sir, are a liability."

The tip of my tongue pokes at my third molar to keep from laughing. "Do you always listen that closely when the flight attendant gives safety instructions?"

"Without fail," Paisley confirms.

Thinking back to the night she made the comment about being a stellar pedestrian, I ask, "Are you a people pleaser, Royce?"

"It's a flaw I'm working on."

I nod, lips pushed out. "I'm insecure sometimes. It's a flaw I'm working on."

"To being works-in-progress," she says, miming lifting a glass in the air.

We pretend to toast.

She opens her book. I take out my notebook and a pen, jotting down notes for another plot that's been wiggling around in my brain for a few months.

The pilots position the plane for takeoff, and then we're picking up speed and ascending.

There's a *bump bump bump* after a minute, and Paisley drops her book, white-knuckling the armrest.

I nudge her. "Are you ok?"

"Why is it bumpy?" Panic flashes in her eyes.

I pry her fingers from the armrest, keeping her hand in mine. "It's the change in air temperature as we ascend. Think about how much hotter it is on the ground than it is up here as we go higher and higher. Air travel is bumpier in the summer."

She nods as I speak, her eyes trusting. What is it about that look that gets me right in the feels?

She looks down at her hand in mine, appearing to be surprised that it's there. Smiling sheepishly, she retracts her hand. "Sorry about that."

"I don't mind making you feel better about something that frightens you."

"I appreciate it," she murmurs, reopening her book.

Paisley loses herself in the story. Her small smiles, the way she chuckles under her breath, the tip of her tongue that intermittently wets her lips, are all indications of how much Paisley enjoys what she's reading.

Per Cecily's instructions in a text she sent me this morning (*Take pictures!!!*), I snap a photo of the world outside the airplane window, making certain to keep the window frame in the picture.

We're halfway through the flight when I lean over and whisper, "Did you make it to the hand job yet?"

She whips her gaze at me, eyes threatening. "Don't make me regret telling you that."

I lift my palms in innocence. "I didn't say there's anything wrong with hand jobs."

Paisley makes a vibrating noise with her lips. She glances at my crotch, the faintest rose blush blooming on her cheeks. "Obviously."

She goes back to her book. I go back to outlining.

Eventually, I notice Paisley hasn't turned a page in awhile. "Did you fall asleep, Royce?"

"Hmm?" She looks at me in surprise. "No," she answers, setting her book on her lap so she can untwist her messy bun. She finger combs her hair, then re-ties it on her head.

"All good?" I ask her.

She nods once, tight-lipped. I'm not buying it. I grew up with two women. They might say they're good, but it doesn't mean that. Oftentimes, it means the opposite.

I also learned pushing a woman who doesn't want to talk can sometimes lead to a sharp-tongued comment, and very likely an insult to accompany it.

In the interest of starting out this trip on the best foot possible, I keep my mouth shut.

We land and head for baggage claim. When Paisley spots her luggage, she moves forward to grab it, but I'm faster.

"I can get it," she insists, but I shake my head.

"I may be your fake boyfriend, but I am a real gentleman."

This comment should've earned me a retort of some kind, in that playfully sassy way of hers, but she barely manages a shaky smile.

To make it clear I meant what I said, I handle her heavy-ass bag through the airport. Her maid of honor dress, encased in a thick garment bag, drapes over her shoulder.

We grab mediocre sandwiches from a little place in the Raleigh airport, and by the time we've picked up the rental car and are headed to the town where we will catch the ferry, my antennas are up.

"Paisley," I start, watching her fingers drum the steering wheel.

She glances at me. Her blue-green eyes are sick with worry.

"What's going through that head of yours?"

"I'm starting to feel nervous," she admits. "I've been okay up until this point, but now"—she takes one hand from the wheel and runs it down her face—"I'm wondering if this is the dumbest thing I've ever done."

"Bringing me to the wedding, you mean?"

"All of it. What if none of this works? What if everyone feels sorry for me that I'm the maid of honor in my little sister's wedding to my ex? What if everyone finds out you're not really my boyfriend and I look like an even bigger loser?" Tears well up in her eyes, thickening her speech. "And even worse, what if I hate the island now? It used to be my favorite place in the world, but then bad stuff happened there, and now I don't know if I love it anymore." Her head shakes, as if the confusion she feels can be wrung from her mind. "I want to love it."

Her shoulders shake as she cries, and all I want to do is haul her over the console and into my arms.

I'm thinking of a way to persuade her to pull over when a sob wracks her body, and I say, "Paisley, pull over right now."

"I'm"—hiccup—"fine."

"Now, Paisley."

Miraculously, she signals to move into the right lane and then takes the exit. Coasting to a stop on the grassy shoulder, she shifts into Park.

"I'm sorry." Tears strangle her voice.

"You're on your way to a wedding you probably should've said no to, and you're about to participate in a week of wedding events that culminate with standing beside the bride during the ceremony. Honestly, I'm only surprised you haven't cried about it before now."

Paisley turns her gaze on me. She looks lovely with her tearstained cheeks, her nose a rosy pink. "You probably think I'm insane for agreeing to this."

My head tips side-to-side as I feign considering. "Only a little."

Through her tears she manages a tentative smile. "Pretend you have a brother and he's marrying your ex-girlfriend. What would you have said?"

"My hypothetical answer isn't going to help you. The situation is far more nuanced than that. Cut and dry went out the window a long time ago. And it's not only why you're returning to the island, but the fact you're returning at all." I scratch at my neck, taking a moment to gather my thoughts so I don't say something too offensive. "Your sister isn't marrying your ex at a fancy resort ballroom. She's marrying your ex at a place that holds both good and bad memories for you."

Paisley sniffles. "Best and worst." She reaches into her purse and comes away with a travel size pack of tissues.

"The whole thing is a clusterfuck." It's the nicest way I can think to put it. Everything I think so far has a lot of f-words and character assassinations.

"What if they see right through us?" She blows her nose. "You're a writer, not an actor."

I smirk. "Someone once told me that writing a book is like the longest, most intricate lie. If that's true, acting isn't that far out of my wheelhouse."

A smile ghosts over her face.

"Look at it this way, Paisley. I'm weaving a story, and I'm really damn good at that, so trust me that I'm going to make the story good, ok? When we're on the island, everyone is going to see I'm madly devoted to you. If my adoration doesn't make them nauseous, I haven't succeeded."

Paisley sniffles, nodding, looking uncharacteristically vulnerable.

"I'm going to spin a yarn so elaborate, even you and I might get stuck in it." I don't know where these words are coming from. My heart? Certainly not my head. My head knows better. But my heart? He's a mouthy bastard.

Paisley's throat bobs with a hard swallow. She relaxes into her seat, angling her body toward me. "I'm happy you're here, Klein."

"We're in this together, Paisley. If it's only Monday but you decide you're finished, say the word. I will put you on my back and swim you off the island. You got it?"

Her lips curve upward.

I'll do anything to keep the smile going, to keep the corners of her mouth climbing higher. "I'm not going for any reason but to support you."

My goal is reached. She smiles. "And eat cake," she adds. "I'm definitely going so I can eat cake."

I smile at the joke. "Right. Cake. I'm also here for the cake."

It's in this moment I realize I'd have done this for her without anything in return. No digital marketing. No social media. No cake.

She looks out of the windshield and takes a deep breath. "Klein, listen, I've been thinking about something." Her nervous gaze works over my face.

"Say it," I encourage. "You can say anything to me."

"I don't want our first good kiss to be in front of my family."

Are those angels rejoicing in my chest? A trio of trumpeters? I'd like nothing more than to reach across this console and claim her mouth immediately.

The only thing stopping me is how epically bad our

first kiss was. Our first good kiss cannot just be *good*. It must be phenomenal.

Paisley's focus is on my mouth, and the angels and trumpeters resume.

I settle for taking her hand, holding its soft warmth in my palm. "I was never, not for a single second, going to follow up a drunken mess of a kiss with a fake chaste peck meant to appease onlookers." Flipping her hand over, I trace the lines in her palm. I don't know how she's going to take what I'm about to say, so I keep my gaze lowered. "I intend to make our first good kiss so unbelievably good, you'll have trouble remembering we ever had a bad one."

Her fingers close suddenly, stopping my meandering touch. Our hands intertwined, she nudges under my chin and encourages my gaze to meet hers. "I look forward to it."

All traces of nervousness are gone from her face. In her eyes is a hunger I recognize, because it's like looking in a mirror. My entire body wants Paisley.

She shifts into Drive and pulls onto the road, tossing me a provocative grin. "Bald Head Island, here we come."

---

To be fair, I was warned.

Paisley told me if I stood at the front of the ferry transporting us to the island, I'd get wet. I thought she meant a little spray.

Nope. My shirt is soaked.

Not that I care. I'm too busy taking it all in.

The salt spray assails my face, and I blink against it. In the distance, the island looms. Rectangles and squares fill the view, sharpening into objects the closer we get. Homes.

Two stories, with roofs of gray and light blue, trimmed in white with matching porches. The beach in front of them, and before that, navy blue churning water.

I look for Paisley, wanting to share this with her. Having placed little more than my sight on Bald Head Island, I feel confident in saying this place is special. Unique.

Paisley leans against the boat, feet planted on the water beaten flooring. She wears a yellow baseball cap that says Vitamin Sea, but still the wind whips her hair up and around her jaw. Before we embarked, she exchanged her sweats for light pink and white seersucker shorts. She kept on the white tank top she's been traveling in.

"Come up here," I yell above the sound of the large boat crashing over the choppy water.

She shakes her head, pointing at her white shirt.

As much as I wouldn't mind seeing her white top soaked through, I refuse to share that view with anybody else.

The captain navigates the channel, pulling into the marina.

People file to the exit, waiting to disembark. Paisley waits for me, grinning when I join her. "I liked watching you take it all in. I was taking pictures of you, too. For Cecily."

My face hardens, my insecurity getting the best of me.

What did I look like? Some loser who has never seen the Atlantic? Never been on a ferry?

We're at the back of the slow moving crowd, and Paisley slips a hand over my forearm. She tugs, silently asking me to look down at her. So I do. The wind has pinkened her cheeks, tousled her hair. She's gorgeous.

"I appreciate your openness, your willingness to let yourself feel the island's magic."

I allow her words to move through me, to soak in. How many times does Paisley have to make it clear she's okay with me? With who I am, and what I do for work?

We step off the ferry, but before we can get swept up in the melee of bodies, of people finding their luggage and their way, I fasten my free hand to the hand Paisley still has on my arm. Then I give it a squeeze, attempting to give her a meaningful look in the short time we have.

Paisley smiles like she understands, moving away to seek out our bags, and her grandmother who's scheduled to pick us up.

When we have our bags, we step out of the mostly organized chaos, finding a calmer spot off to the side.

"My grandmother said she'll be here in a minute," Paisley says, glancing at her phone. "A quick rundown on her: she's funny in a way that will probably take you off-guard, my grandpa was the love of her life and she still can't talk about his passing even though it was five years ago, she will almost certainly tell you about the time she went on The Price Is Right and kissed Bob Barker, and she dresses in a style we call 'coastal grandma.'"

I'm fumbling with all the information Paisley tossed

my way, including this being the first time she mentioned her grandpa passing.

"Got it. Be ready to laugh, don't mention your grandpa, let her tell me about Bob Barker, and… *coastal grandma*? That one needs explaining." I spend a good portion of time studying descriptors, and clothing styles, and physical characteristics. But 'coastal grandma'? I'm lost.

"It means she wears white and ivory and cream in cotton and linen. Flowy, unbuttoned button-ups, striped cardigans, a fisherman sweater. It says"—Paisley's palms are pressed out, tipping back and forth—"she's ready for all things beach. She can light a bonfire, sip white wine, prune her garden, maybe even clip hydrangeas and arrange them in a vase."

"That was…descriptive. And effective." I'm impressed.

A woman on a golf cart rolls up beside Paisley. "Excuse me," she calls out in a melodic voice. "You look a bit like my granddaughter, only more beautiful."

Paisley's face splits into a grin before she has the chance to turn around. The woman climbs out from behind the wheel of the golf cart. She wears a navy and white striped blouse tucked into loose white linen pants. On her feet are camel-colored slides and dried sand, like she walked off the beach and onto the cart.

Paisley drops her bag, peels off her hat, and folds her grandmother in a hug. The hug continues, developing into a sway. The woman catches my eye, winks, and says, "Paisley, introduce me to your boyfriend."

Paisley untangles herself from her grandmother's embrace. "Grandma, this is Klein. Klein, this is Lausanne."

"It's nice to meet you, Lausanne." I take her offered hand, cocooning it in both my own. Her smile is warm and welcoming, and she wears three strings of varying length delicate gold chains around her neck. She is regal, stately, carrying herself with a posture that has me correcting my own but is still somehow relaxed. If I wrote all that down on page, she might sound standoffish, but she is affable, offering me a second wink and patting my shoulder.

"Your name is unique. I've never heard it before." I make quick work of our suitcases, stowing them in the third row of the golf cart.

"I've never met another Lausanne," she says happily, settling behind the wheel. Paisley takes the seat beside her, and I slide into the second row. "My father served in the military, and spent some time in Switzerland when he lived in Europe. There's a town there called Lausanne, which means Lake Geneva. So, technically, my name is Lake Geneva, but Lausanne is just fine."

Lausanne lets off the parking brake, and the cart comes to life. We pull out onto the cart path, and while I'm trying to pay attention to the conversation happening in the front seat, it's nearly impossible. There's so much to look at, to understand.

Forget the palm trees, the coconuts. The trees lining the paths are huge, so tall I have to crane my neck to see their tops, but for some I can see only the canopy.

"Maritime forest," Lausanne says, her voice traveling behind her as she winds over the path. "Live and Laurel oaks, mostly."

Paisley looks back at me, grinning. Her tousled hair

takes a beating, wrapping around itself. Her blue-green eyes shine, a sparkle attributable to happiness.

I can see why Paisley called this her favorite place. She's soaking it in, this special spot of hers. It's too bad she has experienced pain here. And even sadder to think that pain is likely not yet finished.

What does the rest of the week hold for her?

## CHAPTER 21
*Paisley*

Watching Klein's reaction to his introduction to Bald Head Island has only made me love it more.

He was in awe, and not afraid to show it. Not afraid to enjoy it. There was a moment, when he caught himself, and I watched the hesitance slip onto his face. Why does he do that? Why does he anticipate me finding something wrong with him?

Right now, watching him absorb the uniqueness of the island as we hurtle over the path, it would be difficult to believe he's the same person who had a momentary freak-out on the ferry.

The same could be said of me, too. Chapped lips and cheeks, snarled hair, and happy as can be, nobody would know I'd had to pull the rental car over and have my own meltdown earlier today.

"Here we are," Grandma announces, driving down the gravel driveway lined in white rocks.

It's the same home I've been coming to since I can

remember. The place where I had my first taste of watermelon, where I missed a bottom step on the outdoor stairs and earned the small scar under my chin. My first kiss was on the beach, with a boy who was here for the summer. I passed my driver's license exam with flying colors because I'd been driving a golf cart for years by then.

Klein carries my overstuffed suitcase up the stairs like it's made of nothing more than feathers. Grandma leads us into the back entrance, straight into the dining room and adjoined kitchen.

Nothing about this place has changed, and I appreciate that more than my grandmother can know. She could easily update the kitchen, install white cabinets and marble countertops, replace the can lights with rattan pendant lights.

It brings me such joy to know she hasn't. I do not want fancy new floors. I want wood marked by scooters and roller skates in the house. I want scratchy sisal rugs under bare feet and sand no matter how meticulously we vacuum.

"Your home is beautiful," Klein comments. It's not a compliment given because he feels he is supposed to. There is a touch of wonderment in his voice, an undertone of gratitude at being here.

A small thought floats across my mind, opaque and shiny like a bubble. *I'm genuinely happy to be here with Klein.*

And then, well, there's what he said to me earlier in the car. *I intend to make our first good kiss so unbelievably good, you'll have trouble remembering we ever had a bad one.*

That line has played on repeat in my mind for hours. When does he plan on doing such a thing? How good are we talking?

Grandma accepts Klein's compliment, showing him around the kitchen. She opens up drawers and cabinets, getting him acquainted with where things are, and showing him how to use the coffee maker.

"I'll need to know that," Klein grins teasingly at me. "Paisley's underpants are in a twist until she is properly caffeinated in the morning."

I playfully roll my eyes and look away. Grandma swings open the pantry door and steps inside, rummaging through boxes.

Klein comes closer, and I whisper, "Did you just say underpants?"

"Better than saying *'panties'* to your grandma."

"Call them whatever you want. She wears thongs."

Klein tries not to make a face, but fails.

"Kidding," I say, to put him out of his misery. "She puts the granny in—"

Klein's palm shoots into the air. "Enough."

Grandma steps out of the pantry. "It's just the three of us here tonight. Everyone else arrives tomorrow, so we better soak up the peace and quiet while we can." She sets a few items down on the counter. "You two go to your room and get cleaned up while I start dinner."

*Your* room?

I shake my head, certain I've heard her wrong. "I'm staying in my usual room." I thumb at Klein's chest. "Where do you want Klein?"

"Arrangements are different this time. Starting tomorrow, this house will be filled to the brim with people for the next week. Your brother and cousins, and Sienna because she's doing the old-fashioned thing and not staying with Shane until the wedding. I'm putting you and Klein in the second main bedroom."

Panic sits at the base of my throat. "But that's where Mom stays."

Grandma scrunches her nose. "Not with that boyfriend of hers. I told her to rent her own place." She throws up her hands. "Why she thinks I want all those details is beyond me."

"I don't blame you for that," I grimace. "The last time we spoke, I hung up wishing for the conversation to have been a dream."

"A nightmare," Grandma corrects. "Anyway, you and Klein will share a room. And you can lose the shocked look. I'm sure you've already done the horizontal mambo. I'm old, but I'm not that old."

She crosses her arms, eyebrows raised, daring me to contradict her.

I grab Klein's arm and lightly shove him toward the exit on the left. "We're going to get out of here before this conversation devolves any further."

Grandma twinkles her fingers at us as I push Klein from the room, luggage in tow.

"Phew," I say, careening with him into the living room. "Two topics I don't want to discuss: my mother's sex life, and mine."

Klein looks around the living room, taking in his

surroundings. "I think your grandma and my mom would be best friends if they ever met."

"They'd probably turn into a formidable team of feisty, crime fighting superheroines."

Klein steps up to a shelf on the media center, peering at the jars of small shells and sea glass my siblings and I collected over the years. The same shelf holds a book on the history of the island, and a second book about the animals and native plant life.

He lifts his arm like he's going to remove the books, then draws his hand back.

"You can read those. They're not one of those doorstop coffee table books nobody ever reads. They're meant to be enjoyed."

Klein takes both books and tucks them under his arm. "Coffee table books are my pet peeve."

"That tracks."

Through the living room we go down the hall, passing a bedroom with two sets of bunk beds. Next up is the bedroom commandeered by me and Sienna every summer. A quick peek as we pass tells me not much about it has changed. Same floral bedspread, same Roman shades on the windows.

The end of the hall is our destination, the second main bedroom with its own, glorious bathroom. And glass shower that faces the window, and beyond that, the beach.

In another time, when this was my mom and dad's room, I'd sneak in to use the shower. Sharing a bathroom with my brother and sister was less than ideal; Sienna stole my products, and Spencer ignored all warnings that if he didn't start flushing the toilet, he was going to be forced to sleep outside.

That feels like a lifetime ago. Does a decade count as a lifetime? That's how long it's been since that final summer with the Royce's vacationing as a family of five. One glance out the bedroom window at precisely the exact moment when my dad and the neighbor slipped into a movie-worthy kiss, and that was it.

But I won't think about that now. Hopefully, I'll think of it as little as possible.

"Here we are," I announce, stepping into the room.

"Wow," Klein says, walking in behind me.

A large window running three-quarters of the length of the wall greets us, the sparkling late afternoon ocean beyond. Curtains frame the window in a delicate white lace. A chair, upholstered in nautical blue and white stripes, is positioned beside the window. I can already see Klein sitting there, reading his books. Outlining his next novel.

One wall houses the dresser, and the entrance to the bathroom. Opposite that is my second favorite part of this room, a shiplap wall where the bed and two night stands are situated. The bed is a king, with a matching headboard and footboard that looks like taupe woven ropes. The bedding is textured, white, with throw pillows to match the blue stripes of the chair. And—

*Oh no.*

I look sharply at Klein.

His hands are in his pockets, his lips pursed.

Klein already knows, but I say it aloud anyway. "There's only one bed."

How in the world did I not see that coming a mile away? Of course there's only one bed. There has only ever been one bed in this room.

My mind races. Is my head exploding? It feels like it.

"Paisley." Klein takes hold of my shoulders. "Calm down. Maybe we can find an air mattress somewhere and I'll sleep on that."

I nod, though I have little confidence. Guilt pokes at me. I didn't haul Klein across the United States so he could sleep on an air mattress.

And yes, he has promised me an epically good kiss, but that doesn't mean we need to share a bed. Right?

Klein opens his carry-on suitcase and sets about unpacking. I do the same, starting with hanging the dress in the closet. With the lightest touch, I admire the fabric. I'm the only person in the wedding party wearing a pattern. Carolina blue roses on a white background, floor-length with a corset top and three rows of ruffles on the bottom. It swings, with a hidden slit that reaches mid-thigh. I have to hand it to Sienna, she has exceptional taste. The three remaining bridesmaids will wear various style dresses all in a shade of blue that matches mine.

With a final look at the stunner of a dress, I close the closet and make my way into the bathroom with my toiletries.

"Do you mind if I put on some music?" Klein calls.

"Go for it," I yell back from the shower, where I'm lining up my various bottles.

The Beach Boys start playing, and it makes me smile. My grandpa loved The Beach Boys.

"Good choice," I tell Klein, returning to the bedroom

to begin unpacking my clothes. Klein stands at the window, gazing out.

"I can't believe you spent every summer here," he says. His voice is a mix of awe and forlorn. "We went to California a few times when I was little, but then—" He cuts off.

Was he about to talk about his dad? Or whatever else it is that makes him close down?

"—we stopped going, " he finishes lamely. "And I'm sure you already know this, but there are far better places to be in the summer than Phoenix."

"It's not so bad," I say, placing a stack of pajamas in a drawer. "You stay inside in the air conditioning, and you go from one air-conditioned store to another. It's the reverse of winter in cold climates where they stay inside seeking warmth."

"I guess that's true."

"It gets hot here, too. And humid."

"But there's a beach."

"You got me there."

"You were right Paisley, this place is magic. There's an ocean out there," he points, then swivels, "but oak trees that way. And animals. Did you know there are deer on the island? And foxes?"

I deposit my underwear in a drawer and close it with my hip. "Someone's been reading one of the books he swiped."

"When you were putting your stuff away in the bathroom," he says, pointing at the book propped open on the arm of the chair. "I guess we should probably go to the beach and take a picture to send to Cecily."

"Whatever you say, Klein the writer."

I scoot from the room to give Klein time to change and freshen up, and he meets me in the kitchen where my grandmother has her homemade chicken noodle soup simmering in a dutch oven.

"Lausanne, would you like to come with us to the beach?"

My grandma beams at Klein's invitation, but says, "You two go. I've been dying for a chance to make my homemade biscuits, and this seems like a good reason. Do you like biscuits, Klein?"

"I like homemade biscuits a lot more than a man should."

Grandma titters. She shoots me a look. "Oh, Paisley. I like this one. You should keep him."

I wink at Klein. "I'm considering it."

There isn't a doubt in my mind Klein is one of the good ones. This would be a perfect time for him to lay a passionate but respectable kiss on me, but since we're in need of a re-do before the fake kisses can begin, I force myself to calm down.

Donning a hat and sunglasses, I follow Klein outside to the covered porch. I point out the wood plank private walkway to the beach. He takes my hand as we go, threading his fingers through mine.

"In case your grandma is watching," he explains, squeezing my hand. "There are about fifteen windows on the backside of that house, and she can probably see through at least eight of them from where she's standing in the kitchen."

"You missed a golden opportunity to kiss me back

there in the kitchen. Just something sweet and small, a little more than a peck but not too much."

"I know," he says gruffly. "But I made my intentions clear."

"You'd better cash in on those intentions pretty soon, because my entire family is descending upon us tomorrow."

"I'm aware."

We take three steps up to the next part of the walkway. Klein halts at the end when we reach the top of the sand dune. The ocean, as stunning as it is powerful, hurls itself at the shore. "I've always loved listening to the ocean."

"Are you a Pisces?"

"March 4th."

"Pisces."

"How is that relevant?"

"You're a water sign." Relief cascades through me. "How did we forget to ask about one another's birthday? Kind of important to know."

"What sign is January 11th?"

I startle. "That's my birthday."

"I know."

"How did you know that?" He must've asked Paloma, or Cecily.

He shrugs, and not only do I see it, but I also feel it because he's still holding one of my hands. "I used to see you sometimes in the cafeteria before our class started. Someone walked up to you one day and handed you a cupcake with a candle in the center of it."

"Marie," I say, the memory draping over me. "It's been

so long since I thought of that day. I can't believe you remembered the date."

He shrugs again, tugging my hand up once more. "I have a good memory. Plus having 1/11 as your date of birth is kind of cool. Are you still friends with Marie?"

"I wish I could say yes to that, but no. She started seeing a guy and moved to Chicago for him after college. We grew apart. It happens."

Klein looks out at the ocean. "Ready for that walk?"

The wooden stairs leading from the sand dune to the beach are old and narrow. Klein darts in front of me, saying, "That way, if you trip, I can catch you."

"Is this your way of telling me you have eyes in the back of your head?" I'm teasing to cover up the thrill racing around inside me.

His shoulders shake as he laughs. We reach the bottom, kicking off our shoes and digging our feet in the still-warm sand. All down the beach families are packing up, and a few kids run around, their bright kites billowing in the wind.

Klein walks to the water's edge and lets the sea foam tickle his toes. I do the same, closing my eyes and taking a deep breath. It's a body wide inhale, the wind a salt water smack across my cheek.

Five years have passed since I was last here saying a final farewell to my grandpa. I'm ready for this place to start feeling effortlessly good again.

"Klein," I say suddenly. He looks down at me, eyebrows lifted. "How do you feel about me showing you around the island tomorrow? All this week, really, when we're not doing wedding stuff. I'll show you why I love this place."

"I'd say it's a date. Though I already see why you love this place."

My smile stretches wide enough to hurt. "Just you wait. It gets better."

"That's hard to believe," he says, his eyes on me. "But I'll take your word for it."

We resume walking. The evening sun drops lower, growing a darker orange, deepening into pink and purple.

Klein falls back. "Keep walking," he instructs.

When he catches up a minute later, he shares the photo he took. It's surprisingly good. My hair tumbles down my back, and my head blocks a fraction of the setting sun.

"You have some talent with a camera," I say, "but what do you think about me getting a picture of you? Give Cecily some options."

Klein agrees, and I have him sit near the water's edge, facing the ocean. "Pull your knees in and wrap your arms around them."

He does as I say, and I snap a handful of pictures. Handing back the phone, I say, "Hopefully there's one in there you like."

I start to step away, but Klein grabs my wrist and twists me back into him. His phone is extended, ready to take another photo.

"You and me," he says.

I'm already standing in front of his chest, so I lean my head back and let it rest on the hard planes. Klein's chin dips lower, the bottom of his face hovering above the top of my head.

"Say, *fake dating*," he singsongs, making me laugh.

He takes the photo.

"Ugh," I groan. "I hate pictures of me laughing."

The skin between Klein's eyebrows pleats. "Have you seen yourself laugh?"

"Only about one hundred thousand times, give or take."

"If you really hate it, I'll delete it, but I promise you the sight of you laughing is beautiful. And in case anybody has ever told you otherwise, let me be the first to disabuse you of that belief."

Something warm and heavy settles in my chest. Emotions, to be sure, but I can't put a name to them. They are a bit dodgy, these emotions, desiring to not yet be known.

"Keep the photo, but I appreciate you offering to delete it. And for the other stuff you said."

Klein slides his phone into his pocket. "Dinner will be ready soon." He wraps an arm around my shoulders, turning me in the direction of the beach house. "You're not very good at receiving compliments."

"I'm not used to it," I clarify.

"Do you know how somebody gets used to something?"

"How?"

"Repetition."

"I guess it is a good idea for you to compliment me in front of my family."

We reach the stairs that lead back to the beach house.

"And kiss you," he points out. "Something sweet and small, a little more than a peck but not too much." He smirks, looking proud to repeat my sentence verbatim.

Sliding my shoes on my feet, I pause on the first stair and look back at him. "The clock is ticking, Wordsmith."

Do I throw a little extra side-to-side motion into my hips as I go up the stairs? Possibly.

We might be fake dating, but the enjoyment I get from taunting him is genuine.

Klein Madigan
@kleinthewriter

Lovely at 37,000 feet. The view outside the window isn't bad, either.

◯ 14     ♥ 1k     ↺ 3

## CHAPTER 22
*Klein*

Cecily texts to tell me she posted my airplane photo. It reminds me to add the photos from my and Paisley's walk on the beach. I do as I'm supposed to, then switch my phone to Do Not Disturb for the remainder of the night.

"Alright, Klein," Lausanne says, "people tend to be opinionated about chicken noodle soup, so let's hear it. What did you think of mine?"

I sit back in my porch seat and pretend to think. My standards for chicken noodle soup are astronomical. I can't recall a childhood sick day that didn't carry with it the aroma of chicken broth and sage. My mother, inexplicably to my immature brain, always had on hand the ingredients.

"It ranks up there with my mom's," I answer, and Lausanne beams.

She goes on to claim it's because she took the ferry to the mainland and shopped at a farmers market, where the carrots had been pulled from the ground the day prior.

It might be that, but my money is on the third beer I had. Everything tastes better after you pop the top on beer number three.

Paisley and Lausanne polished off a bottle of white wine at dinner, and uncorked a second on the way out to sit on the porch.

"Klein," Lausanne says, staring dreamily at the dark sky with her glass pressed to the front of her light sweater. "Did Paisley tell you I once kissed Bob Barker?"

Paisley and I share a look, a playful smile running across her lips.

Sitting back, I prepare myself to hear the story. "Paisley may have mentioned you kissed Bob Barker."

"There I was," Lausanne launches into her narrative. "In Los Angeles visiting a friend. We were invited to the studio taping of The Price Is Right. This was in the 80s, so the show had been on-air for a while by then. What I mean to say is that the precedent to kiss him on the cheek had already been set." She grins at her memory. "I could not believe it when my name was called to come on down. And then I guessed the closest price for a terribly ugly armoire, and suddenly he was inviting me onstage! I knew it would be the only moment in my life when I'd be on TV, and in the presence of Bob Barker at the same time, so I went for it." She laughs, eyes sparkling.

Paisley sighs. "I love that story."

"My mom will, too. She watched that show when I was a kid."

Lausanne lifts one shoulder and does a playful little shimmy. "Alright, granddaughter of mine," Lausanne narrows her gaze at Paisley. "Tell me the truth."

Paisley looks at me in alarm, but Lausanne follows it up with, "Is it weird that your sister is marrying your ex?"

Paisley softly chuckles. "Yeah." She drops her feet to the floor and rocks back in her chair. For a moment there is only the reliable sound of the waves kissing the shore, then she says, "I want Sienna to be happy, and Shane, too." She shrugs, glancing at me with a look I can't decipher. "It would have been nice if Sienna had thought of my feelings," she admits.

Lausanne shakes her head back and forth. "I couldn't believe it when your mother told me you're in the wedding. Why did you say yes to that?"

"I thought about the future, sometime down the road when they've been married for a long time. I had to ask myself if I would still care about it all by then, or if I would regret it if I really put my foot down. And, honestly"—Paisley's gaze flicks to Lausanne—"it was easier to say yes."

"Easier on her," Lausanne points out.

"Yeah."

"What about you?" she presses.

Paisley's attention is on me now, swift and sure. "I'm doing fine."

The desire to touch her right now is strong, but Lausanne sits between us. I settle for a dip of my chin, a slow acceptance of her claim.

Lausanne pushes off with her feet, rocking her own chair, and nods. I'm not sure if it's in agreement, or acquiescence.

After a long moment, Paisley announces she's going

inside for water and she'll return with enough for everyone.

When the door closes behind her, Lausanne says into the dark night, "Paisley should've told her sister to go fuck herself."

I couldn't agree more.

···✿✿✿···

PAISLEY DOWNED THREE GLASSES OF WATER AND DECLARED it bedtime. Lausanne kissed both our cheeks and climbed the narrow staircase to her second story bedroom.

On our trek in from the beach earlier, I'd located an air mattress in an unattached shed, hidden off to the side of the house. When I'm positive Lausanne has closed her bedroom door, I sneak outside and remove it from where I hide it behind the billowy hydrangea bush.

Upstairs, Paisley turns on the shower while I use the handheld motor to inflate the air mattress.

Or, as I attempt to inflate the mattress. Ancient and missing instructions, this is likely going to end up with me in a MacGyver situation. Short on tools and extra sticky bubblegum, I'll have to rely on my intellect.

Paisley sits on the edge of the bed as she waits for the water to heat, watching me. In five second intervals, her longing gaze finds itself in the bathroom, where the shower runs.

"You can take a shower," I tell her, wrestling with the small metal piece that is supposed to fit into the mattress.

"We need the sound. I wouldn't be able to close the door."

"You afraid I'll sneak a peek?"

"Klein," her head tips sideways. At some point this evening she tied it into a messy bun identical to the one flopping around her head when she showed up to the airport. Was that only this morning? It feels like it could've been yesterday.

As if spurred into action by my thoughts, the exhaustion sinks into my bones. I sit back on my knees and fight a yawn. "Yes, Paisley?"

"We're sharing a room. And a bathroom. I'd say it's likely that at some point this week, you and I are going to see one another's bits."

If I didn't feel like I'd recently swallowed a mouthful of melatonin, I'd be laughing out loud at her use of the word *bits*. "This feels like a set up. Like you're planning to rip away my towel after I step out of the shower."

Paisley pushes herself off the bed, the shadow of a sly smile playing on her face. "If I do, just know it's for research purposes. I'm still trying to figure out if it lights up."

A laugh takes me by surprise, causing me to cough. Paisley sails into the bathroom, leaving the door open. There isn't a single part of me that does not want to lean back, just a little, *just enough*, in the hopes of catching a glimpse of Paisley in a state of undress. I'm not picky. Any state of undress will do.

Those sexy legs of hers not covered up by shorts? I'll take it.

A shirt missing from her upper half? Doesn't matter that I'll probably see her in a bikini before the day is over tomorrow. I could die a happy man, envisioning her breasts gathered in the lace of her bra.

I can't let my mind go any further, can't let myself even begin to think of what she would be like under her bra and panties. The shorts I changed into before our walk on the beach don't hide a damn thing, and if she comes out here before the blood flow redistributes to the other parts of my body, there will be no hiding what the idea of her naked in the bathroom does to me.

With the laser focus of a man trying to get rid of an erection, I throw all my attention into figuring out this air mattress.

And, what do you know? Without the distraction of Paisley perched on the bed watching me, I get it working and inflated in no time.

Paisley appears in the doorway, a fluffy white towel wrapped around her body, her hair wound into something small and lavender and turban-like on her head. Her skin is flushed from the heat of the water.

"The shower is free," she announces, scampering into the room.

My eyes are on her body as she crosses to the dresser.

"New rule," she says, rummaging through the top drawer. "Take your fresh clothes into the bathroom with you when you shower."

"In that case," I respond, stepping up to my side of the dresser and opening my top drawer. "I guess I should grab my things."

"Mm hmm," Paisley hums, rummaging through the contents of her drawer. Thongs in every color stare teasingly back at me.

"You going to choose something, or stir it around like a soup?" I don't intend to sound so gruff, but that erection I worked to get rid of is back in full force.

My tone rolls off Paisley's smooth, tan skin. She grins. She's enjoying this.

"Oh, Klein. So grumpy sometimes." Using two fingers, she plucks a delightfully poor excuse for an undergarment out of the assortment and holds it aloft. "These will do," she says.

Sliding fisted hands into my shorts pockets, I do what I can to press out on the fabric and give the front some breathing room.

I give Paisley a dead-eye expression, as if the color of the sheer thong she's holding out is not an exact match to her eye color.

She steps back. "Shower time," she says playfully. "Might want to make it a cold one," she adds, looking pointedly at my crotch.

Grabbing something to sleep in, I roll my eyes at her as I hustle past. It's either that, or I'll end up turning our first good kiss into our first fantastic fuck.

Unlike Paisley, I close and lock the door to the bathroom.

Because I didn't sneak a peek, I can't say for sure what Paisley did in the shower, but I know for damn sure what I'm adding to tonight's agenda for my shower.

Between Paisley's moist post-shower skin wrapped in that towel, and her little show with her thong, I find relief in almost no time.

It's acceptable, but not nearly good enough.

I'm out and dressed when there's a soft knock on the

door. I open it, and in steps Paisley wearing an oversized sleep shirt that falls to mid-thigh.

"I need my moisturizer," she says, pointing at an array of tubes and bottles on the counter. "And to brush my teeth."

We stand beside each other in front of our respective sinks. She shares her tube of toothpaste, and we trade bubble paste grins and fleeting glances in the mirror with toothbrushes stuck out of the sides of our mouths.

Paisley is picking through her toiletries bag when something clatters to the tiled bathroom floor.

Bending, I pick it up. It has a handle like a wand, and a rounded head covered in tiny nodules.

"Paisley," I smirk. "Am I holding your special friend in my hand?"

She swipes the rubber tool from my grasp. "Wipe that amused grin from your lips. It's a facial cleansing device." Held an inch above the surface of her skin, she demonstrates by running it in concentric circles.

When I say nothing, she makes a face, daring me to challenge her. I hold up my hands in a show of surrender. She tosses the device into her bag and stomps from the bathroom.

I finish up, then follow her. All I want is to face-plant that giant bed Paisley is pulling back the covers on.

Alas. The already wilting and cracked plastic air mattress will be my bed.

All the lights in the room are off, save for an ambient glow from the nightstand lamp. The window is propped open, the soft cadence of the water filtering into the room.

Charcoal gray sheets cover the air mattress, and a pillow. Nudging the mattress with my foot, I say, "Those weren't there when I went to take a shower."

"The bedding fairy visited in your absence." Paisley, content with her sheet arranging and pillow fluffing, climbs into that big, soft-looking bed. The night shirt rides up her thighs, exposing her shapely muscles, her creamy skin.

She has one leg poking out from the cover, and I swear that leg is begging for my fingertips to run up its length, my hands to knead the muscles, my lips to blaze a trail.

I could do it, right now. Lean over her where she lies, deliver that kiss I've promised her. She's right. The clock is ticking.

But I want it to be perfect. The remainder of our touches this week will be for show, so this one that I get with her? I'm setting a bar, for whom I don't know, but I have to be superior. I'm already her worst kiss. Now I need to be her best.

The air mattress makes awkward noises as I settle in. "Thanks, bedding fairy."

"You're welcome." Paisley's face appears over the edge of the bed. She's frowning, her gaze running the length of the mattress. "I'm not certain that bed will hold up all night."

"It'll be fine," I assure, the lie floating through my teeth. This bed is ancient, and likely has a number of fissures.

Paisley's frown deepens. "If you wake up during the night and find yourself on the floor, you have my permission to come up here. But don't be a hog," she warns. "Stay on your side."

I fold my pillow in half and blink up at her. "Parameters noted and accepted."

She stretches across the nightstand and turns off the lamp. The room falls into darkness. "Good night, Wordsmith. Get your beauty sleep. Tomorrow, the real hoodwinking begins."

"Sleep tight, Ace."

## CHAPTER 23
*Paisley*

Lie. That was my vibrator.

## CHAPTER 24
*Klein*

A cocoon.

This bed is a collection of angel kisses, a cloud that—

Oh shit.

Last night's fantasy about being in this bed somehow became a reality at an unidentified point during the dark hours.

Orange blossoms.

A scent burned into my memory.

*Paisley.*

My leg twitches, a movement that forces a swift run along a thigh too smooth to be mine.

The sleepy fog in my brain clears, and now I'm remembering my middle of the night wake up, how every part of my body except my head was on the ground, the air mattress a pancake beneath me.

If it weren't for Paisley's offer, I'd either have significant back pain from the ground or be on the couch risking someone finding me.

As directed, I stayed on my side of the bed.

Paisley may have issued the memo, but she did not abide by it. She is not only on my side, she's curled around me.

My gaze drifts down, to where the top of her head fits under my chin.

The parts of my body that are connected to Paisley's suddenly come alive.

My chest... and her back pressed against it.

My knees... tucked into the space behind hers.

My nose... buried in her hair.

And last but so very far from least, her lovely backside curled into my center like a double rainbow.

*Oh, for the love.*

Her T-shirt bunches around her lower back, revealing the top of that sheer thong that matches her eyes. It hugs her flesh, round and firm and disappearing into the concave space made by my body.

Waking up like this is a dream I didn't dare have, but here she is, tucked into me, the lines of her body pressed to mine like she was made to be there. Like she was made for me.

*Whoa. Slow down. What kind of thought was that?*

I mean, yeah, Paisley is the total package. She's funny and kind, whip-quick and intelligent. She'd do anything for her family, as is evidenced by the fact we're here. I'm learning that while she may seem unruffled on the outside, she's softer on the inside. She has a figure that makes my body groan from head to toe.

But, made for me? That's intense.

I have to get out of here. Go downstairs and pour caffeine down my throat. I'm Paisley's fake boyfriend who promised her a make-up kiss because my ego can't handle being her worst. That's all.

Fighting my desire to carry out *lascivious acts*—thank you, drunken Paisley—I retreat from the warm, soft bed. Footfalls quiet, I slip out of the room.

Though Paisley remains in bed, her body heat simmers on me, her smell lingering on my skin.

···🐚🐚🐚···

A BITTER, SMOKY SCENT GREETS ME IN THE KITCHEN. A coffee carafe, filled to the brim with dark liquid, sits on a gold cart at the end of a counter. Also on the cart: six types of flavored syrups, sugar cubes in a glass canister, and a stainless steel creamer.

Wow. This family takes their caffeine seriously. Not that I'm complaining. At any given time of day I am likely to be some degree of caffeinated.

I grab a mug and prepare my coffee the way I like, and by the time I'm stirring creamer into my cup, Lausanne is walking into the kitchen.

"Good morning. Sleep well?"

I nod, noting that once again she's dressed exactly the way Paisley described her yesterday.

*Coastal grandma.* I'll definitely be tucking that one away and using it in a future novel.

"I did, thank you."

"How was the bed? The mattress is new. You two are the first to sleep on it."

"Just right," I assure her. Thanks to my middle of the night bed switch, I don't have to lie.

"Good," Lausanne remarks, adding a splash of vanilla syrup to her coffee. "The rest of the family will descend upon us today. You need to be well rested for them."

She joins me at the table in the eat-in kitchen. The bay window to my left showcases the sunrise over the ocean.

"Thirty years of waking up to that view, and I've yet to tire of it."

"Pictures don't do it justice." I'd looked up the island online, searched the images. Good photography isn't a replacement for the real thing. Tomorrow morning, I plan to be out there when the sun first peeks over the horizon. For now, I need to be here talking to Lausanne and learning more about the Royce family before they arrive.

"Paisley told me her parents have a tumultuous relationship."

Lausanne laughs softly. "That is one way to put it. My daughter spent a few years wanting to kick her ex-husband out of her life for good, but calmed down when she saw how much it was hurting her children. Paisley, especially." Lausanne looks at me with concern, as if perhaps she's said too much. I nod knowingly, to mollify her. I knew most of that already, though learning it hurt Paisley the most is a new detail. I stymie the desire to probe, to ask why Paisley more than her siblings. It feels like something Paisley should tell me, not Lausanne.

We talk about my job as a bartender, and the book.

Lausanne is warm and funny, and reminds me of my mom. She has an ease about her, and I'm immediately comfortable in her home, and in conversation with her.

Paisley creeps into the kitchen, eyes squinting.

"There's my bright-eyed, bushy-tailed granddaughter," Lausanne teases.

Paisley grunts. She fixes her coffee, coming our way with the cup nestled between cupped hands.

I rise, pulling out the seat beside mine and guiding her into it. "Good morning, Ace," I say, keeping my tone light as I press a soft kiss to her temple. It's what a boyfriend would do, or at least, it's what *I* would do if I were her boyfriend.

She leans into me, my touch, pushing back against my lips with her head.

"Ace?" Lausanne asks, bending a leg and tucking it beneath her. "How cute is that? I need the background on that nickname."

Paisley looks to me to answer. She sips her coffee, and it's as if I can see the cobwebs begin to clear. I hold her gaze. Her eyes widen, a realization creeping into them. Is she remembering how I made my way into her bed during the night? Maybe she's thinking about the way *she* made her way into *me*.

"Well," I answer, my eyes on Paisley and her messy ponytail, her rumpled pajamas. "Paisley strikes me as a capable person. You should see the way she walks down the hall at P Squared Marketing. She strides confidently, like she knows she's the boss. She's the best. Skilled. An ace."

A delicate shade of pink blooms on Paisley's cheeks. "He's overselling me," she assures her grandma, lifting her coffee to her lips.

"I doubt that," Lausanne responds.

Tracing her pink cheek with my fingertip, I say, "Just be happy I chose ace instead of virtuoso. Or champion."

Paisley's shoulders bob as she laughs at the same time she swallows her coffee. Coughing, she says, "Ace is preferable."

My finger travels another inch, gathering a shorter piece of hair that has fallen from her ponytail and tucking it behind her ear. "Ace," I nod with finality.

Her lips part slightly, inviting me in, then she suddenly breaks the connection of our gaze, asking her grandmother, "What time does everybody arrive today?"

"Eleven. Your mom is planning to make her favorite soup for lunch. I'll make a salad."

Paisley nods. "Good. There will be enough time for me to take Klein on a bike ride."

"Old Baldy?"

My mom, if she were here, would make a joke about calling someone out for being advanced in age and also lacking hair.

I'm guessing Old Baldy is the name of something, a place maybe, and Paisley says, "Later in the week. Today I want to help Klein get a lay of the land. And take him to Nauti Bowls."

"Nauti Bowls?" I ask.

Paisley answers. "Smoothie bowls. Açai bowls. Coffee. Baked goods."

I leave Paisley to finish her coffee while I get ready. We trade places, with her getting ready and me checking the bike tires. They are flat, but have no fear, I also spotted a bike pump near the air mattress in the shed.

The bikes are a matching pair of beach cruisers, one

carnation pink, and the other mint green. Fastened to the pink bike is a white basket, with colorful lights wound through the spokes.

Paisley finds me under the house, finishing the last tire. She's wearing a white dress that hits just above her knees and ties at the back of her neck. Eyes on me, she says, "You've done a lot of pumping over the last twelve hours."

Standing up straight, bike pump in hand, I search her face for a hint she's making a sexual joke. Worse, that she somehow heard me last night despite the fisted hand I pressed against my mouth in an effort to be silent.

Paisley grabs a bike handle and swings her leg over, adjusting her dress so she can sit properly. "Get your mind out of the gutter, Madigan. First you accuse me of bringing a vibrator on this trip, and now you can't handle hearing the word 'pump'?"

She's teasing me. I like it.

She continues. "I saw your bed deflated during the night. That made it easier for me to push under the bed when I got up this morning, but probably wasn't so great for your sleep quality."

I scratch my forehead with my thumb. "About that. Turns out I only got half a night of bad sleep."

"Why is that?"

"I woke up in your bed this morning. I don't actually remember climbing in. But, yeah. I woke up next to you."

Her eyes scrunch closed. "I thought it was a dream. When I woke up, I assumed I'd dreamed it."

"So you remember me getting in?"

She nods. "It's hazy, but yes. You pulled back the

covers and climbed in. You didn't say a word, but you"—her eyes flash, something dawning—"you pulled me into you."

I'm shaking my head before she's done with her sentence. "You suctioned yourself to me sometime during the night. I know because you were on my side of the bed when I woke up."

Now she's the one shaking her head. "Lies. All of it."

I stare at her. She stares at me with the same determined expression I feel on my face. A stalemate.

"Agree to disagree?" I offer a hand.

She looks at it, turning her chin sharply. "Never." She pushes off, pedaling over the driveway. Her knee-length white sundress flutters in the breeze she creates.

She looks cute as hell on the bike, ponytail swinging and sun shining down on her. Quickly, I pull my phone from my pocket and snap a pic. I'll send it to Cecily later.

Swinging my leg over the green bike, I take off after her.

We head north, away from the beach. Soon the vegetation gives way to the live oaks, thick and green. Sunlight reaches through leaves, stretching around branches to dapple the path. Golf carts pass, each driver lifting a hand in hello.

I ride a foot behind Paisley, and a little to her left, so that I'm more in the road than she. She smiles as she rides, her face bright and open. Carefree and happy, Paisley leads the way, slowing as we approach a lawn.

I come to a stop beside her, my gaze lifting up up up until it reaches the top of the lighthouse in front of us.

"Old Baldy," she announces. "It's the oldest standing

lighthouse in North Carolina. It's been out of commission for a long time, but people can climb to the top."

"Are we climbing it?"

"Another day," Paisley says, repositioning her bike to get on the path. "Nauti Bowls awaits."

In the middle of the island sits a row of shops. Clothing, café, grocery, wine, and Nauti Bowls. We slide our bikes into a rack out front, and I look around while Paisley walks ahead on the brick walkway. Sun soaks the front patio, dropping over potted plants bunched at the entrance.

Paisley waits with the door propped open, watching me. "I like watching you catalog everything you see."

"I want to remember everything." My gaze drops from the trees lurching overhead, finding Paisley. Her head tilts, the slightest tug of her mouth on the left side.

*Everything.* Especially the softness in Paisley's gaze, the oceanic color of her eyes, the way her dress melts over her curves.

Pressing a hand flat on the open door above Paisley's head, I wait for her to walk in the shop. She doesn't. She spends a moment that feels more like ten standing under my gaze, close enough that her orange blossom scent washes over me.

She blinks, and the spell breaks. I nod for her to go into the store, and she pushes off the door, walking in ahead of me.

The space is small, sharing a pass-through with the sundries shop next door, and smells of hazelnut and sugar. A long butcher block counter is loaded with individually wrapped baked goods, and two hanging signs list the specialty drinks and bowls.

"What do you want?" I ask Paisley. She's swaying beside me, hands clasped as she reads the menu.

"Hmm. The Original sounds good. You?"

"Two Originals, please," I say to the girl behind the counter, removing my wallet from my back pocket.

"I can get mine," Paisley says, stepping in closer.

I hand over cash and look down to Paisley. "On dates, I pay. Yes, you're independent. No, you don't need me to buy you stuff. But if I'm your boyfriend, I'm paying. End of story."

She thinks for a second, grins, and says happily, "Okay."

I was expecting more of a fight, and I'm relieved not to be getting one.

We take our açai bowls to the sunny patio. I finish mine in record time, but Paisley eats slowly. She places the spoon in her mouth, leans back in her seat with her eyes closed and the sun spilling over her, and sighs contentedly as she pulls the spoon from her mouth.

At this point, it hurts. Her beauty might actually be painful. I might be begging for mercy before the week is over.

"Everything tastes better here," she says, opening her eyes and nudging the half-empty paper cup on the table. "Everything feels better here. It's vacation, but it's home, too. That's how it felt every summer. I was visiting, but the island was mine." A blush spreads over her face. "That probably sounds ridiculous. Too emotional."

"If you want to talk about emotions, I'm your guy." I

take her leftover cup, motioning with the silent question *can I finish this?* Paisley nods. "Emotions are my thing, Ace. I like them big, I like them small, I like them messy, I like them all."

A zip of laughter bursts from her. "Are you quoting Dr. Seuss?"

I polish off her bowl, saying, "I'm quoting Klein Madigan."

She pushes her sandaled foot against mine. "That guy sounds like he means what he says."

Stacking our cups, I toss them in a nearby trash and hold out a hand to help Paisley up from her seat. "He does."

Paisley places her hand in my grasp, allowing me to hold it while she stands. I'd like to keep holding it, but we don't have an audience. Nobody for whom we need to convince of anything.

"Ready to continue the tour?" I ask, pulling Paisley's bike from the rack and wheeling it to her. She takes the handlebars, and that's when I notice a tiny purple smudge at the corner of her lips.

Without thinking, I reach out, thumbing at the color. Paisley tenses, her bike frame between her thighs, then relaxes.

"Açai," I explain.

Softly, I rub at the spot past when it has disappeared.

"I think you got it." Her voice is low.

My thumb makes two more passes. "It's stubborn. But it's getting there." One more swipe and I step back, climbing onto my bike with an uncomfortable tightness in my chest. Being close to Paisley is exquisite torture.

We ride around the island, and Paisley points out landmarks we pass. The boardwalk, where ferries come in. The Conservancy, where scientists work to protect sea turtles and conserve barrier islands. The chapel (a beautiful place, Paisley says, but not where Shane and Sienna are getting married). We take a break beside the golf course lagoon, drinking from the water bottle she brought and trying to spot alligators in the water.

"It's amazing here, right?" Paisley's throat moves as she drinks. "It's a secluded island, but it has everything a person needs."

"There's a surreal quality to it," I confirm, taking the water bottle from her outstretched hand and keeping an eye on the water. We're twenty feet away, but it's creepy, especially to this Arizona man. Even after five minutes, when nothing rises to the surface, I'm still vigilant.

Paisley tips her head to the sky, basking in the sun. "No alligators today, Wordsmith. Are you ready for our mission to really begin? By the time we get back, everybody should be there."

Reaching out, I run a single fingertip up the length of her exposed throat. She flinches, eyes open, but doesn't move away. "I'll play my part so well, by the end of this week, even you will think I'm your boyfriend."

She looks like she wants to say something, but the words aren't there. Using the tip of her tongue, she licks her lips. "Good. Make sure you're sending pictures to Cecily. You're not playing the role of a lifetime for nothing, right?"

She mounts her bike and pedals away at a leisurely

pace. Using her reminder, I pull out my phone and take a photo of her back as she wheels away.

Before I can forget, I send Cecily the photo. She responds immediately.

> I need more.
>
> Send me everything you have, even when you don't think it's good. There might be a part of it that's good when cropped.

I gave her a thumbs-up, then take off after Paisley.

# CHAPTER 25
## *Paisley*

Dread has an acidic flavor.

For the final five minutes of my bike ride with Klein it is all I can taste, overpowering the lingering sweetness of my breakfast. My stomach swirls, apprehension cloaks my thoughts. All the good feelings from being here with only Klein and my grandma are muted, colored over by the reality of why we're here.

"Are you good?" Klein asks when we ride under the house and leave our bikes leaning on a wall.

I nod. I'm not good, but the only way out of all this is through the middle of it.

Pointing to the additional golf carts in the driveway, I say, "They're here."

My mom and Ben. My aunt and uncle. My little brother and younger cousins. Sienna and Shane.

Ugh. Shane.

I start for the house, but a grip on my arm pulls me back.

"Paisley," Klein says, gently bringing me in closer. "Our

relationship might be for show, but my friendship is genuine. You're not alone this week."

His declaration mollifies me, bringing comfort to my heart, easing my worry. I like the way his eyes search mine, how they drop lower and take in the rest of my face, lingering on my lips.

"Thank you," I whisper.

He releases me, and walks with me up the stairs. Stepping in front of me to get to the door first, he opens it at the same time his hand finds the small of my back.

And... curtain.

My sister is the first to spot us. She sits on a counter height stool, one knee tucked up into her chest, while the other leg keeps her steady on the chair rung. Her eyes light up when we walk into the room. She bounds from her seat, clapping her hands twice.

"Big sister is here!" Exuberance presses into the sides of her tone, filling out her words. She releases me from her hug and turns to Klein. "And her boyfriend, too. Thanks for making the long trip."

"It was nothing," Klein says. "It's nice to see you again."

Sienna presses her lips together. "About that. I'd like to apologize. I wasn't myself that night."

Klein waves away her apology. "I've seen plenty of drunk brides-to-be. You fell in the harmless category."

"Right." Sienna looks relieved. "Since I was harmless, there's no need to mention it to Shane."

My eyebrows cinch. Why does Sienna feel the need to keep something so innocent from her fiancé?

"No problem," Klein assures her.

"Yes, problem," I say with a low volume. The suspicion

I'm feeling has my tone coming out more forceful than I mean it to be. "You didn't do anything wrong that night. Why can't Shane know? What is there to keep him from knowing? You were inebriated and ate fries at two a.m. Some people call that a normal Friday night."

Sienna clears her throat and smoothes her hair. "That's not how I typically conduct myself."

"We are crystal clear on that," I mutter, and then, because I dislike how stiff she's acting, I add, "It was the penises, wasn't it? Or is it pen*i* when it's plural?" I look to my fake boyfriend/real wordsmith for guidance.

He shrugs. "I'll have to look into it and get back to you."

Sienna narrows her eyes. "Leave that detail out of the stories."

I roll my eyes at her. "Can you please provide me with a script for what to say if your fiancé asks for additional details about the bachelorette party I threw for you?" I hold up a palm. "Wait. Let me give it a shot. First, we drank a glass of champagne while we discussed your flight and lamented the status of air travel these days. Next, we moved on to dinner, where we dined on salad and the collective air of superiority around the table." I know I should stop talking, but I'm offended and *worried*. Why doesn't Sienna feel comfortable telling her future husband the truth?

She sniffs. "I don't know what your problem is, but you're being really mean to the bride."

I know what my problem is from a high-level, but I also don't know what it is in this precise moment. Overwhelm, I think, and indignation. Repressed feelings.

Suspicion toward Sienna's editing of her bachelorette party. Not a great combination.

Unsurprisingly, Shane chooses the worst time to stride into the room. Sienna swipes under her eyes quickly, blinking twice and plastering on her face a smile faker than my relationship.

"Pais," Shane calls, frat boy style, like I'm his bro. We haven't seen each other in three years, and this is how he chooses to greet me?

Crooking one arm around my shoulders, he pulls me in for an awkward side hug while also shaking me. "Hey, Shane," I say quickly, stepping out of his embrace.

Klein reaches for my hand, pulling me until my back meets his chest. Shane looks over my shoulder at Klein, recognition lighting up his eyes.

"I know you from somewhere," he says, pointing at Klein. His finger taps the air like he's hitting a piano key.

Klein puts us all out of our misery by saying, "We were in the same creative writing class in college." His arm snakes around me possessively. "Paisley, too."

Shane's eyes dart from Klein to me, then he snaps his fingers. "That's right. You made Paisley cry. Not an easy task." He pretends to punch my arm. "There might as well be a force field around this one."

I stiffen.

Klein chuckles, but the sound is less *that was funny* and more *keep saying things like that and see what happens*. "Interesting thing about force fields is that they're effective at keeping out the bad. But the good? That penetrates."

Shane's forehead wrinkles with his struggle to make

sense of Klein's words. "Right," he says slowly. "Anyway, thanks for coming to our wedding. Wasn't sure Paisley had it in her."

My foot lifts, and I have every intention of stomping on his toes, but Klein hauls me in closer. He nuzzles my hair. The stream of air across my skin as he breathes, his nearness, his damn scent, it combines to distract me. Soothe me.

Then he says, "Paisley and I debated about coming this week, but she reminded me the beach is still on our list of places we want to have sex. So"—I feel his shrug—"here we are."

Normally a comment like that would mortify me, but the look on Shane's face? The mortification is worth it.

Shane's head rears back. It actually, measurably moves. He recovers by grabbing my sister by the waist and kissing her temple. "Did you hear that, babe? They're in that new relationship infatuation stage. It took us forever to finally get through that, remember?"

"Mm hmm," Sienna says, nodding along.

"I think you put us back into it with this 'no sex the week leading up to the wedding' nonsense."

Irritation flickers over Sienna's expression, but she quickly stows it. "I just thought it would be fun and romantic."

Shane frowns. "It is neither."

Silence settles over us. Somewhere else in the house are the sounds of a television, a low buzz of conversation, but here in this kitchen it's only awkward air, thick and sliceable.

"Oh!" Sienna throws up her hands. She looks grateful

to have remembered something, to have a reason to rush to her oversized bag slung on a kitchen chair. "I have your itinerary for the week."

She presses an ivory sheet of textured 8.5 x 11 paper into my hand. It matches the stationery her wedding invitation was printed on.

> Wedding Week Itinerary:
> Sunday - Travel + Beach/Bonfire
> Monday - Dad arrives; Dinner
> Tuesday - Assemble 'thank you' gifts; Mixer at Shane's house.
> Wednesday - Sunset cruise
> Thursday - Spa day for girls, chartered fishing boat for boys
> Friday - Rehearsal dinner
> Saturday - Wedding

"This looks"—I find my sister's eyes, lit up like a Christmas tree—"fun."

I'm not lying. It looks like a week of laughter, of hair that smells like smoke and sunscreen and salt. Sun-kissed skin and sandy toes.

"That's good to hear," Sienna says, "because I've already booked everything. And Klein—" She glances above my head. I can't see the man, but every part of me knows he's there, feels it with a heightened awareness I'm not sure I'm comfortable with. "I know you're not a part of the bridal party, but I've included you in everything. I hope that's alright."

"Thanks for including me," Klein responds politely, the deepened voice tumbling down around me. "That was kind of you."

"Are you kidding?" Sienna's eyes widen, happy and excited. "It was my pleasure. Paisley hasn't dated anyone in a long time." She looks at me accusingly. "That I know of, anyway. You being here is a big deal. She must be serious about you."

It's like there's an alarm in my limbs. Everything is on high alert.

But then there are warm hands on my upper arms, long fingers wrapping around my skin, squeezing me softly, reassuringly. "That's good to hear," Klein says, voice warm and spicy like cinnamon. "I'm serious about her, too."

The wailing siren stops. Later, I'll have to thank Klein for that perfect response.

"Whoa," a voice says from the entrance. "Is this awkward, or what?"

Swallowing my groan, I rip my gaze from Klein and to the voice.

"Spencer," I greet my little brother. "Hey, dude."

Spencer grins, leaning against the wall, arms crossed and staring at the four of us. He loves poking at people, their pain points and weak spots. Triggering people is a favorite pastime.

His hair is dark, like our dad's, and messy on purpose. He wears linen khakis I'd call too short, but I know is the style for boys his age. At seventeen, I was nothing like

Spencer. I was serious about school, focused and ready to follow in my dad's footsteps. I was going to major in business finance and be his right-hand woman.

I envy Spencer, the carefree way he behaves. The carefree way he lives. What a gift it is, to be young and unsaddled with the secrets your parents keep.

Klein holds out a hand to Spencer, introducing himself. They make conversation about the player changes in the English Premier League. From listening, I gather they're talking about soccer. Shane has nothing to add to the conversation because he was never interested in the sport, but he hangs on the periphery of their conversation.

"You ready to see Dad tomorrow?" Sienna asks.

I shrug. "As ready as I ever am."

He's not cold to me, per se, but he's standoffish. He cannot get over how I forged my own path. I can't get over how swiftly he blocked me from his life once I did it. I wonder if he realizes he set it all in motion? If I'd never seen him cheating, if he'd never asked me to keep it from my mother, I would have stayed on the path he laid out for me. His lying, his duplicitous behavior, was like a tree falling in the path. It was the roadblock I needed to see there was another way for me. It went against the person I'd been until then, the girl who bent over backward to make sure everyone in the Royce family was happy.

At the end of the day, I am his biggest regret. And he is the cause of it.

Spencer grabs a soccer ball from the room he's staying in, returning with our triplet fifteen-year-old cousins. He makes quick introductions, which includes them grunting a hello. Spencer asks Klein to go outside and kick the ball around. Klein agrees, and Shane joins. That should make for an interesting sight.

Shane turns back on his way out the door, pausing to say, "Hey, Pais. My mom said she's looking forward to seeing you." Then he's gone, no response needed from me.

His mom, Rebecca, was always kind to me. It will be nice to see her.

Before Sienna has a chance to say a word about her soon-to-be mother-in-law, our mom breezes in wearing a Lilly Pulitzer maxi skirt and fuchsia tank top, Ben in tow. When is he not attached to her side?

"Paisley, I didn't realize you'd returned from your bike ride." She offers a perfunctory hug in greeting, stepping back and looking into the kitchen behind me. "Where's Klein?"

"Downstairs playing soccer with Spencer and the triplets."

"And Shane," Sienna adds.

"That's nice," Mom says. Ben kisses her cheek and tells us he's going to join them. With a wave to me that is a hello and a goodbye, he exits.

Mom stares, heart-eyed, at his retreating back. "He is so handsome."

Sienna and I share a look, silently warning *Gird your loins.*

"Uh-huh," I say.

"And a real man in bed, you know?"

"Gross, Mother." Oops. That was out loud. What is with me today?

She frowns at me. "You're grown now, Paisley. I'd like to be able to talk to you like we're girlfriends."

I want to tell her how dysfunctional that is, but the fear of losing her keeps me from speaking up. I already have one parent who can barely stand me. I'm not going for two out of two.

"Sorry, Mom. Please, detail how he rings your bell."

"We'll save that for later when we've had wine."

Please, no. Any filter she has disintegrates when alcohol is involved.

She sidesteps me and Sienna and walks all the way into the kitchen. "I'll get started on lunch."

· · · 🐚 🐚 🐚 · · ·

SPENCER AND THE TRIPLETS HAVE SET THE TABLE WITH bone-colored soup bowls and shiny silver spoons. A bottle of red and a bottle of white sits in the center of the table, to the left of the enameled stockpot and ladle.

My mom, hips pressed to the edge of the table for leverage, lifts the lid off the pot. The fragrance of tomatoes and spices, the briny scent of crab permeates the room.

She breathes deeply, audibly, and sighs a happy, "Mmm."

Ben rubs a hand absentmindedly over her backside. My brother sees this happen and looks away.

A stab of sympathy assails me. Does their behavior upset him? Likely.

Mom ladles soup into everyone's bowls. Grandma pours wine. To Klein, Mom says, "I hope you like it. I made this at least once a week every summer when my kids were growing up."

Klein looks down at the mixture, his eyebrows tugging.

I fill my spoon halfway, lifting it midair and pretending I'm going to feed him. "You've probably never heard of it before, I know I haven't seen it on restaurant menus in Scottsdale, but—"

Klein leans away from my spoon. "What is that?"

I freeze. "Crab soup."

Klein shakes his head. "I'm allergic to shellfish."

*Oh shit.*

I drop my spoon in my bowl. The entire table sends me one long, accusatory look. "You didn't think to mention your boyfriend's shellfish allergy to me, Paisley?" my mother huffs.

"I... I—"

"She must've forgot." Klein relaxes his posture, pressing back into his chair. "We don't go to seafood restaurants on our dates. Landlocked state, and all. Not a lot of opportunities for my allergy to come up."

Mom nods slowly, regarding me with shrewd eyes. "Well Paisley, you'll have to miss out on your favorite soup. Can't have you eating it and then kissing Klein."

I grab two dinner rolls, trying to shake off the embarrassment. "More carbs for me."

"Hah," Spencer snorts. "Paisley tried to kill her boyfriend."

Shane laughs.

My face flames.

My grandmother, bless her heart, asks Sienna a question about the wedding ceremony. Klein brushes the outside of my thigh with one hand. He looks at me with apology and I attempt an imperceptible nod.

Sienna and the wedding dominate conversation for the remainder of the meal. She details for my grandma the bridesmaids dresses. Goes on and on about the centerpieces (vases with pampas grass and dried fronds). Laments she wasn't able to get the arch she wanted (a custom made piece done by a man in a small town in northern Arizona who wasn't taking new clients because his wife was having a baby). I tune her out when she discusses how she and Shane chose their first dance song.

Klein and I retreat to our room after the late lunch is over to get ready for the bonfire listed on our itinerary.

I head for the bathroom, and Klein follows. He closes the door, and I whirl around, glaring. "You came to an island and forgot to tell me you're allergic to shellfish? How? Did you see the way they all looked at me?" The moment was my current worst fear, nearly realized. "That could've ruined everything. Now at least one of them is probably suspicious. Spencer can be smart at the most inconvenient times." Hot tears prick at my eyes.

Klein's jaw tenses. "Yeah, that wasn't great."

"To put it mildly."

"Are you mad?"

I shift, uncomfortable. Am I mad? That's not the right word. I'm... I'm... *oh*. "I'm embarrassed. What kind of girlfriend doesn't *remember* their boyfriend's shellfish allergy? What if I'd eaten crab some other time and kissed you? I could've put you in danger. And"—maybe I am a little mad—"how could you not give me pertinent information?

We spent all that time getting to know each other and you forgot to tell me about something that big? Is there a part of you that wants me to be found out?"

I know Klein wouldn't do that, but I feel like a supreme fool right now.

Bracing my hands against the edge of the bathroom counter, I haul myself up onto it. Staring down at the tiled floor, at the tightly looped bath mat, I try to stop the fear from taking hold. That was close. Too close. Maybe it wasn't enough to make them think this relationship is fake, but it was certainly enough to make them wonder why I tried to spoon-feed my boyfriend something he's allergic to.

"It was an oversight, Paisley. Or have you never had one of those?" One eyebrow quirks in an infuriatingly endearing way. "You're just perfect all the time, perfect Paisley walking around doing everything perfectly?"

My arms cross. "What are you talking about? That's nonsense. You know I'm not perfect. Or do you not remember the terrible story I wrote in college?"

"How many times do I need to say I'm sorry? *I'm sorry.*" Klein drags his hands through his hair, leaving it sticking up in some places, and my indignation melts away. He makes frustration look good.

He continues. "The way I see it, you have two options. The first, you forgive me and move on."

*He really does have Peter Facinelli lips.*

"Second, you harbor all that anger, and let it affect the way you act this week."

*Can a throat be strong? Masculine? Why is his throat attractive?*

"Or, I guess there's a third option where—"

"Klein."

"Yeah?"

"What will it take to make you shut up and kiss me?"

He's on me before I can have another thought.

"Paisley," he growls, fitting his big body between my legs. Two hands cup my cheeks, my jawbone slicing through the middle of his palms.

A fire, so big and bright, burns in his eyes. If I could place a single word in those irises, it would be *devour*.

That's what I think he's about to do to me, but then he pulls back. He keeps his hands on me, but he studies my face, his eyes roaming over me.

"What are you thinking about?" My voice is a hoarse whisper. "Please don't change your mind."

I'm embarrassed to admit how much I want this. How much I want him to give me my best kiss. I already know it will be.

He shakes his head. "I was thinking about how I'd describe you on the page."

"Tell me."

Klein's eyes darken. His gaze roves over my shoulders and up again.

"Paisley's honeyed hair tips down her back. Her chin tilts, exposing her thrumming pulse."

His words tumble over me, spurring my heart to beat faster.

He comes closer. His hands leave me, settling on my hip creases. He drags me forward in one rough motion. His head dips, and then his lips meet my neck. Back and forth they swipe, only an inch of ground covered, and his tongue darts out over the rush of blood beneath my skin. "Her skin is sweet, like sugar, a taste so delicious he could lose himself in it. In her."

I gulp. The tip of his nose runs up my neck. Over my jaw where his hands had been. I reach for him, his waist, my touch winding around to his back.

His lips travel across my skin, the corners of our lips meeting. "Her mouth is one he's kissed before, yet somehow it feels like a first. The time before was a joke, a game, a trick played by fate." His words vibrate against my cheek. I squirm against him, trying to get closer, to make all parts of us touch.

His left hand journeys around my rib cage, flattening against my back. His right hand lifts, snaking through my hair, coming to rest on the back of my head. He leans me back slightly, tipping up my face, pulling me in closer so the want between my legs meets his lower stomach.

A cry slips between my teeth at the friction I'd been desperate for. It's temporary though, a momentary salve, and now I'm wanting *more more more*.

Klein's lips brush over mine—*finally!*—and he hovers there. "What am I going to do with you, Ace?"

*Everything*. His hands, his mouth, I want him all over me.

"Kiss me, Klein," I manage to say, in a voice too breathy, too wanton to be me. And yet, that's me. Wanting Klein. Practically mewling, rubbing myself against him.

There's a groaning sound low in his throat, almost feral, and then he lowers his mouth to mine.

I don't respond gently. I don't have it in me. I'm filled

with need for this man, a desire that has me rolling my hips, seeking relief deliverable in only one way.

His tongue dips into my mouth, tasting me, and my hands traverse his back, working their way into his hair.

We kiss like we're needy.

We kiss like we're desperate.

We kiss like people who've been dancing around their attraction for weeks, who've been coming to the thought of one another.

Our frenzied kisses slow, and Klein nips at the side of my lower lip. My grinding against his stomach ceases. Our chests rise and fall as our breath comes back to us.

His forehead falls against mine. "Damn, Paisley. That didn't only put *our* first kiss to shame. That put *all* first kisses to shame."

My sense returns. Klein straightens, bringing me upright. "Yeah," I manage. "That, um, more than made up for it."

My gaze finds the front of his pants, the massive outline pushing against the fabric, and a fresh round of blood flow sends an ache to my lady part. His hands go into his pockets and he shifts, making room in the front of his shorts.

I laugh, meeting his eyes. He shrugs, but he's blushing, and why do I like that so much?

"I guess I should let you have some privacy so you can get changed for the beach."

I nod. "I guess so."

He strides out, closing the bathroom door behind him. I rush over to lock it, and reach into my toiletries bag.

If it weren't for this *facial cleansing device,* I might melt into a puddle right here.

## CHAPTER 26
*Klein*

HERE'S THE THING ABOUT PEOPLE LIKE ME. WORDSMITHS, as Paisley creatively called me. We're always creating stories in our heads. Or, taking a developing situation and finishing out the scenario.

Sometimes this storytelling parallels catastrophic thinking.

Maybe that's what I'm doing now, lying here on this bed waiting for Paisley to finish changing.

Catastrophizing.

*Was Paisley only pretending to enjoy that kiss? What if that's all it was, and she did it so she didn't hurt my feelings because I have to be here with her for the rest of the week, and maybe if I realized she hated our second kiss more than our first I would run (swim? somersault onto a boat?) off the island and leave her here to face the week on her own.*

Catastrophic thinking, or storytelling? Depends on the reader, I guess.

For me, that kiss was earth-shattering. It was an answer to a long held question. *Are Paisley and I physically incompatible?* The answer, for me, is a resounding no. Paisley's soft skin, the smell of orange blossoms, the little noises in the back of her throat, and *help me God* the feel of her lips. Soft and supple, perfect, melting against mine.

Paisley steps from the bathroom wearing denim cutoffs and a thin white tank top. Her eyes find mine, a peachy-pink flush stealing over her cheeks. From me? Our kiss?

She smiles shyly at me. Does this mean I won't need to catapult myself onto the next vessel off this island?

"Paisley—"

She holds out a hand. "You look worried, Wordsmith. Don't be."

"It wasn't our second worst kiss?"

She shakes her head slowly, her smile small but genuine, her eyes alight. "Not by a long shot."

Is my smug feeling showing on my face? Probably. Years spent self-flagellating over that terrible performance, and now I've shown her I'm better than that.

Righted a wrong.

She comes to a stop beside the bed, pushing her hip against the side of the mattress and looking down at me. "You ready for some beach volleyball and a bonfire?"

"Only if I can pop my collar. This feels like an ultra-preppy event. Let me grab the keys to my sailboat. Will there be photographers present? Ralph Lauren has been incessant about putting me in their summer issue."

Paisley beats back a laugh. "Don't make me kiss you again just to stop your mouth from running a mile a minute, Madigan."

*Won't you, please?*

"Wouldn't dream of it, Royce." I swing my legs off the bed. "Besides, you can't kiss me now. We're supposed to be saving our lip locks for the audience."

She gives my clothing a once-over. "Correct. Bring a sweatshirt with you. It can be chilly on the beach at night."

She pulls a forest green zip-up hoodie from the closet where her dress hangs. I do the same, grabbing the only sweatshirt I brought from my dresser drawer.

Sweatshirts in hand, we head out of our room. We pause to say goodbye to Lausanne, who tells us Paisley's mom and Ben have gone to the place they're renting. Paisley invites Lausanne, but she declines, claiming she'd rather cook dinner.

"Don't worry," Lausanne reassures, "she took the soup with her."

We leave for the private walkway, the roar of the ocean filling my ears with every step we take closer. For the twentieth time since I arrived, I marvel at the fact I'm here.

It's late enough in the afternoon that most families are gone from the sand. Individuals, and some couples, walk at the water's edge. It's earlier today than it was yesterday when we came out here, the sky still a lemony yellow but darkening into dandelion at the edges.

We pause at the bottom stair on the other side of the dune. A handful of people—*fifteen?*—gather around. I recognize Paisley's brother, Shane, and Sienna, but everyone else playing volleyball is a mystery to me.

The game is men versus women. The men wear chinos in muted pinks, blues, and greens, and matching white polos. The women wear dresses in linens and eyelets, and oversized sunglasses.

I glance at Paisley. "What in the Vineyard Vines is going on here?"

A laugh bursts from her. "Did I forget to tell you? Ralph Lauren canceled your shoot. Vineyard Vines replaced them."

"Hardy har har." We schlep over warm sand and deposit our things on one corner of the enormous light blue and white gingham beach blanket. On the opposite corner sits a cooler, propped open to reveal water bottles, cans of soda water, wine, and beer.

The game pauses. Shane makes introductions to his groomsmen, none of whom I have a snowball's chance in hell of remembering except for *Tag*, because it may as well be *Scooter*.

Tag, with his curly sandy brown hair that flops in his eyes, informs me he is Shane's brother, and also the best man. Recognition flares when he spots Paisley. His lean body slants back, arms open for a hug.

Paisley's greeting is warm, genuine. They spend a few minutes catching up as Sienna introduces (more like re-introduces) me to her bridesmaids. I recognize them from the bachelorette night, and if the light in their eyes is any indication, they remember me, too. Sienna must have them on the same gag order, because none of them call me Klein the stripper.

We join the volleyball game at the next rotation. Paisley surprises me by being pretty damn good. It isn't until later, when we're sitting and watching the sun sink lower in the sky, that I learn she played varsity volleyball in high school.

Behind us, Spencer yells at the triplets who joined late. Paisley glances at them over her shoulder, watching. She is different around her family. Watchful. Careful. Almost like a mother hen. She is not the laid-back and funny Paisley I know, with the saucy mouth who likes to poke lighthearted fun. Family dynamics can be difficult and multi-layered, and the Royce family has succeeded in piquing my curiosity.

Why is Paisley guarded, tense, and far too agreeable with her family, but perfectly willing to tell me when she doesn't like something?

Our shoulders are nearly touching, so when she draws her gaze away from Spencer, it stops on me. The corners of her eyes soften, crinkling, and I believe that warm look in her eyes is gratitude.

I wrap an arm around her, my fingertips trailing over the part of her arm left bare by her top. She blinks at me, and I wonder if she is remembering earlier in the bathroom. I've thought of it at least a dozen times, to the point of distraction. I missed my contribution to *bump set spike!* in the game earlier, because my mind had been elsewhere. We had a bad first kiss to make up for, but was that it? Did Paisley need to make those little noises of enjoyment? Rub herself against my stomach? Hold on for dear life and give one hundred and ten percent of herself to that kiss?

My fingers on her arm drift higher, rounding over her shoulder, traveling into her hair and running up behind her ear. She leans into my touch, nuzzling my hand. Her eyes flutter closed, eyelashes thick against her cheek. Like she is lost in the moment, in my touch, in whatever it is she's feeling.

"We have an audience," she murmurs.

Her words swipe the air from my lungs. What a fool. Here I was thinking she was simply enjoying me. She is not. This is a performance. And that kiss in the bathroom earlier? That was nothing more than a kindness shown to our past selves.

"Right." I stare out at the waves. "Let me know when nobody's looking. I'll stop touching you." There's an edge to my voice. It's not rude exactly, but it's not warm and fuzzy either. Firm, I suppose. It's all I can muster right now.

"Will do," she whispers, eyes still closed.

Shane calls me over after that. He's standing in a semi-circle with his groomsmen, holding a bottle of top-shelf tequila. He extends it like an offering, and I'm preparing to decline, but he says, "Why don't you be our bartender, Klein? Isn't that what you do now?"

I'm no stranger to uppity frat boys acting like fools. That's just another Friday night at Obstinate Daughter. The trick is to stare at them like they are basic and boring, then apply a thin film of disdain to the glare.

"Among other things," I answer.

"Like my ex," he says, winking and smiling like we share a secret. The other men (term used loosely) snicker and guffaw, as though Shane has issued a veiled burn.

Shane doesn't know me. Therefore, he is without the knowledge that I will never, ever stand for someone commenting on a woman in such a way, suggesting she is something we *do*.

I'm standing close enough to Shane that I can put my hand on his shoulder, turning him away from his group until his back faces them.

"Shane." I tighten my hold on his shoulder, pressing my thumb into his flesh until he grimaces. "If you ever talk about Paisley like that again, I'm going to make you a eunuch. I doubt Sienna will have much interest in you after that." I could soften my threat with a sunny smile, but I don't want to.

"Bro," Shane says, adopting a cordial tone. But I don't miss the tremor. "I don't know what that word means, but I get your point."

"Have fun looking it up later on tonight when you're alone." I slap his upper back twice, hard. "Pour your own tequila."

Paisley stands next to the bonfire, holding tight to a clear plastic cup half-filled with wine. The flames illuminate the front side of her body, warming up her features, highlighting her curvy profile. She watches me approach, and I don't slow down. I step right into her, gather her in my arms, and tip her head back. Then I kiss her, and yes, it's for show, but underneath the surface of this performance, I'm kissing her because I can't imagine not putting my lips on hers. The need to have her mouth, to stake my claim, is something raw and animalistic.

Yes, we're fake dating. No, Paisley isn't mine.

But she damn sure isn't anybody else's.

The world falls away in an instant. Ocean waves become white noise. Chatter ceases. Paisley's mouth responds to mine immediately. She kisses me back, matching my pressure, my intensity. I don't go so far as to taste her with my tongue, but I let my mouth linger on hers, and against her lips, I whisper, "That was our second best kiss."

Her lips curve into a smile I feel. "What was that for?"

"Your ex needed to be reminded you're someone else's girlfriend now. Mine."

I let her go, but keep an arm wrapped around her side.

We stick together for the rest of the night. My arm stays around her. When she talks to me, she touches my chest, my arms, some part of me.

I understand we are in front of people, and this is part of the charade.

But is it totally? Completely? Should it be this effortless?

---

Despite re-inflating the air mattress, it deflates by the middle of the night. I'm hoping last night's invitation extended by Paisley still holds true, because I don't feel like having back pain tomorrow.

Paisley rouses when I slip between the covers, making cute little sleepy noises. "Klein," she softly groans my name, backing up into my body. I freeze in place, waiting for her to fully wake up and elbow me in the stomach. She snuggles deeper, adjusting her head on the pillow. "I think while we're here for the week, we should give in and have fun together. Really enjoy this place." She yawns. "We should have sex. A lot of sex."

She falls fast asleep after that.

Not me. I stare at the ceiling, wide awake for the next hour.

Klein Madigan
@kleinthewriter

The sun, the sand, a drink in my hand. And a beautiful woman on the beach.

◯ 18    ♥ 2k    ↑↓ 7

## CHAPTER 27
*Paisley*

I start by flexing my foot.

When I don't hit a warm, solid mass, I creep out a few inches further.

Nothing.

Leg extends. Still nothing.

Opening my eyes confirms what I already knew. Klein isn't in my bed.

An odd emotion fills me. Not sadness but more… bereft. Did I want to wake up next to him? What does that mean?

The bedroom door creeps open. Klein walks in slowly, a smile spreading across his face when he sees I'm awake.

I push myself to sitting, attempting to work my fingers through my bed head. "Morning."

"Good morning," he answers, gently closing the door with his foot. He wears a bright smile and holds two mugs.

He brings me the coffee, my arms already outstretched.

"I hope this is okay," he says, handing over a cup decorated with brightly painted seashells. "This is how you prepared your coffee yesterday."

He remembered how I prepared my coffee yesterday? He was paying attention? I blink hard and sip, pushing away the pinches of pleasure assailing my heart.

There's a lot happening here I'm not used to. Waking up around somebody? That hasn't happened in years. Having someone pay attention to me so closely they remember the way I made my coffee? Possibly never.

Klein settles onto his side of the bed, facing me. Rumpled hair and sleepy face only makes him more handsome. He's been wearing a plain white T-shirt to sleep in. Is he doing that for my benefit? How do I tell him it would benefit me more if he lost the shirt? What if I—

*Oh my gosh.*

A mouthful of hot coffee threatens to fly onto the white bedspread.

The panic must be evident in my eyes, because Klein says, "It's all good, Paisley."

I gather my thoughts as I swallow. "That's what we always say, isn't it? We use that word, over and over. *Good.*"

Klein nods. "We do seem to use that word often."

"About what I said in the middle of the night," I hesitate, and Klein says firmly, "Paisley, don't worry. I won't hold you to it."

I lift my coffee cup to my lips, just to have something in front of me, a makeshift shield. I can't believe I'm about to do this. "What do you think about holding me to it?"

Klein opens his mouth. Closes it. Considers something, then opens his mouth again. "Do you think you're in a vulnerable place right now?"

"Yes," I answer honestly.

"That's what I thought," he sighs. "It took me an hour to fall back to sleep last night after you said that. I kept going over it in my mind, trying to figure out if your idea was very good, or very bad." He winces, probably at the poor word choices.

"You can do better than that," I say, frowning. "You are not very sad, you are morose!" I raise a fist, adopting the call-to-action tone of voice Robin Williams used in Dead Poets Society.

A smile plays on his mouth. "Did I tell you that was one of my top five favorite movies?"

"No, but it doesn't feel that far a leap to make."

He stays quiet, doing that thing where he knits his brow. By now I know it means he's thinking hard about something, and he isn't likely to say out loud what it is.

"I was trying to figure out if your idea was excellent, or ruinous." He smirks. "Was that better?"

I nod emphatically.

"I like how you challenge me."

"I like to challenge you." My chin tips up. "So, did you come to a conclusion?"

He shakes his head. "Nothing concrete. I don't want to take advantage of you, though, I know that for sure."

"I appreciate that, and I don't think you would be. This is a tough week for me, but it's nice having you here. It's nice to have someone on my side, not that sides need to be taken. And I know my grandma would be on my side, if forced to choose." I shrug, attempting to put into words what I'm feeling. What I'm asking for. "It's different with you. It's almost like I have a partner. A... friend?"

Klein nods, telling me that yes, we're friends.

It feels weird to finally call him my friend, when really that's what we've been for weeks now.

Sipping the last of my coffee, I set the cup on the nightstand and throw back the covers. My nightshirt has ridden up, and my eyes are on Klein the moment he spots the tattoo at the top of my thigh. His eyes flare, his lips part.

Innocently I stand, bunching my hem in my hand and lifting it to reveal the ink. "Surprised?"

His eyes darken, his jaw tenses. There is hunger on his face, a basic instinct to devour. *Me.*

He remains silent. Internally, I rejoice at having stolen all the words from a wordsmith.

I drop the hem, and he asks, "What does it say? I wasn't able to read it."

"I guess you'll have to find out another time. I need to get ready for hiking Old Baldy." Through the dresser mirror I watch his eyes follow me.

Am I smug?

Oh yes.

···🐚🐚🐚···

WE EMERGE FROM THE CANOPY OF DEEP GREEN LEAVES TO find the sky overhead is dark, the clouds heavy with moisture.

"We're almost there," I say to Klein, on his bike beside me.

He nods and glances up at the sky, not a trace of worry in his gaze.

The first raindrops, large and heavy, fall as we're guiding our bikes into the racks at the visitor center. We pay the fee and make a break for it, running across the grass lawn and up the handful of stairs through the wooden door and into the lighthouse.

Klein tugs a hand through his hair, shaking out the moisture. He looks around, getting his bearings. "This place was built in 1817," he tells me studiously.

Brushing rain from my face, I say, "Someone's been reading their *History of Bald Head Island* book."

He meanders to a wall, touching it with tentative fingers. "It was made out of red bricks, then covered in stucco and painted white." His hand moves up and over patches that have been worn away through time to reveal the red brick beneath.

Walking to the middle of the small area, he looks up at the wood plank ceiling. In the center is a rectangle of space that goes all the way up to the very top of the lighthouse. "One hundred and eight stairs," he says.

I look up with him, surveying all the stairs. "You ready for a butt workout?"

"Never say no to training your glutes," Klein jokes, starting on the stairs ahead of me.

The lights mounted on the walls give off a yellow-orange hue. During the day when the sun shines, the sunlight filters in through the top.

At the moment I don't have a preference over electric versus natural light. I'm a friend of any light that allows me to appreciate the fantastic ass two stairs in front of me.

"Do you go to the gym?" I'm trying to keep my tone light, offhand, as if I'm just making conversation.

"My apartment complex has a pretty decent gym. I use that, and then playing soccer helps." He pauses to glance back at me, smirking. "Why? Do you like what you see?"

"It would be hard not to see it," I grumble. "Since it's all up in my face right now."

We stop at the third landing. Klein motions to the next set of stairs. "Would you like to go first? I'm more than happy to stare at your ass."

A smile pushes at my lips. "Actually—"

A crash of thunder bangs into my sentence. I screech, throwing myself into Klein's arms. I'm not afraid of storms, but that was louder than anything I've ever heard.

"It's okay, Paisley," Klein soothes, rubbing my back.

"Sorry," I step back, getting my bearings. "Thunder doesn't usually bother me, but I felt that one in my bones."

"It's probably because we're inside here. There isn't anywhere for the sound to travel." Klein peers up at the top of the lighthouse. "We don't have to keep going, if you don't want to."

"I want to," I insist. "I've never been to the top during a storm."

"After you," he gestures.

I take the lead. After two flights, Klein says, "For somebody whose legs are shorter than mine, you seem to cover the same distance as me."

"I put my head down and power through."

"Kind of what you're doing here. At the wedding."

Huh. Insightful. "I guess you're right about that." I stop suddenly, pivoting on the stair. Klein freezes, two stairs down and nearly the same height as me. "But I don't think I'm putting my head down and powering through as much as I would be if you weren't here. You make all of this feel less… sharp."

"Sharp?"

"Yeah. It hurts less." Maybe even not at all. In fact, I think it might be enjoyable. I like having him around, showing him what I love about the island. And the tension between us? It's intoxicating.

"Well, Ace," he offers a half-bow. "I am at your service."

"That"—I lean closer, our noses separated by only a few inches—"is a place I think I like having you in."

I half-spin on the stairs, going the rest of the way up without stopping.

"Wow," Klein breathes in appreciation as he emerges through the small rectangular cutout and onto the top floor. "This is… *wow*."

"Cape Fear," I point east.

Klein joins me at the window, looking out at the darkened water. "Everything is lush. The treetops, so deep and green. Even the water. It's like a grayish-blue without the sun making it sparkle."

I like how he sees the world and describes it, and the tone of wonder in his voice as he does so. This is a man who is not afraid to feel awe. And even better, to show it.

The sky rumbles. Raindrops fall harder, tapping the outside of the lighthouse. The air inside is dank, the cobwebs in the corners moving with the breeze as it whips through.

My gaze lowers back to Klein, and I find he is already looking at me. The bruised sky makes his green eyes darker. His tongue slips out to run over his upper lip, then retreats, and he swallows. Hard. The undulation of his throat flips a switch inside of me. Thoughts of running my tongue over his Adam's apple consume me. I'm flummoxed by how attracted I am to this man. All of me wants to touch all of him. It's not just his body, either. It's his mind, the way he thinks. His heart.

I turn into him. He reaches for my hips, and when his hands find my skin, I tremble.

"Paisley," he says, but that's it. Just my name, delivered on a husky exhale.

My hands slip over his shoulders, roaming his upper back, converging at his neck and gliding up into his hair. My lips part, and my chin tips up. "Please kiss me, Klein."

His gaze settles on my mouth. "This wouldn't be making up for our bad kiss."

"No."

"Or kissing in front of people for the sake of our charade."

"No."

"This would be for us."

"Yes."

He cups my head, holding me, and lowers his mouth to mine.

Our first kiss was terrible, our second was hungry and desperate, our third was him staking a claim, but this one? It's decadent. Slow. A note of reverence, a touch of relief.

I moan into it, vibrating our lips, and Klein quirks a smile against me. He licks over the seam of my lips, urging me open. My tongue mingles with his, tasting the shock of peppermint and the sting of bitter coffee.

His thumb turns a heavy circle behind my ear as the rest of his palm keeps me secured in place. The heat of him in my mouth, of his hands on me, sends want racing through my body, into every crevice. Fingers curling into his hair, I arch up, desperate to be closer to him.

He pauses to look at me, eyes hooded, before coming back in for more, deeper, rougher, still torturously slow.

One hand leaves his hair, curling around to his neck, where his pulse thrums against my heated palm. His mouth drops, his hand fists my hair, angling my face to the shallow ceiling. His lips skim my neck, sucking delicately over my collarbone. Dropping lower, leaving tiny fires in his wake. His journey halted by the fabric of my top, he pulls it between his teeth and lightly tugs.

I arch higher, desperate for his mouth on me.

"More," I whisper.

Klein listens, gathering the top swell of my breast in his mouth, sucking and licking and kissing. A single finger dips into my top, finding its way into the cup of my bra.

This is *oh so good*, and almost painful because this is all that is available to us up here at the top of this lighthouse. If only I could transport us to—

"Just a few more steps and we'll be there," a woman's voice reaches up from below. "You'll have to hold it. There isn't a potty up here."

The word 'potty' may as well be a bucket of ice water. Klein lifts his head from my chest. Drops his hand. His lips are swollen. My fingers rub my lips, finding them swollen, too.

The sounds below us grow louder.

"If we don't get down now, we're going to have company up here, and I'm not particularly interested in being in a small space with people right now."

Klein turns for the rectangle cut out in the floor. "I'm not particularly interested in being in a small space with people *ever*. After you."

I lower myself through the cut out, and Klein follows when I reach the last stair.

A woman and two children stand off to the side, waiting. "One more coming down," I tell her.

She gives me a thumbs up and bends to tie a child's shoelace.

It's steep, and we're slower going down. A broken leg, or worse, would really put a damper on our time here. More and more, I'm starting to want to squeeze every drop of good times from this trip.

We reach the bottom, and Klein peers out. "The storm has passed. We should go. Your dad will be here soon."

The unbridled happiness falls off my face. My shoulders droop, squashed by an unseen weight. Dread comes over me as I recall the text message I saw just before I hopped on my bike to ride here. "I forgot to tell you. My dad is refusing to go to the house because my mom is there with Ben. I told him we'd meet him at The Beach Club for dinner instead."

Klein rubs the back of his neck. He looks like he wants to say something, but he's conflicted.

"What is it?" I ask as we step from the lighthouse and into the grass, slick with the rain clinging to the blades.

"Your grandma's making cowboy spaghetti for dinner, and you said it's basically your second favorite meal after tacos."

We reach our bikes. "Uh-huh."

Klein swipes a hand over his bike seat, brushing off the water that has pooled. "Why are you giving up your favorite dinner, cooked by one of your favorite people?"

I do the same to my seat. "Because my dad doesn't want to see my mom with her boyfriend. Nobody else volunteered to meet him, so—" I shrug. "I guess I will."

Sienna and Spencer simply bowed out, saying *I'm not going to accommodate him*. I know I could say the same, but there's a part of me that won't allow it. No matter what he believes, I never hurt him on purpose, and I won't start now.

Klein looks at me with tenderness. "You don't have to."

I laugh without any sound of happiness. "Yes, I do."

"I get that, but Paisley," Klein presses a hand to the small of my back. "Why?"

An uncomfortable huff comes from my throat. "Klein, I said why three seconds ago."

Klein shakes his head slowly. "You recited the reason your dad gave for not wanting to attend a family dinner. You didn't say why you agreed to miss out on having one of your favorite meals cooked for you by your grandma."

I look at my hands, gripping the bike's handles, knuckles turning white. "I don't want to force my dad to see something he doesn't want to see." I know where

Klein is going with this, and I do not want to follow him there.

"So you're going to accommodate him?"

"Klein, please." My voice tunnels. "I can't, okay? I can't take on all the family dynamics in one week."

Klein rubs a warm palm over my back. "I hate that you're going to miss out on something special with your grandma. My grandma passed away when I was a teenager, and I'd do just about anything to make sugar cookies with her again."

I parse through the jumbled mess of my thoughts, and can only come up with, "I know, I know. I'm the floor."

"That's what you said to me that first night we saw each other again. I assumed you were really drunk and that's why you said that. But unless you have a flask hidden somewhere on your body—"

"I might," I supply, to which he grins.

"Please help me understand what you mean by calling yourself the floor."

"Paloma was trying to tell me that I let my family walk all over me. She called me the floor, but she meant to say doormat."

"That makes a lot more sense than what I thought."

"What did you think?"

"That you were mentally unstable, but hot enough to excuse it."

I stick my tongue out at his joke, and he wraps an arm around me, pulling me in to his side. "You don't have to be a doormat."

"If I'm not a doormat, what will they do?"

"If you keep being a doormat, what will *you* do?"

I've never thought about what it does to me. Or what it's already done. "I just want to keep everyone happy."

Klein tucks a strand of hair behind my ear. "At the expense of your own."

"I don't know how to be different."

"Do you want to be?"

"Yes. Absolutely. I don't want to feel like I'm responsible for keeping them happy when they're doing something shitty. I never wanted to. I hated it every single time." Tears press at the backs of my eyes.

"It doesn't have to happen this week. Or this year. It takes time to implement change." He picks up my hand, pressing his lips to my knuckles. It's a soft kiss, yet it manages to sear me nonetheless. "Realizing it is the first step. Wanting to is the second."

I gaze up. Klein knows what I want, and meets me halfway. The kiss is slow, sweet, a gentle pressing of lips.

"Are we still meeting your dad tonight?" he asks when I pull away. "You can say yes. No judgment from me."

My answering nod is small. "I already told him I would, and it's almost too late to cancel."

"Then we'd better get back and get changed."

## CHAPTER 28
*Klein*

THE BEACH CLUB IS AN UPSCALE RESTAURANT CONNECTED to Nautilus, the hotel where Shane and Sienna will be married. White tablecloths drape over tables, and the mirrored bar reflects the ocean back at us.

Paisley leads the way, weaving through the full dining room. At a table near the back, beside the streak-free glass window, sits a man with his back to us.

If I were waiting for people, I'd sit where I could see them.

"Dad," Paisley greets, in a voice I've never heard before. Kind, but restrained. Polite. Crafted.

He stands when he hears her, depositing his linen napkin on his abandoned seat. "Paisley," he says, offering a stiff hug.

The difference between the way he hugs his daughter, and the way my mother hugged his daughter, is stark. "Dad, this is Klein. Klein, this is my father, Andrew."

We shake hands. "Nice to meet you, sir."

"Likewise, Klein. Interesting name."

I nod but stay silent. Not much can be said to me about my name that I haven't already heard. The underwear jokes abounded in school. Kids can be cruel, and when it came to me, they had more than enough material. I would've been happy if my name was all they had to make fun of me about, but, well, that's not the road I walked.

We settle in our seats, Paisley beside her dad at the square table, and me across from him. I'd pictured her dad as a titan, a captain of industry, but he's a regular guy, a *Joe*.

Judging a book by its cover is supposedly frowned upon, but I don't think very many people would take a look at this average-size man with a receding hairline and think it plausible he cheated on Robyn.

Andrew orders a bottle of cabernet for the table without asking if that's acceptable to anybody else.

"So, Dad," Paisley says after we've ordered appetizers and dinner. "How have you been?"

"Working my fingers to the bone."

Figurative language, of course. White-collar fingers stay intact and silky smooth.

Paisley leans back in her seat and sips her wine. "How's Perri?"

"Perri is fine."

Paisley explains to me, "Perri is my dad's administrative assistant. She's been working for him for twenty years."

"That's… nice." Lame, but what else am I supposed to say? Perri deserves a raise, no matter the figure of her current salary?

"Klein, what do you do?"

I'm surprised it took us this long to get to this point in the conversation. Here we go. Before I can say anything, Paisley answers.

"Klein is an author."

I know Paisley is trying to save me from having another experience similar to the one I had with her mother the night I met her, but it's fine. She doesn't have to lie for me.

"An aspiring author," I amend.

"Not for long," Paisley shoots back. She looks at her dad. "My company recently launched a digital marketing campaign centered around Klein's work, with the goal of creating and fostering his online footprint to appease an interested publisher."

Our appetizers arrive, and I squeeze Paisley's hand where it sits on top of the table.

"Nothing against your book, Klein, but Paisley, if you worked for me you wouldn't be delivering overly curated sentences about making stuff up and posting it."

Paisley's eyes drop down to her plate of melon wrapped prosciutto. "That's not what I do."

"What is it that you do, Andrew?" I'm changing the subject for the benefit of everybody at this table. If I have to listen to him put down his daughter even one more time he won't like what I have to say.

"I own a wealth management firm." Pride creeps into his voice. "Remember the housing bubble? I saw it coming and I shorted it."

He must assume I know what that means, but I don't.

Nor do I want to, so I nod along to keep him from explaining it to me.

"Made my clients very wealthy," he continues. "And me, too."

"Congratulations on the, uh, shorting."

Paisley lets out a garbled laugh. Andrew releases a tight smile, his first one since we arrived.

"Paisley here could have followed in my footsteps, but she decided to have a rebellious phase." He sighs, giving her a look, meant to let her know he is still disappointed in her. "I could have eventually given her the keys to the castle, but she didn't want them. She wanted to move across the country, and take classes that wouldn't get her anywhere." His cheeks are rosy from wine. "Did she tell you she took creative writing, Klein? Not surprisingly, she did not like it." He points at her with his wineglass. "Just like I told her she wouldn't."

I'm waiting for Paisley to stand up for herself, but she doesn't do it. She only sits there, quiet, gazing out the window.

If she won't, I will.

"Andrew, have you ever been to P Squared Marketing?"

"What is that?"

The guy doesn't know the name of his daughter's business? Doing my best to keep my already low, but still plummeting, opinion of Paisley's father from my tone, I answer, "The name of Paisley's firm."

He glances at Paisley over the rim of his wineglass. "No."

"You should visit her sometime and take a look at what she's built."

"I'm waiting for her to come to her senses and join me in my business."

"I won't," Paisley says, her voice small but firm. "I love what I do. The people I help."

"You can help people by managing their wealth."

"Before Klein, I had a client who owns three local coffee shops and was struggling to connect with her customers, and—"

"It's *coffee*," Andrew interrupts, "how hard can that business be? People are already addicted to your product."

"That's not what this woman saw for her business. She wanted an inviting environment, a meeting place, friendly faces and employees and patrons who developed rapport. But she didn't know that was what she wanted, only that something was missing from her business. My team and I helped her figure out her vision, and use it to show people what she had to offer."

Watching Paisley speak, gesturing with her hands, it's clear she's passionate about what she does. I have so much respect for that, for someone who loves what they do.

"That's nice, honey," Andrew says patronizingly. He's not giving up, he's merely switching tactics.

A fire lights in Paisley's eyes, and just when I think she's about to tell her dad off, the fire dies.

Someone clears our appetizers, and our server appears with dinner. We eat quietly, awkwardly, until Andrew says, "Is your mother about done embarrassing herself with the man-child?"

"He has a name." Paisley cuts into her steak with a little too much force.

"I don't care about his name."

Andrew went from patronizing to petulant. I think we know who the man-child really is.

"Mom's happy." Paisley chews her bite.

"Your mother isn't happy. She's throwing the world's longest fit."

Paisley takes another bite and avoids eye contact. "You're divorced."

"What's that?" He angles an ear toward her, but I'm betting he heard her just fine.

Paisley places her utensil on the table and attaches her gaze to his. "You're divorced."

"And whose fault is that?"

My fork clatters to my plate. Under the table, Paisley stomps on my foot. A warning.

"I'm not the one who was caught with my tongue down the neighbor's throat," Paisley says cooly. Andrew's nostrils flare.

"Is this your doing?" He spears a bite of steak and points his fork at me. "This attitude of hers?"

"No, sir. I believe this is *your* doing."

The muscles in his cheeks tighten.

Paisley continues. "I know you're sad. I know you're alone, and all you do is work. But you're only hurting yourself by acting this way." Paisley's tone is soft but firm. Respectful, but take no shit. "Of your three children, I'm the only one who came here tonight. Think about that. Sienna and Spencer aren't busy. They just don't offer themselves up as your punching bag like I do. But even I will eventually stop doing that."

I'm so proud of her I could applaud. Maybe stand up from the table, slow-clap, make a show of it. I wouldn't dare, because Paisley would be embarrassed, but I want to show her what an accomplishment this is.

Paisley pushes to her feet, grabbing her purse. I follow.

To her father, she says, "Dad, I love you, but I don't like you. I haven't for a while. It's up to you to figure out why."

Paisley strides away from the table. Anger turns the tips of Andrew's ears red, but I'm betting there's another emotion adding to the color. *Shame.*

That's good. It's okay to feel shame when you've done something shameful. It also means he's not completely unaware of the effects of his behavior.

I catch up to Paisley at the hostess stand. She's handing her credit card to the hostess and asking her to have the manager run the card. The baffled hostess hurries away, and Paisley turns to me, hand tapping the side of her leg.

"That felt good in the moment, but now I'm starting to feel scared."

Slipping my arms around her waist, I pull her in and kiss her forehead. "If it helps, I'm so damn proud of you." Gathering up my courage, I say, "If I had the opportunity to look my dad in the eyes and tell him off, I would. In a heartbeat."

Paisley's eyes widen. "You never talk about your dad."

"I know."

"Ms. Royce?" A man in a pressed white shirt extends Paisley's credit card.

She steps from my arms to take it from him and slide it back into place in her wallet. "Thank you."

His brows furrow. "Is everything alright?"

"Yes," she answers, using a pen from a cup on the

hostess stand to sign the check. "The service was fine. The food was delicious. The view was spectacular."

His head tips as he tries to understand. "What was the problem?"

"The company," Paisley responds, tossing down the pen. "Have a nice night."

Paisley strides out into the balmy evening. We're nearly to the golf cart when someone calls her name.

She whips around, seeking out the voice in the lighted area strewn with golf carts.

A woman walks closer, her sandy brown hair pulled into a bun. She looks familiar, though I'm certain I've never met her. I notice Tag climbing from a cart and put it all together. This is Shane and Tag's mom.

"So lovely to see you again, Rebecca," Paisley says, arms open for a hug. She pulls away, saying, "This is Klein. My boyfriend."

We shake hands, and I see where Shane got his eyes and nose. Tag, too. I offer him a wave as he strolls up behind his mom, and he does the same.

"It's good to see you, Paisley. I always liked you." She places a vertically held hand beside her mouth like she's telling a secret. "Kind of weird that Shane's marrying your sister."

Paisley laughs. "Agreed."

"Mom," Tag gusts a sigh. "You promised you weren't going to say stuff like that."

"I promised not to say stuff like that to *Shane*."

Tag looks apologetically at Paisley. "I'll have to rework the wording on that promise."

Rebecca shrugs. "Too bad. No retro-fitting."

Tag shakes his head. "We're going to miss our reservation if we don't get in there. I had to donate a kidney to get the ocean view."

Rebecca hugs Paisley again. "Wouldn't want that donation to be for nothing. Good to see you again, Paisley. Nice to meet you, Klein."

They head inside, and Paisley hands me the keys to the cart. "Back to the house, but I don't want to go inside. I want to sit on the beach and decompress before I face anybody."

We arrive back at the place, but I ask Paisley to wait for me while I run inside and grab something. I'm back five minutes later with a glass Tupperware dish, two forks, and a bottle of wine.

Paisley claps her hands. "Is that cowboy spaghetti?"

Adopting a terrible twang, I say, "Sure is, darlin'."

Paisley kisses my cheek. "All you need are boots and a hat. Klein the cowboy."

She grabs a beach blanket from the second row of the golf cart, and we carry our haul out onto the beach.

"Another day gone." Paisley plunks down on the blanket after she has spread it out.

I lay out the food and drink as she stares at the fraction of sun visible on the horizon. She grabs a fork and removes the top from the Tupperware, bending her head to inhale. "Smells just like I remember." She twirls the fork and loads spun noodles on her utensil. She sighs happily while chewing, capping off her huge bite with, "Tastes like I remember, too." She takes a few more bites and passes the container and fork to me.

While I eat, she says, "I wish they would all leave my

happy place alone. Why did my dad have to come here and bring all that up? Real life stays on the mainland. This island is for the good life, and the good life only. My sister shouldn't be getting married here."

I swallow. "Maybe it's her happy place, too?"

"Whose side are you on?"

"Always yours. But I wouldn't be much of a friend if I didn't offer ways to see or think of something differently."

Paisley bumps me with her shoulder. "What's the deal with your dad?"

I knew this was coming. I've only managed to avoid it this long because Paisley has been respectful of my boundary, careful to step back when she has sensed she came too close.

I set down the nearly-empty spaghetti container. Here we go. "Growing up, I had severe dyslexia."

Paisley blinks in surprise. She stays silent, waiting for me to continue.

"I know you wouldn't think that considering how much time I spend around books. I worked really hard to overcome it." I look out at the dark water, easily seeing my dad's face, feel his presence as he stood over me at my desk. "Overcoming it was the easy part. It was the time leading up to the diagnosis that was painful. It was caught a little late, in the second grade. I'd listen to the people around me and memorize what they were saying about a book. I came up with ways to work around the fact that when I looked at a word, the letters mixed themselves up. But then it started to show up in math, because we had word problems. My grades were really bad, and I remember the way my dad stood over me when I was doing homework. He'd watch me attempt the problems, and it made everything worse." In my mind's eye I see my small fingers trembling with a yellow pencil in my grip. "He was cruel. He'd ask me if I was an idiot. If I was blind. He once asked my mom why she gave him a son who was stupid."

Paisley gasps, lifting a palm to cover her mouth.

"I know. It's terrible. What he said. How he acted. He left soon after that. I felt like it was my fault, but my mom said he was doing us all a favor. Anyway, she's the real champion in this sad story. She went through the process of getting me an IEP. She got me accepted at a school specifically for dyslexia. It was expensive though, and even with help from the state it was nearly impossible to pay the remaining portion of the tuition. She did it, though. I don't know how. When I think of what she must've went without"—stinging starts in the backs of my eyes—"knowing how she sacrificed? It makes me want to find my father and look him in his eyes and tell him he didn't win. He's the loser in all this."

"He is," Paisley insists passionately.

"I know."

"Have you heard from him since he left?"

"Here and there. My mom had sole custody. He paid child support until we turned eighteen."

"When was the last time you saw him?"

"I ran into him at a high-end car show. He was there with a friend. A woman." I see him easily now, what he looked like that day. The way the event brochure stuck out of his back pocket, curved inward by his hand before he tucked it away. I'd known it was him immediately, even from the back. "He looked unhappy, and all I could think was that he'd done it for nothing. What was the point of him running out on his family if he wasn't even going to be happy?"

"Did you speak to him?"

"No. He looked up and saw me. He nodded at me." I pull the cork from the wine and take a drink from the bottle. "He just *nodded*."

To this day, I cannot decide if I'm happy he left me alone, or horrified.

"What the hell is that?" Paisley says, voice raised. "If I thought I was invested in marketing you before? Now I'm doubling down. We're going to make you a published author, Klein." She stabs at the ground with a pointed finger. "And I'm going to find your dad's address, and I'm going to send him a copy of your first book. With a photo of my middle finger."

I can't help but smile at her stern eyebrows, her ardent expression. "It's sweet the way you're defending me."

"Nobody gets to treat you that way, Klein. Nobody. And I'll gladly find your father and tell him he missed out."

The half-moon sends an arc of light on Paisley's face. Her eyes steel like a warrior, a woman with internal fortitude and strength, ready to engage in battle. I reach for her, caging her in my arms. She holds onto me, trusting me as I guide her back onto the blanket. Leaning on one forearm, I gaze down at her, drinking in the beauty in her face and in her soul.

"I like the way you want to stick up for me."

She frowns. "I don't like the idea of someone being unkind to you, even if it was almost twenty years ago."

"I didn't care for how your dad belittled your job tonight. Among other things."

She nods, and her hair settles on the blanket. "I could see how difficult it was for you to stop yourself from saying something."

"You stomped on my foot just as I was about to lose it." Using a fingertip, I brush aside a piece of hair from her forehead. "You did a good job holding your own."

"It was the first time I stood up to him like that." Her eyes search my face. "It felt so damn good."

"I'll bet."

Paisley's head turns, her gaze finding the ocean. The waves lap at the shore, the most soothing of sounds. She's quiet for a full minute before she says, "How do you feel about kiteboarding tomorrow morning?"

"Kiteboarding?"

"A big kite pulls you over the water while you ride on a board."

"Hmm." I don't love the idea of not knowing what's underneath me, but I'm fast becoming addicted to Paisley's smile when she introduces me to another of her beloved island activities. "I'll do it," I confirm.

"Klein?"

"Yeah?"

"I'd like you to kiss me for a while. And then later, when we're going to bed, don't even pretend to sleep on the air mattress we know is going to deflate."

My heart expands in my chest. "As you wish."

I do exactly as she's asked.

How could I not?

**Klein Madigan**
@kleinthewriter

Future setting: a rainy lighthouse.

◯ 21   ♥ 3k   ⟲ 8

# CHAPTER 29
## *Paisley*

"How badly does it hurt?"

My arms encircle Klein's waist, allowing him to lean on me as he limps off the golf cart in front of the house.

Klein winces as he puts weight on his right foot. "More than a bee."

I've been stung by bees three times in my life, so I understand at least a fraction of what he's feeling.

"I still can't believe you were stung by a jellyfish. I've been swimming in the same waters my whole life and never been close to one."

Following our kiteboarding, Klein and I decided to spend some time on the beach. I stayed on the shore, while he ventured out into the water. At a depth barely deep enough for wading, Klein's eyes suddenly flared and his head reared back. With a hand tented over my eyes to block the sun, I watched Klein head for me with a grimace twisting his face.

"Lucky me," he manages, twisting to look at his right

calf. An angry looking long line shines red and swollen on his skin, lashed by a tentacle. "Fucker," he manages.

"Yeah," I chant, getting in on the name-calling. "Asshole jellyfish." We arrive at the bottom of the stairs. "How do you feel about making it up those?"

Klein blows out a breath. "I don't have much of a choice unless I plan on sleeping outside."

"I'd sleep outside with you. It might be chilly, but we can grab a couple extra blankets and be alright."

"You're sweet." Klein leans over and kisses my forehead, and my insides melt a tiny bit. "You were really worried about me when it happened."

"Well, yeah. At first I thought maybe it was a shark."

Klein pales. "A shark? Are those common around here?"

"Uh. No?"

"You're a terrible liar."

"I sure hope you're not right about that or we're facing an uphill battle for the remainder of the week."

Klein attempts a smile, but only manages a grimace.

"Come on," I urge him gently. "The sooner we get you up to our room, the faster I can give you pain medicine and get hot water running in the bathtub."

I'd looked up how to treat a jellyfish sting as soon as I could get my phone from my beach bag.

It's slow going, but we make it into the house. First, we encounter my mother, who tells us to apply vinegar to the sting. Then my grandmother tells us she'll leave hydrocortisone cream outside of the bedroom door if he'd like to use that. Shane asks if Klein would like a shot of tequila, and Klein glares at him. Shane backs off, and I make a mental note to inquire about that exchange later. We find Spencer sprawled out on an armchair, staring at his phone as we pass through the living room. Phone still positioned in front of his face, Spencer looks at Klein's calf, and says in a voice devoid of emotion, "Sucks, bro."

It actually makes Klein laugh, which makes me laugh. I shake my head as we walk down the hall. "Later he'll probably tell you that the jellyfish that got you must've been a banger."

"Sorry, I don't speak cool kid. What does 'banger' mean?"

"It means something that's exceptional. I had to look it up the last time I heard him say it. I'm only twenty-six and I'm already having to look up what the young-uns say."

"We get old fast these days." Klein winces when his leg brushes the bedroom doorframe on our way through. "Fuck, that hurt."

"Just a little further," I urge, taking him to the bathroom and helping him sit on the edge of the tub.

I turn on the hot water and run my hand through until it's almost too hot to bear. "The medical website I found said to soak it for forty-five minutes in water that is as hot as you can stand it. Is this temperature okay?" Klein tests the running water and nods.

I grab two pain reliever tablets from my toiletries case while the tub fills halfway. He swallows them without water, and I get him situated with towels behind him so he can lean on the glass shower that is connected to the tub. He slides his hurt leg into the water, sucking a breath between his teeth when the hot water envelops his calf. Standing back, I survey the scene to see if the set up works. "Do you think it would work better if you were all the way in the tub?"

"Probably," he agrees.

"I can help you undress. Or, I mean, I'm sure you can undress, but I can turn around and give you privacy and just be here if you need assistance."

Klein looks up at me through his lashes. He looks tired. Disappointed. Slightly beaten down. "I'm not worried about you getting an eyeful if there's future fun on our agenda."

I stop, surprised. "*Fun* fun? Or more kiteboarding fun?"

"I've had my lifetime's fill of kiteboarding. I'm talking about two-person only fun." He points at me, saying, "Person one." His finger swings back to his chest. "Person two."

Anticipation slices through me. Am I going to get exactly what I've asked for? "I guess that means you've either decided you're done being a considerate gentleman, or that it wouldn't be taking advantage of me after all."

"I determined it is not taking advantage of you. And I will only be a considerate gentleman when you want me to."

The grin splitting my face is borderline embarrassing. I swear, if this man wasn't nursing a jellyfish sting, I would pounce on him right now.

I step up to the side of the bathtub. "Shirt first, Word Daddy."

Klein makes a face. "Word Daddy?"

"Cecily," I explain, and Klein nods. "That actually makes sense."

Klein can take his shirt off by himself, so I'm really only there for moral support. I want to touch him so badly though, to run my hands over those abs that were on full display at the beach earlier, that I force upon him my unnecessary help. He laughs when I drag my fingernails over his chest. The shirt clears his head, and I arrange it nicely on the stool beside the tub so he can put it on when he gets out.

"Shorts next," I say, and I try to act nonchalant, like I'm some kind of nurse and I see this stuff so frequently I'm immune to it.

Klein hooks his thumbs in the waistband of his shorts, then pauses. "These are swim trunks, so I could probably just wear them."

I act like it's no big deal, but if I'm being honest with myself, I most definitely would like a sneak preview. "You do you, Wordsmith."

He lowers himself all the way in the tub, shorts on. "The sting has made it, umm, *difficult* for me to look the way I want to look for you the first time you see me."

I swallow a rock hard lump in my throat. Am I spending too much time picturing Klein, smooth and long and hard and ready? If the moisture between my legs is any indication, the answer is yes. "Understand that. It would be like me undressing in front of you for the first time and wearing nude colored full-butt underwear."

Klein looks up at me from the tub. For someone in a moderate amount of pain, he doesn't look to be too put out. "For the record, I'd be perfectly happy to see you in any and all undergarments."

"Even pantaloons?"

His arm shoots out, taking me by surprise, and smacks my ass. I yelp and hop out of his reach.

"Per the itinerary, I have to go help my sister and the 'I do' crew with the favors for the wedding guests. I'll be back soon though. Can I bring you anything?"

His gaze drops to my backside. "Just your fine ass."

I sashay from the room, giving him a show on my way out.

---

"Sorry I'm late," I call, walking into the home down the road the three bridesmaids are sharing.

"In here," Sienna calls from the back of the house.

I follow voices until I find everyone gathered around a white-washed oval table. I say hello to Farhana and Maren, seated at the table with my sister. Wren has her back to me, bent over a box as she parses its contents.

My sister waves from her seat, and when I take the empty seat beside hers, she surprises me by reaching out and hugging me. After a second of stiffness, I melt into it. My sister isn't a hugger by nature. Even when she was a baby, she preferred to be put down on her play mat, left to bat at the toys that hung overhead.

Sienna releases me, but looks me in the eyes and says, "I'm happy you're here, Paisley."

I nod like a bobblehead. I don't know what to say. My sister can't start being nice now. I need her to be self-centered and self-absorbed, so I can be mildly antagonistic and low-key disagreeable while still meeting her expectations.

"Me too," I answer. It's not a lie. I don't want to be left out or left behind. And I like having Klein here on the island.

"I had lunch with Dad just before I came here. He told me what you said to him last night."

I nod slowly, rubbing at my dry eyes as a trickle of dread filters through me. Where is this going?

"He said he's proud of you, Pais." She takes in my shocked expression and adds, "He also said all this would've been a hell of a lot easier if you'd stayed on the path he set for you." She rolls her eyes. "He's still *Dad*. But I think maybe he'll come around."

Wren sets an armload of ribbon and other supplies on the table and asks, "Who wants champagne?" We all raise our hands.

Farhana, Maren, Sienna and I work on unboxing the favor components. We separate them into sections, taking place along the large table and forming an assembly line. Wren makes two trips into the kitchen and back, delivering champagne.

Farhana turns on Taylor Swift, and we listen while we work. Maren talks about a guy she matched with who claims to be an environmental lawyer. She says she has her doubts about his truthfulness because he won't tell her the name of the firm where he works. Everyone, with the exception of my sister, trades online dating horror stories that make me happy I've never joined an app.

I'm quiet, listening to them chat. There isn't much for me to add that wouldn't be a lie of some degree.

Sienna brings me into the conversation when she says, "Klein seems like a really good guy, Pais."

"He is," I nod, doing my job of tying light blue ribbons around the tops of the small glass candy jars. Klein should be out of the bathtub by now. I wonder how he's feeling, or if he needs anything? *Besides my fine ass.* The thought brings a smile to my face.

"Ohhh, look at that grin," Wren says, polishing off her champagne. Mine is long gone. There wasn't much else to do while they all talked. "That's the smile of a woman in love."

I finish tying the next ribbon. "I don't know about love. We haven't talked about all that yet."

"You don't have to talk about it. Just watch the man's actions."

"The way he looks at you," Maren says dreamily. She affixes the personalized tag to the little knob on the top of the candy jar after I've tied the ribbon.

"That," Wren says, a smile sliding from one side of her mouth, "and the fact he threatened to castrate Shane."

I freeze. "What?"

To my right, Sienna echoes me.

Wren shifts uncomfortably. "I assumed you both knew." Her eyes dart between us. "Shane made a tasteless joke about Paisley, and Klein didn't appreciate it. Tag was standing next to them and overheard Klein."

My eyebrows creep up my forehead. "Tag heard Klein threaten castration?"

"In a manner of speaking. He used the word 'eunuch.' We had to look it up."

Maren nudges her. "Who's 'we'?"

"Me and Tag."

Maren smacks her forearm. "Was he in your room last night? Is that what I was hearing?"

Wren blushes. "Maybe."

Farhana gasps. "You ho."

Wren cackles. "We're on a secluded island for five more days. You should both be trying to get laid, too."

While they argue back and forth about the merits and pitfalls of a fling with people they might have to see again in the future, I nudge Sienna's foot under the table. Her furrowed brow worries me.

*I'm fine*, she mouths.

But she's not, and we both know it. We also know a conversation about Shane is off the table. Their highlight reel is all I'm allowed, and I understand. I don't know that I want more than that, but I *want* to want more. I want to be there for her.

Wren gets my attention by saying, "I bet Klein is laying Paisley out every night. And every morning too, probably, right Paisley? Is Klein a morning guy?" Excitement widens her eyes. "I bet that's why you were late arriving!"

If only that was the reason. "More like taking care of Klein's jellyfish sting."

They groan collectively. Farhana asks, "Is he okay?"

"A typical reaction, thankfully. Not severe."

"Paisley's going to have to give him the good loving tonight," Wren quips. "The guy took a plane, car, and ferry to spend the week with your ex, and ends up stung by a jellyfish."

I keep my eyes off my sister on purpose. I don't want to see whatever look is on her face, and I don't want her to feel like she has to plaster on a certain expression for my benefit. I hadn't thought about how this might feel for her, having Shane around his ex all week. In my head, he's my ex. I never think of myself as his.

To be fair, it's not as if I invited myself here. And it's true that none of us would be in this position if my sister weren't marrying him. But this is the first time we've all three been in the same room. And it's not just one room, one time. It's a weeklong party. There's an *itinerary*.

Is Sienna, now that she is in the thick of it, regretting any of this?

The conversation moves on. We finish assembling gifts.

By the time I'm climbing back on my golf cart, my sister and Shane are far from my mind.

But Klein? He's at the forefront.

And I have an idea.

## CHAPTER 30
*Klein*

I lied to Paisley about how much the sting hurt. It killed me the ride back to the house, and going up the stairs was agony. But leaning on her small frame, watching her prepare the hot water, and offer to help me undress? There were anesthetic properties in her care.

I'm on the bed in the towel I'd wrapped around myself when I got out of the bathtub and shucked my wet shorts. The sting looks mean, red and angry, but on the bright side it's not keeping me from lying down. The pain when it happened was shocking, almost like electricity at first, and then a hot throbbing. It has dulled now, thanks to Paisley nursing me.

I wonder how much longer Paisley will be gone? I should probably get dressed. Looking out the window though, at the glimmering blue ocean, it's not easy to make myself get up. I won't have this view forever. I'll spend a few more minutes savoring it, then I'll dress.

We've been on the island for three days, and I haven't been able to figure out Paisley's family yet. It's hard to put my finger on it, but they're missing something. A cohesion, perhaps? They seem like satellites, existing in the same orbit, but never touching. I've always understood that people can be rich in a variety of ways, and now I'm seeing firsthand what it means to have monetary wealth, but be lacking in love and belonging and acceptance.

It's not a topic I like to think about, but even with my dad—

"Hey," comes a soft, tentative voice.

I'm smiling before my eyes meet hers.

Paisley hovers in the open doorway. Her hair is tied on the top of her head, messy, still windblown and beach matted from earlier. She hadn't cleaned up before going to meet her sister. She'd only taken care of me.

"How are you feeling?" Paisley closes the door softly behind her. She bites the corner of her lower lip nervously, but her eyes dance, mischievous.

"You didn't get dressed?" she asks, coming closer.

I look down at the towel. "I thought I had a little more time before you came back. If you want to bring me my clothes, I'll get dressed."

Instead of walking to the bathroom for my things, Paisley comes closer to the bed. She settles down at the end, sitting the same way I sat yesterday morning when I brought her coffee.

"May I?" she reaches for me, fingers brushing my ankle. "Just want to check on the patient."

I turn my right leg over, just enough so she can see the red line. She sucks air through her teeth at the sight. "My grandma left that cream, if you want it." Paisley pats her shorts pocket. "I picked it up before I came in here."

"Maybe later," I answer, because at this precise moment I'd rather not smell medicinal.

"I feel terrible this happened to you," she says, her voice on the jagged end of a whisper.

"It's just a jellyfish sting. Could be worse."

"True. You could be made a eunuch."

The corners of my mouth curve as I try not to laugh. "He's lucky I stopped there."

"Good to know you're not above medieval torture methods." With a fisted hand propped under her chin, she asks, "What did he say?"

I'd rather not tell her, only because I don't want to watch her face absorb it. But I'm not going to lie. "He suggested he and I had both"—my fingers lift for air quotes—"*done* you."

"Ahh." She nods, nonplussed. "So he woke up and chose to be classy."

Her sarcastic comment draws out my laughter. I'm relieved she's not upset.

Paisley repositions herself so she's sitting back on her heels, knees bent and thighs pressed together. "I shouldn't be surprised you rode in on your white horse and gallantly fought for my honor." Her hands clasp, resting on the crevice formed by her legs, and there's something about the tenderness evident in her expression that steals my breath.

"Klein." My name on her lips is ragged, harsh, silk over broken glass. "You've been so good to me since we arrived on the island. And somehow I know you're going to keep being good to me."

There's that word we keep using. *Good.*

My mouth opens to speak, but whatever I had to say is halted by Paisley running her fingertips up the inside of my left leg. Her touch travels higher, meets the hem of the plush towel.

I swallow the boulder in my throat, unsure of what to do or say.

"And I was thinking," Paisley continues, a lone fingertip swooping over my thigh muscle, "that I'd like to be good to you, too."

"You already are," I grit out. "We're each holding up our end of the deal." I know because I check the account regularly, I see the photos and captions Cecily is creating.

Paisley rubs my thigh. My midsection coils, blood rushing into a part of my body I've maintained near-perfect control over when I'm around Paisley.

Through a fringe of golden lashes her gaze tumbles down to me. She looks vulnerable and tentative, and seeing Paisley less than confident rips at my chest. I don't know why, only that it does.

The tip of her tongue pokes out and swipes over her upper lip. "This wouldn't be a part of our deal." One corner of her mouth lifts in a lopsided smile. "It would be a part of our new deal. Our *fun* deal."

My heartbeats pick up pace.

Paisley rises, still on her knees but no longer sitting on her heels. "Klein, what do you say? Will you allow me to be good to you? Help you forget about your sting for a little while?"

Sting? Oh, right. All this talk, this tension, shoved the sting and its pain to the back of my mind. But with Paisley's mention of it, the searing heat on my leg flares.

I don't want Paisley doing anything with me out of guilt. Or anything else that's not purely because she desires to.

Sitting up from the mountain of pillows, I place two fingers under her chin and align our gazes.

"Paisley, I know this week has been a lot for you emotionally, and I don't want you to—"

She shakes her head, a tiny movement that causes her messy bun to bounce. "That's not it, Klein. This is something I want to do. Something I've"—her jaw shifts under my touch as she bites at her lower lip—"thought about already."

Of all the words I thought might come from Paisley Royce's mouth today, that admittance was not one of them.

"I've thought about you, too. That way." I breathe a short laugh. "Every way."

Paisley grins. She moves her chin left, breaking my touch on her. Her palms are on my thighs, her warmth seeping into my skin. Her hands glide up, disappearing under the towel.

My muscles flex at her soft touch, and in anticipation.

"Lie back," Paisley whispers.

I do as she says. Using my thighs to steady her, Paisley leans in, pressing her lips to my lower stomach. Her lips move over the muscle slowly, and she murmurs, "I like your body, Klein. The way your hips have this 'v' shape," she shifts left, running her tongue along the diagonal, until she's stopped by the rolled top of the towel. "It was very distracting on the beach earlier."

"My apologies."

She fists the top of the towel and tugs, and the end of the towel that was tucked in gives way. She looks up at me, gaze wickedly playful.

"Poor Klein," she pouts, batting her eyelashes.

"Poor me," I say, trying not to smile. "So sad."

Paisley sits back enough to grab both ends of the towel. Slowly, she pulls them apart, like opening the blinds on a window.

As if driven by a spring, I surge forward.

Paisley licks her lips, saying impishly, "Would you look at that? It doesn't light up."

I've never been in this position and laughed before, but here I am. Chuckling at Paisley's wit, even on the precipice of something so intimate.

Paisley grips the part of me that's throbbing. Her fisted hand climbs, gathering dew, and says, "I hope this takes your mind off things."

My mind is already taken off *things*. What pain? Where?

And then Paisley leans forward. Wraps her mouth around me, warm, wet, and perfect.

Stars. That's what I see. My head tips back and I look up at the ceiling as my brain adjusts to the simple fact this is Paisley—*Paisley!*—with her mouth on me.

My gaze snaps back down. I can't miss a moment of this. Paisley's sunshine hair, the sun illuminating her right side, the diamond stud in her ear casting prisms of light on the wall.

My thumb rubs over her cheek. Her ocean-eyed gaze meets mine. She looks sexy as hell, a vixen, but somehow sweet.

What have I done right in this life to deserve Paisley on her knees, mouth filled with me, gazing up at me with an intoxicating mix of sweetness and desire?

Paisley's eyes flicker closed, her gaze drops, and she gets to work.

My entire world fades into the background, and there is only this moment, beautiful Paisley's head bobbing in my lap, letting down her guard and offering this piece of herself.

My focus narrows, becoming a pinpoint, and the pleasure ascends. I look around for a tissue, a T-shirt, but there's nothing in supply. Only the towel trapped under my body.

"Paisley," I groan, stroking her cheek with my knuckles. "Soon. I'm going to—"

She hums, not letting up. The peak nears, my muscles tightening, and I attempt to move away from her, but she locks my hips into place with her hands and pushes herself further down on me.

My eyes close as white flashes across my vision. "Paisley," I croak, my hand wrapped around the side of her neck.

My body jerks, and under my palm Paisley's throat undulates.

*Oh.*

*Fuck.*

Paisley releases me tenderly, and my eyes blink open. She returns to sitting on her heels, and if it weren't for the leftover shock of my orgasm, I'd consider everything that just happened one of my many fantasies about this woman.

Paisley's eyebrows lift, gaze watery. "Feeling any pain?"

Struggling to find my way out of my post-fellatio haze, it takes me a moment to decipher what she means. "I'm feeling everything but pain." I'm not only feeling the afterglow of pleasure, I'm feeling all kinds of things I'm not supposed to. Feelings that weren't a part of our deal. Feelings that make me want to tell her to forget our deal and just let me be here, on the island, in some capacity that isn't fake.

What would she do if I said that? Should I say that?

"Klein, can I be honest with you?"

"Always," I hurry to confirm. I throw the towel around my lap. No need to be the only naked one here. Also, my thigh muscles are twitching.

Paisley captures the side of her lower lip between her teeth. "I feel a little shy now."

"You?"

"Yes. Me."

"Why?"

"Well," she twists the comforter. "That was probably the boldest thing I've ever done."

"I don't think that's true."

Her head snaps up. "Until now, that act was a perk reserved for boyfriends."

I reach for her hand, stilling the twisting motion. "You coming here with a fake boyfriend in tow was bold. You coming here at all was brave."

She crosses her arms and looks away, playfully haughty. "You're saying that because I just blew you."

I shake my head, laughing once again at something this woman has said. Leaning forward, I wrap my arms around her and lift. She gasps, then lets herself be lifted, tucked against my chest. She's careful of my right leg, and I'm grateful. The pain has come back, but I know it was actually always there. The distraction she provided was effective.

Paisley's head settles on my chest. Using the palm of her hand, she drums a beat on the center of my chest. "That's the sound of your heart, Klein. It's still beating fast. I made it race."

"No past tense."

Paisley lifts her head, staring deep into my eyes. "What do you mean?"

"Present tense. You *are* making my heart race."

She shakes her head as much as she can in this position. "It's the effects of—"

"You, Paisley. It's the effects of you."

"Klein." But that's all she says. Just my name.

"Paisley, we've agreed to have fun this week. And we are. We will," I amend. There is so much more I want to do with this woman. I want to make her body sing, her eyes search the ceiling unseeingly. "But that doesn't mean my heart can't beat faster around you."

She looks at me for a long second, and then says, "I'd do well to remember you are a wordsmith. You spend your days immersed in language, toying with words, adjusting them to elicit emotional response."

She doesn't get it. She doesn't want to get it, either. She wants to make light of my words, to not allow them their weight.

What is she afraid of?

I'll give her this one. I'll let her have a pass. This week

we'll have the kind of fun she is asking for. But will that be enough for me?

"Klein the writer," I say, using one of the nicknames she's given me. I'm giving her an out, something to fall back on.

"Klein the writer," she echoes. "I'm going to rinse my mouth out."

From where I lie I can see Paisley standing in front of the bathroom mirror, squeezing a pea-sized amount of toothpaste onto her fingertip. She adds the toothpaste and a handful of water to her mouth and swishes. Through the mirror she meets my eyes, and I swear even from across the room a faint shade of pink blooms on her cheeks.

She spits, rinses, and blots her mouth with a hand towel. Exiting the bathroom, she comes to stand in front of me. Her lips are pursed for a second before she asks, "Are we good?"

"Good?" I repeat disbelievingly, like a dummy. I'm James Bond realizing his life's purpose, finally closing his decades-long story arc. I'm Spiderman kissing Mary Jane upside down. I'm Klein Madigan, fresh off a *lascivious act* with the object of his affection. "Paisley, I'm better than good."

"Glad to hear it." She adjusts the P on her necklace. "I'm not going to lie, I don't know what to do now." Her floundering is endearing.

"Maybe grab some clothes for me out of the dresser? I'll get dressed and we can go downstairs."

Without another word she gets clothes from the dresser and hands them over, then goes into the bathroom to brush her hair and make herself presentable (her words—I think she looks perfect as is.).

I dress, careful of my sting.

Paisley returns, hair wrapped into a bun at the nape of her neck. I reach for her hand, ignoring the pain in my leg.

"Let's go spend some time with your family before we have to go to Shane's place tonight."

"Ugh," Paisley groans. "The mixer. I forgot about that."

Taking her hand, I open the bedroom door for her. "Maybe it'll be better than you think."

Paisley presses up on tiptoe, delivering a kiss to my cheek. "You're going to be there, so it's already better."

Klein Madigan
@kleinthewriter

A jellyfish bested me. It wouldn't be a story without a plot twist, yeah?

◯ 32   ♥ 4k   ↻ 10

## CHAPTER 31
*Paisley*

Following a late afternoon spent playing board games with my family, Sienna and I broke off from the group to get ready. Klein stayed with Ben, my mom, and grandma, locked into a serious game of Catan.

When Sienna and I were younger, we'd be in the same bathroom getting dolled up for an event. Now the ever-widening chasm between us had us going our separate ways to get ready.

Sienna was stiff all afternoon, smiling perfunctorily but not really a part of the action. I hadn't worried because I'd been too busy laughing, too busy smiling, too busy enjoying Klein's presence around my family. Everybody likes him, it's easy to see. Who wouldn't?

So much for that tiny step Sienna and I took while we were assembling favors earlier. Was it Wren's story about Klein and Shane? I'd purposely kept my attention from her after Wren told us, it's possible I missed an important non-verbal reaction.

I'm pressing a mascara wand to my lashes when Sienna slips into my bathroom.

"You look pretty," she says, fingering the fabric of my ruffled mini-dress. Her voice is hesitant, but soft, like she's silently amending this afternoon's behavior. "I love the deep neckline." She mimics the cut on her own chest. "And the color."

Hot pink and bright orange floral is a color combo that can't be pulled off just anywhere, but here it works.

"I like your dress, too," I say, leaning into the mirror and applying a second coat of mascara before the first coat dries.

Through the mirror Sienna sends me a dismayed frown. "Don't tell anybody, but I'm getting sick of wearing white."

"Just because you're the bride doesn't mean you have to wear white all week." I finish applying mascara to the corners of my eyelashes and secure the wand in the tube.

"I thought it would be fun." She looks longingly at my outfit. "But I miss color."

Grabbing her wrist, I say, "We could trade. You wear mine, and I'll wear yours." It's not me being a pleaser, it's me being kind, and it makes my offer feel good instead of many other negative emotions.

Sienna considers it, then shakes her head, her red-beaded chandelier earrings swinging. "You can't show up in white, Paisley."

She's right, but only kind of. Technically, I can show up in anything I want. But convention says white is verboten.

"But I'll take it with me on my honeymoon, if you don't mind."

"I'll give it to you when we leave."

"Thanks." Sienna leans into the mirror, running a fingertip along her lower lip that's already perfectly lined and lipsticked.

"I asked Shane about what Wren said. His comment," she clarifies, not that a clarification is needed. "He said it was a joke Klein took the wrong way."

She looks like she needs me to believe it, or at least say I believe it. I could make a fuss, state my opinion, but for what? I know I'm trying to be more assertive with my family, but this doesn't feel like a hill I need to die on.

"Sure," I say agreeably.

"I just don't want you to feel like Shane is being weird or anything," Sienna adds, her words at 1.5x speed.

"No weirdness perceived," I assure.

Together we walk to the living room. Early evening sun streams through the large window. The Beach Boys plays from a speaker on the side table.

Klein places the last of the game pieces in the box. His eyes zero in on me. "Your grandma won. She has no mercy."

"No fucks given," she sings out from the far side of the couch.

"Grandma," I admonish, but it's playful. She's wearing her happy smile.

Through the living room window I spy my mom and Ben, sitting on the padded wicker love seat sharing a cocktail.

"You ladies look beautiful," my grandma says, smiling at us.

"Why don't you come, Grandma? Mix it up with the bridal party?" Sienna sits beside Grandma and takes her hand.

Grandma waves her off. "You must be joking. That group can't handle me."

Klein stands, coming to me in the center of the room. The look on his face is predatory. He twirls me around once, a slow revolution. "You're beautiful."

"It's nothing."

"It's something," he whispers. "You're something."

I press into him, lightly.

I haven't been able to stop thinking about what happened between us earlier. Even though I planned it, even though I spent the ride from the bridesmaid's house thinking it through, it somehow managed to surprise me.

By the time I made it to our bedroom door, I'd second-guessed myself and had nearly talked myself out of it. But then there Klein was, lying on the bed wearing a towel, and my rational thought disappeared.

There wasn't an ounce of me that didn't want to have him in my mouth, to feel him unravel on my tongue.

And then I did exactly that. And it was... phenomenal. I meant what I said, that before today, that act had been a boyfriend perk.

But there's something about Klein that makes me want to come out of my skin, to shed the person I've known myself to be until now. He makes me want to try new things. Maybe it's because I don't feel judged by him. It's safe. He's safe.

Though I admit, looking at him now, the emotions he's eliciting? They are dangerous.

We've agreed to have fun this week, but like Klein said earlier, that doesn't mean our heartbeats can't quicken their pace around one another.

Is that what this is? Thrill?

Klein nuzzles the side of my head. "You're having some deep thoughts, Royce."

"Tell me, Madigan, how could you possibly know that?"

"When you're thinking hard about something, your lips pucker the tiniest amount"—he draws a finger across my lips—"and your eyebrows draw together in the center." His touch ghosts the bridge of my nose, smoothing the skin between my eyebrows.

"I was thinking about earlier," I admit.

"What about it?" Low and grumbly, his voice vibrates over my skin.

My hand runs up his arm, then back down, fingers intertwining with his. "How much I liked it."

"I liked it too."

My mind plucks the memory, serving it up to me. Thick and heavy in my throat, the way I had to relax my muscles to accommodate him. "I remember."

He tucks a lock of hair behind my ear. The man hasn't had a single drink, but the way he's looking at me now, there's a drunkenness to his eyes, a haze.

"Paisley." His touch slides over my jaw, halting at my chin. He leans in, his lips tickling my lobe, his words a low hum against the shell of my ear. "When we get back here tonight, I am going to fuck you so well, so *good*, I'll have to clamp my hand over your mouth to keep everybody from hearing your screams."

The air in my lungs thickens, becoming sticky. A shallow breath drags through my nose, and I whisper, "If you don't, I will. That face washing device is a vibrator."

He grins, slow and sexy. "I know."

"Um. Hey." My sister's face pops into my field of vision. "Not to burst your bubble, but there are other people in this room right now, and it's super awkward that you guys are standing here whispering."

"Sorry," I say, but I don't mean it. Not even a little.

"I'm not sorry," Klein says, eyes on me even though his words are meant for Sienna. "When your sister is in the room with me, she might as well be the only one. That's something I'll never be sorry for."

I smile at Klein, then look at my sister. I wish I could say she looks happy for me, and I guess she does, but she looks other things, too. Envious. Resentful.

Why? She's the one getting married in a handful of days. She's the one who should be glowing.

"Very sweet," she clips. "It's obvious you are a great writer."

"Anyway," I break in before Sienna gets any more acerbic. "We better get going. At this point, you will be fashionably late, but anything past that is considered rude."

Sienna pivots and walks away. What the hell? Her behavior is giving me whiplash.

I wave at Grandma, and wish her a nice night. She wears a knowing smirk, offering me a saucy wink. Did she hear my conversation with Klein over the crooning of

The Beach Boys? Probably not. Maybe it was our body language she was reading.

Grandma shoos us out. "Your brother and cousins should be up from the beach soon. We're going to make dinner and watch a movie. You kids have fun. I won't wait up for you."

Klein grabs me by the waist, turning and gently pushing me so I can follow Sienna. Swiftly, in a move that startles me at first, he brushes aside my hair and plants a soft kiss on the dip of skin where my shoulder meets my neck.

Shivers tumble down my skin. I hope tonight goes by quickly so we can get back here. My thigh muscles are already aching, clenching in anticipation.

---

KLEIN DRIVES US IN THE GOLF CART. SIENNA IS QUIET, AND when Klein sends me a concerned look, I make an attempt with her.

"Is everything okay?"

"Everything is fine," she replies, but she sounds tired. Of what?

I look back to Klein and shrug. I could push the issue, but I don't think it's likely she'll open up in front of Klein. Or, maybe, to me.

Shane has rented a house further down the island, closer to Cape Fear. Judging by the number of golf carts parked out front, we are the last to arrive.

Sienna says not a word as we park and weave through

the other carts. She walks ahead of us on the stairs, footfalls light and quick.

"Maybe she's nervous about tonight," Klein suggests, reaching for my hand as we climb the stairs together.

"That's probably what it is."

We reach the top of the stairs, and I pause. "Cecily texted me while I was getting ready for tonight. She said the response to your account is better than she hoped it would be. Did you know that already?"

Klein shakes his head. "I've been doing what I was told to do. I take a lot of pictures and add them to a shared album." Klein rubs at the back of his neck. "I've been preoccupied."

"By the jellyfish sting?"

"Hah. No." He runs a hand over my bare arm. "By a beautiful woman. And her sassy little mouth. And her playful nature. And the way she loves the ocean, and the grains of sand that gets stuck in her hair." He waves a hand back and forth above my head, like he could keep going. "And on and on and on."

"I'm surprised you've overlooked that, considering it's half of the reason you're here."

He steps closer, taking up space, stealing my breath. "Is it?"

"Well, that, and the secondary deal we made."

"That secondary deal is a recent development. It can't be counted."

My head tips up so I can really take him in. The slightly messy hair, the light dusting of facial scruff. Intelligent eyes, irises darkening with lust.

Pushing up on tiptoe, I press my lips to the space

below his ear. "It does sweeten the deal, though, doesn't it?"

"Paisley," he says, pulling back, tucking the pads of two fingers below my chin so he can look directly into my eyes. "I could have a G-rated week with you, and it would be just as sweet."

I drag my gaze to the side, needing a break from the intensity. He's only waxing poetic, right? He's doing what he does so well. *Weaving words into emotional prose.* Isn't that what Sienna was picking up on earlier?

"Lovebirds," someone yells. We turn in unison, seeking out the voice in the dark.

Shane flickers the front light as he stands in the doorway, holding the door open. "Are you planning on joining us this evening?" He points at Klein. "I have a Cuban with your name on it."

Klein is the first to move, but he keeps a hold of my hand. We pass by Shane as we step into the house, and I feel the weight of his gaze on my face.

"Everyone's in the kitchen," he says, following us inside. "That's where the food is." We follow the sounds of music and talking.

Farhana is the first to spot us. She waves me in, grabbing a flute and filling it with bubbly. "For the maid of honor," she says, handing it over. "Klein, can I get you anything?"

"A beer, if you have it."

"Of course we do," Shane interrupts. "Hope you like IPA."

"That works," Klein says, nodding his thanks when Shane hands it over.

"Do you like IPA?" I whisper, poking at the sailfish on the paper covering the bottle.

"This one is good. Some are obnoxious in their attempt to be burly." He tips the bottle so he can study the branding. "This one is... nautical. Fitting."

Shane pulls Klein into conversation with his groomsmen, bloviating about venture capital. Klein doesn't give two shits about anything related to the financial services industry, but he politely listens. My sister complains to her half of the bridal party about a guest who declined, but reached out today, asking if there would be room for them after all. "And a plus one!" she exclaims, shuddering at the wedding etiquette faux pas.

I look over at Klein. He's leaning against the island, his posture relaxed. When he takes a drink from his beer, his eyes find mine, and stay there. The corners of my lips lift automatically, without me having to think much about it. Just looking at him puts a smile on my face.

Retrieving my phone from my purse, I type out a message to him.

> How are you feeling? Your sting ok?

He takes his phone from his pocket and reads my message.

> What sting?

He winks at me.
Suppressed laughter ripples my shoulders.

> My lips did the job then? Literally.

He grins crookedly.

> Yes. They did.

I make a big show of sighing silently, lifting up my shoulders and dropping them dramatically.

> I hate to break it to you, but I think you may have impregnated me.

He sends me a concerned look, teasing.

> Perhaps you missed that day in reproductive education, but those body systems don't connect.

I lick my lips and shrug, one-shouldered.

> After that? They might.

Klein hides his laugh behind the back of his hand, but Shane catches on.

"Something funny on your phone, Klein?" He makes a gimme motion. "Now you're going to have to share it with the class."

Klein shakes his head, eyes meeting mine. "Not happening," he answers firmly.

Shane follows his gaze, straight to me. Understanding comes into his eyes. "Gotcha." Spinning, he grabs a box from the counter and holds it open, announcing, "Cigar time." The men *ooh* and *ahh*, with the exception of Klein.

Shane passes the open box under my nose and I nod politely.

"That's right," he says. "I forgot you hate the smell of cigars." He grins in a way that is too on purpose, too *Oh yes I remember that about you.* "And the taste."

This fucking guy. I really hate him. Deadpan, I say, "I never did enjoy eating cigars."

Farhana laughs. So does Klein. Shane smirks. "Look at Paisley with a sense of humor. When did you develop one?"

A vein in Klein's temple throbs, and the sight of it is what I need to remind myself not to allow Shane's remarks to bother me. For whatever reason, it seems Shane wants me to be sad. Upset. Aggrieved. But why? Who knows. Something to do with his ego, almost certainly.

"Shane," my sister cuts in, wrapping her arms around him, pressing her body into his. I'm trying to hide my surprise at her public display of affection, but Shane doesn't do so well at first. It takes him a second to tuck back his surprised expression. He pats Sienna's back, saying, "Is my bride-to-be tipsy?"

Sienna giggles in a very un-Sienna like way. "Maybe," she trills, fluttering her fingers in the air. "And I think we should play a game."

He leans in, nuzzling her nose with his own. "What game would that be?"

"Hmm," she pretends to think. "Spin the bottle!"

"Hard pass," Klein announces.

Sienna pouts. "You can't say no to the bride."

"I can say no to kissing anyone who isn't Paisley."

A chorus of *aww's* come from the bridesmaids.

Sienna looks hard at Shane. "You wouldn't kiss anyone who isn't me anyway, right babe?"

"Of course not, Blondie."

Shane looks at me as he says this. Is he hoping I'll hear the nickname he first used on me, and react? I don't care. At all. Besides feeling bad for my sister at her fiancé's lack of originality.

"Sardines?" I throw out the game, hoping my sister will remember that it was our favorite game to play growing up.

Her expression brightens. "Yes!"

Shane's eyebrows tug as he looks at Sienna. "You want to play Hide and Seek?"

She squeezes his shoulder. "A variation of it. Everyone?" She looks around the group of adults. The women nod. The men shrug. Wren elbows Tag, and he nods dutifully.

Sienna recites the rules for those who may not know them. "I get to hide," she announces, taking a drink directly from the champagne bottle.

Per Sienna's instructions, we all close our eyes and count to one hundred. When I open my eyes, I find Shane staring at me with an expression I don't understand.

Klein squeezes my hand. "May the best man win, Royce."

"Good luck, Madigan. I know how my sister thinks. So I already know where she is."

He winks and takes off out of the kitchen. We trickle out, except for Tag and Wren, who mysteriously head toward the front door.

So here's the thing. I knew how my sister thought when we were kids. But I'm on my second pass through the house and I haven't found her yet, so apparently I don't know how she thinks as an adult. I've run into a number of other people while looking for her, so most of us haven't found her yet either.

I stop in the kitchen to eat a few chocolate covered blueberries, and down half a glass of champagne. I'm passing the pantry door when it opens suddenly and a hand sticks out, clamping onto my wrist.

I cry out as I'm hauled inside the small, dark space.

## CHAPTER 32
*Paisley*

"Wha—" I say, cut off by a hand pressed lightly to my mouth.

"Shhh, Ace."

I smile against Klein's palm. He releases me, and I whisper, "Why are you in here?" My eyes haven't yet adjusted, and it's too dark for me to see anything. "Wait. Is Sienna in here? Did you find her?"

"No," he whispers. "It's just you and me and our own little game."

I cover up my laugh. "How did you know it was me when you grabbed me?"

"I know your gait."

"Be real." I playfully shove him.

"Ok, the truth is I was looking under the half inch of space at the bottom of the door. I saw your shoes."

"You were lying in wait."

"I knew you'd be along soon. Chocolate covered blueberries are your third favorite food, after tacos and cowboy spaghetti."

"I never told you that."

"You don't have to be told something to learn it, Royce. You need only watch."

My hands find his chest, running up and over the hard planes, snaking around to the back of his neck. "What else have you learned by watching?"

"You wiggle your toes in the sand because you like the feel of the warmth between them. You're the caretaker of your family." His hands go to my hips, fingers curling into my skin. "You have one speed in the morning: sloth. Your family and that asshole are surprised to find you're funny, and I'm still working out why you don't show them your sense of humor."

"It's your fault."

His breath of laughter tickles the top of my head. "How's that?"

"You make me funny. You bring it out in me."

He tightens his hold on my hips. "So I bring out your sense of humor, and you gave me a boyfriend perk. Royce, I think you might like me."

"That's the problem, Madigan. I know I like you."

His thumbs stroke my hip bones. "How's that a problem?"

"I don't trust myself with men. The last one I chose turned out to be a carbon copy of my father. In case you were sleeping during dinner with him, that's not a compliment."

"In case you've been sleeping since the day you met me, I'm nothing like either of those people."

I know he isn't. I know it as certainly as I know the sun will rise and pierce through my curtains in approximately eight hours. But it's not him. It's me. I have emotional baggage to work through before I can move forward.

Klein's hand leaves my hip, settling on my forehead. He runs the pad of a finger between my eyebrows. "Creased," he announces quietly. "I bet if I felt your lips, they'd be pursed."

I force my lips to relax. "I don't know what you're talking about."

He lowers his touch, thumb tracing my mouth. My mouth opens slightly, capturing his thumb and biting down. A hiss of air comes from between his teeth.

I release him, and his touch lowers, to my chin, pinching it between two fingers. He lifts my face, and his lips find mine.

The kiss is better than good.

It's fulfilling in a way I've never had, but always wanted. He kisses me like he wants me desperately. Not only my body, but my lips.

He tips me up, supporting the back of my head, and tastes me. This man is ravenous for me, and I think perhaps I've been parched for the feeling. For him.

I push into him, pressing myself against his chest as much as I can. I hate these clothes. I hate this pantry. I hate being here in this house at this precise moment.

Klein's hand leaves my hip, sliding around to the front of me. Up over my rib cage, skirting the swell of my breast. I arch into him, asking for his hand. He smiles against me. "So eager."

"For you," I say, as quietly as I can.

"Is that right?" There's arrogance in his tone, and I love it. "Let's find out if that's true."

His touch is at the hem of my dress, his fingers traveling beneath it. He feathers over the inside of my thigh, inching higher.

Higher.

Higher.

Stopping at the apex. He runs a hand over the fabric. "Oh, Paisley," he says, his tone playfully chiding. "What have we here?"

"Paradise," I respond, in a voice so low and throaty I can't believe it belongs to me.

He sweeps the thin fabric aside, running his fingers over me. "It is, isn't it?"

His flattened palm comes up over me, exerting pressure. His hand slides down, his middle finger slipping inside on his descent.

"Ah," I choke on my gasp, surprised at the welcome addition.

Klein's nose and forehead press to mine, hot breath mingling with my own. "I've discovered Shangri-La between your thighs, Paisley, and I want it."

"It's yours," I pant as he works slowly, torturing me with an unhurried rhythm, as if we're not hiding out in a pantry and we have all the time in the world.

"Mine," he whisper-groans, increasing his pace.

It turns out I like possessive Klein as much as I like arrogant Klein.

Gripping his shoulders, I press my face into his neck and inhale the clean scent, holding on as my heart thunders in my chest.

"So. Close," my strained whisper is warm against his neck.

"I know," he murmurs into my hair, his tone holding something akin to reverence.

There are noises in the kitchen now, voices, loud recapping of where Sienna had been hiding.

Alarm races through me.

"You're tensing around my"—he adds a second finger—"fingers. Don't focus on anything but this. Me. You."

His pace increases, the rhythm creating a bundle of heat at the base of my spine. In the kitchen, someone says my name. Another person responds, saying *I don't know where they went.*

My fingernails claw at Klein's arms. Lips pressed to my ear, he whispers, "You can come quietly. Or you can scream and give away our location. I'm a proud contributor to either response."

His words tip me over the precipice, and with people on the other side of an unlocked door, I shatter under his hand, biting at his shoulder to stay silent.

"That's my girl," he says, his words rumbling against the side of my head. The bicep on his right arm continues to flex as he slows but doesn't stop, bringing me down slowly from the crescendo.

"Paisley?" he says.

"Mm-hmm?" My thighs are a quivering mess, and so is my voice.

"The next time you come, I want the lights on so I can watch your gorgeous eyes roll back in your head." His fingers, still inside me, curl and flex, the sensitivity making me buck.

"Yes," I agree, as his fingers disappear from me.

I adjust my dress, my hair, swiping under my eyes. I haven't the faintest clue what I look like right now.

The kitchen is quiet again. Perfect. Everyone has gone somewhere else, and we can step from this pantry undiscovered.

Klein turns the handle, an arc of light appearing as he slowly pushes it open an inch. "After you, Ace. Or maybe I should start calling you a siren."

I look at him in the modest light illuminating his features. His cheeks are flushed. He looks happy. Pleased.

"Siren?"

"You call to me like a siren luring in a sailor."

"I have no intention of drowning you."

"And yet, you seem to be."

"Drowning you?"

"Don't you know, Paisley?" Klein drops a swift kiss to the corner of my mouth, lingering there to say, "You are a dangerous woman."

"I doubt that."

"You pose a threat to every part of me."

My heartbeats falter. Does he mean these things he says?

"After you." He inclines his head.

Pushing open the door, I step into the kitchen, blinking against the harsh overhead light. Klein steps out behind me, his chest brushing my back.

My eyes adjust, then widen.

"Hey," I squeak.

Shane stands opposite us, casually leaning back against the counter with one ankle crossed over the other. He's peeling an orange, which strikes me as odd when there's an island laden with platters of prepared food.

"Guess I found one of the missing couples." The smirk on his face quickly dies. "At least someone around here is getting laid."

The corners of my lips turn down. "It's only for a week leading up to the wedding night." My sister isn't here to defend her decision, so I'll do it for her.

"Right," Shane says dryly. "Did you two have fun in there?" His lip twitches like he's fighting a sneer. "Sure sounded like it."

He's baiting me. Baiting Klein. Stirring for a fight, or at least a reaction. Klein doesn't know Shane very well, but he's already seemed to figure this out. He ignores Shane, grabbing a handful of chocolate covered blueberries. He takes my hand and flips it over, forming a cup and dropping the sweet treats into my palm.

"I know how she can be," Shane says, not letting up.

Klein meets my eyes, and I shake my head slowly, a warning. I can't even muster up anger about his crassness, because he looks so damn pathetic.

Shane keeps going, peeling his orange slowly, eyes cast down on his task. "When Paisley decides she's ready, you'd better hop to it, right?" He chuckles quietly, as if he knows, he *remembers*, he got there first and left his ghost to save his spot.

Shane wants attention, though I can't understand why. He's the groom. Isn't he at the center of everyone's attention, second only to his bride? *My sister*. In this moment, I would love nothing more than to send a heartfelt *fuck you* directly to Shane's face. But not for me. For

Sienna. For the disrespect he's showing her *and* their relationship.

"Hey Shane," Klein says, nonchalantly throwing a few blueberries in his mouth, "You keep going on like that about Paisley and I'll break your jaw." He takes my hand. "Let's go."

We leave Shane in the kitchen without a backwards glance. My sister and the rest of the bridal party are crowded on the front porch. One of the groomsmen holds a joint to his lips, then passes it to the guy beside him.

"We're going to take off," I tell Sienna. "Can somebody bring you back when you're ready?"

"Yeah," she says dismissively.

I have no idea what I did to upset her, and I'm not interested in finding out. There's so much more on my mind right now.

"Bye, everyone. See you all tomorrow."

Klein and I make our way back. He drives the golf cart, and I sit beside him, his hand in my lap. What happened in the pantry felt illicit and delightful, but also, it felt *right*. Like Klein's hands are the only hands I want on me.

I don't know what that means for our agreements. Maybe it doesn't have to mean anything. Can it just be us, on this island, having fun because real life feels like it exists elsewhere?

We're quiet going through the house. Light filters under the door as we pass the boys' room, and from what I can tell by the sounds, they're playing video games.

Klein leads me into our room. He closes the door softly behind me, heated gaze locked onto me.

And I kind of, sort of, just... *lose it.*

I launch myself at him. He catches me easily, my legs wrapping around his waist and his hands gripping my ass.

I lower my face, and he lifts his. We are nose to nose, breathing the same lusty air.

A nip at his lower lip. A pass of my tongue along the bite. A shallow breath. Klein grins, lazy and arrogant and teasing. "You didn't get enough in the pantry, Ace?"

My fingers thread through his hair. *I don't think I'll ever get enough of you*. It's a stupid thought, and it would be even stupider to admit out loud. "I want that lights-on orgasm you promised me."

Klein adjusts for our height difference by lowering me down his body, then captures my mouth in a brief kiss. "Then I guess I'd better deliver. Can't have a broken promise on my record, can I?"

"I get the feeling you don't break promises."

"Never," his deep voice grounds out against me.

Something about his words, spoken clearly and confidently, tells me he's a man who means what he says. That alone makes me feral. I want him in a way that shocks me. I've never been like this before. Klein isn't my boyfriend. We're nothing more than temporary as we carry out mutual favors. And yet, there's something about him. Something primal, basic, a calling. I… *want* him. Is it too plain? Not layered enough? Could it really be so easy?

"Overthinking," he murmurs, rubbing the pad of his thumb between my eyebrows. "What's going on in there? Are you having second thoughts?" Now his eyebrows are furrowing. "You can. You know that, right? You can change your mind at any point, even if we've already…" he trails off.

I burrow into him. "It's not that. Not at all. It's just... does this seem too easy to you?"

Klein squints one eye as he tries to understand. "Are you asking me if I'd like you to play hard to get?"

I smile. "No. Despite the fact we're here pulling off one hell of a charade, I don't enjoy playing games when it comes to dating." With my legs still wrapped around him, I slip one hand around his upper back and use the other to stroke a path through his hair and behind his ear. "Me and you. Physically, it feels so easy. Going down on you earlier today, not only was it bold of me, but it was like I wanted to, so I did, and there wasn't anything else about it. Mentally is easy, too. Talking to you, joking, laughing, I'm not used to it being simple. Seamless. It's like, like... sitting with my best friend and never running out of conversation."

"It was like that the first night we met. Do you remember?"

"I'd assumed it was the copious amount of beer, but that wasn't it."

"I felt an immediate and deep connection to you, Paisley. Like your curves fit my dips, and I filled out your shallow parts."

"Like we fit."

He nods. "Yes."

We stare at each other, both painfully aware we are dancing on an invisible line. Physically, we've already crossed it. But emotionally? We're still playing a safe game.

Maybe that's ok. Maybe that's what both of us need right now.

Terrified and exhilarated by my feelings, our mouths meet and fall apart. A small kiss, and then something deeper. Our tongues dance, then collide.

When we break, I say, "We've gotten a lot better at kissing each other since our first kiss."

He hoists me higher on his midsection. "I remember every moment of that kiss."

"Every bad second of it?"

"Even the worst kiss is the best if it's with you."

My smile wobbles. "Klein the writer."

The muscles in his jaw tighten.

I search his green eyes. "Do you want me to stop saying that?"

## CHAPTER 33
*Klein*

"It's not that I want you to stop saying that," I inform her, staring into her eyes, the prettiest shade I've ever seen. "It's that I want you to stop thinking when I say something you like, it should be attributed to that."

Color gathers in her cheeks. "I didn't realize that's what I was doing."

"It's a defense mechanism."

She nods. "Yes."

"What is it that needs defending against me?"

Clearly, and with confidence, she says, "My heart."

The very same organ that sits in my chest begins to squeeze. I wish Paisley could feel what she does to me. I wish she could know the way she's marked me, changed me, the way watching her struggle with her family torments me, how deeply I want to shake them all and tell them they're hurting the best person I know.

"Paisley," I center our faces so there is little else in our fields of vision. I need her to not only hear my next words, but absorb them, too. "There is no safer place for your heart than with me."

She moans, a tiny garbled noise. "Klein, I can't stop thinking about you." Her words carry the softness and fragility of a confession, and perhaps that's what it is.

My hold on her tightens. "You occupy every one of my thoughts, and my dreams, too."

In response, Paisley's thighs squeeze me. She arches, pushing her breasts into me. "Show me what you think about."

I capture her mouth and walk us backward to the bed, lowering her when we get there. Her dress rides up her legs, giving me the shortest glimpse of her tattoo.

My hand runs up her thigh, pushing the fabric higher. Using a fingertip, I trace the word written in cursive.

*Attraversiamo.*

"What does it mean?" I lean down, brush my lips on the inked flesh.

Paisley squirms, fingernails raking through my hair. "It's Italian for 'let's cross over.' It's a way to describe transition or movement. I got it after my first year of business, when I went to Italy for two weeks." Her nails leave my hair, swooping over my neck. "I paid for the trip myself, and I was proud of that. It felt big, like I'd made the transition to adulthood. I'd done it on my own, the way I wanted to. I had defied my father, and my natural inclination to please, and it wasn't for nothing."

I stare down at her, unable to keep the wonder from my eyes. "You are something else, Paisley. Something really fucking special."

My lips drop to her thigh, to that word. Attraversiamo.

The tip of my tongue traces the cursive. I look up, my mouth still pressed to her skin. Paisley looks at me, eyelashes fluttering.

"Klein," she says, but there's nothing else after it. Not a request. Nor a question. Only my name, because she can. Because she wants to.

I suck at her thigh, at the tattoo, drawing the skin into my mouth and biting down. She gasps, and her hand finds my hair again. My mouth drops from her thigh, sliding down a hill, to that place where my fingers explored earlier. Her thighs, still locked together, form a 'v.'

Sitting up, I look down at her closed eyes. "Paisley, if you want me in here, you're going to have to open up for me."

Her eyes open. Gaze on mine, she parts.

Settling between her knees, I run my hands up her thighs, watching them disappear under the hem of her dress. Higher I push, until the fabric settles at her hip bones.

I stare down at her, exposed for me. "Now that," I say, appreciating the light pink lace.

Paisley smiles. "That is underwear worthy of removing."

Hooking my fingers into the waistband, I tug them down her body. They were pretty while they lasted.

And there, right fucking there, is my paradise.

"So pretty," I admire, a blush of crimson stealing over Paisley's cheeks.

Settling in, I press my mouth where I want it. Where Paisley wants it. Hidden in the pantry earlier, we were short on time. Now I have her on her back in a big, soft bed, and I take my time. Her fingernails scrape my scalp until it's too much and she cups a hand over her mouth to muffle her mewling. Her hips buck, and I press a forearm low over her stomach to keep her in place.

One pass over her. Then another. A lazy drag, a roll. A slow circle that has her thigh muscles tensing, and then I suction my mouth to her until her body bows off the bed. Thigh muscles quaking, she remains silent while her bucking body screams for her.

"I wish you could see how beautiful you look," I say when I sit up. Her hair swirls around her head, her cheeks are the loveliest dark pink.

"If it's anything like the way you looked when I took your mind off the pain, then I already know."

"And you call me the wordsmith."

She smirks. "That mouth of yours has many talents."

"For my next act..." Sliding my hands in the waistband of my shorts, I push them down swiftly.

Paisley's eyes are glued to the part of me that springs forth. "I don't have condoms. I wasn't expecting anything like this to occur."

"I brought some."

Paisley feigns surprise. "Klein Madigan. How dare you make such assumptions about a lady."

"Precautions," I clarify, grabbing my shorts. I stowed one foil packet away in my wallet before the party. "No expectations."

Sitting back on my knees, I guide the condom onto my length. Paisley, propped on her elbows, watches me. The low light from the bedside lamp spills a deep yellow over the bed, and over Paisley.

She reaches for me, and I settle myself into the cradle of her hips. Lowering my mouth, I take one pert, pink nipple between my lips. Continuing on with the theme of taking my time, I sink into the task, cupping one breast while I work on the other. Paisley grows impatient beneath me, and I smile.

She releases a feminine growl of frustration, and I smile wider. It's adorable.

Paisley reaches between us. Her grip locks onto me, positioning me right where I need to go, and she says, "Please."

Is there anything I like better than hearing that word on Paisley's lips? Right now, nothing comes to mind.

She gasps when I press inside, her chest rising with her inhale. Trailing kisses over her collarbone, up her neck, and finally, to her mouth. I set a tempo that is not fast nor slow, but something in between. Paisley likes it. She folds her legs so they parallel our bodies, her fingers running up my back and into my hair.

"Look at me," I ground out.

Ocean blue gazes into forest green.

It is only me, and her.

Her hands on my back, kneading at the muscles.

The tiny droplets of sweat gathering in crevices.

The slickness of our bodies.

"It's never been this good," Paisley whispers, her body rising up to meet mine. "Why haven't we been doing this for the past eight years?"

My hips roll with hers, her breasts tumbling with the movement. "Because we are very, very stupid."

Paisley laughs, and it makes her walls clench.

I draw back and sit up, pulling Paisley up with me. She sinks onto me, knees on either side.

My lips are on her neck. "The lights are on, so I can watch you this time."

Paisley nods, guiding my hand between her legs. I do as she silently asks, and she treats me to a show. Her hands on my shoulders, head tipped back, nipples scraping my chest, and just like I said earlier, I get to watch her eyes roll back in her head.

"Beautiful," I groan, nuzzling her neck as the pulsing and quaking of her muscles subside.

She clenches around me, lifting her hips before dropping them down, and presses her lips to mine. She is directing the show, leading me there.

Primal, raw, shared breath and slick bodies. There's no one else in this house. On this island. It's only us. We're not kissing, but her mouth moves over mine in tandem with where we connect.

The edge nears, rising up. Paisley jerks, squeezing me, silencing her cries. It catapults me to the end, and now she kisses me, and I kiss her back, and I don't know what we've done or what we're doing, or what we may have started.

I only know that Paisley feels perfect in my arms, and perfect in my chest, and for now that is enough.

## CHAPTER 34
*Paisley*

HEAT FROM THE SAND RISES UP THROUGH THE TOWEL I'M lying on. It's a perfect day, balmy, the slight breeze lifting my salt-dried hair from my shoulders. The sun is proudly displayed in the middle of the sky, like a superhero revealing their uniform.

Klein lies beside me.

Ahh. *Klein*. My whole body smiles when I think of him, from the tips of my toes to the crown of my head. Last night was perfect. This morning, too, as he gathered me into his chest. He was slower this morning, lazy and sleepy, nearing decadent.

Klein slides his sunglasses down his nose, eyebrows raised as he asks, "Do you need me to reapply your sunscreen?"

I probably don't need a re-application for a little while longer, but turning down Klein's offer to rub his hands over my back? I'd be a fool.

"If you're offering, I'm accepting." Sitting up, I rifle through my beach bag and hand him the coconut scented sunscreen. He takes it from me, squirting a quarter size amount in his palm as I push my bikini straps off my shoulders.

His touch is cold at first, but quickly warms up.

"Your muscles are tight," he remarks, kneading at the top of my back. "I think I might know why."

Looking back at him flirtatiously over my right shoulder, I say, "Somebody worked me out last night."

"And this morning," he adds proudly. "We should hydrate. The day is young."

His comment makes me laugh. He's mostly finished reapplying, so I snap my straps on my shoulders and turn, lunging for him. It knocks him back on his towel, and I lean over his chest, dropping a kiss onto his lips. "I like your wit."

"I like your everything."

His words send a flush of pleasure throughout my body. He claims there is no safer place for my heart than with him. I hope that's true.

After a second, slightly longer, kiss I return to my previous position on the towel.

A beach volleyball game is being played a short distance from us. It's the entire wedding party, plus my mom, Ben, and Grandma. My dad has been silent since dinner, and is absent from today's beach fun. At what point is he planning on joining us? Normally I would care more about his absence, or feel responsible for including him.

Klein has been the best distraction.

My mom yells over, asking if Klein and I want to join the match. Klein tells her we'll get the next one.

I crook one eye open. Klein is on his back, shades covering his eyes, a book held aloft. It's a murder mystery, something taken from my grandmother's collection. He sees me looking and sets down the book. Rolling onto his side, he presses a light touch to my lower back.

Wearing a look I can only describe as adoration, he says, "There are freckles emerging on your cheeks."

"From the sun." I point needlessly at the giant lantern in the sky.

He nods, his gaze roaming over me. His hand explores my back, bumping over the ties of my bikini top. He begins using a fingertip, looping and swirling, crossing and dotting.

"What are you doing?" I ask, propping the side of my head on stacked hands.

"Plotting a story."

I smile lazily. "What kind of story?"

"A love story." He writes something on my back, something I can't decipher.

"The book you're reading isn't giving you murder mystery inspiration?"

He makes a show of eyeing Shane. "Maybe."

"Hah." Even my laugh is slow, molasses pouring from a jar. It's the sun. I don't have a fast speed under its rays. "What's giving you inspiration for this love story?"

He surveys the beach. "The island vibes." Eyes on me. "And a certain woman."

"My grandma? Is it a love triangle with Bob Barker?"

Klein's plotting halts. "You got it. I travel back in time and face off with him to win a young Lausanne's affections."

"You're the obvious choice." I roll over and prop myself on an elbow. My fingers trace his chest, his pecs, pausing over his heart. "I'd choose you."

He kisses my shoulder, lingers, nibbling at the warm skin. "Are you catching feelings for me, Ace?"

My heart beats double time. "Do you want me to?"

He pulls back, leveling me with a tender look. "Yeah. Maybe I do."

I'm hit unexpectedly with emotion. Klein's question, the sun and the sand, the island paradise, it feels the closest to perfection I've ever been.

I want to lie here in this moment forever, soaking up the sun and this man who has knocked me off my axis for a second time in my life.

I prepare to pull Klein in, ready to embark on a partially indecent beach make-out session, but I'm stymied by a shadow looming over us. I tent my hand to see who it belongs to.

Sienna, wearing a white bikini (naturally), looks down at us. "Klein, I need a break from volleyball. Can you sub in, please?"

Klein drops a reluctant kiss beside my ear before standing. "Sure. No problem." He walks off through the hot sand, and I watch him go. His calves are filled out, shapely, a result of those weekly soccer matches. The lash mark of his jellyfish sting is still red, but a fraction less angry.

Sienna lays out beside me on Klein's towel. She tips her face to the sun. "You two seem to be getting along well."

I watch Klein take his place on Shane's team. "We are."

"Shane is jealous of Klein."

The despondence in her voice makes me roll over, bending my elbow and propping my head on my hand.

I'm so confused. Hadn't she made it a point to tell me in my bathroom yesterday afternoon that whatever had gone on between Shane and Klein was a misunderstanding? What has happened or been said to cause this jealousy she claims Shane feels?

"Why would Shane feel that way?"

She shrugs, hands folded in her lap. In her profile I see her younger self, the little girl who loved making chocolate pudding and hated waiting for it to set.

I try again. "Why, Sienna?"

"Because it's glaringly obvious you're beyond happy."

Maybe my acting skills are better than I thought. *Or maybe I'm beyond happy.*

"It would be hard not to be happy with Klein," I say, aiming for pragmatic when all I really want to do is gush about how incredible he is. "He's a good person."

"I'm happy for you, Pais, really."

I sense she wants to say more, so I stay quiet.

Sienna's grasped hands twist. "I feel awkward asking you this, but would you and Klein mind toning down all the lovey-dovey behavior?"

My initial reaction, my knee-jerk response, is to immediately say *Yes, of course I'm not interested in causing my sister grief, especially during wedding week.*

But.

I hear them. Paloma and Klein.

*You're the floor.*

*If you keep being a doormat, what will* you *do?*

Indignation simmers in my blood. "Have you asked your fiancé to stop being jealous? Or have you asked yourself why your fiancé is jealous in the first place?"

Sienna's mouth drops open. "It's easier for everyone if you act differently since you're the one creating the problem."

My hands clench. "How am I creating a problem?"

"You're making Shane jealous."

My eyes squeeze shut as I shake my head. This is too crazy to be real, right? "How do you know this, Sienna? Is this your opinion?"

The set of her shoulders is firm. "It's an opinion formed by watching him last night."

She doesn't know what Shane said to me and Klein after our tryst in the pantry, so on what is she basing this?

"He was his typical obnoxious self last night, Sienna. That's it."

"That you saw," she mutters. "He was a real asshole after you and Klein left."

"His behaviors are his choice, you know that, right?"

"I can't believe how disagreeable you're being about this."

At this point this conversation is almost *laughable.* "That's not how I see it."

She glares at me. "How do you see it?"

"I'm not letting myself be pushed around."

She scoffs. "Because you've been pushed around until now?"

"Yes."

It doesn't feel like it's me having this conversation. I'm

floating somewhere up above, swooping down like the cormorants, listening in.

"Whatever," Sienna blows out a harsh breath. "I'm going inside the house to take a nap. See you at six for the cruise."

My heartbeats slow as I watch her stomp off through the sand. Farhana calls to her, and Sienna turns, yelling that she wants to rest. She continues on, but her walk has less stomp and more whimsy. She's remembering she has a crowd, and now she's playing the role of jaunty, unbothered bride-to-be.

It appears I'm not the only one behaving a certain way in the name of meeting others' expectations.

## CHAPTER 35
*Paisley*

Climb aboard a boat for a sunset cruise, they said.

It'll be fun, they said.

They lied.

Sienna forgot to mention my dad would be on this boat. My mother and Ben's attendance? She left that out, also.

Waiting on the dock for the boat to arrive was torture, the sticky humid air made thicker by my mom and Ben's steamy canoodling. My dad kept his distance, waiting twenty feet away with his cell phone pressed to his ear. I'm not sure if his call was business or personal, because I busied myself by catching up with Shane's mom while we waited.

Now here they are, sharing the same space for the first time since the divorce was final. Mom and Ben snuggle at the back of the boat, my father at the front. He cuts an interesting figure, alone up there in his khaki pants rolled at the bottom and navy woven half-zipped pullover, hands tucked in his pockets. Forced to face the fallout of his bad choices.

The bridal party huddles around the table on the top of the boat. A platter of fruits and cheeses sits half-eaten on the table, surrounded by nearly empty beer bottles and glasses of wine.

They're mid-debate, volleying the merits of twist-off wine versus corked. Klein, seated across from me, looks bored to tears.

When I catch his eye, he offers me a reassuring wink.

I try to do the same, but my stomach is in turmoil. The water is choppy today, the result of high winds. The boat responds to the waves in a way my stomach doesn't appreciate. I don't know the specifics of seasickness, but I'm not appreciating its symptoms right now.

Standing up from the table in an effort to get control of my ill feelings, I step from the group and grip onto a railing. The first mate, Crew, comes up from the galley with a fresh round of drinks for everyone. He finishes handing them out, then joins me at the railing.

"Did you want a glass?" he asks. "I can go below and grab one for you." He offers an eager smile. He's handsome, with deeply tanned skin and jet-black hair. When we'd first climbed on and met the captain and first mate, Maren commented that Crew should be in the marketing material for the sunset cruise.

"No, thank you," I answer. "I'm not feeling great at the moment."

"Ahh," he nods knowingly. "You need to get your sea legs under you." He rubs my back, and I'm too precariously close to vomiting to step away from his inappropriate touch.

My stomach sloshes. "I might need to get a bucket under my face soon."

He grins, thumbing over his shoulder. "I have some ginger candy on hand. It's below deck with my stuff, if you'd like to come with me to grab some?"

The boat bounces. My body stretches, one way and then the other, like pulled taffy. Another wave slaps the boat, rocking us.

Sustained nausea has weakened me, and though my grip tightens on the railing, it's not enough to keep me in place.

I stumble, and Crew grabs my waist, fingers digging in and keeping me upright. "Whoa," he says, eyes glinting.

"If you want to keep your soft hands, I suggest you take them off my girlfriend."

The voice reaches deep into my belly, ribboning through me. He could be a knight on a white horse, arriving to rescue his fair maiden. And threaten bodily harm to his opposition, of course. Even in my sickened state, I can take a moment to appreciate his possessive behavior, his menacing tone. "Klein," I murmur, reaching for his shoulders.

I don't know if Crew has a response, I'm too busy attempting to get control of this feeling. Crew releases me, his hands replaced by Klein's. He twists me into his broad wall of a chest, holding me still while the boat rocks. "I think I'm going to be sick."

He guides me down the stairs, leading me around the corner to a quiet place.

Gingerly, he gathers my hair and holds it back while I grip the rails and lean over the boat. The dark water dips and swells, splashing the boat. Droplets smack my face, cooling my skin. Oddly, it makes me feel better.

A minute passes as I wait. Nothing happens. "False alarm," I say, taking a step back from the railing as the nausea subsides. "Sorry."

"Don't be," he murmurs, releasing my hair, only for his hand to drop to my lower back, where he begins rubbing circles. "It happens to the best of us." A small smile tugs up one corner of his mouth as he gazes down at me. The waning light darkens his green eyes like a maritime forest.

My tongue darts out to wet my lips. "Why are you looking at me like that?"

"Like what?"

"Like you adore me." Should I have chosen less meaningful words? Something that would've given Klein the chance to have a less impactful response?

For several seconds he stares, eyes riveted and glimmering and thoughtful.

"Tell me to stop," he says hoarsely.

"Don't stop."

Whatever sickness I've been feeling is long gone now. An incredible surge of something that used to feel foreign, but is now familiar with Klein, comes from somewhere deep inside me.

What is happening to me? To us?

## CHAPTER 36
*Klein*

Why was I looking at Paisley like I adore her?

Short answer: because I do.

Long answer: because her evident vulnerability when she thought she was going to be sick made me feel a caveman type of protectiveness over her. Like somebody imperative to my own survival was weak and I needed to stand guard and ensure her safety, barring predators from absconding with her.

Predators in the form of revoltingly good looking first mates.

*Crew.* The name is too perfect for the job. It must be a pseudonym.

Since we'd climbed aboard he'd been staring at Paisley a little longer than what I consider friendly. And then he put his hands on her in the guise of steadying her.

I went caveman. And I don't regret it.

Paisley is feeling better now. I located a ginger ale in the galley, and she munched on leftover crackers from the platter on the table. The wind has died down, and the ocean with it.

Paisley's dad has remained at the bow of the boat, visiting only with Spencer, who is right now staring at his phone and doesn't appear to be much for conversation.

Bending, I brush a kiss onto Paisley's cheek and say, "I'm going to go talk to your dad."

She looks at me with a question in her eyes. "Why?"

I shrug. "He looks lonely."

Paisley leans left, peering past the captain steering the ship. I know what she sees, because I saw it myself a few moments ago. Her father, sitting alone and staring out at the Atlantic.

"Do you want me to come with you?"

"You don't have to. I think I can hold my own with him."

Paisley smirks. "I know you can."

I make my way down to where he sits. "Mr. Royce," I call out as I come up behind him, so I don't startle him.

He grips the arms of his chair, leaning forward and swiveling at the waist to look at who's speaking to him. "Klein," he greets blandly, turning back around.

There's an open seat beside him, and though he hasn't invited me to join him, I sink down into it.

"Beautiful evening," I remark. I'm not sure what else to say, and I'm still trying to figure out how to get the guy to do something besides scowl and look put out.

He side-eyes me. "I wouldn't think you'd be impressed with sunsets, given where you're from. Isn't Arizona known for its sunsets?"

"Among other things." I shift in my seat. "A sunset over an ocean is something special though."

"Did you come down here to wax poetic about sunsets?"

I breathe a laugh. I guess there is something to be said for getting to the point. "I did not."

He turns, assessing me full on. "My daughter then, I take it? You want to talk about my daughter?"

"Just want to tell you how great she is."

"I already know that."

I stay silent, but raise my eyebrows.

"I do," he insists.

"You have an odd way of showing it."

"Awfully bold of you to come down here and start this conversation with me."

I shrug, crossing an ankle over the opposite knee. "I'm a bold guy."

He studies me. I can't tell if that's begrudging respect on his face, or if he's calculating how much work it would take to attempt to toss me overboard.

Finally, he says, "I'm not as bad as you think I am."

"Mr. Royce, at the end of the day, I am not interested in disrespecting you. After all, you are still Paisley's father. Paisley has opened up to me about some of her experiences with you, and though I am automatically on her side no matter what, those belong to her. So far, my singular experience with you has supported what Paisley has talked about. So, forgive me, sir, but if you want me to think you are not as bad as I think you are, you're going to have to start behaving differently."

He turns his gaze to the ocean. My heart smacks my breast bone. I knew I was thinking all those things, but had no plans to say them. Once I started talking the words took on a life of their own, and marched out like they grew feet and wore combat boots. Sitting by and watching somebody mistreat Paisley is unacceptable to me. Family member or not, real girlfriend or fake, I won't stand by while someone says she's anything less than amazing. Even her dad.

"Klein." Paisley's voice sails down to me. I look up. She's standing at the rails of the top deck, fingers curled around the metal. Her hair floats around her face, her orange tank top glowing against the tan she has picked up over the last few days. Gone is the greenish hue she wore on her face earlier.

I wave, and she yells, "We're going to play a card game." Her gaze darts to her dad. His back is to her, but he leans forward, prayer hands between his knees and his shoulders hunched. Gaze dragging back to me, she asks, "Should I deal you in?"

"Yeah," I yell back.

And then, in a move that shocks everyone, Paisley's dad turns around and hollers, "Deal me in, too."

Paisley takes a full three seconds to recover, before a grin breaks onto her face. "Done," she says, happiness in her tone. She steps away from the railing and disappears.

Mr. Royce stands, adjusting his pants that have bunched up around his legs. "No time like the present to turn things around, right?"

We walk around the side of the boat, heading for the

stern where the stairs are located. "They say sunsets are an opportunity to reset."

He pauses with one foot propped on the bottom stair. "You really are a writer."

**Klein Madigan**
@kleinthewriter

Priceless things: the sun burnishing her shoulders, her laugh when she knows she has told a good joke, the way she examines me from the sides of her eyes, lighthouse kisses, ocean eyes, her carefree smile when she rides a bike.

◯ 179   ♥ 22k   ↺ 127

# CHAPTER 37
*Paisley*

It's Thursday, also known as spa day for the women and chartered fishing day for the men. I wake up to a text from Cecily.

> Girl. GIRL.

>> What's wrong?

> Don't you mean what's right? Klein is getting all kinds of traction. Likes, shares, comments, mentions. If this doesn't get the attention of an editor, I will personally walk into their office wearing a sandwich board of his book cover and nothing underneath.

>> I'll drive you. But let's hope it doesn't come to that.

> How are things going on the island? Paloma said you've been incommunicado and she's going to pour boiling water in your ear.

Toggling over to my long-running text conversation with Paloma, I type out a semi-serious threat.

> I'm officially removing the tea kettle from the office.

I have a mini kettle in my desk.

> FFS. How's it going with the architect?

Very well, thank you. Architects' desks are multi-purpose, did you know?

> Very nice. Just stay off my desk.

How's Word Daddy?

> Very wordy. Very daddy.

I KNEW IT.

> Don't make it a thing.

Oh, but it is. It is a thing.

---

"I CAN'T BELIEVE THE WAY DAD PLAYED CARDS WITH US LAST night," Sienna says, stretching her legs out on the chaise lounge beside mine.

We've been at the spa for the last three hours. From head to toe, we are exfoliated, moisturized, massaged, and our nails are a neutral pinkish-taupe. The bridesmaids are finishing their last treatment. Sienna and I are alone in the nap room. So far we've pointedly ignored the topic of our interaction on the beach yesterday.

I push my sleep mask onto my eyes, and my view goes dark. "Weird, right? But good."

"I'm not sure what I'm going to do if he starts being likable."

"Hah," I say. "I wouldn't go that far. He managed to give Mom and Ben at least three stink eyes. Likability is still low."

"True. They stayed far away from that card game."

"Self-preservation," I joke.

My dad had played four rounds of To Hell With Your Neighbor, a not-very-nice card game where each person is in it for themselves and invariably causes people to cry out in indignation. It was the most fun I've had with my dad in years.

We've been having a nice time today, so I decide to go out on a limb and ask, "How are you and Shane leading up to the wedding?"

My sister is quiet, and then says, "Fine. Why?" There's a defensive edge to her tone.

"No reason." I force breeziness into my tone. "It can be a stressful time for couples, that's all."

"Not us." Her voice takes on a sharp, irritated edge. "We're fine. Stress free."

"Good."

"By the way, I talked to Shane. I was wrong. He is not jealous." She laughs, and though it's melodic, it's forced. "That was just me seeing something that's not there and being dramatic."

I've never been more grateful for a sleep mask in my life. I allow myself a massive eye roll, and say, "Glad you got that squared away."

"Mm hmm."

The door to the nap room opens, and I push the mask off my eyes to see who it is. The bridesmaids walk in, wearing robes and looking blissed out.

"Mimosas by the spa pool to end the day?" Maren asks.

I'm up from the lounge chair quickly, ready to be away from this conversation with my sister. "Count me in."

One mimosa before I head back to Klein sounds perfect.

···🐚🐚🐚···

I STEP INTO MY BEDROOM AT THE HOUSE AT THE SAME TIME Klein comes from the bathroom. He wears powder blue shorts, no shirt, hair glistening with damp. Heat blooms in my chest at the mere sight of him. This man is criminally attractive.

A smile springs onto his face the second he sees me.

"How was fishing?" I ask, watching him run a hand through hair that is a shade darker than normal.

"Good. I caught two King Mackerel, and an Amberjack."

"I don't know what that means, but"—I raise two fists in the air and shake them—"yay."

Klein grins. "Shane caught a small shark."

"Fitting."

"How was the spa?" Klein comes closer, and I tip my head up for a kiss. Like we are a couple, and I'm arriving home.

"It was the spa. My muscles that were relaxed from my massage are already bunching up again." Probably due to that conversation with Sienna. It'll take more than a mimosa to work the irritation from my body.

A wicked gleam appears in Klein's green eyes. "The massage wasn't enough to relax you?" He takes a step toward me.

I back up playfully. He takes another step.

He wants to catch me? Well, guess what? I want to be caught.

"Unfortunately, the massage is only a temporary relaxation technique." Another step back.

Klein grins devilishly. "Do you know of any other relaxation techniques with more lasting effects?"

"Possibly." Another step. "You look like a predator."

He's close enough to grab me now. "You look like prey."

My back meets the wall. My eyes widen, and Klein's eyebrows lift once, dropping back down. "Gotcha."

He leans in, nipping along my jaw, tasting my neck. "I missed you today. The ocean is bland compared to you."

I laugh throatily. "It's the ocean. Nothing can compare to that."

He pulls back to look at me. "You do."

My first inclination is to laugh off his words, to believe he can't help but speak that way, but only two days ago he asked me to stop doing that. He asked me to believe that when he speaks like that, he means it.

So this time, I do.

"I missed you today. The nap room would've been way more fun with you."

He quirks an eyebrow. "Nap room?"

I nod.

His head drops, and he licks over my collarbone. "I would've locked that nap room door and showed you how I like to nap."

My fingers stretch through his damp hair. "I think I have an idea."

He leans right, locking the bedroom door with a simple turn of his fingers. "Let me get my point across." He drops to his knees, looking up at me as he tugs my shorts down over my hips. They slide down my legs, pooling at my feet. My underwear joins them.

My tongue runs over my lips in anticipation.

"Do you know what's coming Paisley?"

"Me," I manage to say.

Klein smiles. "How do you always make me smile or laugh in situations like this?"

"It's a talent."

"So is this." He leans in, pressing his nose to me. His hands are on my thighs, running their length. "Your skin is soft."

I squirm as he runs his nose up and down me. Through my lust-filled thoughts, I register footsteps in the hallway. Then a knock on the door, only two feet away from where I am against the wall.

"Paisley?"

I look down at the top of Klein's head, frazzled. He looks up at me. "It's Shane," I mouth, careful not to make any noise. My body is confused. It's like I was running a sprint, and then somebody yanked on my collar.

One side of Klein's mouth curls up, arrogant and possessive. He leans forward and softly kisses me. "So?"

"Paisley, are you in there?" Shane's voice infiltrates my moment.

My head bobbles, my hands shake in front of me. What am I supposed to do right now? And Klein, well, he is not stopping. He is getting started.

"Answer him," Klein murmurs, the words a vibration against me.

I swallow. "He-ey," I call out.

"Can you open up?" he asks.

"Not right now. I'm… changing."

"Are you alone?"

I look down at Klein's head, moving up and down, then in slow circles. "Klein's taking a walk on the beach." I sound like I'm being strangled. Death by cunnilingus.

"Good," Shane says, relieved. "Can we talk?"

Klein, mouth attached to my body, chuckles. "This isn't a great time," I manage to say, but only barely.

"Pais, please. Everybody went for ice cream and this is the only chance I'm going to get."

"Let him talk, *Pais,*" Klein whispers, breath hot against me. "Nobody said you have to listen."

Turning my cheek so it's pressed against the wall and my mouth is closer to the door, I say, "I'm going to keep the door closed, but say whatever it is you need to say."

From Shane's silence, I gather that he's thinking about arguing with me. The thought spends little time in my brain, however. Klein is doubling his efforts, devouring me. If it weren't for him helping me stay upright, I would melt to the floor.

Shane speaks. "I thought you should know I'm having a hard time seeing you this week."

Klein grips the back of my knee, urging my leg up and propping it over his shoulder, increasing his access.

"Uh-huh," I respond, my voice jerking.

"I don't know, Pais, it's hard to explain. Maybe if I could say it to your face—"

The handle on the door moves.

"No," I bark.

Klein doesn't let up. The man does not even pause. I don't believe he entertained a single thought about stopping.

"Okay, okay." Shane sighs. "Are you having a hard time, too? Seeing me?"

Klein inserts a finger, relentlessly lapping at me. My hips buck. A scream of *Yes!* sticks in my throat.

"Sorry"—eyes on the ceiling as I squirm—"Shane. We're not on the same page."

"Is it him? Is that what this is about?"

My hands run through Klein's hair, nails scraping over his scalp. My blood is flowing to that one central point, the pleasure building on itself.

"It's not about him," I ground out, forcing the words. Pretty soon I will no longer have the ability to speak. "It's. About. You."

"Ouch," Shane says, but it barely registers.

With his free hand splayed on my stomach, Klein holds me still as I fall apart. I shake. I convulse. I lose myself to the moment, to Klein. Sure, it's his mouth doing the work, but so much of what he's done for me so far this week has been emotional. It takes an already great orgasm and amplifies it, sending the high all the way to the tips of my toes.

"Yes," I call out, slapping a hand over my mouth. Klein pulls back, grinning at me, lips glistening.

"What? Yes what?" Shane asks.

Klein's face presses against my sex, and he chuckles into me. Why is that hotter than hot?

"Nothing," I call out, my voice returning to somewhere closer to normal. "I'm hopping in the shower now, so, uh, bye. Nice chatting with you." I make a face at Klein, silently saying *I don't know what to say, but that probably wasn't it.*

He laughs and goes to sit on the bed.

Shane doesn't say anything else. I assume he's gone. I don't know, and I don't care.

"You," I say to Klein, stalking toward him. "You are a very naughty man."

He falls back on the bed and holds out his arms for me. "I'm not done with you yet."

"I was hoping you'd say that."

Lifting his hips, I make quick work of his shorts. Wearing only my tank top from the spa, I settle onto him.

He grips my hips, pushing me down until I'm full. "There you go." He rocks my hips back and forth. "Right where you belong."

It is. It really is.

## CHAPTER 38
*Klein*

Tonight at dinner, Paisley's mom snapped a photo of me and Paisley. My elbow is propped on the table, my body turned into Paisley. She's pressed into me, eyes closed, a hand cupping her mouth that doesn't at all hide the way her laughter tugs up her cheeks. I'm smiling down at her.

Afterwards, when Paisley had gone to help Lausanne serve strawberry shortcake, Robyn asked me for my number and sent me the photo.

I made it my backdrop.

This afternoon Paisley called me a naughty man.

She has so many names for me. I have a few, too.

Whipped.

Fallen.

Fool.

I am a whipped fallen fool for Paisley Royce.

**Klein Madigan**
@kleinthewriter

New trope: the whipped fallen fool.

◯ 41     ♥ 7k     ↻ 68

## CHAPTER 39
*Paisley*

I WAKE UP TO A TEXT FROM CECILY, SENT LAST NIGHT AT midnight.

> Boss. You sexy thing, you.

Checking the time on my phone, I decide it's an acceptable time in the morning to send a text message.

> Elucidate.

> KleinTheWriter is fire.

> I haven't looked at yesterday's content. I will as soon as I get a chance.

> I don't have to look to know you're killing it though!

··· 🐚 🐚 🐚 ···

THE WEDDING REHEARSAL IS TAKING PLACE ON THE LAWN OF Nautilus, at precisely the location where tomorrow's wedding will be held. The hotel's wedding coordinator, Raelynn, meets us in the lobby. She ushers us outside, where the green lawn overlooks the ocean.

White folding chairs are already set up, as is the square arch. Raelynn informs us the vines and flowers will be wound around the arch in the morning, in an effort to keep them from wilting overnight.

Raelynn claps her hands, ready to get the show on the road. Her eyes search the group, looking for the bride and groom, but coming up empty. "Where's Shane and Sienna?"

Tag, eyes scanning his phone, holds up one finger. "Shane says they'll be here in a minute. They had a problem in the parking lot."

My father sighs audibly and sits down in one of the chairs in the front row.

My mother takes a seat on the opposite side. So much for the guests of the bride on one side and the groom's on the other.

Shane appears a minute later, holding Sienna in his arms. He strides down the aisle, toward everybody waiting with questions in their eyes.

"I think she rolled her ankle getting out of the golf cart."

Tag steps out of the group to look it over. "Slightly swollen. Can you put weight on it?"

Shane sets Sienna down gently. She winces as she attempts to set her right foot down. "I can if I have to, but it hurts."

Tag nods. "Sit down, and put your foot on another chair." He turns to Raelynn as Sienna follows his instructions. "Can you grab a bag of ice from the hotel?"

She hurries off to do as he's asked. My eyes find Klein, sitting in the back row. He lifts his chin, acknowledging my look, silently asking what's wrong with the tug of his eyebrows.

I walk down the aisle toward him. He has one leg folded over the other in a figure four, hands folded in his lap. "What's going on?" he asks when I get closer.

"Sienna rolled her ankle. She's resting it and the coordinator went for ice."

"That's unfortunate, but at least she'll be fine by tomorrow." Klein unhooks his leg and pats his lap. "Sit down."

I make a show of peering at all the open seats around him. "Are all these chairs unavailable to me?"

"The only place for you"—he widens his arms and glances down—"is right here."

"Well then," I say, sinking onto him as if I'm riding sidesaddle, "I guess that's where I'd better park myself."

Turning to face him, I wrap one arm around his shoulders and press my free hand to his chest. "How are your posts going? Cecily texted and told me I'm a sexy thing? What was that about?"

A smile slides across Klein's face. "I've been taking all those pictures and adding them to the shared album, but I'm guessing she's talking about the pictures I took of you sitting at the shoreline with all that sand stuck to your bite-worthy ass."

"In my teeny bikini?"

He nods once, slowly, lips pushed out.

Leaning in, I place a tiny peck on him. Pouty lips call for kisses. I don't make the rules.

"I can delete it, if you want me to," Klein offers. "If you're not comfortable with her using it. I don't know that she will, but it's your call."

"As long as my face isn't part of the photo, I'm fine with it."

Klein's hands on my back begin to move, kneading at the muscles. "Do you think—"

"Paisley?" my sister shouts.

I twist around, still holding on to Klein. Sienna looks back at us from her place at the front. Her leg is propped on a seat, and I'm assuming there's an ice pack on her ankle.

"What?" I ask.

"Can you sub in for me for the rehearsal?"

I frown. Subbing in for my sister means walking down the aisle to Shane. My ex. A man I dislike on a normal day, and have only grown to dislike more as this week has progressed.

Sienna is bracketed by our parents. Behind her stands the bridal party. Every one of them. Shane's mother. And, of course, the coordinator who is only trying to do her job.

All eyes are on me.

I really don't want to do this, but if I say no, I'll look like I have a problem. An issue. People will assume I don't like Shane. Or I don't like Sienna. Or that I don't like Shane and Sienna together. I can't throw away all my successful ignoring of Shane's remarks only to fall down in the eleventh hour. I can do this. I can show up for my sister in her time of need.

Again.

After she's failed to consider how I might feel about the situation.

Again.

Klein's hands move off my back, like he's letting me go.

I don't know if it's that motion, like he's assuming I'll do what's asked of me when I don't want to, or if it's Sienna's exasperated expression, like she thinks I'm taking too long to comply. Maybe it's a combination of the two, but here's what I know for certain: I'm opening my mouth and saying the word. "No."

So powerful, this word.

No, I will not walk down the aisle to your fiancé who's been disrespectful of you and me this week.

No, I will not do as you ask simply because you've asked and expect me to.

No, I will not be a doormat while you never stop to consider my feelings.

A sizzling energy extends to my fingertips, pride filling my chest.

Sienna's mouth drops open. "Are you serious?"

Klein's arms wrap around my waist and he exerts a tiny amount of pressure, just enough to let me know he's here. He supports me.

"Yes, I'm serious. No, I don't want to step in for you and walk down the aisle and stand in front of my ex. Why would you ask that of me? There are three other women standing beside you." I motion to Farhana, Wren, and Maren. All three have mouths agape. "Ask one of them."

Sienna spends a full five seconds staring at me, stunned, before she turns around slowly and says something to the group. They fall in line, all walking around the set up of chairs and gathering near the back. It's quiet, awkward, and they shoot me glances I don't care about enough to decipher.

I press my hands on Klein's shoulders and push to stand.

"Proud of you," he murmurs. "That's my girl."

His praise causes a flush to spread across my cheeks. *His girl*. Is that what I am? Klein's girl?

I wink at him, then join the bridal party. Maren is playing the role of the bride. Raelynn lines us up. I'm second to last, as I should be. She tells us when to go, and I walk with Tag, the best man, down the aisle. Shane catches my eye, so on purpose it's embarrassing, but his expression startles me. Where I thought I'd find irritation, there is only wonderment.

The rehearsal trips on. Despite the death rays shooting from my sister's eyes, I'm enormously pleased to not be her stand-in.

···🐚🐚🐚···

THE REHEARSAL DINNER IS HELD IN THE PRIVATE DINING room at The Beach Club. Despite having been placed with the other ladies in the bridal party, I've made a space for myself next to Klein. Sienna shoots me a dirty look when she spots me spooning leek and potato soup into my mouth from my place beside Klein. I ignore her.

She's not happy with me? Well, guess what? I'm not happy with her either at the moment.

Dessert is served, a white and dark chocolate mousse, and coffee for those who've requested it. A tray of espresso martinis is delivered to those who forget, or don't care, that tomorrow is a big day.

Sienna sits, foot propped on Shane's lap. She's been icing twenty minutes on, twenty minutes off. This is her off time.

Tag looks down the table at me, martini glass raised as if to toast. "Paisley, do you have your maid of honor speech prepared? I've got to warn you, mine is spectacular. I plan to show you up."

Oh. Shit.

The speech.

*The speech!*

Did it slip my mind, or did my subconscious bury it on purpose? Either way, I don't have a speech. I don't even have the beginning of a speech. For that matter, I don't know that I have a single nice thing to say about the couple.

Klein closes the inches separating us, his lips brushing my ear. "Your face is giving away everything you're thinking right now."

I force the panic from my eyes. The irritation from my taut cheekbones.

Lifting my coffee cup in the air, I say with false bravado, "I see your spectacular, and I raise you an outstanding."

"Good recovery," Klein murmurs.

Tag winks. "We'll just have to find out who wins tomorrow, won't we?" He drinks. I sip my coffee.

Conversation moves on. But Sienna? Her gaze turns shrewd. She knows I'm bullshitting.

···🐚🐚🐚···

Klein drops Sienna and I at the house, sending us a wave on his way out of the driveway. He's returning to Nautilus to collect the trio of rowdy, drunken groomsmen. And, drunkest of all, the groom.

The hour is late, nearing midnight. The air, thick with the sounds of chatty bugs, takes on an awkwardness now that it's only the two of us.

"So," I start, stepping down on the first stair. I have nothing else though. Nothing to say that can have any meaningful impact on the shit show that was this evening. "I'm glad your ankle is better. Do you think you'll still wear your heels tomorrow? Maybe we could find some fancy flats or sandals if you need—"

Sienna, one step higher than me and gripping the wooden railing, turns to face me. The light of the moon reflects off her blonde tresses, giving her an ethereal quality. Despite appearing to be at least partially healed, she favors her left foot. "Paisley, we need to talk."

I nod. "Yes," I agree. There's so much I have to say, so much I want to get off my chest. Maybe once that happens, we can work on our relationship. We can improve it, and grow stronger.

"I don't think you should be a part of the ceremony tomorrow."

Her statement hangs, suspended in the humid air.

"I... You... *What?*"

She sighs. "I realize now I never should've asked you to be my maid of honor. It was dumb of me."

Dumb isn't the word I'd use. Foolish, maybe. Inconsiderate, most definitely.

"Sienna, don't you think it's a little late in the game to switch up the batting order?"

"I realize this will throw a wrench in things, yes. But I can't have you standing beside me if you have feelings for the groom."

My stare is rock hard, my gaze attempting to penetrate her brain. I've never spoken the same language as someone and felt like all the words mean something else to them than they do me.

"You think I'm not over Shane?" Now I'm sputtering.

"You couldn't even stand in for me during the rehearsal."

"Because I didn't want to! Because you never should've asked me to be in your wedding in the first place. It's *weird*, Sienna. What were you thinking?"

Sienna palms her chest, her head flinching back. "Excuse me for thinking my big sister might like to be a part of my wedding day."

"With my ex," I say slowly, incredulous. Is she truly this unaware?

"I thought you were over him."

"I *am* over him." Pinching the bridge of my nose, I look up at the starry sky and think about how I was ever with him in the first place. "I've been over him for a very long time."

"Then what's with you bringing Klein here?"

"Why did I bring my boyfriend to your wedding?"

"No," she shakes her head. "Why did you bring a fake date to my wedding?"

Her chin tips up, so pleased at herself for learning my great big secret.

"How did you know?"

"You're not even going to deny it?"

I shrug. "What's the point?"

"One of the women I work with sent his post from today to our group message. I recognized your tattoo in the photo. And then I spiraled into the rest of the account, and couldn't believe what I saw."

I stay quiet. What is there to say?

"You must have enlisted Klein in an effort to make Shane jealous. You two are just so... so... *hot*. All over each other. Watching one another. Whispering and laughing. Klein might want to take up acting."

"Sienna, I—" Wait. Something about the timing of this is odd. "You knew all this before the rehearsal, yet you asked me to step in for you?"

A smug smile curves her lips. "It was a test. You passed. Or failed, depending on how you look at it."

I've never seen Sienna this devious. It's like she's possessed... or desperate. For what, though? "I'm less than interested in Shane."

"You couldn't stomach the idea of walking down the aisle and standing next to him. Because you care for him."

I'm already shaking my head before she finishes speaking.

"Yes, Paisley," she insists.

Vehemently, I say, "No, Sienna." Frustration threatens to topple me, and I press the pads of my fingers to my eyes until I see spots. "This is all so stupid, Sienna. You shouldn't have asked me to be in your wedding. I shouldn't have agreed. Everything else is details."

"Details I don't want." Sienna steps up to the landing. She makes it to the door before she looks back briefly. Her mouth opens like she's going to speak. She hesitates. Mouth closes. She walks inside.

I don't know what to think. What to do.

The reason I'm on the island has vanished.

## CHAPTER 40
*Klein*

"Do you know what I mean, man?" Shane slurs the question for the third time.

Do I care about the purr of an engine in a Mercedes versus a BMW? Not one damn bit, but I say, "Yes, I know what you mean."

Anything to make him stop talking.

We come to a stop in front of his place. He slides out of the golf cart, slow and viscous like the slime Oliver likes to make.

Shane gives walking a fifty percent effort, then abandons the attempt and lies down.

To be clear, I don't like Shane. Never have, and that feeling has followed through the entirety of this week. My best guess is that I'll never like him.

That's okay. People can't all like each other all the time.

But just because I'd rather spend time with a chipped cinder block wall than this guy doesn't mean I'll leave him lying on the gravel in the front of his rented house. Though I must admit, his current position suits him.

Slipping my arms under his armpits, I lift him. "Come on, dipshit." Can't resist the opportunity to call him a name or two while I can. I'd say it to him sober, too, but this way I don't have to deal with that bloated look he gets.

I haul him inside, but only to the living room couch. I'm not nice enough to tuck him into his bed with warm milk and a bedtime story. Not when he's spoken poorly of Paisley.

He sits on the couch, looking around the room with half-mast eyelids.

His head lolls back on the couch, his gaze on the ceiling. "Pretty fucking scary how someone can change, right? It's like... like... you owe it to me to stay the same." He runs a finger under his nose, sniffing. "Bait and switch, but in reverse."

Pre-wedding jitters must've grabbed onto this guy and inserted its hooks. However, I'm not interested in being his therapist. I can't wait to get the hell out of here. Paisley is waiting for me, and if tonight ends like last night, it means the opportunity to show her how quickly I've become obsessed with running my hands over the small of her back and tracing her tattoo with my tongue. It's my new favorite pastime, and I'll destroy anybody who gets in the way of it.

"Yeah, weird how people change when you think you know them. Sorry that's happened with Sienna, but—"

Shane levels a bleary one-eyed gaze at me. "Paisley. Not Sienna."

Ok, now he has my attention. "What about Paisley?"

He tosses his hands in the air, slumping down when they fall back to his lap. "She's different. She's *fun* now. She's *fun-ny*. She wasn't either of those things when I was with her. She was *there*, but nothing colorful. A background person. I needed more." He sighs. "And now she's *more*."

I could challenge each statement he has made. I could cite examples to contradict him. But in the end, he's very drunk and I very much don't care what he thinks. "Agree to disagree," I offer amicably.

"You must remember," Shane insists. He raises a pointed finger and stabs at the air between us. "You knew her back then, too. Not very well, probably."

It would be beyond satisfying to hear the thwack of my hand up the side of this dumbass's head, but it wouldn't get us anywhere. The pen is mightier than the sword, so it must also follow that a verbal assault is more lasting than physical. I take a seat on the coffee table in front of Shane. He looks like shit. "As the ex, it's your right to remember Paisley as the person you believed her to be." Not that she was what this idiot thought she was, but I digress. "And it's Paisley's right to be whomever she wants to be in reality. You get to remember her as you perceived her. She gets to go on to be whatever she wants on the road to becoming whomever she wants. Make sense?"

Shane's eyes drift closed. "Clear as mud."

I leave him there on his couch, possibly passed out. I did the nice human thing already. I made sure he got inside, but he probably would've been served a much needed slice of humble pie if he'd woken up in the morning with gravel indentations in his cheek.

Here's the thing: I wasn't the lucky bastard who dated Paisley for three years, and I get the feeling I knew her far better than he did. Paisley was never simply *there*. Shane was, and still is, too shallow and self-involved to see. Paisley wasn't a background character. She was the whole damn story. A complicated plot, interwoven with subplots. A riveting main character. Internal conflict mixed with shifting goals.

Shane was never man enough to read her story.

But me? I'm immersed in it. Forget slowly diving in, I'm already lost in her pages. I was hooked on page one, sentence one.

Do I have a favorite book?

Sure do. The tale of Paisley Royce.

And I'll be damned if it doesn't end in a happily ever after.

---

Paisley is waiting up for me. Cross-legged in the center of the bed, wearing a gray jersey T-shirt of mine. Her face, free of the makeup she wore to the rehearsal dinner, is dewy with her nighttime moisturizer.

My hands ache to touch her, to lean her back on the pillows and kiss the hollow of her throat. The look on her face tells me to press pause on my desires.

"What's wrong?" I ask, toeing off my shoes and kicking them beside the door.

Paisley sniffs. "If you want to try kiteboarding again, tomorrow would be a good day. Turns out I'm available."

I settle on the bed, one leg bent and the other extended to the ground below. "Something happened with Sienna after I left?"

"You could say that." Paisley exhales a terse breath of disbelief. "She kicked me out of her wedding party."

My head rears back. "She... What?"

Paisley, hands folded in her lap, begins to rub at the top of one hand with the opposite thumb. "That was almost my exact same reaction."

I reach for her hands, gently squeezing to let her know I'm here for her. She didn't want to be a part of this wedding in the first place, but she gathered up her courage, and she made it here, only to be kicked out?

"What happened?" I ask cautiously.

"Sienna thinks I still have feelings for Shane." She rolls her eyes. I roll mine too, but internally.

"I'm going to be honest, I thought we did a damn fine job selling our relationship this week."

"Sienna saw your account. She knows our relationship is fake." Paisley's eyes meet mine, flustered by the admittance. "Or was, anyway. Whatever. I don't know."

"Was," I confirm.

Her smile is small, but it's there. It's also grateful, and relieved.

"How do you feel about what Sienna did?"

Her cheeks fill with air, like a puffer fish, and she lets it out in one noisy breath. "I felt angry at first. Indignant. Like, *how dare you? Do you know what I went through to get here?* And then that feeling subsided, and I felt sad."

"Because you're going to miss your sister's wedding?" Will she? Does getting kicked out of the bridal party mean you're also barred from the wedding? I haven't a clue, and this doesn't feel like the right time to ask. Right now is for listening.

Paisley shakes her head. "Maybe to a certain degree, but not really. It's more that I can't believe how quick my family is to cast someone out when they don't do exactly as they're told. And then I started to think about it, and I realized it's only me they do that to. I'm the one my dad expected to follow in his footsteps and attend his alma mater, I'm the one he wanted to take over his firm. Sienna expected me to do as she said, no questions asked." Paisley blinks twice, staring down at the comforter until she lifts her gaze and meets my eyes. "Why? Why me? My dad did this super awful thing by cheating on my mom, and then asking me to hide the truth from her. And it's not like he begged me to do it. He *instructed* me. He assumed that once he spoke, I would follow. Like a commandment."

I've been where Paisley is now, staring into the reality of loved ones' shortcomings. Nobody is perfect, but when someone's flaws cause you harm, it hurts a little extra when you love them.

"Paisley, I don't know your family well enough to form concrete thoughts about this, but here's my two cents: some people are inherent manipulators, and sometimes the intention is not malicious, but habitual." She nods, and I take that as my permission to continue. "Also, there are some people who cannot see their own shortcomings. Some people call them narcissists, some people might say they have narcissistic tendencies, or, they can simply be called selfish."

Paisley looks at me in wonder. "How do you know all this?"

"Research for my book. It ended up helping me a lot, also."

She smiles in a not-happy way. "It looks like I'm a benefactor of your knowledge."

"Remember when we were in the car driving to the coast after we landed? I told you I would put you on my back and swim you off this island. The offer stands."

She rises, uncrossing her legs and placing her weight on her knees. Her arms pretzel around my neck and she pulls me close. Nestling my nose into the dip of space at the bottom of her throat, I breathe in deeply.

"You smell divine."

"Describe it, Wordsmith. What do I smell like?"

I groan into her skin, the sound reverberating. "You smell like you're mine."

She sits back on her heels, looking into my eyes. "Am I yours?"

Her beautiful eyes, her heart-shaped face, her sun-dappled freckles, they undo me. This woman, *this woman*.

"We joke that I came here for the cake, right?"

She nods, waiting.

"Paisley." My fingers slip through her hair, curling around the back of her neck. Here we go. "You are the cake. I'm here for you. I'm here for your hard times, and I'm here for you as you grow as a person and I don't know about you, but all this fake dating stopped feeling fake as soon as we landed."

A smile that could rival the midday sun over the ocean outside our window lands on Paisley's face. "Klein," she breathes my name. "I wish there was a way to open up my mind and let you read my thoughts over the past week. You'd see just how perfectly you crept into my heart." Paisley leans forward, placing a kiss on my forehead. "I like your storyteller mind, your vivid imagination, the way you see a situation and poke through it instead of taking it on its face." Her lips move lower, to my chest, where she places a kiss on the center of the space. "Your heart is so big, Klein, and so interested in me. In being in my corner. It hardly seems like it's been enough time, but I've never felt somebody's investment in me the way I feel yours." She rises, her lips hovering over mine. "And this mouth." She dives in, kissing me briefly, leaving me begging for more. "Don't even get me started on this mouth. You say big, lovely things, and you make me feel even bigger and lovelier."

I push forward, capturing her lips with a searing kiss. "This mouth?" I ask, teasingly nipping at her lower lip.

"Yes," she whimpers.

In one swift motion I flip us over, so she's straddling me.

Paisley blinks in surprise, recovering, and then she's reaching for my shorts, unbuttoning them and pulling me out. She rears up onto her knees, lifting my oversized shirt from her body, and I shove aside her underwear. Positioning me at her entrance, she sinks down.

"Ahh," she breathes, like it's a relief to be where she is.

For me, it is not only a relief, it is my whole world. What does it mean, this barrage of feelings? Is this the big

L word, the feeling I'm not supposed to feel yet, because it hasn't been long enough? Long enough according to whom? Two weeks ago, I read an article about a man who risked his life to save a stranger, and for the rest of the day I thought about how a person must have a basic love for humanity to do something like that.

If that's true, why can't I already love Paisley? Be *in* love with her? She's no stranger, and I'm not only referring to the fact I'm inside her body right now. Our lovemaking does not require her to enter me, and yet, she is there, infiltrating me from the center of my chest all the way to my extremities. Shades of Paisley, throughout.

"Ace," I say, and she nods.

"I know, Klein," she nods, lifting her body. "I know." Sinking. "Not yet, okay?" Hips rolling. Soft moaning.

"Roll over with me," I instruct, and she lies down on my chest, her hair splaying out over my face.

We spin, until she's on her back. Hooking her legs over my shoulders, I drive inside, gripping her hips and picking up the pace. Her head tips back, mouth open.

"My Paisley," I say, watching her enjoy what I'm doing.

"My Klein," she responds, and my heart bursts like a confetti cannon. Are we our own people? Of course. But do we belong to each other? Absolutely.

Using my thumb, I rub tight circles around the middle of her. Eyes on me, she shatters silently. Her release prompts my own, and I fall down onto her. Her nails lightly scratch over my back as I empty.

"Forgot," I huff. "A condom." Everything happened so suddenly. I hadn't even thought about it.

"Don't worry," Paisley croons, her hands making their

way up into my hair. "I'm on birth control. Plus, you know, we're together now, so..."

I grin against the T-shirt on her body that I never want back. "Boyfriend perk?"

Her soft laugh filters down over me. "Yes."

I know I should get up, take us both to the bathroom to get clean, but everything about Paisley is so warm and inviting, I want to stay here another minute.

"About, um," Paisley falters. My head lifts so I can look at her. "My feelings for you are very strong. But this week is a lot on me, and the way I feel about you should have its own time. Its own place. I don't want to share big words with other feelings. Does that make sense?"

I press a kiss to the first spot I can reach, which happens to be her heart. "Total."

Sliding out of her, I get off the bed and offer her a hand. "I don't know about you, but I'd like a shower. Care to join me?"

Paisley follows me in, holding my hand like she can't let me go. When the water is hot, we step in together. I wash her hair, something I've never done for a woman before. She shows me what to do, how to focus on her scalp, teaching me to condition her ends.

We're exhausted after a long night, but being in the shower together, and knowing I don't need a condom, invigorates us. Paisley turns around, propping one foot up on the built-in shelf seat, and shakes her rear end at me.

I point at her. "Siren."

She laughs, then goes quiet.

I wrap a hand around her mouth when she comes, and she bites down on my finger.

This woman.

I know what I'm not supposed to say to her yet.

So, when she turns around and cuddles into me while the water washes away the evidence from between her legs, I say it silently in my head.

For a guy who believes in the power of words, I have to admit, these three are superior.

Klein Madigan
@kleinthewriter

When I was little, I believed I had more than one heart. My wrist, my arm, my thigh, in front of my ear, on my neck. I touched these places and felt my many hearts beating back against my fingers. I later learned these were my pulse points. The belief was naive and innocent, that of a child, and I left it behind. Until I met her. Under her gaze, my heart multiplied, spreading out around my body. Here I am years later, once more believing I have many hearts.

◯ 23   ♥ 9k   ⟲ 25

## CHAPTER 41
*Paisley*

Waking up to 'Klein the boyfriend' is, in a word, *magnificent*.

I must've run him ragged last night because he's usually up before me. He never misses a chance to bring me coffee and remind me what a sloth I am in the mornings.

I peek at his prostrate form, his chest rising and falling in even intervals. He's on his back, unfairly long eyelashes dusting his cheeks, mouth slightly parted. A small birthmark darkens a patch of skin on his ribs, and an even smaller mole dots the landscape beside it.

I want to know everything about this man. Map his body, learn his ticklish spots.

My response to him is strong, and if I'm being honest with myself, it has been since day one. Not just that first night he walked into my apartment when we were eighteen, but six weeks ago when I sidled up to his bar.

Was it only because I harbored hurt feelings? I don't think so. Looking back, I see what I couldn't in the moment. It wasn't only me responding strongly to him, it was my soul.

My soul wants Klein.

My body? That's a given.

And my heart?

I've been a terrible judge in the past, choosing Shane when he is almost a carbon copy of my father. I know Klein is nothing like Shane or my dad. Down in the depth of my heart, and in the shallows, I know this truth.

In his hands, my heart is safe.

What a relief. What a joy.

With one last longing look at the handsome man in my bed, I slip from under the covers and grab my robe. Tying it around my waist, I grab my phone and tiptoe from the bedroom.

The house is quiet. It is still early, the sun just beginning its climb into the sky.

Suddenly I have the urge to talk to my mom. I send her a text.

> Are you up?

> In the kitchen drinking coffee. Come over.

In my pajamas and robe, I hop on the golf cart and drive the short distance to my mom and Ben's place.

I step inside without knocking. My mother sits at the kitchen island, wearing a lavender silk robe and holding a cup of coffee.

"Hi, Mom," I greet.

"Good morning." She points at the coffee maker. "Make yourself a cup."

I do as she's said, joining her at the island when I'm done. "So... have you talked to Sienna?"

She gazes at me over the brim of her coffee cup, nodding. "She called me late last night. She was on her way out to stay the night with Shane."

"I'm sure that pleased him," I grumble.

She places her cup of coffee on the table. "Real talk, Paisley?"

I quirk an eyebrow. "Are you sure you can handle it?"

In this family, there is everything but real talk.

My mom ignores my question. "Sienna told me about Klein."

Great. Just fucking great. All that work this week, for nothing.

I flip my hair over my shoulder, and the smell of Klein's body wash comes over me. No matter what happens with my family, this week was not for nothing. No matter how messy it has been, or will be for the next forty-eight hours until we leave the island, this weekend was the beginning of mine and Klein's relationship. Our *real* relationship.

"Klein and I may have not started out in a very conventional way, Mom, but there's nothing fake about us anymore. In fact—"

My mom holds up a palm. "You don't have to tell me. I have eyes. I can see how smitten you are with each other."

A smile tugs up one corner of my mouth. "Yeah?"

She nods once, slowly. "Yes. He's obsessed with you. In a good way."

"I'm obsessed with him, too."

"Yes, you are. It feels good, doesn't it?"

Sipping my coffee, I ask, "Is that how you feel about Ben?"

At the mention of Ben, my mother's eyes light up. "Oh, yes. Yes. He's..." She searches for the word. "Everything I always wanted."

I try to nod my encouragement, to be supportive, but it feels weird to hear my mother say these words, and have them not be about my father. Not because I think they should be, necessarily, but it's just odd.

"Did Sienna tell you she kicked me out of her wedding?"

Irritation flickers over my mom's features. "Yes. And I told her she was wrong to do that."

"You did?"

"Of course, Paisley." Her eyebrows pull together in the middle as she gazes at me like my surprise confuses her.

"You tend to think Sienna can do no wrong."

She frowns. "That's not true."

"You thought it was okay for Sienna to date my ex. You thought it was fine for her to get engaged to him. You thought it was acceptable to ask me to throw her bachelorette party."

Mom sits back in her chair. "Honey, you don't know what I thought. You didn't ask me."

"I'm asking you now."

"I thought the choice was odd, and when I questioned Sienna, she said you were fine with it. She even said you were happy for her. Honestly, we'd had so much upheaval in our family that I felt relieved. I didn't want to deal with more pain in my children's lives. But," she sighs, brushing her fingers through her hair, "I should have pushed. I should've called you and asked you outright. I'm sorry I didn't press the issue, Paisley. I wish I'd looked harder at your blasé attitude."

My breath sticks in my throat. An apology? From my mom? Is this real?

She holds up a lone finger. "However, why didn't you speak up sooner, Paisley? Why didn't you tell Sienna you weren't comfortable with her relationship?"

I blow out a heavy breath. "In this family, when I speak up, I get kicked out."

"Are you referring to your father and college and your choice of career?"

"Yes, but it's more than that. I finally told you about Dad cheating on you, and it broke our family. Sienna and Spencer blamed me, Mom. It affected my relationship with them."

She starts to argue, but I cut her off. "They both told me they wished I'd never said anything. I've been carrying around guilt about it for years. *Years*. So when Sienna told me she'd run into Shane and I heard the happiness in her voice, I couldn't deny her. I just *couldn't*."

"Guilt is a powerful emotion. It can make people behave in all sorts of ways. It can even make a woman stay in an unhappy marriage years past when she's ready to leave."

My fingers tighten around my cup. "Are you saying—"

She's already nodding. "You didn't break up your dad and I by telling the truth. If anything, you gave me the out I'd wanted for a long time."

"But… but…" I'm sputtering, unable to form a sentence.

"I'll talk to your siblings, honey. I'll make sure they know you're not to blame." She wraps a hand around mine. "I'm sorry you've been shouldering this for so long."

Not one apology, but two? I'm not sure what to make of this conversation.

"And," she continues, "for what it's worth, nobody believes you have feelings for Shane except Sienna. And only she believes that because she can't accept the fact Shane is struggling to see you here with Klein."

"Dad can't stand seeing you with Ben, either."

She rolls her eyes. "Could he make it any more obvious?"

I bark a laugh at my mother's irreverence. It's the little bit of comedic relief I need in this atmosphere laden with old truths.

"One day," my mother says, picking up her coffee cup and bringing it to her lips, "your father and I will sit down and have a heart to heart, but that day is not today." She walks to the sink and rinses out her coffee cup. "I have to get changed to go to the club and start getting ready for the ceremony. The makeup and hair team will arrive soon, and I'm up first."

I feel a stab of pain and a pinch of envy, knowing I won't be a part of this family memory. That I've been blocked from it.

My mother wraps me in a quick hug, taking me by surprise. Physical touch is her last-place love language.

"It's all going to work out," she says, shocking me even more by chucking me on the chin.

A memory wiggles to the front of my mind, and I ask,

"This is random, but do you still have those Halston wrap dresses?"

Her eyebrows tug. "That is random. And yes, I do."

"Would you be willing to part with one?" Briefly I recap the story of Halston and her mother. "Halston's probably the reason Klein and I are together right now. All of it was her idea."

"That's a lovely gesture. I'd be happy to send you a dress."

"Thanks, Mom."

I drive back to a quiet house. Coffee has been brewed, but my grandma isn't in the kitchen or living room. Sienna isn't here, and the teenage boys will sleep until noon.

What will I do with my free day? How will I fill my time?

A restless energy surges through me. Pretty soon Bald Head Island will be in the rearview, taking its place in my daydreams and memories.

Klein opens his eyes when I walk in our bedroom. "Hey," he says in that thick, sexy morning voice. "What happened to sloth mode?"

"I transfigured into whatever animal wakes up early and wants to"—options race through my mind—"walk on the beach."

"Seagull." Klein runs his hand through his bed-mussed hair.

I nod decisively, resisting the urge to pounce on him. An early morning walk on the beach will disappear if I give in to my desire. "Seagull. Do you want to come with me?"

Klein hauls himself from the bed.

"I am persistently impressed with your ability to fly out of those covers."

Klein stops for a kiss on his way to the bathroom. "Just wait until you see all my other tricks."

He runs a toothbrush over his teeth, then pulls on a T-shirt. On the way out of the house we make two coffees to-go, and then we're on the beach, toes curling in the wet sand, foamy water crisp around our ankles.

We hold hands, and I tuck myself into his side as we walk. He's unusually quiet, so I ask, "What are you thinking about?"

"How we only have forty eight hours left here. Despite the crazy week this has been, I'm anticipating leaving this place behind and it's not a great feeling. It's just like you said. This place is magic. I feel sad to leave."

I squeeze his hand. "We can always come back. Maybe next time without the wedding shenanigans, though."

He stops short, guiding me into his chest with the twirl of our clasped hands. He looks so damn happy, and all I can think is *I put that look in his eyes.* When did making Klein happy become paramount? Sometime between him consistently being in my corner, and giving me the support I needed to stand up for myself to my family.

His green-eyed gaze heats, his chin dips, and his mouth lowers to mine. Flavors of bitter coffee and cool peppermint swirl around on our tongues, our lips yielding to one another.

He smells incredible, and he tastes divine. He's so

handsome it sets an ache to my chest. This man is *everything*.

We come up for air when a large wave sends water around our calves.

"How are you feeling about the wedding, now that you've had the chance to sleep on it?"

"Great question." I intertwine my arms around his neck, deeply breathing in that spiced apple scent of his. "My feelings are very hurt that Sienna would leave me out so easily, and for a flimsy reason. It's clear Shane is the one with the problem, but Sienna doesn't want to see it, and it's easier to blame me. I think—" Movement in the ocean catches my attention. "Dolphins!"

One jumps first, then two more. Klein and I watch them move parallel to the shore before they disappear from sight.

My excitement wanes. "Those dolphins don't care about the disaster that is this wedding day."

"Not at all."

I return to snuggling into Klein. "I wish my sister wouldn't blame me for something I didn't do, nor have any control over, but I see why she's doing it. If I imagine today as my wedding day, and my fiancé is acting the way Shane's been acting, maybe I would protect myself and my ego by placing blame on the wrong person. It's easier for her to disinvite me than it is to disinvite him."

"Divorces are expensive though."

I snort and swat Klein's arm. "I hope that's not the outcome, but yes. They are expensive."

We keep walking, and when the sun warms us a bit too much, we head up to the house. We're walking over the dune when Wren appears at the end of the private walkway. She breathes heavily, bosom heaving as she pushes hair from her eyes. "Paisley, come quick. It's a disaster."

"What's wrong?"

She gives me a look that says *you won't believe me even if I tell you.* "Sienna. Cut. Bangs."

My eyes grow so wide it actually hurts, and my hand flies up and covers my mouth with a dull smack.

"I know," Wren says gravely. She grabs for my hand. "Sienna's asking for you."

Klein presses a kiss to the side of my head, murmuring, "Just tell me what you need and I'll be there for you."

"Thank you." I respond with a kiss on his cheek. Pangs of already missing him hit my chest.

Wren leads me to her waiting golf cart. "You're lucky," she says when I climb on. "He's hot, intelligent, and cherishes you. Basically everything a woman wants."

Am I lucky? I guess I am, to a degree. Lucky to have chosen Obstinate Daughter from the hundred other restaurants in the area. Lucky to have gone on a night Klein was working. Lucky to have decided to drown my self-pity at the bar instead of following the bachelorette party out the door.

"There is some measure of luck to it all," I agree, holding on as Wren careens around a bend. "But I deserve to be loved well, Wren. And so do you." So does my sister. Is Shane the man to love her well? I don't know. I can't even tell. I know little of them, only what I've seen this week. The representation has been poor, admittedly. Maybe this week has been an anomaly in their relationship. The stress of the wedding, and all that.

Wren stays quiet for the remainder of the ride. By the time we arrive, my hair is windblown in a not-cute way.

"Paisley," Wren stops me beside a hedge. "What you just said about deserving to be loved well? That hits." Using two fingers she taps the center of her chest. "I hope you have a few more gems like that up your sleeve for Sienna. She's going to need them. I don't know what happened after I picked her up from Shane's this morning and brought her here, but it's not good."

I take a deep breath and enter the bridal suite.

# CHAPTER 42
*Paisley*

"You were right." Sienna, seated at a vanity with a gold-framed mirror, stares at me in the reflection. Her eyes track me as I close the door and make my way through the small room. A round pink velvet ottoman is nearby, so I snag it and drag it over to her.

"What was I right about?" I ask cautiously, while trying not to make it obvious I'm looking around for the cutting tool she used on the blunt edge bangs flopping unevenly on her forehead.

They look *bad*.

"Shane. He came here to talk to me after he woke up."

"Did he smell like espresso martinis?"

"He smelled like a barn animal."

"Delightful."

A sad smile tugs at her mouth.

"He's not over you, Pais."

I sigh. I saw this coming, and I have a rebuttal. "He only thinks that, Sienna. He was thrown for a loop when I arrived with Klein. He didn't expect to see me happy. To be honest, I didn't expect to *be* happy. Klein was here to provide moral support, and make me look like less of a loser at my little sister's wedding to my ex-boyfriend." I shoot for a wry smile, but it doesn't quite reach my ears. Baby steps.

My sister sniffs. "He wasn't brought along for the purpose of making your ex jealous?"

"Not at all." I take her hands. "You have to know that no matter how all this turns out today, none of this was my intent. Klein and I were barely friends when we boarded the plane in Phoenix a week ago. His job was to make people stop looking at me with pity. That's it."

"Nobody was looking at you with pity."

"At your bachelorette party I overheard the bridesmaids basically say I was a loser."

"No way," Sienna draws out the 'y' sound.

"Yes way," I confirm.

"Now people will be looking at me with pity." Sienna stares into the mirror. "I cut bangs, Pais," she whispers, features twisting into disbelief and horror. "And they're not even cute."

"Uh, no. They're uneven and unfortunate."

Tears spring from her eyes. "What am I going to do?"

"About the bangs?"

She begins to sob. "About everything."

I wait for her sobs to subside, then ask, "How did you and Shane leave it this morning?"

"He said he still wants to marry me today. Can you believe that? Why would he want to marry me if he believes he's not over you?"

Heat rises up in my limbs. That fucking bastard. Fuck

him for putting my sister through this. Fuck him for wanting what he can't have. For not wanting me until someone else did.

"I don't know. Shane is," I falter, grasping to find the correct way to word what I'm thinking. "He's a lot like Dad, I think."

Sienna winces. "That's foul. But not untrue. And it's not the first time that thought has crossed my mind."

My laugh is empty. "It's not great. It's also not uncommon, you know? For people to seek out partners similar to their parents. Especially parents who've hurt them."

"Klein is nothing like Dad," Sienna points out. Her beautiful face is streaked with tears. Thank goodness the makeup artist hadn't started on her yet, or she'd resemble a clown.

"True. But Shane is, and, well, you know how that story goes."

Sienna wipes her face with the backs of her hands. "This is so messed up. It's my wedding day. My *wedding day*. It was supposed to be perfect."

"It still can be." Locating tissues across the room, I pick them up and deliver them to her.

She plucks two from the box and looks at me gratefully. "I don't think so. I'm—" She takes a deep breath and gathers herself, pulling strength from somewhere deep inside. "I don't want to marry a man like Dad."

"Sienna, I didn't mean to dissuade you. Do whatever you want. Whatever you think will make you happy."

"That's the thing. I don't believe Shane is that person." Her words exit her mouth with hesitation. "He was great when we started dating, but after a while it felt false, like a wrong note played on an instrument." Words trip from her mouth, faster now. "I felt stupid for dating him, Paisley. Because he was your ex. If I was going to be so audacious as to date him, I had to keep dating him."

"Doubling down on a bad decision is never the right choice."

Her hand flips into the air. "Now she tells me."

Sticking my feet out, I cross my legs at the ankles. "So, the wedding isn't happening?"

Sienna winds her engagement ring around her finger. "No." Her voice is a mix of many emotions, but dominated by shock.

"It's all going to be okay. Just keep that in mind."

Sienna groans suddenly. "I don't want to tell Dad."

Tapping my nose, I say, "Not it."

"What do you think Mom will say?"

"Who knows? She might not even notice. The hearts in her eyes probably block her vision."

A smile attempts to find its way onto Sienna's face. "This day is going to get worse before it gets better."

"For you," I point out. "For me, this day can only get better from here."

"Thanks," she deadpans.

"Look at it this way," I sing, fighting my desire to finger brush her bangs over her forehead. "Untrained bangs are a vibe. "

## CHAPTER 43
*Paisley*

"Dearly beloved, we are gathered here today to join, er..."

"Robyn Royce and Ben Patel," I stage-whisper from my place beside my mom.

The reverend nods in short, annoyed head movements. He does not find the switcheroo amusing.

My dad's grandmother, who's almost deaf, says loudly in her creaky voice, "Who's getting married? I'm confused. What the hell is going on?"

Behind me, Sienna laughs her happy laugh. She's sad too, under all the layers, but right now she's happy for our mom. Happy someone got to use this beautiful wedding she planned.

With the help of bobby pins we were able to force back her bangs. Sienna's first call when she gets back on the mainland will be to her hairstylist.

Sienna had barely recovered from announcing the wedding wasn't going to happen when Ben stepped in and suggested he and my mom get married instead. At first my mom was shocked, but then tears began pouring from her eyes and she said yes and kept crying and then they kissed and she kept crying.

Sienna borrowed Wren's bridesmaid dress. Mom was already decked out in her elegant mother-of-the-bride dress, and ready with her hair and makeup done. Ben was in his suit.

I beam at Klein, standing up for Ben and looking so handsome in his khaki woven suit and pressed white shirt. All I can think about is taking it off him. Me and my lascivious acts.

As if he can read my mind, Klein narrows his gaze and shakes his head slightly, playfully admonishing me. I can't help it. I'm a fool for that man.

The ceremony continues.

There aren't rings to exchange. Sienna returned hers to Shane when she drove to his house, bad bangs bouncing in the breeze, and told him the wedding was off.

Ben dips my mom backward, kissing her. The kiss deepens. It's embarrassing. My dad stomps away, straight to the bar.

When he'd learned the turn this day was taking, he'd said, "Absolutely not. I paid for my daughter to get married, not my ex-wife."

Mom looked hard at him for a bloated second, as if reminding him of something, and said, "What was the total? I'll transfer it to your account immediately."

He'd frowned and walked away, but showed up when it was time and pouted in the back. I'm not sure what to make of his attendance.

The reception doesn't go to waste, either. I slip the DJ

a note explaining the name change. A gold cursive S & S sits atop the cake. When nobody is looking, I pluck it from the cake and toss it in the trash.

Speaking of the cake... It is divine. Vanilla with tart and sweet lemon curd filling, and vanilla bean frosting. Worthy of a flight across the country, a rental car, and a ferry. Maybe even worthy of facing the familial pain I've been running from.

Klein spears a giant slice of cake with his fork. "This cake does not disappoint." He wraps his arm around me, feeding me a bite while he snaps our photo.

Swallowing, I say, "Good thing, considering that's all you're here for." I wiggle my eyebrows at him. He feeds me a bite.

"I got everything I came for, and a whole lot more."

"You can do better than 'a whole lot more,' Wordsmith."

"Plethora."

I shake my head.

"Profusion."

I raise an eyebrow.

"Superfluity."

"I don't know what that means, but I accept."

"I got everything I came for, and a superfluity more."

I wrinkle my nose. Klein grimaces. "Never mind."

I finish my cake and set the plate on the table. "Maybe wordy isn't always better."

Klein's hand slides up the inside of my thigh. Even covered by my dress, it blazes a hot trail on my skin. "Wordy is *always* better."

I nod solemnly. "Yes, Word Daddy."

He sighs and shakes his head.

This is too fun, though, so I continue. "Hot Hemingway?"

He delivers an exasperated look and stands, hand extended. "I believe this next song is ours."

"If you're suggesting our song be the Macarena, I will take off my high heel and cheerfully beat you with it."

"Patience, Ace." He leads me out to the wood dance floor in the middle of the lawn.

The current song ends, and the DJ says, "This goes out to a Miss Paisley Royce from Word Daddy." The DJ shakes his head like he can't believe what he just said.

I whirl on Klein. "I knew you liked that!"

The music begins, and I recognize it instantly.

She's In Love With The Boy.

Fisting the front of the shirt, I laugh and sway. "I can't believe you remembered."

He holds my face in his palms and glides the tip of his nose over mine. "If you say it, I remember it."

Klein spins me around. Neither of us know what we're doing, but we're a happy little mess. I belt out every word of the song.

It's hard to believe that through all the turmoil of the day, there is still joy. Through the high highs and low lows of the week, and everything in between, two people managed to come together.

To fall.

The song ends. Klein dips me back, kissing me senseless. When he lifts me upright, my face is pink and happy.

Sienna, sitting alone at a nearby table, catches my eye. A shadow casts itself over my happiness. I wish my sister had gotten her perfect day. I wish Shane had been her soulmate.

Sienna sends me a wink, downs her glass of champagne, and marches out into the night.

Klein and I dance until our feet hurt. We dance with my mom and Ben. We dance with my grandma, and I force Spencer out onto the floor for a two-step lesson led by the DJ. The female half of the 'I do' crew has stuck around. The men are missing, likely aiding Shane in whatever he's doing to get over having his wedding canceled the day of.

Klein carries my shoes on our way to the golf cart. He drives me and my grandma back to her house. She goes upstairs to her bedroom, and Klein and I make our way to ours.

We undress, and Klein waits for me in the bathroom as I unwind my hair and wash my face.

"Crazy day," he remarks as we slide under the covers.

"The craziest," I agree.

We come together quietly, each knowing what the other wants. What the other needs. When it's over, we lie in bed with the window open and listen to the waves crash to the shore.

Klein runs his fingertips down the length of my arm. "I'm going to miss that sound," he says, forlorn.

I press my back to his chest, snuggling in deeper. "We can come back. The island isn't going anywhere."

Klein Madigan
@kleinthewriter

Best cake I've ever had, and I think maybe She's In Love With A Boy.

◯ 175    ♥ 17k    ↱ 72

## CHAPTER 44
*Paisley*

I've yet to have a final full day on Bald Head Island that wasn't both happy and sad. It's an interesting dichotomy, to experience these opposing feelings simultaneously.

Klein wakes up before me. He brings me coffee. I stretch out in bed, the caffeine slowly bringing me to life, and join Klein for a walk on the beach. It was his idea, though I would've suggested it, too.

Tar Heel gulls laugh over the water, diving for their breakfast. An osprey joins the fun, leading feet first into the water and coming away with a wriggling fish.

Klein gazes out over the ever brightening surface of the water. "I've lived in the desert my entire life, and coming here this week has made me realize that I am—"

"Thirsty?" I ask, unable to stop myself from making the joke.

He laughs, pausing to drop a kiss on my lips. "In more ways than one."

"And now?" I ask, tipping up my face, asking for more. "Has your thirst been quenched?"

"Not at all." He obliges me, kissing me again and again. The ocean reaches for us on the shore, the cool water enveloping our ankles. We break apart, watching the water recede. "I think she wants you to come in one more time. She's beckoning you."

"Not a chance."

Turning around suddenly, I start running backward and twirling my fingers at him. "Come in, Klein. Come *iiin*."

He bends his knees and ducks, rushing me. I have time for only half a shriek before I'm in his arms, thrown over his shoulder.

Laughing, I run my palms over his back. He does the same to my backside.

"What do you want to do today?" he asks, setting me down.

"Nothing that can be found on an itinerary."

"Agreed."

We make good on that agreement. We ride bikes to get ice cream, and I stop at the little grocery store for chicken necks. Klein grimaces, but I refuse to tell him what I'm up to, asking that he trust me.

I take him out to a dock in the marsh, producing two lines of durable string I found in the shed when I was putting Klein's malfunctioning (lucky us!) air mattress away earlier. The find led to me spending copious amounts of time on the internet learning if someone with a shellfish allergy can go crabbing. The conclusion was affirmative.

"You're not doing a very good job keeping the disgust off your face," I say, laughing at his contorted features.

"Maybe it's because you're tying a knot around a chicken neck."

"Raw chicken neck," I clarify.

"The designation does not help your case."

"Here." I hand him a line. "Drop that in the water."

"Am I going to catch a water monster?"

"Yep."

"For real?"

"If you consider a crab to be a water monster, then yes."

Excitement widens his eyes. "I'm fishing for crab?"

A peal of laughter slips out of me. "You're *crabbing* for crab."

He nods once, decisively. "Fishing for crab, then. It's not an issue with my allergy?"

"I spent twenty minutes this morning reading about it. It appears to be fine, but if you're worried, we can scrap it."

"I want to stay. I just won't touch them."

"Good idea. They pinch."

"I—" His line jerks. "Fish on!"

"Crab on," I correct, jumping to my feet so I can help him. "You have to be very quiet." I say this with almost no volume. "The crab will let go if they hear you."

He goes silent. His muscles are tense as he takes the line from the water inch by inch. His thrill at the activity has my heart twisting.

The claw clears the water first, then the remainder of the body.

"It's a blue crab," I whisper. "A female."

"How can you tell?"

"Her claw tips are bright red."

His neck twists so he can see. "Why isn't she letting go if she can see us?"

"She's feisty."

After another inspection, Klein lowers her into the water. I drop my own line, and we spend the next hour crabbing.

"Who taught you how to do that?" he asks as we ride back to my grandma's.

"My dad, if you can believe it."

My grandma has sandwiches and potato salad ready when we arrive. We wash our hands with hot, soapy water and dig in.

The afternoon is spent on the beach with my grandma, Sienna, and Spencer. The newlyweds join us halfway through the afternoon. I have to look away when their kisses surpass a socially acceptable amount of time.

Sienna assures me she hasn't told anybody besides our mom about me and Klein. Someday I will. It'll be a great story. But that day is not today.

The sun grows heavy in the sky, and my mother suggests we go up to the house and eat whatever is left in the fridge. It's exactly the same thing she said on the final day of every trip when I was a kid. Everyone eats something different, or little pieces of everything.

My mother, my grandmother, and I settle in the rocking chairs on the porch. Sienna walks out with a bottle of wine in each hand, and takes the fourth chair.

My mother and I share one bottle, Sienna and our grandma the other.

The sun dips lower, and we stay quiet, lost in our own thoughts until Sienna says, "I came here to get married."

Her hand rests on the arm of the rocking chair, and Grandma reaches over to gently pat it. "If you wanted to get married, you probably should have chosen a better groom."

We are stunned into silence, but then Sienna laughs. It's a deep belly laugh, the kind that folds a person in half. My mother and I laugh, too, and Grandma shrugs sassily.

She turns her gaze my direction, and I shrink. "Don't start on me."

Her eyebrows raise. "You seem to have found your voice."

"Klein brings it out of her," Sienna says.

Grandma shakes her head, disagreeing. "I don't think he brings it out. More like he doesn't suppress it."

My mom tips the bottle to her lips. Following her swallow, she says, "Does anybody else feel like they just received a verbal spanking?"

Sienna nods. "Absolutely."

"That's one of the perks of getting older." Grandma takes the wine from Sienna. "Your filter is worn out and lets more through."

We talk into the night. Klein joins us with a bottle of beer. My mom asks him to describe his book, and then mentions Ben's best friend works at a publisher. "It's always good to have another option," she says when Klein explains there is already interest. "Even better when one publisher thinks another publisher is after your work."

My phone vibrates in my back pocket, and when I pull it out, I have to blink twice at the name on my screen. When was the last time my dad text messaged me?

> Hey, hon. I had to head back unexpectedly today. Emergency at work. I was hoping to get a chance to talk with you tonight, but it doesn't look like that's going to happen.

I stare at the phone, reading the message over and over. Klein leans against me, brushing a kiss over my temple.

"Did you read it?" I ask quietly.

He nods against my skin. I type out a response before I can spend too much time considering it.

> Sorry to hear that, Dad. I'm always just a phone call away.

> And a flight.

I freeze. Klein rubs circles on my thigh, a majority of the skin left bare by my shorts. He pauses the movement, replacing it with the gentlest squeeze. I know what it means. *I'm here for you. It's ok.*

I type my response.

> You're welcome in the desert anytime. The saguaros and I would be happy to have you.

> I love you, Paisley.

> I love you, Dad.

I look up at Klein. The porch light is on behind him, but the navy blue night casts his face in shadow.

He motions to my phone with his chin. "How do you feel about that?"

"Good," I answer, reading over the conversation.

"Good," he repeats.

Soon after, Klein and I head for bed. After hastily packing because neither of us feels like being neat and methodical (our own rebellion against the end of our trip), we slip under the covers one last time.

This week has been a roller coaster from start to finish, but I'm ending on a high note. For the first time in a long while, my heart feels like it's heading in the right direction.

We have a long day of travel tomorrow, and it begins early. But when Klein's fingers trail up the inside of my thigh, I respond with vigor.

One more time with the window cracked, listening to the waves hit the shore at the same time Klein's hips roll against me.

Another opportunity to have Klein in my favorite place, to let him carve himself into my memory of this room.

He holds my hips, my legs thrown over his shoulders, fingers disappearing into the crease at my thighs. His abs flex and ripple with the effort, and I trail a hand over his chest and midsection, feeling the muscles under my palm.

"Paisley," he groans almost soundlessly, letting go of one hip only to capture a hardened nipple between two fingers and pinch it lightly. He bottoms out inside me, leaving me and then filling me again, until I press a hand to my mouth but keep wide eyes on him.

He drinks in my orgasm, his lips open and his eyes half-closed. With a chin tipped to the ceiling, he finishes with jerky movements.

We go to the bathroom to get cleaned up, and Klein presses a warm washcloth between my legs.

When we get in bed, he wraps an arm around my waist and tucks me into this front.

It's the perfect ending to a tumultuous week.

**Klein Madigan**
@kleinthewriter

Leaving the island, though it is my hope that with you, there will never be a last time.

---

◯ 212   ♥ 27k   ↺ 334

## CHAPTER 45
*Klein*

A golf cart.

A ferry.

An automobile.

An airplane.

Those are the modes of transportation that land us back at Sky Harbor International Airport in hot and dry Phoenix, Arizona.

We stand in baggage claim after collecting our bags, hands intertwined. I can tell Paisley doesn't want to let me go. I don't want to let her go, either.

"Eight days ago when I was here, I had no idea what the week would hold. I thought there would be sun, sand, and—"

She grins impishly. "Cake."

"Yep. But the trip turned into more than I could've dreamed of."

"What now, Klein?"

My thumb runs over the top of her hand. "What do you mean?"

Worry pulls at the corners of her eyes. "Now that we're back. What now? On the airplane, I started wondering, what if it was the magic of the island? Will the desert negate it all? Normal life?"

"Eight years ago I liked you when I met you living normal life in the desert."

A breath of relief pushes from her chest.

I lean in, pressing a kiss to her lips, letting it linger. "Do you have a car parked here?"

"Yes."

"Do you want to give me a ride home? Otherwise I have to call Halston, and I'm not ready for her questions and attitude." I'm scheduled to work with her tomorrow night, so it's not like I can avoid her much longer.

Paisley drives me home. We linger in front of my apartment, trading kisses over her console. She brushes a fingertip over her lower lip, saying, "It's going to be weird not to be with you tonight. To wake up without you tomorrow morning."

I stroke her face, tuck her hair behind her ear, rub my thumb over the apple of her cheek. This past week changed my life, and I think I'd live in a home built out of Palo Verde twigs if it meant waking up and pulling her body into mine. "I'm off tomorrow during the day, but I'm working tomorrow night. I can come over after? It might be late." Even that is too much time for me. I miss her already.

She leans into my touch. "Late works for me."

I haul my bag from her back seat, turning to wave goodbye before I climb the stairs to my apartment. I let myself in, and unbelievably, everything is the same. So odd for it all to be waiting for me the way it was when I left, but I am returning a different man.

I unpack and start the laundry. Paisley and I text all evening, about everything and nothing.

My chest aches with how much I miss her.

## CHAPTER 46
*Paisley*

"It's good to have you back, boss." Cecily dips a carrot stick into a dish of red pepper hummus.

"We're going to need you to tell us all the things," Paloma informs me, biting into a crisp endive leaf.

We're at our favorite lunch spot. It's my first day back after returning home yesterday. I'm exhausted, and my body clock is on Eastern Standard Time, but there's something to be said for adrenaline. I missed work. I didn't spend much time thinking about it while on the island, but now that I'm back, I'm excited to be in the middle of things again.

I miss Klein more, though. I miss his smile, his expressive eyebrows, the way he drags the pad of his thumb across his lower lip.

"What do you want to know?" I ask innocently, dunking a sesame cracker in the hummus and popping it in my mouth.

"We're going to need to know how Klein went from

fake to *daddy*." Paloma's eyebrows stay elevated on her forehead as she stares at me.

"It sort of just… happened?"

She shakes her head. "That's not good enough."

"It was the captions, wasn't it?" Cecily wipes her mouth with her napkin.

I scoff. "Yes. The captions you wrote for his social media posts made me lose my bikini. Especially the one about thinking you had hearts in different parts of your body." I snap a carrot stick in half. "Who knew you were so poetic?"

Cecily's head tilts, trying to understand. "I don't mean my captions. I mean his."

I'm confused. "You're managing his social media."

"All the photos, yes. And responding to comments, and all that. But Klein took over the captions halfway through your trip."

My carrot hits the table. "What?"

Cecily's gaze bounces from me, to Paloma, and back to me again. "I assumed you knew."

Pressing a hand to my stomach, I pull in a deep breath to calm myself down. Those posts were beautiful. "He didn't tell me."

Cecily's lips purse. "Is this a good revelation?"

I picture Klein below me on the bed last Friday night, the words he wanted to say but swallowed at my request.

I didn't let him say those three big words to me, but he went ahead and did it anyway. In the only way he knew how aside from speech. Through story.

"I have to go." I push off from the table, fumbling for

my purse. Paloma unwinds it from my seat when my shaking hands fail at the task.

"Here you go," she says serenely. "Go get your man."

··· 🐚 🐚 🐚 ···

WILL HE BE HOME?

What am I going to say?

Am I a fool? Is it too soon? Too soon to love a man who puts me first? Who offered to swim me off an island, talked sense into my dad, tolerated Shane and all the other shenanigans of the week?

*No.*

It can't be. It's too good. Too right.

Maybe falling for someone isn't a process. It isn't meted out, like bullet points in a timeline. Maybe it's a thing that happens quietly, when you're watching them hug their mother, or pedal a bike under a canopy of trees, or climb a lighthouse during a storm. When they're reaching for your hand when you're struggling, just to let you know you're not alone. Is it when they learn how you like to be kissed, and then to do it well, and often?

If so, I have my answer.

I thunder up the stairs to Klein's apartment. Four knocks on the door and it opens.

"Paisley?" Worry creases Klein's forehead. "Was that you on the stairs? What's wrong?"

He holds out his arms, and I do not fall into them, because I've already done that. I *float*.

"Paisley," he hums, stroking my hair. "Is there a problem? You're dressed in work clothes."

My head shakes, nose rubbing the front of his soft T-shirt. I want to bury myself in this man, get lost in him, never come up for air.

"Your captions," I murmur.

Klein moves us out of the doorway, closing the door with his foot. He walks us to his couch, and when he sits, I crawl onto his lap.

His gaze searches my face, falling down my body. "I take it you're happy."

"So happy. Sublimely."

He wraps a section of hair behind my ear, rubbing my earlobe between two fingers. "Does this mean I can say what I want to say out loud, to your gorgeous face?"

"Yes." My hands run through his hair, sliding down and over to cup his cheeks.

"Paisley, I'm in love with you. And it feels like a flash, and also a throb. You are a place where my heart can settle, but still be itself. Your laughter prompts my own, and I didn't realize how important that was until I met you. To be connected, loved, cherished, to be inspired, to be grounded but not tethered, I knew none of that until you walked back into my life." Klein grips my face the same way I have his, absorbing the moisture on my cheeks. "We had something back then, Paisley, and we have something today, and that tells me we'll have something in twenty years. In forty. In fifty. We are evergreen."

Moisture forms behind my eyes, a salty sting.

"I believe I'm your soulmate, Paisley, but I don't believe I complete you. I think you do that on your own, and I'm here to share in that. I think the same is true of me. We're here to learn and grow and be better, and I'd like to do that with you, unconditionally. What do you say?"

Tears tumble down my cheeks. I'm not a crier, and yet, here I am unable to stop. "I thought I was coming here to tell you I love you," I sniffle. "Instead I got the most heartwarming declaration of love I've ever heard." More tears arrive. Wiping at my cheeks would be useless. Klein has a hold of me, and I'm not about to break that contact.

He grins crookedly. "Yeah, well, I thought I went to Bald Head Island for cake."

I breathe a laugh. "Klein the writer, you have a mouth that says beautiful words, and a heart that feels beautiful things. I can only hope I'm as good as you, as thoughtful, as expressive. And when the time comes I don't say words the way you do, I hope you'll see my actions and know how much I love you."

"Communication has many forms." Klein gently eases me closer. He kisses me like I'm sustenance and all he desires is survival.

When I take a break to breathe, he says, "There's another form of communication I know of that's as effective as the written word."

My hips wriggle. "Oh yeah?"

He hooks his hands around my backside and presses me harder against him. "Hold on," he instructs.

I wind my arms around his neck, and he carries us to his bedroom.

Pressing kisses to the scruff of his neck as we go, I whisper, "Klein *the guy I'm in love with.*"

"Of all the nicknames you've given me, that's my favorite."

"I'll get it tattooed on my other thigh."

"And I'll bite it. Every. Damn. Day."

We tumble on his bed together.

Pulling his shirt over his head, I rasp, "Please tell me that's a promise."

"Everything I say to you is a promise."

He unbuttons my black work slacks. I tug off my blouse. He buries his face between my breasts, humming happily.

"Paisley the everything," he murmurs against me.

"Is that my second nickname?"

He nods, taking my nipple in his mouth. "It's perfect for you," he murmurs around the hardened peak. "You are my everything."

My heart fractures, splits, making room for something newer, bigger. He lines himself up with me, notches in, his gaze on mine.

"I love you," he husks when he's all the way inside me. He sets a perfect pace, the one he knows I prefer, and his *I love you* echoes through me like it was shouted into a cavernous hall. I hear it over and over, with each of his withdrawals, and every return.

I kiss along his jaw. "I love you, Klein. So much, you don't even know."

He pulls back, then in again. "I know, Paisley. Believe me, I know."

I don't return to work until the next day. Paloma tells me I'm glowing. I ask her for a double date with her architect. She's cagey, insisting they're only casual, but I see through her vehemency.

My mother's package arrives, and I wrap it in pearlescent paper and attach a note.

*A Halston for Halston.*
*Thank you for everything.*
*- Paisley*

Klein gives it to her at his next shift, and texts me saying she got teary-eyed, then punched his arm when he pointed out the tears.

The following weekend, Klein's mother has us over for dinner. Eden and Oliver are there, and Eden swears she knew we were going to develop into something real. "I saw the way he looked at you, and I knew my brother was done for."

Under my breath, I say to her, "Next we'll work on that soccer coach."

"He posted a video of bridge lifts. Do you know what those are?"

"I'm picturing hip thrusting."

She nods, slowly and with lips pushed out. "It was almost pornographic."

"That's disgusting," Klein complains as he kisses the side of my head.

"Get over it. I read every one of your social media posts since your account was created. I've liked, shared, commented, printed them out and glued them to my car, the whole nine."

I burst out laughing. Eden grins.

"I appreciate the support," Klein says dryly. "Let's hope the interested publisher is at least a fraction as enthusiastic."

# CHAPTER 47
*Paisley*

THREE MONTHS OF CECILY MANAGING KLEINTHEWRITER, and Dom calls.

"It worked. They want a meeting," he says, voice rising in volume and tone. "Am I on speaker?"

"Yes," I answer, glancing at the glowing phone screen on Klein's coffee table. Klein sits on the couch, silent. He appears to be in a trance.

"Paisley, tell Cecily I want to take her out for a drink when I'm in town next week. She should be in on the celebration."

I give Klein a look and wiggle my eyebrows. No response. "Dom, Klein might be catatonic at the moment."

"Perfect time to remind him to pay up. He lost our bet and still owes me a hundred dollars."

I eye Klein, who's at least blinking now.

"Bet?" I ask.

"Before he left for the island he said you guys weren't going to be anything but friends." Dom laughs. "Wrong."

Still nothing from Klein. If anything was going to kick him in gear, it should be his cousin demanding his due.

"Klein's going to have to call you when he finds his voice, Dom."

We hang up, and I crawl onto Klein's lap.

"Klein?" My fingertips graze his shoulders. "Are you alive?"

"They want a meeting," he says, coming to life. "A meeting. It worked." His voice goes from breathless to a shout.

I gasp as he stands up suddenly, spinning me around. "You beautiful, incredible, intelligent woman." He has one hand locked around my waist, the other tenderly cupping my head. "You believed in me. Without reading the book, you believed in me."

I read the book soon after we returned from the island, but that's not what he means. He's referring to how we launched a marketing campaign, book unread.

Running my knuckles over his cheeks, I say, "I remembered how talented you were in college. I knew you'd only become better since."

For the record, his book was incredible. I never saw the plot twist coming.

Against my lips, he says, "You are my favorite story. The best I've ever heard, and the best I'll ever tell."

# *Epilogue*

THE SAND IS WARM BETWEEN MY TOES. THE DAY IS CLEAR, bright and beautiful. The ocean is the color of Paisley's eyes.

Her face, wet with tears, shines up at me. "I do," she says, the strength in her tone slipping into the crevices around the letters, filling them out.

"By the power vested in me by the state of North Carolina, I now pronounce you husband and wife. Klein, you may kiss your bride."

I kiss Paisley well. I dip her backward. I hold her as tight as she holds me.

When I'd proposed eight months ago after asking for her father's blessing, we'd known immediately where we wanted to say our vows.

Bald Head Island is where we fell in love, so it was natural we'd return. There wasn't an itinerary, or a week full of activities. "On the beach," Paisley had said when we started planning. "Small, attended by our family and closest friends. In fact, nobody has to be there at all. I only need you."

"And cake," I amended.

Paisley laughed. "And cake."

I take a moment to myself during the reception, watching Paisley from the sidelines. She's a stunner in that white dress, but it's the soul I see in her eyes that gets me. A soul that calls for me, reaches for me, yearns for me. What a gift it is to have been given this woman to walk beside. She has been my biggest cheerleader, my advocate, proudly telling everybody she knows about my book.

Thanks to Paisley and her team, my debut novel was well-received. So much so that we are due in New York next week for a meeting with my publisher about my next book idea: a fake dating murder mystery set on a beach. Spoiler alert: the conniving fiancé is the first to meet his maker.

After that meeting, Paisley and I will fly to Europe, where we will see the real Lake Geneva on the first stop of our honeymoon.

As I watch, Paisley's dad approaches her. He holds out a hand, asking her for a dance. It has been a journey not without difficulty for Paisley and her dad these past two years. She is open to his love, but he struggles to give it. He is working through that, and I suppose that's the most you can ask of a person. To recognize flaws, and work on them.

When I get Paisley back in my arms, I lean down and breathe in her sweet smell.

Sighing contentedly against me, she says, "Klein the husband."

# EPILOGUE

"Paisley the wife."

She rises on tiptoe, delivering a kiss.

I am the luckiest man alive.

*** 

Want more Paisley and Klein? Visit www.jennifermillikinwrites.com to read a bonus epilogue. Go here to preorder Jen's Sept. 5th, 2024 release, What We Keep.

*Also by Jennifer Millikin*

## **Olive Township Series**
## **(A contemporary twist on The Princess Bride)**

*Penn (February 6th, 2025)*

*Hugo (May 1st, 2025)*

*Ambrose (Fall 2025)*

*Duke (Early 2026)*

## **Hayden Family Series**

*The Patriot*

*The Maverick*

*The Outlaw*

*The Calamity*

## **Standalone**

*What We Keep*

*Better Than Most*

*The Least Amount Of Awful*

*Return To You*

*One Good Thing*

*Beyond The Pale*

*Good On Paper*

*The Day He Went Away*

## **The Time Series**

*Our Finest Hour - Optioned for TV/Film!*

*Magic Minutes*

*The Lifetime of A Second*

### **Green Haven Series**

The Least Amount Of Awful

Better Than Most

To be in the know about new releases, receive exclusive sneak peeks, and get

a Hayden Family prequel novella for free,

visit jennifermillikinwrites.com and subscribe to the newsletter.

*Acknowledgments*

Readers, thank you for picking up Here For The Cake! I am humbled and grateful by your love of my work.

Luke. You lift me up when I'm struggling to stand on my own. You are my fiercest protector, and my most ardent supporter. I love you.

Erica. Your running commentary scribbled in the margins of your beta read bring the brightest smile to my face. Thank you for continually helping me make my work shine.

Crystal. Bald Head Island is pure magic, and I wouldn't have been able to write about if you hadn't planned our family vacation there. Thank you for inviting us to your favorite spot, a place that has a heartbeat and a pulse. And no cars!

# About the Author

Jennifer Millikin is a bestselling author of contemporary romance and women's fiction. She is the two-time recipient of the Readers Favorite Gold Star Award, and readers have called her work "emotionally riveting" and "unputdownable". Following a viral TikTok video with over fourteen million views, Jennifer's third novel *Our Finest Hour* has been optioned for TV/Film. She lives in the Arizona desert with her husband, children, and Liberty, her Labrador retriever. With sixteen novels published so far, she plans to continue her passion for storytelling.

Printed in Great Britain
by Amazon